The Academy

QUINN ANDERSON

RIPTIDE
PUBLISHING

TABLE *of* Contents

Chapter One

Outside the car window, trees slid by in a green and brown blur. Nick let his eyes go unfocused, mind wandering. Today was the day. Today, he'd have a shot at a fresh start. Today, everything would change, possibly for the worse. His stomach acid churned.

"Mr. Steele."

Nick twitched in his seat, making the leather creak. He glanced at the driver: a woman, dressed in a sharp pantsuit, who had even sharper features. Dark-red lipstick, a pointed chin, and skin that was thin and white like paper. She'd introduced herself as Dr. Finn, but Nick had been calling her Jane Austere in his head.

One of her finely penciled eyebrows rose above the top of her black sunglasses. She alternated between glancing at him and watching the road. "Are you excited for your first day?"

"Yes."

She probably wanted him to elaborate, but instead he pulled down the sun visor and checked his appearance. Blue eyes stared back at him, bloodshot from lack of sleep and framed by unkempt strands of blond hair. He'd attempted to make himself look presentable that morning, but there was nothing he could do about the smell of public transportation that clung to his clothes.

Pretending to be absorbed in running fingers through his messy hair, he prayed she'd lose interest in him.

He had no such luck.

Dr. Finn cleared her throat. "This is an extraordinary opportunity, you know."

"Yeah, I know."

She'd told him as much no fewer than a dozen times over the course of the past few months. Officially, Dr. Finn was part of the admissions board for the Academy of Holy Names—a private Catholic university in Evanston, Illinois—but sometimes she seemed more like the Academy's PR rep. She'd done nothing but extol its virtues since Nick had first put in a transfer application.

"Sorry I couldn't pick you up sooner," she said, not sounding the least bit sorry. "There was so much to do to prepare for the new semester."

"It's fine." Nick meant it. He hadn't expected someone from the college to pick him up regardless. He was twenty-one. He could have taken a cab. Though his bank account appreciated the gesture, and the delay had given him a chance to say goodbye to all his favorite places in Chicago. His home city. Now his past.

"Your first class isn't for a few hours, so you have time to settle in. When we arrive, I'll take you to the administration building, where Dr. O'Connor—your student advisor—will be waiting for you. She'll go over everything you need."

"Student advisor" seems like a fancy way of saying "guidance counselor for baby adults."

Nick had gotten an email from the Academy—as the university was colloquially known—that'd explained all the same things Dr. Finn was telling him now, but he didn't mind hearing them again. There had been a lot of new information to absorb about classes, the town, and the college itself. Thankfully, the administrators had held his hand through all of it, probably so he wouldn't have a breakdown before he'd even arrived.

This car ride alone was proof of that. A higher-up like Dr. Finn had better shit to do on the first morning of a new semester than pick him up, and yet here she was. Judging by the thin line her lips had been pressed into since they'd met, she thought so as well.

Then again, they need me almost as much as I need them.

After a lifetime of being bullied for liking science, Nick had found a way to put his nerdiness to good use. He'd majored in physics at his old college, and the Academy, which focused more on the arts than hard sciences, was trying to bolster their STEM programs. One full-ride scholarship later, Nick had agreed to finish out his degree at the Academy.

Thank God too, or I'd be fucked.

His thoughts drifted to the circumstances that had led him to transfer, to being unable to pay the tuition at the University of Illinois. But the second they did, his eyes stung in a way that had become embarrassingly familiar this past year.

He slammed a mental door shut on the subject and stared hard out the window again. It was impossible to pick out any individual features as the car sped down the country road, but trying kept his mind off things.

Dr. Finn continued. "If you have any trouble adjusting to campus life, there are plenty of resources available to you. The Academy takes the wellness of our student body very seriously. We have counselors, academic advisors, peer mediators, and more. There's no reason you shouldn't find your niche."

Despite her reassuring tone, Nick heard a message underneath her words: *if you fuck this up, it's not our fault.*

But Nick had no intention of fucking up. Not after the year he'd had. He was going to keep his head down, get a diploma, and graduate at long last. After that . . . Well, he'd figure the rest out when he got there. The way he saw it, he was already a year behind. First, he had to catch up. Then, he could worry about everything else.

Dr. Finn seemed to take his silence as acquiescence. She didn't prod him for a response. Fifteen minutes later, the trees melted away, and they pulled up to a large, redbrick building with a white stone sign out front: the admissions building. Nick could make out other structures off to the side, but from this angle, the campus didn't look terribly impressive.

As if reading his mind, Dr. Finn said, "The front entrance is much more picturesque, with the stone arch and the famous wrought-iron gate. You looked at the brochures I gave you, right?"

"I did."

"Then it should come as no surprise that the Academy is considered one of the most beautiful campuses in the country. The redbrick edifices date back to the 1800s, and the original buildings are still in use today."

Nick didn't care if the walls were gold and beer came out of the drinking fountains. But Dr. Finn seemed determined to get him to say something nice about the Academy, so he relented. "The photos in the brochures were stunning. I'm sure the real thing is even more impressive. I can't *wait* to see my new school." He plastered a smile onto his face.

She pursed her lips. "Your enthusiasm is truly infectious."

I never was much of an actor.

Dr. Finn cut the engine and popped the trunk. Nick took the cue to exit and grab his shabby duffel bag. By the time he'd shut the trunk again, she was waiting for him on the sidewalk, arms crossed over her starched navy suit.

"This way, please." Her heels clicked on the brick path leading up to a set of glass doors.

Nick scrambled after her, shouldering his bag. It housed all his worldly possessions: a few sets of clothes, his dinosaur of a laptop, and the MP3 player he'd gotten for Christmas years ago. Dad had scrounged for months to—

His eyes prickled, and he shook that last thought off. He'd done enough blubbering in the past year. Today wasn't the day for more. Stuffing his free hand into the pocket of his jeans, he fingered his smartphone. The cracked screen nipped at his finger.

Soon as he got through this impromptu orientation, he needed to find his dorm and plug it in. All the outlets at the bus depot had been taken. He hadn't charged it ssince he'd left home at the crack of dawn. Or rather, what had once been his home.

What is it about today? I can't go five minutes without depressing myself. Must be because this whole transition is finally real.

The glass door caught his heel behind him, nearly pulling his sneaker off with it. Dr. Finn led him down a series of carpeted hallways that looked like they could have been transplanted from any administrative building in the world. Same went for the banal artwork on the walls and the fluorescent lights. Eventually, she dropped him off in front of a closed office door that read *Dr. O'Connor* in black letters.

"Here you are." She stood back and gave him a once-over, as if determining if she wanted to change anything before handing him over. "Please don't hesitate to contact me if you have any questions."

"All right. Thanks for the ride. It was nice meeting—"

But Dr. Finn had already waltzed off, her heels somehow managing to sound sharp even on carpet.

Nick fought the urge to stick his tongue out at her retreating back. *So much for caring about the wellness of the students.*

Sighing, he hefted his bag—which felt like it weighed twice as much as it had that morning—and rapped his knuckles against the frosted glass.

The door opened immediately, revealing a black woman with a big, pretty smile and even bigger glasses. Her eyes were huge behind the thick frames as they darted across Nick's face.

"Nickolas Steele?" She didn't wait for an answer before opening the door wider. "You're right on time. Come in."

"Thanks." Nick walked through the door and took in his surroundings. His suspicions that Dr. O'Connor was secretly a grown-up guidance counselor seemed confirmed by the inspirational cat posters on the walls and the dog bobbleheads lining her desk.

Better than Dr. Finn, though. No contest.

He set his bag on one of the patterned chairs across from the desk and threw himself into the other. As Dr. O'Connor settled behind her desk, Nick studied her as discreetly as he could. There was something about her that made him relax. Something that felt parental, which was funny, considering he had only the vaguest memories of his mom from when he was little. Before they'd lost her. Though he supposed there was no "they" anymore.

Keep it together, Nick. Crying in front of the guidance counselor on your first day won't make the best impression.

"So, Nick." Dr. O'Connor turned to her sleek computer and tapped on the keyboard. "In case no one has said it yet, welcome to the Academy. We're very pleased to have you."

"Thank you."

"Do you go by Nick, or would you prefer Nickolas?"

"Nick is fine."

"And you're coming into the fall semester as a junior, correct?"

"Yes." *Is this necessary? She obviously knows who I am.*

Dr. O'Connor hit a few more keys, and the printer next to her sprang to life. She reached for the pages the moment they'd been spat out. "Here's a map of campus and a copy of your schedule. You can review it at any time using the online student portal, which I'm sure you're familiar with by now."

She selected a pink highlighter from a mug shaped like a cat head and marked several buildings on the map. "The dorm you signed up for is here: Powell Hall." She held up the map and pointed with the tip of the highlighter before moving it to another section. "And your first class is here. You can pick up your student ID in this building, three doors down, on the left. Use that to check into your dorm, get your room assignment, and settle in before class. Any questions?"

"No." Nick reached for the paper in her hand, but when he tugged on it, she tightened her grip.

"No questions at all?" Her large eyes searched his face. "I realize you've had all summer to prepare for this transition, but surely there's *something* you'd like to know. It doesn't have to be about the Academy. Maybe you'd like to hear about Evanston? What there is to do for fun around here? Anything?"

Nick suppressed a sigh. All people did these days was ask him questions. How was he doing? Was he holding up okay? Irritating as it could be, they meant well, and considering Dr. O'Connor's vocation, she likely did as well.

His eyes skimmed over the dog figures on her desk. *Cooperate, and she'll let you go.*

He let his hand drop. "Actually, I do have a question."

She smiled, perking up like a sunflower at dawn. "Yes?"

"This is a Catholic school, right?"

"It is." She gave him a quizzical look. "Is that your question? Because Dr. Finn should have given you brochures explaining the history of the Academy, and—"

"Oh, she gave me brochures all right." *If I never see another tri-folded paper.* "I was wondering if I'm going to have to attend Mass or anything? There was nothing in the brochures about that, and when I googled the Academy, I couldn't find anything on your site." *Besides enough pictures to start a school Instagram account.*

Dr. O'Connor nodded. "The Academy is a Catholic university in the sense that a large portion of the students are Catholic. Notre Dame is the same way, along with a few other big-name schools. But no, you're not required to attend Mass, and you won't be considered strange for abstaining. Students of other faiths are welcome here, so long as they conduct themselves respectfully."

"Okay, good." Nick grimaced. "I mean, thanks for clarifying." *Thank fuck, because I'm about as Catholic as a sock monkey. And queer to boot.*

"You're welcome." She eyed him in a way that made him feel transparent. "Well, if that's your only question, I suppose I should let you go. You have lots of preparing to do before your first class. Remember, you're here on a full scholarship, so you must—"

"—maintain a high GPA, especially within the Physics Department, or I'll lose my scholarship, be unable to afford the tuition, and get tossed out on my ass. Yeah, I know."

Nick regretted the words as soon as they were out of his mouth. *You're supposed to be keeping your head down, jackass, not pissing off the administration.*

He braced himself for her reaction. Anger, he could handle. Or being reprimanded for his language. But unfortunately, when Dr. O'Connor looked at him, it wasn't with annoyance. It was with something much worse. Pity.

"I'm sorry, Nick." She sounded like she meant it. "You're under an extreme amount of pressure right now, not that you need me to tell you that. Rest assured, everyone here at the Academy wants you to succeed, and not just because more students majoring in STEM fields means more funding."

"Why then?" Nick blurted out before he could consider the wisdom of such a question. "There are hundreds of students at this school. What's it matter if I succeed or not?"

I'm getting myself a muzzle as soon as this is over.

Dr. O'Connor looked off into space for a moment before she answered. "I've seen your file. I know what you've been through in the past year. Losing one parent is bad enough, but to have your father die so many years later . . . It can't be easy. Especially when the law considers you an adult and expects you to magically have all the answers. For what it's worth, if you ever need to, you *can* talk to me."

Nick glanced down at his lap and didn't respond.

Dr. O'Connor cleared her throat. "I also saw in your file that your grades were phenomenal before you took your bereavement leave.

You should have no trouble getting back into the swing of things and maintaining your GPA. If you find yourself struggling, here's my contact information." She plucked a business card out of a ceramic holder shaped like a weiner dog and slid it across the desk.

Nick took it and stuffed it into his pocket without looking at it, face burning. "Thank you. I'll keep your offer in mind."

"Please do." She stood up from her desk and held out a hand. "I'll let you get going so you can find your dorm and settle in. It's been lovely meeting you, Nick. I'm certain we'll see each other again soon."

That was probably intended to be comforting, but to him it sounded ominous. He rose to his feet and shook her hand regardless. "Thanks for taking the time to meet with me."

With that, he left her office and pulled out his map. It looked like his dorm was located near the center of campus, which was fine with him. He liked to sleep in, and this way, he could roll out of bed five minutes before class and still make it on time.

He started to head that way, but then remembered what Dr. O'Connor had said about picking up his student ID. Navigating down the hall, he followed her instructions to the correct room.

Inside, a bored-looking guy sat at a folding table with a smattering of student IDs lined up in front of him. After showing him his driver's license, Nick was given a blue plastic card that had his name, student number, and the photo he'd submitted printed on it.

Nick stowed the card in his wallet and exited back into the hall. Instead of heading to the front of the building again, he followed the hallway down the other way to an exit.

Pushing it open, he stepped outside and was given his first real look at the Academy of Holy Names. The campus was small—especially considering he was used to UIC, one of the biggest colleges in the state—but what it lacked in size, it made up for in aesthetic.

The buildings were all redbrick, like the admissions building, with white stone columns and eaves. A number of them had ivy growing across their faces and stained-glass windows. They looked old too, but not in a dilapidated sort of way. Seeing them made Nick self-conscious about how little time he'd been on this earth.

People milled down the stone paths that sliced through the manicured grass. They looked more or less like proverbial college students. Even on the first day of a new year, they all had tired eyes and backs that were hunched from carrying textbooks.

Nick took a deep breath. *You're going to be fine. No one knows you here. You can be whoever you want, or no one at all. Once you make some friends and get into a routine, everything else will fall into place.*

His internal monologue did nothing to calm the razor-winged butterflies in his stomach. Taking another breath, he consulted his map. According to it, the music building and the gymnasium were the big, fancy-looking buildings to his right. Beyond them, there was the science building—where Nick would attend most of his classes—and the dining hall, in which he hoped to spend a lot of time.

To his left lay classrooms, the arts building, an auditorium that housed both classes and student plays, and then two dorm houses. At the center of it all was the quadrangle in which he now stood. Mossy willow trees cast shade on the many picnic tables dotting the grass, and there were flowers planted everywhere. Nick imagined he'd spend a good bit of time hanging out quad-side, eating lunch and talking to his friends, once he had some.

For now, however, he headed in the direction of his dorm to unload. His shoulder was starting to ache from carrying his bag. He kept his head down as he trotted along the path he'd selected. He wasn't interested in meeting anyone until he'd had a chance to find a mirror. His hair had a tendency to turn into a straw Gordian knot at the slightest provocation, and he always looked exhausted these days. When was the last time he'd slept through the night? Probably a year ago.

Halfway down the path, the smell of roasted coffee beans stopped him dead in his tracks. Off to the side, at the base of a tree, was a sight so beautiful it had to be a mirage: a food cart. He'd *kill* for a good cup of coffee right now. The shit at the bus station had been no better than murky water.

The girl operating the cart saw him staring and flashed an amiable smile. "What can I get you?"

"Um." He scanned the small menu board. There were six options, and none of the drinks had prices. Not that it mattered, considering his wallet currently contained his IDs, a debit card with a zero balance, and a colorful assortment of lint. "How much is a regular cup of coffee?"

"Two dollars. Got your student card on you?"

He pulled out his wallet and tried to slide the ID out of its new home. It stuck, of course, and took an embarrassingly long time to pry free. "Sorry. It's hot off the press. Here."

"Thanks." It was out of his hand and into hers faster than he could blink. She swiped it through a machine and then handed it back with a smile. "It looks like you have the meal plan. The cost of the coffee will come out of that. Since your ID is new, I figure you are too. Are you a freshman?"

"Not exactly." Though he was certainly acting like it. His last university had used student IDs for multiple functions as well. Had he been away from school for so long he'd honestly forgotten how things worked? He'd known his scholarship came with a meal plan. Bet that would have come rushing back to him the moment his stomach gurgled.

The girl smiled kindly at him as she snapped a plastic lid onto a steaming cup of coffee. "Well, welcome to the Academy anyway. Need any milk or sugar?"

"No, thanks." Nick took the coffee, shoved his ID into a back pocket, and scuttled off. As he walked, he took a sip and immediately scalded his tongue. Fuck. Off to an excellent start.

He stopped in the shade of a willow tree, popped the lid off his coffee, and blew on it until he felt confident taking a second, albeit more tentative sip. His tongue stung, but the rest of his mouth—and his exhausted psyche—welcomed the warm liquid.

Digging in his pocket, he pulled out his phone and checked the time. He still had two hours before his first class. If unpacking went quickly—which it should, considering how little he'd brought with him—he might have time to see what the food here was like. Judging by the greener-than-green lawns and well-kept buildings, he was expecting more than the usual cafeteria slop.

While he pondered his plan of attack, his eyes drifted across campus. There were a dozen or so students within sight, scattered around the quad. Compared to his last school, the place was a dead zone. But then, he'd read in one of the dreaded brochures that the

Academy only had about nine hundred students. His high school had been bigger than that. He'd never experienced life outside of a big city before, but he'd watched enough TV to know what to expect. Everyone here probably knew everyone else, and word traveled fast. He'd do best to avoid attracting attention to himself, lest he end up in the rumor mill.

Right as he thought this, his eyes landed on a group of guys sitting at a picnic table beneath a nearby tree. They weren't doing anything to catch his notice, but all three of them were attractive. Like, teen-TV-drama attractive.

One had dyed-red hair and skin that could give Snow White a run for her money. The guy next to him was black with prominent, symmetrical features. He was what Nick would have called "Instagrammable." Beautiful in a classic way that was destined to go viral.

The last guy was sitting on the table with his feet propped on the bench. Messy dark hair like a stray brushstroke topped his aristocratic face. Between his Roman nose and pink cheeks, he might've climbed out of an old oil painting. Gangly and lean to the point of looking underfed, he was the farthest from Nick's type of the three.

So why was Nick staring at him like he had winning lottery numbers scrawled across his face?

Nick, he scolded himself, *you can't check out boys on your first day at a Catholic college. The religious types tend to frown on that. Save the gay shit for another day.*

He ordered himself to look away, but his eyes disobeyed. He frowned. What the hell was his problem? The guy was cute, sure, but so what? His friends were cuter, and he was far from the first attractive man Nick had ever seen. Why couldn't Nick move on?

As if sensing Nick's stare, the guy looked dead at him.

Shit. Turn away!

But Nick didn't. He met the other student's gaze unflinchingly. Close as he was to the table, he was able to make out his eye color. Gray. *Deep* gray, like storm clouds or rain water.

Damn. There was a word to describe eyes like that. Something Nick had read in a poem once. What was it? He scrambled to remember, but the best he could come up with was that he thought it started with an *L*. His thoughts were so scattered, he couldn't smash them together well enough to remember.

Does he . . . remind me of something? Yeah, I think that's it. But what?

Three of the longest seconds of Nick's life passed before he managed to jerk his head away. Holy shit. Having just come from a bus station, he was inured to making uncomfortable eye contact with strangers, but that'd been something else.

The weird thing was, right before he'd broken eye contact, Nick could have sworn the other student had smiled. In a smug way, though. More like a smirk.

Nick brushed off the odd encounter and started walking again, though his feet dragged with reluctance.

Jesus. If this were a movie, I'd think that was some kind of fated meeting. I mean, our damn eyes met from across the way. Doesn't get much sappier than that.

Nick shook his head and took another sip of coffee. The bitterness and heat brushed away the last of the cobwebs clouding his thoughts. He had way too much going on to get sidetracked by a pretty face. One that could be attached to a Catholic boy with some deep-seated ideas about Nick and his preferences, he reminded himself.

Best to put the whole bizarre moment behind him. Small school or not, he'd probably never see that guy again.

Chapter Two

P owell Hall—Nick's new home for the foreseeable future—was a four-story, moss-covered building that resembled an old man who had hair growing out of . . . well, everywhere. It was located smack-dab in the middle of campus, no more than a five-minute walk from everything. Nick instantly loved it. Looking at its brick-and-stone façade, he saw a lot of late mornings in his future.

As he walked inside, his expectations were low. The last dorm he'd stayed in had been all prisonlike cinder block and fluorescent lighting. To his surprise, he was greeted by hardwood floors, ivory walls, and a tastefully decorated foyer.

Peering through the doorways on either side, he spotted a lounge with a fireplace and some sort of rec room. All in all, it was a big improvement. He could have done without the paintings of stern-faced saints on the walls, however.

According to Dr. Finn, orientation had been last week, so everyone else had already moved in. A few students were lounging in chairs near a large front window, and they peered at him curiously. Nick peeked around for some sign of where he should go. Before he could move, a man in a blue shirt that read *Resident Assistant* appeared.

"Hi there, I'm Don." His tone said he'd done this a hundred times in the past week and was operating on autopilot. "I'm the RA for Powell Hall. Are you moving in?"

"Yes, I'm—"

"ID, please." Don held out his hand.

Nick pulled his ID from his pocket and handed it to him. He'd expected Don to consult a list of room assignments, but at the sight of the card, Don nodded.

"I thought as much. You're the last one to check in, Steele. Welcome to Powell Hall. You're on the fourth floor. Head up the staircase until you can't anymore." He pointed to a polished wooden staircase set along the far wall. Then, he reached into his pocket and pulled out two identical keys on a simple metal ring, which he tossed to Nick.

"Got it." Nick caught the keys. "How will I know which room is mine?"

"Easy." Don flashed a prepackaged smile. "It's the only one up there. You're in the attic."

Nick was about to ask if it was, like, a *spooky* attic, but there came a muffled crashing sound from somewhere in the back of the building. With a knowing sigh, Don darted off.

Guess I'm on my own.

Nick did as Don had instructed and headed up the stairs. He was winded by the third floor and made a mental note to add some cardio to his next workout. Panting, he forced himself up the last flight and came upon a short hallway that led to a single door.

He set his bag down and started to unlock it, but no sooner had he inserted the key, the door opened. Standing on the other side was a tall brown boy with the prettiest eyes Nick had ever seen. So dark they were nearly black and ringed by lashes like ink smudges.

"Oh hey." The stranger blinked at him. He was dressed in black slacks and a button-down shirt. His formal attire was offset by bare feet and silky hair that was sticking up like he'd been shocked. "You must be my new roommate. Cutting it a little close, aren't you? I was beginning to think you weren't going to show."

Damn, he's handsome. Is everyone at this school preternaturally good-looking? Or have I been single for way too long?

"Um." Nick fiddled with his bag's strap. "Hi, I'm Nick."

"I'm Deenabandhu. Nice to meet you."

Panic punched Nick in the gut. "Nice to meet you too, um, Deena . . . Deenaba . . ."

Deenabandhu held up a palm. "No offense, but I can't listen to another white person butcher my name. Just call me Deen. Everyone does. Unless you're a bully, in which case, call me Deena."

Nick snorted. "Deen it is."

Deen stepped back, allowing him to enter the room. As soon as Nick did, he whistled, eyes sweeping from the high, steepled ceiling to the large windows. Two beds had been set up on opposite sides of the room, along with identical desks, nightstands, and bureaus. To the right, by the entrance, was a closed door that must lead to a closet or a bathroom.

His unspoken question was answered a second later when Deen waved at the room. "Everything's pretty self-explanatory. Feel free to use my minifridge and microwave if you like." He pointed out the appliances before jabbing a thumb at the closed door. "Bathroom's through there. We have to share with the whole floor, but fortunately, the whole floor is us."

Nick snorted again, and Deen beamed, like he wasn't used to people laughing at his jokes. He walked over to the bed on the right. It was piled with textbooks, and judging by the tangled sheets, it'd been slept in. "I hope you don't mind, but I got in a week ago, and I had to sleep somewhere, so I staked my claim."

"No worries. I'm just glad there aren't bunk beds. My last dorm had those, and I got stuck beneath a snorer." Nick deposited his bag onto the left bed and took a seat. The mattress was the perfect combination of soft and firm. If he didn't know any better, he would think the university had spent actual money on the dorm rooms. "Though honestly, if I've got a blanket and a horizontal surface, I'm happy."

"Awesome." Deen hopped onto his bed, facing Nick. "So, you're new here, but you're not a freshman. Are you a transfer?"

"Yeah, and I'm a junior. How'd you know?"

"Well, I've never seen you around before, for one thing. This is a tiny school, and everyone knows everyone else. Most of the students came here from the same feeder Catholic high school and have been classmates for years. I would have assumed you were a freshman, but you said you'd lived in a dorm before. Ergo, transfer student."

Nick whistled. "Damn, that was some Sherlock Holmes shit."

"Elementary, my dear Nickolas." He pretended to puff on an imaginary pipe. "It is Nickolas, right? And not like, Nickstopher or something?"

Nick laughed, relaxing for the first time since he'd been on campus. It seemed he'd lucked out in the roommate department. If the rest of the year went this smoothly, he'd be set. "Nah, it's Nickolas. Nickolas Steele. What year are you?"

"I'm a sophomore, so I'm a year younger than you." Deen waggled his eyebrows. "That makes you my senpai."

Nick started to correct him—thanks to his year off, he was older than most juniors—but at the last second, he clamped his mouth shut. That would invite questions he didn't have the energy to answer right now. Not on the first day of a new semester.

Instead, he repeated what Deen had said earlier. "So, everyone knows everyone else? I'm going to stick out, huh?" *So much for keeping my head down.*

"Pretty much. Where are you from?"

"Chicago. Born and raised."

"What made you decide to go to school in Evanston?"

Fuck. Avoiding the subject is going to be harder than I thought.

"The Academy offered me a full ride," Nick answered truthfully. "Without that, I wouldn't be here. What about you? Did you go to that feeder school you mentioned?"

"No, I moved here from out of state, believe it or not. I got a great scholarship, since I'm studying engineering."

"Oh, hey. I bet we got similar scholarships. I'm in the STEM department too." Nick figured he might as well unpack while they spoke, so he hopped up and opened his bag.

"No shit. What's your major?"

"Physics. That makes us science bros."

"*Excellent.*"

Nick deposited his clothing into the bureau, pulled out a tangled charger, and plugged his phone into one of the outlets above his desk. Then he tossed his bulky laptop onto the mattress.

Deen eyed it, lips puckering like he'd bitten into a lemon. "You might want to invest in some new tech, buddy. That thing looks like it's on its last legs."

"Once my disbursement gets in, I'll see if I can swing it. Until then, I'm stuck with what I've got. But honestly, even with a full ride, it's not like I'll be eating filet mignon. Like any other college kid, I microwave my noodles one cup at a time."

"I hear that. The scholarship I got was good, but I still have to pay out of pocket for a lot of shit. My parents are helping me so I won't have to apply for loans. Are yours helping you?"

Nick pretended to dig in his now-empty bag so Deen wouldn't see the way his face contorted. "Nah, the Academy hooked me up. They offered me the freest of free rides. Tuition. Room. Board. I won't have to get a part-time job like I assumed I would. I can focus totally on my degree. Some of the big state schools offered me money too, but I couldn't pass this up."

Deen *oohed*. "That's awesome. You must be a genius to get a full ride."

"Uh, no. I mean, I did pretty well at my last school, but nothing newsworthy. It helps that I've always liked science and math."

"Same. My parents wanted me to be a doctor, but considering my older brother went to art school, they're not going to push the issue. Are yours excited to have a future physicist in the family?"

Fuck. Was there no way to get to know someone without talking about the past? Nick supposed he should give up the avoidance routine, especially since Deen and he were going to be *living* together. Plus, Deen seemed cool. They might genuinely become friends.

Taking a breath, Nick turned around and shrugged. "My parents don't think anything of it, actually. I don't have any family."

Deen's beautiful eyes widened. "Oh shit, man, I'm sorry."

Nick waved him off. "Don't be. You didn't know. My dad actually died last year, and I took time off to deal. But life marches on, so here I am."

"I'm legit sorry though. I didn't mean to dredge up bad memories."

"Don't worry about it. I mean it. Anyone would have asked me the same questions. It's not your fault my answers are so depressing." He offered Deen a smile. "Although, I'd appreciate it if you didn't tell anyone."

"Of course!" Deen seemed to cling to that as if it were a life preserver. "Thanks for being cool. I've always wanted a chill roommate. And hey, if you need a bright side to look on, you're going to be *super* popular."

Nick raised a brow. "What makes you say that?"

"You took a year off, right? That means you're twenty-one. You can buy *beer*."

They both laughed, and the tension in the room dispersed.

Deen stood up and stretched. "When's your first class?"

Nick checked the time on his phone. "At 10:40, so about an hour from now."

"Perfect. How about I give you a quick tour that ends in the dining hall? We can grab some breakfast, and then I'll show you where your class is."

Nick could figure it out on his own, thanks to his map, but he wasn't about to pass up on a chance to bond with his roommate. Besides, he didn't want to be that guy navigating campus with his nose buried in a map. He'd been mistaken for a freshman enough already.

"Sounds great. Give me five minutes, and we'll go?"

"Deal."

Deen grabbed his own laptop off his desk—a sleek MacBook that was thinner than Nick's pinky finger—and started typing at lightning speed. Nick booted up his dinosaur, and the fans made sounds like an old man wheezing for breath. If any of his classes involved quiet note taking, he was going to be embarrassed.

Once his desktop had loaded, Nick connected to the university's internet and pulled up his bank's website. He'd been checking it fanatically for the past week, waiting for his financial aid to come in.

He was no stranger to disbursements, but this was the first year he'd had no backup money to rely on in the meantime. There had been some life insurance money, but that had gotten eaten up by medical bills, cremation, the funeral, et cetera. Plus bills and his bus ticket here. Everything cost money, and he was well and truly on his own. He'd thought he'd been independent when he'd first left for college. Now, he realized how much help his dad had been.

Time was running out too. There were certain things he could only put off buying for so long. Like textbooks for the classes he was starting *today*. As far as school supplies went, he had a broken pen and a crumpled napkin to his name.

With aching slowness, his laptop loaded his account statement what seemed like one pixel at a time. Finally, a number appeared in the column representing his checking account. The breath left his lungs in a *whoosh*. His disbursement had come in. After his tuition and board had been paid, he had a few thousand dollars leftover to get him through the semester. Thank Christ.

"Good news?"

Nick looked up and found Deen watching him. "Yeah, my financial aid came in. Just in the nick too."

"Nice. If you want, we can drop by the bookstore for anything you need."

"I might pick up some notebooks there, but I prefer to buy used textbooks. New ones are *so* expensive." Speaking of which, Nick quickly loaded some pages he'd had bookmarked for weeks now and ordered a few much-needed texts. He'd have to shell out for expedited shipping, but he'd finally be prepared for class. One more thing he could tick off his to-do list.

"You don't have to tell me," Deen said. "My organic chemistry class made me buy a supplemental note package that was legitimately just printouts of our slides, and it cost *two hundred dollars*. I'm not ashamed to admit I wept in the checkout line."

Nick grabbed at his throat, pretended to gasp for breath, and collapsed onto his bed, tongue lolling out of his mouth.

Deen smothered his laughter with a hand before climbing to his feet. He rooted under his bed for a pair of shoes and pulled them on. "I don't want to jinx anything, new kid, but I think this is the start of a beautiful friendship."

"It could be, provided you never call me 'new kid' again."

"Spoilsport. If you're all finished, let's get going. We have a lot of ground to cover on our tour, and I'm starving, so we'd better get started."

Deen led the way out of their dorm and downstairs, nodding to several other students they passed on the way. They all ignored him, but that did nothing to flatten the spring in Deen's step.

Once outside, Deen swept his arms out as if to encompass the whole of campus. "This, my dear Nickolas, is the Academy of Holy Names. It has a rich history, surpassed only by its party-school reputation."

"Really? With this being a Catholic school, I kinda assumed everyone here was pretty tame."

"Dude, no. It's *because* it's a Catholic school that everyone's a hedonist. You can practically smell the repression. Plus, college is already a perfect petri dish for growing debauchery, and everyone here has money. Money means outlandish partying." He shrugged. "Not that I would know. I never get invited to the parties. Which is a good thing, of course, because I'd become the most popular boy in school, and then I'd never get anything done. I'd drop out, join the circus, and the world would be short one brilliant engineer."

Nick laughed before he could stop himself.

Deen punched him on the arm. "Hey, it could happen."

"Are most of the students here Catholic?"

"In name, yeah, if not in practice. But you have your atheists and your new-age types. And your Muslims." He pulled the collar of his shirt aside, revealing a tattoo of star and crescent moon just under his collarbone. "Like me."

Nick nodded. "Cool. I didn't think Islam allows tattoos."

"It doesn't, and that's why it's so deliciously ironic that I chose to affirm my faith this way. I crack me up."

"Do you feel like you have to keep your faith a secret?"

"Nah. I wouldn't have come here if they weren't tolerant. So long as I don't go around preaching my faith to others, they leave me alone." He patted his shirt back into place. "Let's begin our tour. Our first stop is the bookstore. We can buy school supplies and get high off an artificial sense of productivity."

The bookstore was yet another old-looking redbrick building. Inside, floor-to-ceiling windows let in plenty of sunlight, and the smell of fresh coffee emanated from a little café tucked behind the dozens of shelves.

Nick picked up a couple of notebooks and a pack of his favorite pens—the fancy gel kind—along with a messenger bag to stow everything in. His total was nearly fifty dollars, which made him want to sob, but he'd picked the cheapest items he could find. He would have had to go into town to find a better deal, and without a car, there was no way he'd make it there and back in time for class. This was one expense he'd just have to eat.

Nick stuffed his new supplies into his bag and then slung it across his chest.

Deen seemed to scrutinize him, his index finger and thumb placed beneath his chin in a sideways L shape. "Very broke-college-kid chic."

"Thanks. That's what I was going for."

Laughing, they exited the bookstore and headed back to the quad. Once there, they circled the perimeter. Deen named every building as they went, giving Nick a chance to learn where the rest of his classes were. With the campus being so small, he doubted he'd have trouble finding any of them, but better safe than sorry.

As they walked, Nick allowed himself to feel his first real glimmer of excitement. There was nothing quite like the energy of a college campus, or the first day of a new school year. It was like there were little sparks dispersed in the air, and every now and then, one would zap him. In a new town, at a new college, he almost felt like a freshman again.

As they strolled, Nick checked out the student body—somewhat literally. He was here to get an education, but that didn't mean he couldn't enjoy the view. His earlier theory about everyone being attractive was disproven, but several of his now-peers caught his eye. Though none so powerfully as the three boys he'd spotted earlier.

In general, the students were outfitted with the typical college fare—backpacks, casual dress, and coffee cups in every other hand—but something niggled at him. He couldn't quite put his finger on it.

Deen unwittingly supplied the answer. "You can tell this is a private school from all the name brands." He gestured to a nearby cluster of coeds. "It's like walking past a Coach display at the mall."

Understanding lanced through Nick. From the backpacks to the polo shirts, designer labels abounded. One guy who passed them on the sidewalk was sporting a briefcase that bore a Medusa head Nick recognized from billboards he'd seen back home.

"Damn." Nick surveyed the people around them in a whole new way. "You weren't kidding about everyone having money, huh?"

"Well, not *everyone*. There are scholarship students, like us, and people who took out loans. And the ones who are wealthy aren't necessarily millionaires. They're here on their parents' dimes, and some are middle class. But exceptions aside, college is already expensive, and if you make it private on top of that?" He mimed an explosion with his hands and imitated the sound. "You tend to attract a certain tax bracket."

"Yikes. Are the students stuck-up about it? You mentioned bullies earlier. Am I going to get shit if I wear off the rack?"

"For the most part, no. We're all adults here. But on occasion, you do get your elitist assholes, same as you would anywhere else."

"Is that why those guys in the dorm ignored you?"

"No, they ignored me because I'm a geek." Deen winked. "Don't fret. An athletic-looking guy like you is bound to fit in. And I promise no one's going to stone you for the crime of being poor. Besides, you're new. Everyone's going to be interested in you."

God, I hope not. Attention was the last thing Nick wanted. Unless it was from that guy he'd seen earlier. Gray Eyes had been drifting into his thoughts at regular intervals, though Nick still wasn't sure why.

He toyed with the idea of asking Deen about him—since everyone allegedly knew everyone—but he discarded it. What would he say? *Hey, I know we're relative strangers still, but I saw a guy earlier who looked like a French aristocrat and had rain eyes. Know anyone like that?*

Yeah, no.

They finished their tour of the quad and ended up outside the dining hall. The smell of pizza emanated from it, and right on cue, Nick's stomach growled. He hadn't eaten since dawn, and his vending-machine breakfast hardly counted. Through the glass façade, Nick could see his new peers sitting at tables, chatting and smiling and stuffing their faces. Any one of them could be a friend in the making.

Deen gestured at the swinging doors. "Ready for food?"

"Hell yeah."

They walked inside and were greeted by a sight that Nick would have sworn was familiar, despite never having set foot in this building before. Some places were glitches in the Matrix. The same no matter where in the world you went. Malls. Convenience stores. Bus depots, for sure. And college dining halls.

A man at a desk swiped their IDs, and they were in.

Nick moved a few feet away and breathed in deeply, almost feeling at home in the familiar setting. "Oh, man. I'm so down for pizza."

"Let's see if they've started serving lunch yet first." Deen trotted off toward a steel serving table with a clear, plastic partition separating them from the food. Nick was taller than everyone ahead of them, and so he was able to see delicate pink fish fillets set out with lemon slices and capers.

"All right!" Deen grabbed one of the plates. "Salmon piccata. Score! Do you like fish?"

Nick blinked. "Is this place for real?"

"I think so, barring the usual theories of alternate-yet-parallel universes. Why?"

"No reason. I'll stick with the pizza."

"Suit yourself, but FYI, they only serve the fancy food at the beginning of the semester, when parents are still dropping off their kids. It's to con the grown-ups into buying an overpriced meal plan. Next week, it'll be all burgers and mac."

Thank God. I only have to make it to next week.

Nick headed over to the pizza station, piled a plate as high as gravity would allow, and then followed Deen to an empty table near the front. From there, they could look out the windows at the students strolling by. It was funny to people-watch and think that in the course of the next two years, one of them could become a friend, an enemy, or a lover. A fresh start meant a whole world of possibilities. The idea was equal parts exciting and terrifying.

They enjoyed some peaceful small talk over their food, and eventually Deen convinced Nick to try the salmon. Though Nick still felt it went against the spirit of a campus mess hall, he had to admit, it was restaurant-quality.

He polished off his last slice of pizza and was considering taking a gander at the salad bar—because looking at vegetables was the same as eating them, right?—when a group of guys sailed past the window. Nick spared a quick glance at them only to do a double take. He recognized them in a big way.

Those are the guys from before. The redhead, the handsome guy, and Gray Eyes.

As Nick watched, the three men strolled into the dining hall. They headed straight for the fancy food as if they'd known it would be there. That suggested they were neither freshmen nor new like Nick.

He craned his neck to watch them as they made their selections. Gray Eyes took two plates of salmon with one large hand, grabbed an apple from a bowl, and strode off toward a table in the center of the room without waiting for his friends.

The redhead went Nick's route and headed for the pizza, while the handsome one took a plate of salmon only to dump it onto a bed of greens he'd gotten from the salad bar. Nick's eyes lingered on him. He was so symmetrical, Nick wanted to take an overlay of the Marquardt Beauty Mask and hold it up to his face.

"Nick?"

Deen's voice broke him from his creepiness. He turned back to Deen, heat working its way into his cheeks. "I'm sorry, did you say something?"

"I asked how much time you have left before your first class."

"Oh shit. Class. I almost forgot." He pulled his phone out. "I've got twenty minutes. It's next door in Nassar Hall, so I have plenty of time."

"What's the room number?"

"Uh." Nick checked his schedule. "Five-oh-one."

Deen snickered. "Good luck, buddy! That's on the fifth floor, and there's no elevator."

"Fuck my life. I have that class three times a week!"

"Better invest in some hiking boots."

Grumbling under his breath, Nick snuck a peek over his shoulder again. The two boys had joined their gray-eyed friend, and all three of them were eating together, absorbed in their conversation as well as their food. Which was why it came as such a shock when Gray Eyes suddenly caught Nick's eye.

Nick froze in his seat. *Jesus, not this again.*

Before Nick could defrost, Gray Eyes turned to his red-haired friend and said something. The redhead shot the quickest of glances at Nick and then nodded. Gray Eyes stood up and made a beeline for the exit. He held Nick's gaze until he reached the door. Then, he waltzed outside and headed down a weed-riddled dirt path to the right.

When he was gone, Nick gave himself a shake. Christ, what a weird reaction. It was like his brain clogged up whenever he saw Gray Eyes. What *was* that? If he were a more romantic person, he might read into it, but he didn't have the time or the energy. It was probably a combination of nerves and exhaustion.

Gray Eyes might've left to get away from you. He could be calling you Creepy Staring Guy in his head. That's twice now he's caught you looking at him. Way to make a first impression.

Sigh. He stood up and grabbed his plate. "Well, I'd better get going. Can't be late on my first day."

Deen nodded. "Good plan. You'll want to give yourself extra time in case you need to take breaks on your way up all those stairs. Bring a tent so you can set up camp at the midway point."

"Right? Between class and our dorm, this year's going to be a cardio year." He disposed of his trash, collected his belongings, and with a final wave to Deen, exited the dining hall. But once outside, he hesitated. Gray Eyes floated into his thoughts for the hundredth time.

Nick glanced to the right, at the overgrown path. Gray Eyes was long gone, of course, but Nick couldn't stop thinking about the deliberate way he'd looked at Nick, stood up, and then exited without breaking eye contact.

Did he . . . want me to follow him?

Nick shook his head. That was ridiculous.

But was it? Nick was pretty sure he'd seen that exact move in a movie or two. Then again, why would a complete stranger want to signal Nick?

That's easy: he wouldn't. This is wishful thinking. You saw a cute guy, and you want to believe he noticed you too. Stop being weird, and get to class. You can't afford to be late on your first day.

Nick turned his back on the path, mentally and physically. To his left lay a cement sidewalk that led to Nassar Hall, and by extension, his class. He stared at it, willing his feet to move, but they remained rooted to the spot.

As if of their own accord, his eyes drifted over his shoulder. The path Gray Eyes had taken cut through a patch of trees before curving off behind the dining hall. It was impossible to see where it led from here.

Should I see what's down there? For curiosity's sake? It won't take more than a minute. I have some time to kill before class anyway, and at this rate, I'm going to be distracted if I don't get some closure.

His excuse was thin as tissue paper, but he glommed onto it. After another prolonged pause, he turned right and trotted down the path. The trees weren't thick enough to obscure him from view, but they did give him an odd sense of privacy. Especially as the path wound off to the side, and the main part of campus got left behind.

After thirty seconds of walking, Nick found himself behind the dining hall. The trees thinned into a clearing with an old, disused picnic table in the center.

Sure enough, Gray Eyes was sitting on the picnic table, in the precise same pose he'd taken up earlier that day: feet planted on the bench seat.

As soon as he saw Nick, he smirked again. "Oh, good. You're as smart as you look." He stretched one long leg to the ground and stood up. Nick hadn't realized it before—since one or both of them had been sitting—but Gray Eyes was taller than him. That didn't happen to Nick often.

He scrambled to think of something to say. Unfortunately, his heart was beating so loudly, it drowned out all thought. "Um . . . hi?"

Nice one. Very original.

Gray Eyes slipped his hands into the pockets of his jeans—which looked both new and expensive—and strolled up to him, stopping a few strides away. "I've never seen you around before. Are you new?"

Nick loosened up enough to roll his eyes. "I've been getting that all day. Do they make you guys memorize the student roster, or what?"

Gray Eyes laughed. "You've never attended a small school before. I can tell." He took another few steps forward, bringing them within a foot of each other.

The air left Nick's lungs. From this miniscule distance, he could count the freckles on Gray Eyes's nose.

Limpid. Nick met his gaze. *That was the word I was trying to think of before. He has limpid eyes.*

"You didn't answer my question." Gray Eyes lowered his voice to a murmur, as if they were sharing a secret. "You're new here, right? What's your name?"

"Nick Steele. And you are?"

Gray Eyes studied his face in a manner that was both unnerving and flattering. "Are you a freshman or did you transfer?"

"Now who's not answering questions. And why did you bring me here?"

"Because I wanted to welcome you to the Academy, Nick."

Before Nick could react, Gray Eyes reached out and cupped his chin, sweeping a thumb across Nick's bottom lip.

Nick made a surprised noise. His brain told him to pull away, but his mouth wanted to lean into the soft touch. The very gray eyes Nick had been so focused on latched on to his lip, and for a bleary moment, Nick wondered if this stranger was going to kiss him. Even more confusing was the fact that Nick wanted him to.

Before Nick could decide what to do, Gray Eyes released him. Nick stumbled, weak in the knees and blinking.

"Interesting." Gray Eyes stepped back, eyes trained thoughtfully up at the sky. "You can run away now."

Nick didn't need to be told twice. He turned tail and ran-wobbled away as fast as he could.

Chapter Three

"**W**hat's his name again?"

"Nick Steele." Sebastian glanced across the picnic table at Theo, his redheaded friend. "And he's new here, though I doubt he's a freshman. He looks like he's seen some shit in his day. It's kinda hot."

"You worry me," said Dante. He was fanning himself with a folded copy of the school newspaper, no doubt thanks to the sun beating down on them.

"Want us to move into the shade?" Sebastian had sweat trickling down his own back, but he ignored it. "We could grab our usual table under that one tree. Now that we're upperclassmen, I think we have the right to force freshmen to move if they try to sit there."

"Nah, I'm all right. I have class in the auditorium in a few minutes. It's always freezing in there. I'm soaking up the last drops of summer while I still can."

Sebastian looked thoughtfully up at the clear blue sky. It'd been sunny for weeks now, but the heat of August was starting to wane, as if it could feel September looming closer and closer. If Sebastian closed his eyes, he could pretend he was back home. His parents' house was always a little too cold, probably because there was never anyone in it.

But he wasn't home. He was gearing up for his third thrilling year at the Academy of Holy Names. If it was anything like last year, he could expect partying, depravity, and utter tedium. The usual.

The Academy never changed. The groomed lawns and perfect hedges were present and accounted for. The picnic table behind the dining hall hadn't moved, though there were a few new Sharpie messages graffitied across the surface. And Sebastian was lounging around with his two best and oldest friends. Everything was as it had always been, more or less.

Theo wound a strand of his vibrant hair around his index finger. "On the subject of the new kid, I've already heard some rumors about him. Which seems weird, considering it's been like half a day."

"It was a gossip-light summer." Sebastian shrugged. "Not much else to talk about. Ashley Marr cheated on Dustin Schwartz for the hundredth time, David Patter got a tattoo on his dick, and Chris Rand got caught smoking weed in the dorms. Again. Nothing exciting ever happens around here. Hence, the new kid gets the spotlight."

"If he's not a freshman, then he's a transfer," Dante said. "I heard one of the girls in the registrar's office talking about someone who transferred 'under mysterious circumstances,' quote unquote."

Sebastian frowned. "You're shitting me."

"I shit you not, my friend. Word on the street is, Nick got booted from his last school. Think he got caught cheating? Or fighting?"

"I heard he had sex with a professor." Theo shrugged. "Though obviously none of the rumors are true. He would have been expelled, and the Academy never would've accepted him."

"True." Sebastian stretched his arms above his head. "But that won't stop everyone from spreading gossip anyway. Good to know we've all left our juvenile high school ways behind us. I, for one, am thrilled to be in college, surrounded by adults who never act immature."

Dante scoffed. "You sound awfully bitter for someone who's single-handedly powered the Academy's rumor mill on more than one occasion."

Sebastian didn't dignify that with a response.

Theo cut in. "We don't have to talk about this if you think it's distasteful. How were your early classes?"

"Fine." But Sebastian's brain currently had one track, and it ran straight to Nick. "You guys saw the way Nick stared at me this morning, right?"

"So much for changing the subject," Theo said with a laugh.

Sebastian ignored him. "That was so not subtle. I wonder if he's gay or uncouth."

"Don't stereotype people," Dante admonished. "He could be bi *and* uncouth."

"What about a minute ago? He followed me outside exactly as I thought he would. That's a pretty clear sign of interest."

"What do you care?" Theo raised an eyebrow at him. "You trying to date him?"

Something twanged in Sebastian's chest, but he shook his head. "Don't be ridiculous. I don't date."

"What'd you say to him anyway?" Dante asked. "I saw him run off toward Nassar Hall in a hurry. He looked pale too."

"It's not so much what I said, but what I did." Sebastian grinned, replaying the memory in his head until he imagined he could still feel the softness of Nick's bottom lip against the pad of his thumb. "I touched him. And more importantly, he let me."

Dante grimaced. "Touched him *where?*"

Sebastian glared at him. "His face, you pervert. It was practically innocent."

"Why'd you do that?" Theo asked.

Sebastian considered the question before answering. Honestly, it'd been an impulse, which was strange to admit. He never lost his cool around boys, but the second he'd caught sight of Nick's uncertain blue eyes, he'd *needed* to touch him. It was a little alarming.

Summoning up his best cocky smile, he answered, "Why else? Because I wanted to."

"That's hot," Dante said, pitching his voice high. "Doesn't mean he's interested in you, though. Or interested in men. If some random dude walked up to me and grabbed my face, I'd run for the hills too."

"There's no way he's straight. That look he gave me this morning had something behind it."

"You looked back," Theo said. "Don't think that wasn't obvious."

"Guilty." Sebastian rubbed his chin. "He's cute, that's for sure. He has that whole golden-boy thing going on. Haven't seen one of those since my internship in Cali." An idea rose to the surface like driftwood. "You know . . . he might be a good candidate for our old bet."

Sebastian might have imagined it, but he thought Theo looked stricken for a moment before he blinked catlike green eyes at him. "Seriously? We haven't dusted off the bet in years."

"Yeah, because we've known half our peer group since grade school. There hasn't been a good challenge. The new kid smells like fresh meat to me." Sebastian leaned forward, excitement building in him. "I think we should do it. First one to get a kiss from the new kid wins."

"Might be a little unfair." Dante shrugged a sculpted shoulder. "I mean, obviously one lingering look does not a romance make, but Blondie did check you out earlier. I'd say that gives you an advantage. The subject of the bet has to initiate the kiss, after all."

"Oh, please." Sebastian scoffed. "So what if he stared at me? Everyone stares at me. Besides, I'm *bored*. There's nothing to look forward to this semester. The excitement of freshman year has worn off, we're not seniors yet, and we won't be old enough to buy alcohol for—" He screwed up his mouth. "I suck at math. Theo, how far away is your birthday?"

"Three months and twenty-seven days. Not that I'm counting them or anything."

"Nearly four months! Four long, arduous months before one of us can buy liquor for the rest of us. That's a whole semester still to go before we can stop relying on upperclassmen and fake IDs every time we want to throw a house party. What better to do with our time than revive our old bet? If I remember correctly, the score is tied. We could settle this once and for all."

"Let me get this straight," Dante said. "You're so bored, you want to toy with the feelings of a complete stranger? Over a bet that barely has stakes? Theo, do you find this as disturbing as I do?"

Theo shrugged. "I'm more disturbed that he can't do basic arithmetic."

"Hey now." Sebastian pouted. "My talents are artistic in nature. Bet I can write a better geopolitical analysis of *The Goblin Market* than you can."

Theo grimaced. "Touché."

"And besides"—Sebastian turned to Dante—"the bet does so have stakes. We're competing for permanent ownership of our beloved Barbzilla."

Dante groaned like a dying animal. "Why do we still *have* that thing? It's a million years old and probably soaked in germs."

"I like it." Theo shrugged. "I'm surprised you don't."

"Yeah, Dante," Sebastian said. "Where's your sense of nostalgia? To others it might look like a silly plastic trophy with a Barbie head glued onto it, but it's part of our childhood."

Theo gave Sebastian a dreamy smile. "Plus, I'm currently in possession of it, which makes me the winner."

"Not after I take it from you," Sebastian piped up.

"Try me, Prinsen."

Dante groaned again and let his head *thump* onto the table.

"Sounds like Theo is in." Sebastian clapped his hands together. "That settles it. Nickolas Steele just got one hell of a target painted on his back."

"Before you get too excited . . ." Theo hesitated. "Aren't we a little old for this? I swear, I never should have showed you *Cruel Intentions* when we were tweens. I created a monster."

Sebastian scoffed. "Oh, come on. Our bet isn't nearly as tacky as the one in that movie. It's a simple kiss. No one will get hurt." He paused. "Though for the record, if we *were* in that movie, I would so be Sarah Michelle Gellar."

"Your name is literally Sebastian. Wouldn't that make you Ryan Phillippe?"

"Theo, please. It's obvious I'm Buffy all the way."

"Huh." Theo tapped his chin. "So, does that mean *I'm* Phillippe?"

"You *wish*. You're Reese Witherspoon, and Dante is—"

"I swear to God," Dante interrupted, "if you say Sean Patrick Thomas, I will flip this table."

Sebastian sniffed. "I was going to say Selma Blair, only less gullible and with better fashion sense."

Dante appeared to mull that over. "Acceptable."

"Before we get too ahead of ourselves," Theo said, "we should find out more about Nick. Specifically, we should confirm if he's into men. If he's not, the bet's off for obvious reasons."

"Good point." Sebastian grinned. "Though after the welcome I gave him, I'm really not concerned." He shivered a little at the memory alone. When their faces had gotten close . . . Sebastian hadn't wanted to pull away. Arousal mixed with a note of apprehension blossomed in his viscera. When was the last time he'd reacted to someone like this? Had he ever?

Dante picked his head up with a sigh. "I think it's safe to say this year is going to be interesting."

Nick did his best to concentrate in class, but half an hour after his strange encounter with Gray Eyes, his heart was still jackhammering in his chest.

No matter how many times he replayed the memory in his head, he couldn't convince himself that it'd really happened. A total stranger—who happened to be an attractive guy—had lured him to a secluded spot and . . . and . . .

Nick didn't know how to describe it. He'd touched him? That sounded dirtier than what had actually gone down. It had been a uniquely sensual experience, no doubt. Nick didn't think anyone had ever stopped to touch his lips before. Not like that.

And then Gray Eyes had dismissed him as easily as a professor might. Nick had been all too happy to scamper away. He'd almost forgotten he had class in his haste to escape. Although, considering he hadn't heard a word his professor had said, he could have skipped.

Why had Gray Eyes gotten him alone? Why had he touched him? Was that how people said hello around here, or what? Nick shook his head to himself. Deen had said the people around here were hedonists, but Nick had assumed that was hyperbole. This was still a Catholic university.

There was a chance his expectations about this place were all wrong. The idea was as frightening as it was intriguing.

The professor—a woman in her late twenties who insisted on being called Jessica—turned to the next page in their syllabus. Nick followed suit, along with the other students in the class, before casting his attention out the window. From five floors up, he could see all the way across the lush campus.

Is Gray Eyes in class right now? Is he thinking about me too?

The thought made him squirm. Like clockwork, the memory of the touch played again in his head. It seemed to be getting more vivid with every reprise. He could almost feel the heat from Gray Eyes's skin, the insistent-yet-light press of his thumb. When Gray Eyes had first approached, Nick had gotten a whiff of almond. Maybe his cologne or shampoo. Whatever it was, it had taken up residence in Nick's nose.

Nick wasn't the most experienced when it came to flirting, but he was reasonably sure the stranger had been hitting on him. Why else would he focus on Nick's lips? Heat swept through Nick. He forced himself to think of something else. Cold showers. Screaming children. The mysterious disappearance of Amelia Earhart.

As if sensing his plight, someone tapped his shoulder.

Nick twisted in his seat. The girl behind him still had her hand out, perhaps prepared to tap him again if necessary.

"Hey," she said in an undertone. "I'm Angela."

Next to her, a boy leaned across the aisle toward them. "And I'm Minho."

"Hi." Nick glanced at the professor before giving a little wave. "I'm Nick. What's up?"

"It's nice to meet you." Angela smiled prettily, and Nick's heart skipped a beat. "Are you new?"

"How does everyone— You know what? Never mind." He blew out a breath. "Yeah, this is my first day. It's nice to meet you both. If you're in this class, you must also be physics majors, right?"

Minho nodded. "Yeah, there'd be no real reason to take Principles of Physics otherwise. We probably have a couple of classes together. Hopefully, we'll see you around. All the STEM kids tend to run in the same crowd."

"That'd be great."

There was a pause. Nick considered turning back around before the professor inevitably noticed them talking. But that seemed rude, and he had a sneaking suspicion Angela and Minho hadn't introduced themselves out of politeness.

He checked that Jessica was still occupied at the front of the class before eyeing them. "Was there something else?"

Angela and Minho exchanged a look.

"We hate to ask," Minho said, not sounding like he hated it at all, "but you're the new transfer student, right? Some guys in Powell Hall were talking about you."

Sigh. "Yeah, that's me."

"Mind if we get to know you a little? No one seems to know anything about you."

Nick swallowed. "'We'? Are you two a couple?" He was asking half out of interest and half in the hopes that he could stall.

Angela and Minho exchanged another look and then chuckled.

"Uh, no," she answered. "We're what you might call partners in crime. Now, about those questions." Angela pursed her lip-gloss shiny mouth. "Is it true you were kicked out of your last college?"

Nick was so shocked, he couldn't think of anything to say but the truth. "What? No. Of course not." At the last second, he remembered to keep his voice down.

"We figured that wasn't the case," Minho said. "There's also a rumor going around that you're in Witness Protection." Minho screwed his face up into an exaggerated suspicious expression. "Is Nick your *real* name?"

At that, Nick had to laugh. "Whoever came up with that has been watching too many movies."

"That's for sure." Angela's smile was back. "Sorry about this. A lot of the people around here act like they're still in high school. They don't have enough to do, you know?"

Must be a rich-person thing. At my old school, I was so busy working two part-time jobs to pay for books and board, I didn't have time to make up stories about strangers. Not that I'm bitter or anything.

"I guess," he said aloud. "What else is everyone saying?"

"Not all that much." Minho shrugged. "Though I did hear that you had a steamy encounter with Sebastian Prinsen."

"Who?" Nick didn't recognize that name. It definitely wasn't one of the administrators he'd met that morning.

To his surprise, Angela's brown eyes grew wide. "Wow, you must be new to not know who Sebastian Prinsen is. He's famous around here. Or infamous, more like it."

"And not just because he's gorgeous," Minho said. "He's a huge flirt and a total heartbreaker. He and I have a bit of a past."

Nick looked between them, gears turning in his head.

That must be Gray Eyes. He's the only other person I met this morning, besides Deen.

"I might know him." Nick scratched the side of his face. "Is he kinda tall? Brown hair, and, uh"—*stunning, beautiful, captivating*—"gray eyes?"

"That's him," Angela said. "You scared me there for a second. *Everyone* knows Sebastian. Though some people say his eyes are blue."

Bullshit. They're definitely gray. He must be popular if people discuss his eye color.

"Yeah, I met him this morning." Nick narrowed his eyes. "How could anyone know that, though? It happened less than an hour ago."

"Honestly? We saw you two together on our way here." Minho shrugged. "Sorry for not saying that in the first place. We didn't want to sound creepy, and we weren't sure if it was you or not."

Nick was increasingly wary of Minho's use of *we*. Nick wanted a lawyer present before he answered any more questions.

He asked one of his own. "Why do you care? Are you friends of his?"

"Definitely not," Minho muttered. "Like I said, Sebastian and I have history."

"What kind?" *Were they enemies? Or worse, lovers?* Jealousy swept through Nick, surprising him.

"Nothing textbook worthy, I swear. More like a footnote." Minho eyed him. "Why? Did he mention me?"

Angela elbowed him. "Ignore my nosy friend here. We went to high school with Sebastian, but beyond that we don't really know him."

"Lucky you." *So far, he's been nothing but confusing.*

Angela frowned. "Not at all. He's supposed to be quite the charmer. He was valedictorian of our high school. He paints—*really* well too; he's won awards and shit—he speaks French and plays piano. Oh, and he throws killer parties. Getting invited is a big deal. Plus, there's the whole heartbreaker thing Minho mentioned. Though that's earned him some enemies."

Nick's mind whirred as it processed all this new information. *I'm starting to understand why he thought he could touch me without asking for permission. He's used to people fawning over him. Well, if he thinks he can toy with me, he's got another thing coming.*

At the front of the classroom, Jessica turned another page on the syllabus and looked out over the students. Nick wrenched his torso forward and fixed what he hoped was a look of polite interest on his face. She didn't even glance his way before she turned back to the board.

I should pay attention. I know we're only going over the outline for the semester, but still. This isn't the way to start a new year. Then again, this is a chance to make some friends, and they're fellow physics majors.

Nick waited for the professor to become occupied again before turning back around. "I have a sensitive question for you two."

"We love sensitive questions." Minho winked.

"Awesome. So, when you say Sebastian is a heartbreaker, what exactly do you mean? Is it like a *John Tucker Must Die* situation, and he has a bunch of girlfriends at the same time?"

What Nick really wanted to ask was if Sebastian made a habit of stroking random guys' lips, but that was too specific. They'd know he was talking from experience. And it'd be more gossip, the very thing Nick had rolled his eyes at earlier.

Angela and Minho both fell quiet, and for a moment, Nick thought he'd fucked up somehow.

But then Minho eyed him with increased curiosity. "You seem cool, so I'll let you in on a little secret. The Academy is more secular than it seems, or at least, the student body is."

"What does that mean?"

"It means we're not all good little Catholic boys and girls," Angela said, her smile sharp as broken glass. "A lot of the new students come here expecting it to be a snooze, but there's a lot of intrigue. Through six degrees of separation, pretty much everyone has slept with everyone else, and there's a thriving gay population, including Sebastian Prinsen."

Confirmed. Sebastian's into men. I kind of figured that from earlier, but it's good to know for sure.

Nick did his best to feign surprise. "Are there students who are out?" *Could that be why I was so drawn to Sebastian? I always ended up with queer friends, long before I knew I was bisexual.*

"A few, yeah. Sebastian and one of his good friends are among their number."

I wonder if she means the redhead or the handsome guy.

"You don't look all that surprised, Nick," Minho said. "What did you and Sebastian talk about when we saw you together earlier?"

"Yeah, was he nice to you?" Angela edged closer. "Did he try to seduce you? You can't trust him, you know. He's a total user who never dates anyone seriously. He's slept with every queer boy in the city."

Minho nudged her. "Hey now, slut shame much?"

"Sorry."

But Nick was no longer listening. He was replaying his meeting with Sebastian again, only now it had a whole new light. Nick had encountered plenty of dudes at his old college who were only interested in hooking up. He didn't judge, but casual sex wasn't his speed. If Sebastian thought he could nail the new kid, he had another thing coming.

"Don't leave us hanging," Minho urged. "What did Sebastian say?"

Nick got the distinct impression that anything he told these two would be all over the university by the end of the day. He needed to take evasive action.

"He didn't say much of anything." Not a lie. "Didn't even tell me his name, which is why I didn't recognize it when you brought him up." Also not a lie. "He asked me some questions about myself, like you two are right now."

So there.

Minho made a sour face. "Is that all? Man, that's so *tame*. Oh well. It's only the first day. Give Sebastian time, and he'll do something to make a splash."

They both chuckled, but Nick didn't get the joke. *This Sebastian guy sounds like he's either reckless or in major need of attention. Possibly both.*

"So, Nick," Angela said, "now that that's out of the way, let's hear more about you. Do you live on campus? Where are you from?"

Nick didn't see any harm in answering such innocuous questions—so long as he kept everything vague—and so he did. He even asked a few of his own and got to know Angela and Minho better.

By the time Professor Jessica had finished going over the syllabus, he felt silly for questioning his classmates' motives. They seemed like nice enough people, albeit somewhat nosy. But then, who wouldn't be curious about the new fish in what Nick now realized was a miniscule pond.

The professor dismissed them early, which was all the same to Nick, considering he'd heard a grand total of twelve words she'd said. Angela and Minho walked Nick outside, and then they parted ways.

All in all, Nick's first class had been a social success, if not an academic one. He might have a normal school year after all.

"So, what do you think?"

Dante, who had been chewing absently on the end of his pencil, came screeching back to the present. He focused on the man sitting across from him at a tiny table in the campus bookstore's coffee shop. "Sorry, Theo. What was that?"

"Our theater class. Think you're gonna drop it? I know it's more my bag than yours."

"Oh. No, I like it," Dante lied. "It's very . . . animated. Plus, it'll be nice having a class together again, and I need more gen. ed. credits."

"Uh-huh. I'm sure getting to see me in dorky costumes has nothing to do with it." Theo smiled, bright and beautiful.

Dante's pulse went into overdrive. The bookstore was silent around them; he was convinced the handful of students wandering the shelves could hear his heart pounding away.

"Is something on your mind?" Theo closed the textbook in front of him and leaned back in his chair, stretching his long, pale arms above his head. "You're distracted, and it usually takes a full week for you to stop paying attention to coursework."

"Heh. You got me. I was thinking about earlier." He looked out one of the nearby floor-to-ceiling windows. Late-afternoon light streamed through, warming the old hardwood floor beneath their feet. The sun hadn't started to set yet, but the light was quickly turning from the icy white of noon to warm, burnished gold.

Theo's lips quirked up. "You'll have to be more specific."

"Lunch with Sebastian. When he was telling us about the new kid. Did that seem strange to you?"

"You mean when he proposed we dredge up our juvenile who-can-get-a-kiss-first bet? Yeah, that seemed pretty strange to me."

"Not just that—although, that *was* plenty unexpected. I more meant, did you notice Sebastian's face when he was talking about Nick?"

Theo scrunched his mouth to the side in thought. "Sort of. I guess he looked kinda excited?"

"Not just excited. His eyes deadass lit up. You ever see him look like that when talking about a boy before?"

"No. I don't want to read too much into it, though. Nick's a shiny new toy who happened to catch Seb's eye. He doesn't even know the guy. He'll lose interest before long."

"Maybe." Dante picked up his pen and stared at his open notebook, which was supposed to be full of notes by now. As he gathered the nerve to say what he wanted, he swallowed. "About the bet . . . I wanted to let you know, for the record, that I don't want to participate." He peeked up.

Theo's expression was unreadable as always, but there was a glint of something in his eyes. "Because it's childish and mean, right?"

"Right."

Liar.

"Well"—Theo met his gaze—"if it helps, I don't want to participate either. For personal reasons."

Something unspoken passed between them. Dante wanted so badly to address it, but after dancing around it for so long, could he really come out and say it? Besides, Theo was one of his oldest friends, and his best friend. What if— If they—

He couldn't think it.

Silence fell between them, and Dante dared to hope it was loaded. He mustered up the confidence he was so good at layering on around everyone but Theo. "What should we do, then? Tell Seb the bet's off?"

"I actually think we should play along." Theo stared off into space. "For now, at least."

"Why?"

"I have a feeling about something. It's too early to say now, but in the next week, it should become obvious, one way or another."

Dante frowned. "Mysterious much? I'll bite, though. For all we know, Seb's going to win the bet before the week's out. Nick was definitely staring at him."

"Oh, I wouldn't worry about that." Theo twiddled a pen between his slender fingers. "Sebastian isn't the only one who has a lead in this bet."

"Hm?"

"You know how I requested to live in the dorms this year?"

Dante's eyes widened. "Don't tell me you're—"

"Yup, I'm a resident of Powell Hall, and I've been reliably informed Nick is as well. The real bet should be how long it'll take me to 'accidentally' bump into him."

"Huh." Dante leaned back in his chair, grinning as well. "Then let the games begin."

Chapter Four

A fter the longest first day of classes in history, Nick went back to his dorm and slept for what felt like five years. He didn't even rouse for dinner. When he woke in the morning, he was greeted by the sight of Deen's empty bed. Deen had mentioned he had a few early-morning classes and had followed it with an enthusiastic plea for Nick to kill him.

Damn. I'll have to eat breakfast by myself.

The idea was daunting, considering he wasn't yet drowning in new friends he could sit with. That, and the last time he'd gone to the dining hall, he'd run into Sebastian. He wasn't keen to see him again after their beguiling first meeting.

But Nick couldn't very well avoid the dining hall. He'd have to cross his fingers and hope for the best.

He took a quick shower, threw on clean clothes, and grabbed his messenger bag. It was a lot heavier than it'd been the day before, thanks to online shopping and same-day shipping. Having money was the *best*. He now had all of the supplies he needed and most of the required textbooks. He was still waiting on a few that would have cost more than a new textbook to have overnighted.

Despite his earlier concerns, Nick's trip to the dining hall was uneventful. No one so much as looked at him. It was the closest he'd come to feeling normal since he'd arrived at the Academy. Once inside, he loaded up a to-go box with eggs, bacon, and toast and got the hell out before he could tempt his luck.

After, he found himself at a loss for what to do. He had another round of new classes to attend that day, but his first one didn't start until ten. That gave him over an hour to eat and find the right building, and he could spend it anywhere.

For a second, he considered heading back to his dorm, but he quickly discarded that idea. He wasn't going to be that friendless loser who ate by themselves in their room. There were benches and tables all over campus. Hell, he'd seen a couple of comfy-looking rock outcroppings too. He'd find one and go over the syllabus from his Principles of Physics class, since he'd missed yesterday's explanation of it.

A taunting voice sounded from the back of his head: *There's always the picnic table behind the dining hall. You know that one well.*

He grimaced and marched off in the opposite direction, as if he could distance himself from the memory. Not that it was a *bad* memory, per se. But it was confusing, and he needed to concentrate. He couldn't afford to get distracted this early in the semester. He had to perform well, or he'd be out faster than a day-old meme.

Plus, if what Angela and Minho had told him was true, Sebastian wasn't the sort of boy Nick wanted to get involved with. Not after everything he'd been through. Not when he had so much else going on.

You say that, said the voice in his head, *and yet you can't stop thinking about him.*

He visualized putting a muzzle on his own thoughts. He wasn't going to lose another day of productivity. From here on out, he was all business, no pleasure.

He spotted an unoccupied table by the science building, right next to some aromatic flowering vines. Jasmine? He was pretty sure that was what the white, star-shaped flowers dotting the curly vines were, but he was no expert. Whatever they were, they smelled heavenly and lifted his bleak mood.

After tossing his bag onto the table, he took a seat and flipped open the lid of his to-go box. Inside, a plastic fork and a mountain of cheesy eggs awaited him. With one hand, he shoved food into his mouth. With the other, he dug around in his bag until he found the aforementioned syllabus.

Smoothing it out on the table's (mostly) clean surface, he started reading. It was standard enough. His grade would be based off three exams. There was an optional fourth exam during finals week for students who wanted another shot at a better score. Nick almost never took those, since he tested well, but it was nice to have the opportunity.

Around the time he ran out of eggs, he finished the syllabus and checked his phone. Forty minutes to go before class. That was about thirty-five minutes more than he needed. He had a feeling he was going to have to get used to having downtime on a campus this small. Once classes started in earnest, he'd have plenty to do, but for now, he seized the opportunity to relax and soak in the peaceful morning.

There were no nearby trash cans, so he shoved the last of the bacon into his mouth and set the box aside for now. Then he leaned back in his seat, tilting his chin up. It was another clear, beautiful day. The sky above him was deep blue and unobscured by clouds or birds. It was hotter than it'd been yesterday, but he knew from experience that wouldn't last for long. Wind that bore the jasmine perfume and the indescribable smell of a new school year ruffled his hair.

Students ambled through the quad in groups of twos and threes. Tempted as Nick was to people-watch until it was time for class, he decided against it. After what had happened yesterday, he'd learned a valuable lesson about making eye contact with strangers.

Digging in his bag again, Nick pulled out one of the few possessions he'd brought with him from Chicago: his sketchbook. He was a complete and utter amateur who was convinced of his own mediocrity, but it was a fun hobby. It helped to clear his head when he had something troubling on his mind.

He flipped to a new page—one of few left in the worn book—and pulled a mechanical pencil out of his bag. For a moment, he paused with the lead suspended an inch above the surface of the page. Then, a subject popped into his brain as if planted there. He began to sketch, and within a minute, he had the rough outline of a pair of eyes.

Hard as he tried to tell himself they weren't any eyes in particular, he knew who they belonged to. The gray pencil lead made it even harder to deny.

You're forbidden to think about him. Come up with something else. Class. Deen. The town.

The latter subject inspired a sigh. Between classes yesterday, Nick had ventured off campus to scope out what was nearby. The heart of

Evanston was too far away to walk, but his trip around the neighboring area had confirmed his worst fear. There was nothing fun to do. Evanston might technically be a city, but it was *nothing* compared to Chicago. To Nick, it was like a scale model of what a city should be.

There were no twenty-four-hour coffee places, no skyscrapers, and hardly any public transportation. Nick didn't hate it, but it was going to take some getting used to. There was nothing quite like the frenetic energy of Chicago in the summer, whereas this place was more like an old cat napping on a hot front porch.

When he'd first decided to transfer to the Academy, he'd thought a change of scenery would be good for him, but now it was making him homesick. He never thought he'd miss the noise of the city, or the smell of car exhaust, and pavement so molten he could feel it through the soles of his shoes.

It was too clean here. Too quiet. It gave him far too much time to think.

Which was how his thoughts ended up cycling right back to Sebastian, their strange encounter, and the new "friends" he'd made yesterday. It still weirded him out that people had spotted Sebastian and him talking. Like they were paparazzi hunting for celebrities. He was used to being invisible: one more face in an overpopulated urban sprawl. But here, it seemed someone was always watching.

Luckily, it didn't seem as though Angela and Minho had seen Sebastian get up close and personal with him. If they had, how would Nick have explained that? For once, he knew the answer: he wouldn't have been able to. Sebastian was a mystery, wrapped in an enigma, and a giant pain in Nick's ass.

"Stop fixating," he muttered to himself. "You need to get over it. A weirdo acted weird. That's what they do. Move on."

Easier said than done. The more he thought about Sebastian, the more he wondered how he'd thought Sebastian wasn't all that cute at first. Sebastian's look was classic, and he had this muted energy that buzzed all around him. It'd intensified when he locked eyes with Nick, and spiked when they touched.

There was a good chance he'd never know why Sebastian had "welcomed" him. Hell, he might never see Sebastian again. It wasn't as if they ran in the same circle. From the sound of things, Sebastian was a popular guy, and Nick was a nobody. Honestly, if he had his way, he'd stay that way. He didn't want to make a splash. Just get a few good friends, make some memories, and survive until graduation.

He got the feeling the Academy was like a fishbowl. Everyone within it thought it was the entire world. They had no concept of the big ocean that was out there, or the hardships that awaited once adulthood forced you to swim into it. Anyone who knew what it was like to take care of themself wouldn't waste time gossiping.

You're being a little harsh. It's been two days. Give the Academy a chance. Besides, Deen goes here, and you like him. It can't be all bad.

Nick heard footsteps nearby—probably someone walking past on their way to class. He didn't look up from his sketch as he added fine, individual eyelashes to one of the gray eyes.

A second later, the footsteps stopped, and a shadow was cast across his sketch.

Without thinking, Nick said, "You're blocking my light."

There was a pause. Then, a familiar voice made the hair on Nick's nape stand up. "I'm sorry. I didn't realize."

Nick jerked his head up. Sebastian Prinsen was standing next to the picnic table. He was dressed in a simple black T-shirt and jeans, and yet the clothing fit him so well, it seemed like a fashion statement. Nick had always been attracted to men who were muscular, but looking at Sebastian now, in all his tall, wiry glory, he had to rethink his preferences.

While Nick struggled to remember what words were, Sebastian flashed an apologetic smile. "I didn't mean to block your light. I'm an artist as well, so I understand how important it is. What are you sketching?"

He leaned over, as if to look at Nick's drawing. Nick quickly covered it with his hands and stared at him with wide eyes. "It's not finished."

If Sebastian thought his evasiveness was odd, he didn't comment. "Fair enough. I'm Sebastian, by the way. We met yesterday."

Nick's blood throbbed in his ears. All the times he'd imagined running into Sebastian again, he'd never thought it would be so . . . casual. Tame.

He blurted out, "I know who you are."

The second he said it, he wanted to bite his tongue, but Sebastian looked inexplicably pleased. "Oh? Did you ask around about me?"

Nick stepped right over that. "What are you doing here?"

"I go to school here." Sebastian looked Nick over, as if he were checking him for signs of trauma. "Remember?"

"I know that. I mean, what are you doing *here*"—he indicated the picnic table—"talking to me?"

"Am I not allowed to?"

Much as his insides warmed at the mere sight of Sebastian, he was loath to let his excitement show. He shrugged. "Free country, I guess."

For the past day, Nick had been asking himself a question without really asking it: Did he *want* to run into Sebastian again? The rational side of him had said no, especially now that he knew Sebastian's reputation for partying and playing with people's feelings. But now that the man himself was standing in front of Nick, his rational side had fallen silent.

Didn't mean he was going to make things easy for Sebastian though. Nick was *not* going to fall for the whole handsome, charming, rich thing.

Easier said than done.

Instead of being deterred by Nick's brush-off, Sebastian's smile came back full force. It looked good on him. He eyed the empty seat next to Nick as if he was contemplating taking it, but mercifully, he didn't. "How was your first day at the Academy?"

It was an innocent enough question, but Nick answered with caution. "It was fine."

"Do you like it here so far?"

"It's nice enough."

"Hm." Sebastian wet his lips. "Not very talkative, huh? I thought as much yesterday, but then I wondered if I scared you off by coming on so strong. You're not shy, are you?"

Ah. So, he was flirting with me. There's one mystery solved.

Nick was tempted to be blunt and address the elephant in the room by name. But then, he didn't really know what Sebastian's intentions were. If Sebastian was just making conversation, then Nick might ruin a potential friendship with a well-liked student before it began. That wouldn't be a stellar way to start off the year.

On the other hand, he couldn't picture himself being friends with Sebastian. Something about him—his mannerisms, or the sharp glint in his eyes—both put Nick off and pulled him in. Like a moth who knew he was flying toward fire.

In the end, Nick headed for the middle ground. "I'm not shy. But I think a fruit basket would have been a more appropriate way to welcome me, you know?"

Sebastian chuckled. "You're funny. I like people with quick tongues." His smile grew downright wicked. "Is yours good with more than just words?"

Wow, this guy really is a flirt.

"I'm told I can whistle pretty well," Nick said flatly. "Do you need something? I have class soon. I can't sit around and chat all day."

To his surprise, Sebastian rubbed the back of his head sheepishly. "That was too much, wasn't it?"

Nick blinked at him. "Well . . . yeah, to be honest. Unless being tactless was your goal."

"Sorry. I didn't mean to be so forward, today or earlier. I saw you staring at me yesterday, and then when you did it again in the dining hall, I thought . . ." His gaze dropped down to his shoes. "Well, I wanted to introduce myself and see if maybe there was something here? I'm sorry if I misread things. You're really cute, and it's making me flustered."

Once again, Nick was speechless. His pulse went haywire as he stared at Sebastian, who was now acting nervous and adorably vulnerable, as opposed to the confident, coy man he'd been yesterday.

It was an act. Nick wasn't certain how he knew, but sheepishness looked all wrong on Sebastian, as if he'd pulled on a costume that was two sizes too big. Red flags popped up all over Nick's thoughts.

The apology gave him pause, however. He hadn't expected that, and he wasn't so prideful he couldn't admit that he wanted to talk about yesterday. Closure was what he needed to put this whole thing behind him.

"All right, I'm down to talk about this." Nick abandoned his sketch and fixed his full attention on Sebastian. "Yesterday, when you lured me behind the dining hall and . . . did what you did, you were seeing if I *liked* you? Because you could have asked me to get coffee or something. Why the whole mysterious act?"

Color appeared in Sebastian's fair cheeks. "In retrospect, I realize I was a bit brash. Like I said, I was flustered. I guess I was trying to act cooler than I felt. Before, you said you already knew who I was. What have you heard about me?"

Ouch. There's a question I don't want to answer.

"Not much." Nick coughed.

"Ah. I take it you've heard about my not-so-pleasant reputation. I was afraid of that." His flush intensified. "I'm not proud of it. And I'm less proud to admit that sometimes I try to live up to the legend. It's not the real me, though."

Nick was intrigued despite himself. "Why?"

"Because everyone thinks I'm some kind of Casanova." Sebastian shrugged. "Confident and charming and sexy. Who wouldn't want to be those things? Yesterday, I saw a cute boy on campus who I wanted to talk to. So, I tried to be that guy. It was the only way I was able to work up the nerve to approach you."

"Huh." Nick twiddled his pencil. "I guess I can understand that."

"I'm relieved." Sebastian's smile was back. "So, how about that coffee?"

Nick hesitated. "I don't know."

Sebastian's shy expression fell off his face and was replaced with what seemed like genuine confusion. "Why not? I know you're into me."

The bluntness—and truth—of the statement made Nick's brain go blank. It rebooted, but not fast enough for him to come up with a witty response. He blurted out the first thing that came to him. "Dude, I don't know you. How can I be into you?"

At that, Sebastian chuckled. "There's this thing called 'physical attraction' that people sometimes use to gauge their interest in others."

"I know that." Nick glanced away to hide his embarrassment, and his eyes ended up landing on a group of students sitting in the grass not far from the table. They were watching him and Sebastian and whispering to each other. The second Nick looked over, they pretended to check their phones. They couldn't have been more obviously eavesdropping if they'd tried.

Jesus. I hope they can't hear what we're saying.

In Chicago, he'd always been surrounded by people, and yet it hadn't felt anywhere near this invasive. There, he was one person in a sea of people who were all living their own lives. In this tiny place, it seemed as though the very trees around them were leaning down to hear the conversation.

Irritation prickled up Nick's spine. He glared at Sebastian. "Look, pal, I don't know if this is a game to you or some weird hazing ritual, but I'm not into it."

Sebastian's eyes went wide, but Nick couldn't tell if it was from the accusation or the rebuff. "Why would I haze you? The Academy doesn't have Greek life, and this sure as hell doesn't seem like a frat house to me."

"I don't know, and frankly, I don't care, because I'm ninety percent sure I can't give you what you want."

"What I want?" Sebastian raised a dark eyebrow at him. "Nick, I came over here to say hi and to apologize for being so forward. Nothing more. Clearly, I rubbed you the wrong way, but I promise I have no sinister ulterior motives."

"Why should I believe you?" A combination of uncertainty and mortification made Nick defensive. "You could be lying for all I know."

"Why would I lie to you? As you pointed out, we don't know each other."

Hell if Nick knew, but something was up. He could smell it. You didn't grow up in a big city without learning some street smarts. "I'm going to make this simple, Sebastian. Whatever game you're playing, I'm not falling for it. If you want a hookup, you picked the wrong guy."

Sebastian was silent for a long moment as he studied Nick's face. Finally, he shrugged. "That's a shame."

"What, that I don't want to hook up?"

"No, that you listened to the gossip about me. Why else would you think I want to hook up?"

Nick's tongue tied itself into several complicated knots. "Well . . . you said—"

Sebastian shook his head, and his dark hair fell over his eyes like a shadow. "Don't deny it. I have a past, and I'm not ashamed to admit it, but most of the shit in the rumor mill comes from people who have too much time on their hands. Since you weren't from here, I thought..."

"You thought what?"

Sebastian sighed. "I thought you might be different. I thought maybe I had a shot with someone who didn't have a preconceived notion of me. But you're right. We really don't know each other, do we?"

His words stabbed Nick in the gut. Sebastian moved to turn away. Before he could think it through, Nick said, "Wait."

Sebastian glanced at him, face wary. "What?"

Nick hesitated for a fraction of a second before he looked down at the grass and quietly asked, "Why did you—" Nick swallowed "—do, um, that? Brush your thumb against my lip, or whatever. It was so..." *Intimate*. He couldn't make himself finish that sentence out loud.

There was a stark silence. Nick peeked up.

Sebastian's face was unreadable, but his gray eyes sparked like flint. "Because I wanted to."

Nick's face heated. That was the first thing Sebastian had said to him that seemed like the absolute truth. Sebastian was stating a fact, and the knowledge made Nick tingle. Like it or not, he was definitely attracted to Sebastian.

"Oh. Okay." Nick fished around for something else to say but came up blank.

Sebastian mercifully changed the subject. "I'm curious what exactly you heard about me. It must've been pretty terrible if it led you to reject me before you'd had a real conversation with me."

Nick flinched. "I suppose I owe you an apology for that. I did my best not to listen to what people said, but after what you did yesterday, it all added up. As for what I heard, they said you like to party, and, um, that you break hearts, and you, uh, sleep around."

Sebastian's expression was once again unreadable. "Ah, I see."

"I don't have an issue with that," Nick babbled, suddenly nervous. "The sex part, I mean. Consenting adults can do what they want, and all that. I mean, it's not something *I* would do, but to each their own, and, um—"

"Yeah, I get it. You're Kelly Clarkson, and you don't hook up. You like to make sweet love next to a roaring fire while soft music plays in the background. To each their own indeed." Sebastian's tone was wry. "For the record, my sex life isn't as exciting as everyone thinks. People like to act like I've slept with everyone on the planet, when in fact, there's a whole gender I won't sleep with."

Gears turned in Nick's head. If Sebastian was telling the truth about his sex life—and that was admittedly a big *if*—then what Angela had said *wasn't* true. That meant everything else Nick had heard could be false as well. Nothing but rumors. That put a whole new spin on this conversation.

"I see." Nick glanced at the eavesdroppers, who were still buried in their phones. "I heard that you're out, but is it a good idea to shout that you're gay on a religious campus?"

"Trust me, honey, the administration can't touch me. I'm the son of two pillars of the community and a prominent alumna. Hell, my mom's the state attorney. The university can't discriminate against me without bringing a legal and media shit-storm down on itself."

That rubbed against grains Nick hadn't realized he had. "Well, lucky you, I guess. Must be nice to have influential parents." *Or parents at all.*

Sebastian looked at him askance. "You don't have to worry either, you know. The administration doesn't care, even if they have to keep up the pretense. So long as you're discreet, you'll be fine."

"Damn, there goes my plan to burst into the dean's office wearing a rainbow flag as a cape."

Sebastian crinkled his nose in a way Nick hated to admit was cute. "Yeah, maybe don't do that. But otherwise, there's nothing to be anxious about."

"What makes you think I'm anxious? Or that I have any *reason* to be?"

The smirk was back. "You can pretend all you want, but we had a moment yesterday. I felt something between us. I'd like to feel it again, if you're so inclined."

"That's bold talk considering you know nothing about me. What if I were some meat-headed straight guy who freaked on you for making a move?"

"I'm not new. I was reasonably certain you were into men before I approached you, and if you'd complained to someone, I'd have said it was a misunderstanding, and they'd have made me go to confession. No big deal."

Nick studied Sebastian, unsure of how to respond. Now that he'd dropped the shy act, it was clear why Sebastian was allegedly so popular. He was daring and intelligent, and the whole rebellious, flirt-with-danger thing had major appeal. He had the potential to be attractive to Nick both inside and out.

But something about him was grating, like sandpaper. Part of it was his attitude. A little rebelliousness could be fun, but Sebastian talked like he thought he could do whatever he wanted to people because Mom and Dad were important. That sort of snobby entitlement set Nick's teeth on edge.

There was something else too. Sebastian's disingenuousness. It wasn't just that he'd put on an act; it was how quickly he'd dropped it, like he hadn't thought Nick would notice his sudden change in demeanor.

If he thinks I'm falling for this, he's going to be disappointed. I'm not gonna play his game.

"I have to get to class." Nick closed his sketchbook and shoved it into his bag. Standing up, he shouldered it and gathered his trash.

Sebastian blinked at him. "So soon?"

"I stayed here longer than I'd planned, thanks to you." Nick looked around for a trash can and spotted one. Naturally, it was next to the students who were still not-so-subtly spying on them. He started toward it.

Sebastian fell into step beside him without missing a beat. "Skip class."

Nick stopped short. "What?"

"It's the second day. The professor's going to go over the syllabus and then let you out early. Skip class and hang out with me. I'm enjoying our conversation." His lips curved up into a smile that was charming, wicked, and oh-so-sexy. There were probably people who'd had dreams about that smile, who'd been utterly undone by it.

Nick was not one of them. "I'm not skipping on my second day."

"If it sweetens the deal at all, I might let you kiss me."

Nick's cheeks filled with hot blood. "What makes you think I—" He stopped short. *I can't pretend I'm not attracted to him. I'm not that good of a liar.*

Sebastian's expression took on a hint of smugness that suggested he knew what Nick was thinking. "Come on. It'll be fun. There's a room in the auditorium that's always empty this time of day. We can get out of this heat and get to know each other."

Nick got the distinct impression that Sebastian meant that in the biblical sense.

Nick's eyes strayed to a bead of sweat that had formed on Sebastian's brow. As he watched, it kissed its way down his cheek. Nick was struck by the almost irresistible urge to brush it away with a finger. Sebastian's skin looked soft, unlike his sharp bone structure. What would it be like to touch it?

You're not going to find out. It's your first week at an unfamiliar college that happens to be your last shot. You can't start slacking off, especially to hang out with some boy you don't trust.

Nick shook his head. "I'm going to class. I'm here on a scholarship. I don't want to give anyone a reason to suspect I'm not taking my education seriously."

Sebastian cocked his head to the side. "I guess they have you on a pretty tight leash, huh?"

"Even if I didn't have to keep my grades up, I still wouldn't go with you. Unlike some people, I'm thankful to be here. College is expensive, but private school is worse, and this is a top-ranked university. Being here is a luxury that most people can't afford."

"Christ, you sound like one of their brochures." Sebastian put palms up in a defensive gesture. "Sorry, Dad. Didn't mean to pluck a nerve. I was teasing you, I promise."

"Uh-huh. Weren't you the valedictorian at your last school? You can't act like grades don't matter to you."

This seemed to please Sebastian. "Heard about that, did you? I guess some rumors are rooted in truth."

Damn, I gotta play my cards a little more carefully. I keep giving myself away.

"Well, if I can't convince you to skip, I suppose I'll just have to be patient." Sebastian turned around. After a few steps, he looked over his shoulder and flashed another smirk. "I'm so glad we had this talk. I feel like I know you much better now."

Nick watched him go, wondering why that innocent statement sounded so suggestive.

As he left Nick, Sebastian realized that his heart was *racing*. He could practically feel Nick's eyes on his back, boring straight down to the bone. Sebastian kept his posture straight and his pace slow, as if he were content to stroll away. In reality, his brain was screeching at him to put some distance between them.

Holy shit, Nick was interesting. And a little intimidating. Sebastian wasn't used to feeling outmatched, but Nick had seen right through him almost from the moment he'd approached. It was thrilling in every sense of the word.

Nick was as handsome as Sebastian remembered too. Golden and warm like a day at the beach, right down to his ocean-blue eyes. Sebastian had approached him expecting to flirt and maybe land a steamy afternoon make-out session, winning the bet in the process. He'd get Nick to kiss him, and then Sebastian would report his victory to Dante and Theo. They'd all move on with their lives.

But the second Nick had locked eyes with Sebastian, it'd been game over. It was like Nick could read his thoughts. Sebastian's whole sweet, I'm-nervous-around-you routine had fallen flat.

He'd been prepared for that possibility—acting was Theo's thing, not his—but he hadn't expected to experience an odd urge to tell Nick the truth. Every time he'd opened his mouth, it'd jumped to the tip of his tongue. By the end of their conversation, Sebastian had found himself being more or less straight with Nick. That was something he hadn't done with a guy in a long time.

It was refreshing, and bemusing.

Not only that, but Nick had proven to be both clever and no-nonsense, traits that Sebastian was immensely attracted to. Nick seemed to have some unfortunate puritanical ideas about sex that would need to be removed, but most college kids lost those by the end of their four years regardless.

Grass crunched beneath his feet as he walked aimlessly. A smell he could only describe as "summer" filled his nose. It got him thinking about spending breaks at home, and how painful those often were for reasons he didn't care to think about right now. Or ever. He could have imagined it, but in Nick's cagey eyes and guarded responses, he thought he'd sensed something. Something familiar. Why was Nick so resistant to him? And why had Nick transferred schools? Questions, questions.

Sebastian supposed it didn't matter. Once the bet was over, they'd likely never speak again.

Though things certainly had gotten a hell of a lot more interesting. Sebastian wasn't ashamed to admit he'd figured this all wrong. He'd walked up expecting an easy seduction and instead had gotten one of the more fascinating exchanges he'd had with someone in . . . possibly ever.

A couple of facts stood out to him. One, Nickolas Steele was sharp. Knife sharp. Two, Sebastian's charms appeared to have little effect on him, though that wasn't going to stop Sebastian from trying. And three, this bet was not going to be as easy to win as he'd assumed.

Pulling his phone out of his pocket, he composed a quick text as he tramped off toward the class he'd intended to skip, mind whirring with possibilities.

Theo twirled a pen between his long fingers, eyes unfocused as he gazed at the stern painting of a saint on the library wall. They were the go-to decoration on campus. Anytime there was a blank bit of wall that needed filling, they slapped a dead pious guy onto it. Theo found them macabre, yet strangely arresting.

"Staring off into space again?"

The voice drew Theo's attention to the squishy couch next to him, where Dante was currently sprawled with a textbook open in his lap.

"Staring off into face," Theo replied. "Creepy saint face. I think his eyes are following me."

Dante snickered. "You're not moving. His eyes can't follow you if you don't move." He swung his legs off the couch and pushed himself into a sitting position, his arm muscles flexing.

Theo swallowed his drool. "Good point." He slumped back in his winged armchair and surveyed the books spread out on the table. "It's only the second day of class. Why do we have to study?"

"Because it takes lots of braining to make the grades good." Dante tossed a scribbled-in notebook on top of the pile as if he were throwing a log onto a fire. "For my evening class, I have to read the first six chapters of the text beforehand. Guess how many I've read."

"Zero?"

Dante looked affronted. "What do you take me for? Some kind of shiftless flâneur? I've read one and a quarter."

"Oh, that's much better." Theo's phone vibrated in his pocket. He pulled it out and tapped on the text he'd received. "Seb messaged me."

Dante gasped and clapped his hands to his cheeks. "Oh my stars. He *never* does that! What'd he say?"

"It's about Nick."

At that, Dante's mirth fell away, and he narrowed his eyes. "Oh? He didn't win the bet already, did he? Because if so, I totally called—"

"It's not that." Theo leaned closer and whispered. "Apparently, Seb ran into Nick, and they had an 'interesting' conversation."

"What'd they talk about?"

"I dunno. I'm waiting for him to finish typing. When was the last time Seb admitted he was intrigued by a boy, though?"

Dante tapped his chin. "You mean one he wasn't trying to sleep with? Um, grade school, I think. He playground-married the principal's son and got put in time-out."

"Exactly." Theo's phone buzzed again, and he checked the text. "He says Nick is going to be more of a challenge than he initially thought, and he's looking forward to it. Does that strike you as odd?"

Dante shrugged. "We're having our second conversation about a boy we've never met, whom we're supposed to kiss before our best friend can, all to win a battered plastic trophy with a decapitated doll glued to it. 'Odd' doesn't live in the same state as this."

"Touché."

"Though, if you're referring to Sebastian showing interest in a guy beyond sleeping with him, then yeah, that's odd. You think he actually likes Nick? Because that would be exciting."

"I'm not sure. That's kinda what I want to talk about. Remember the last time we made the bet?"

"Yeah. We were seventeen. Young enough that we still thought that sort of thing was funny instead of gross and immature."

"It's not funny, that's for sure." Theo pushed his laptop away and leaned on the polished surface of the table. "We did it because we were miserable."

Theo remembered that time well. They were all still living at home, trying to survive high school until they could get the fuck out. His father had decided drinking a fifth of whiskey a day was a full-time occupation, leaving his mother to work two jobs to support them. Theo had wanted to leave his expensive private high school and go to public, but Mom had forbidden it. That'd given him heaps of unmanageable guilt and anxiety.

Dante's issues were no better. His big brother had moved back home after losing his job. The same brother who'd never liked the fact that Dante was interested in men. Suddenly, Dante had started showing up to school with bruises and flimsy excuses.

Then there was Sebastian. He was another story altogether.

"Yeah, I suppose we were angstier than the average teens." Dante stretched out on the couch again, on his side this time. He cupped his chin in a hand and batted his eyelashes at Theo. "Do we *have* to talk about Sebastian? I'm here with you, not him."

One look at those gorgeous brown eyes, and Theo almost relented. But he had a point to make, and for the sake of their friend, it needed to be made. "There's something I want to run past you. I have a theory about our darling Seb."

Dante gestured with his pen. "Do tell, psych major."

"What was going on in Sebastian's life around the time he conceived of the bet?"

Dante furrowed his brow. "Um . . . same shit as with us, I think. He came out. Started dating boys. Got bullied. Why?"

Theo glanced at the rows of books around them, checking for eavesdroppers. No one was paying attention to them. "The first time Seb suggested the bet to us was right after his parents started fighting. The next time, they'd separated. See the pattern?"

Dante's eyes widened. "Oh man, that was so long ago, I'd almost forgotten about that. Didn't he think he might have to move if they split up?"

"Yeah, but then his folks went to counseling, and he left for college. Not to go into full-blown psychology mode, but I think watching that go down gave him some warped ideas about love and relationships. Hence, the bet."

Dante scratched his chin. "I mean, that kinda explains why he wanted to do it back then, if he was rebelling against love or whatever. But why start it up again now?"

Theo shook his head. "I think it's because of his parents. I hate to be the one to tell you this, but he's not talking. Seb's folks are finally getting divorced, after years of making everyone in that household miserable."

Dante whistled. "Damn. I wondered about that. Seemed like no amount of couple's therapy could fix those two. Poor Seb."

"He's not taking it well. I can tell by his refusal to talk about it."

"Isn't it a good thing, though? His parents were awful together."

"Yeah. I remember the last time he had me over before we moved for college. It was *brutal*. The place was empty, and Seb told me neither of them were ever home anymore. They were always away on 'business.' I got the feeling he'd pretty much raised himself our last few years of high school. This *should* be a step forward."

"But?"

"I think the damage is done. They should have gotten divorced years ago instead of letting Seb watch their ugliness and nasty legal battles intensify with time."

"Agreed." Dante nodded. "Well, if he's lashing out, maybe we shouldn't enable him. I get that he's hurting, but taking it out on others isn't healthy."

"See, that's where I debate with myself. I think there's a chance Nick could be good for Seb, in a backhanded sort of way."

"I don't follow."

"It's too early to say for sure, but I think Seb's attraction to him is genuine, though he doesn't seem to realize how much."

Dante chuckled mirthlessly. "He has a crush on Blondie, so naturally he wants to lie to his face. Sounds like a stellar plan. What do you think we should do? Save Sebastian from himself, or let him learn an important lesson?"

"I'm not sure." Theo looked up at the ceiling. "I don't want to enable Seb, and I don't want to watch him ruin things with a boy who has potential, but I also have this idea."

"I'm all ears."

"We go along with the bet. At first. For all intents and purposes, we make it look like we want to win."

Dante nodded. "I feel a change of heart coming on. Suddenly, I want that damn trophy. Viva la Barbzilla."

"Exactly. You know how competitive Seb is. If we make him think we want to win, he'll try even harder."

"Okay." Dante frowned. "But how is that going to help anything?"

"That brings me to the second part of my plan, but I want to know if you're in before I share it with you." Theo held out his hand, palm up. "For Sebby?"

Dante didn't hesitate. He slapped Theo five and then let his palm linger. His brown eyes seemed even darker than usual when he met Theo's gaze. "For Sebby."

Theo's heart pounded for more than one reason. He grinned. "All right. So, here's what we do."

Chapter Five

By Thursday, Nick had fallen into a routine. He woke up, went to class, drank too much coffee, and attempted to cultivate a social life, though it largely consisted of hanging out with Deen in their room. Wash, rinse, repeat.

He hadn't made any other friends so far, but he also hadn't had much of a chance. Beyond the first day, classes had hit hard and fast. He was up to his neck in required reading, and his professors fired off information faster than he could type on his ancient leg-burning device. He'd started handwriting notes while he drafted a budget that would justify buying a new laptop.

Angela and Minho said hi to him at the start of class every Monday, Wednesday, and Friday, but when he failed to provide them with gossip—or show interest in what they told him—they stopped reaching out to him. So much for those burgeoning friendships.

If he wanted to make friends, he was going to have to join a club. Or maybe get invited to one of the exclusive parties he'd heard so much about. One of Sebastian's infamous parties.

Sebastian had been absent from Nick's life all week, and Nick couldn't say if he was relieved or disappointed. Their second encounter had done little to clear up his confusion from the first, and while Sebastian had given him a peek at his real self by the end, there was still so much Nick didn't know about him. Including how he could proposition Nick one minute and then disappear the next.

Nick knew one thing, though: he could definitely throw Sebastian's skinny ass farther than he trusted him.

Not that he'd gotten the chance to try. He hadn't seen a single flash of gray eyes since their last encounter. He hated how annoyed that made him.

Maybe Sebastian died, suggested a cheerful voice in Nick's head.

The closest Nick came to a Sebastian sighting was when he walked into his Thursday evening lab. He immediately spotted one of the men he'd seen hanging out with Sebastian: the ridiculously handsome one. The seating chart told Nick that his name was Dante. If neither of them dropped the class, they'd see each other once a week.

Nick toyed with the idea of talking to him, but what would he say? *Hey, you don't know me, but I'm kinda obsessed with your friend. Would you mind telling me, a complete stranger, what his deal is? Thanks.* For some reason, Nick decided against doing that, and so the minutes until the end of the class ticked by one agonizing second at a time.

The lab ended up letting out late. Nick had thought taking an evening class would be easier than taking one of the early-morning options—he knew well the cardinal rule of college: never schedule anything before 10 a.m.—but getting out as the sun was setting was depressing. It made him feel like he'd wasted all day in class and now it was time for bed.

Outside the science building, he stood in the cooling evening air and spent a moment breathing in and out. The sunset was beautiful as it draped itself over the old, ivy-covered buildings like a sheet of gold. If he saw Dr. Finn again, he was going to recommend they add some dusk photos to their brochures.

While he took in the view, he considered his options. If he wanted to, he could stop by the dining hall and grab some dinner. But he'd eaten two meals there already today, and it was getting old.

He had snacks back in his dorm. Nothing fancy. Chips and cookies he'd gotten when he'd raided the vending machines by the gym. It wasn't healthy, but then neither was the pizza he ate for lunch every day.

Resigning himself to a night of processed goodness, he trudged through the quad toward his dorm. His thoughts drifted back to the lab. It seemed like it was going to be a fun class. The professor was a fiftysomething gangly guy whose energy said he'd never left college mentally.

According to the syllabus, they were going to do a lot of "hands-on demonstrations." In physics terms, that meant they'd get to build shit and use sound to measure temperature. Nick was *really* looking forward to it.

As he walked, he passed a group of guys hanging out by a bench. Nick could tell from their build that they were athletes, and he confirmed it when he glanced at their clothes. They were each wearing a crimson shirt that said *AHN Swim Team* in white letters across the chest. Nick had considered joining one of the Academy's sports teams, but he'd never played anything more serious than street hockey. He was a dabbler at best.

His eyes latched on to one guy who was a little taller and leaner than the others. His hair was blond, but from this angle, he almost had the same build as—

"Hey," one of the guys shouted. He didn't sound happy.

Nick startled. *Oh shit. Was I staring?*

"What are you doing gawking at him? See something you like?"

Fuck. Here comes the gay panic. Abort, abort.

Nick backed away, mumbling excuses. He didn't mean anything by it, it was a misunderstanding, et cetera.

But then the guy slid his arm around the slender guy's waist and glared at Nick. "Robby is *my* boyfriend. Go ogle someone else."

"God, Chris, you're so possessive," Robby whined, but he leaned into his boyfriend's meaty arms.

Nick gaped. "Boyfriend?" Was the whole school gay? Was this what happened when people went to Catholic school for too long?

Chris bristled. "You gotta problem with that?"

"No! Not at all." *You have no idea, buddy.* "I'm gonna go." He turned to walk away.

As soon as his back was to them, Nick heard a stage whisper. "Isn't he the new kid Minho was talking about? The *scholarship* student?"

The way he said that last bit made it sound distasteful. Like, *Isn't he the guy who kicks puppies?*

Nick whipped around despite his better judgment. He wasn't a fighter when he *wasn't* hugely outnumbered. If things got heated, he'd need to run. Good thing this was the swim team and not track.

"What's me being a scholarship student got to do with anything?" Nick asked carefully. So far, no one had given him shit for not having money. He'd almost let himself believe that no one cared, that they were all adults.

The swim team guys exchanged looks that Nick didn't like at all. Instead of answering Nick's question, the one who'd spoken up asked one of his own. "Is it true you don't have parents? I heard yours died, and that's why they gave you all those scholarships."

Nick's vision sizzled red. He was actually taken aback by how quickly rage flooded into him, making his heart pound. He clenched his hands into fists at his side and willed himself not to lose his temper. *Calm down. Ignore him. You can't get in trouble in your first week. Or ever.* Even as he thought that, his skin itched with the desire to punch that dick in his smug face. For a split second, he seriously considered doing it; he was so volatile with grief and anger.

Luckily, one of the guy's friends shoved him. "That's not cool, bro. You can't say shit like that to people."

"He started it," the guy muttered.

But the group was already moving. Chris gave his boyfriend a possessive squeeze and shot Nick one final, nasty look before they migrated away.

Nick watched them go, taking slow, deep breaths until the adrenaline left his system. Jesus. He hadn't gotten that angry in . . . ever. He'd never been in a fight before. The idea that he'd been so ready to punch a guy was scary. Clearly, he wasn't dealing with his grief as well as he'd thought.

You should take up yoga or something. It's been a year. You shouldn't still be so raw. Besides, these rich kids would probably sue you into another lifetime if you so much as breathed on them.

With a sigh, Nick returned to his original goal of getting to his dorm. The sun was halfway below the horizon when he got there, and lights were blinking on all around the quad.

He took the stairs at a jog. Between living here and that one class on the fifth floor, he hoped he'd be in awesome shape by the end of the semester. As it was right now, however, he was out of breath by the time he got to his room. What better time to load up on junk food?

Unlocking the door, he prepared to wheeze through a greeting with Deen, but his roommate wasn't home. The sight of his empty bed jogged something in Nick's head. *I didn't tell anyone besides Deen about my parents. How then did those swim guys know? Could Deen have told someone?*

Deen didn't seem like the gossiping sort, but how else could that have gotten out? Then again, people around here seemed to *know* things about him, like the fact that he was new. Nick hated to think he couldn't trust Deen, the only friend he'd made so far. Without him, Nick was completely alone.

God, that was a depressing thought. He'd been trying to keep his chin up this whole week, but in this strange place, cut off from his old friends and the city he loved, he was really starting to feel lonely.

His bed called to him. He made a beeline for it and flopped onto the tangled sheets. He buried his face in his pillow. "Never in my life have I been so eager for the weekend."

Of course, once Friday rolled around, he'd have to deal with the fact that he had no plans, and that would probably send him nose-diving into a pit of despair again. Awesome.

As if cued by his thoughts, there was a knock at the door. Nick picked his head up from the pillow and stared at the door as if he expected it to explain itself.

Had Deen forgotten his key? Or maybe it was one of the swim team boys, come to finish what they'd started.

Cautiously, Nick sat up in bed. "Who is it?"

In lieu of an answer, the person knocked again.

Nick debated with himself for a beat before he tiptoed over and peered out the peephole. All he saw was red hair.

Frowning, he opened the door and stepped back. On the other side was a guy who looked familiar. It took Nick a second to place him. *He's the other one I've seen hanging around Sebastian.*

"Hey there. I'm Theo." He waved. On top of having dyed hair, he also had bright green-gold eyes and a short but muscular frame. His face was boyish, with a big forehead and a pointed chin.

"Hi." Nick wet his lips. "I'm Nick, but I'm willing to bet you already knew that."

Theo laughed and walked through the door without waiting for Nick to invite him. Once inside, he looked between the two beds before turning to Deen's desk and pulling the chair out. He fell into it, seeming as comfortable as if he lived here.

Nick stared at him. "Can I help you?"

"I certainly hope so, Nick. You were right, by the way. I do know you. Everyone does by now. Isn't that annoying?"

Theo's frankness surprised Nick into relaxing a fraction. He nodded. "Yeah. It's been a hell of an adjustment."

"From Chicago to Evanston?"

Nick's eyebrows shot up.

Before he could articulate his question, Theo shrugged. "Like I said, everyone's heard about you by now. Sometimes I think about the fact that we're all legal adults, and I just *laugh*."

Nick wasn't sure quite how to react to Theo's odd mix of mellow and blunt. He also had a quiet, measured way of talking that made everything he said sound important. Nick found himself leaning forward to hear him.

After a pause, Nick pulled out his own desk chair and straddled it, facing Theo. "So, is there something you need?"

"Need? No." Theo regarded him. "But there is something I want."

Nick frowned. "Is it a map to a straight answer?"

Theo laughed again—with enthusiasm—and Nick smiled despite himself.

When he'd composed himself, Theo said, "You're funny. No wonder Seb is so taken with you."

The smile dropped right off Nick's face. "Seb? As in . . ."

"Sebastian Prinsen. The notorious campus heartthrob who also happens to be one of my closest friends. And one of many reasons why I wanted to meet you."

Nick's defenses slammed up. "Did he send you to talk to me?"

"Nope. He has no idea I'm here. In fact, if he knew, he'd probably be all kinds of irritated, so let's keep this tête-à-tête between us. I'm here because I ran into half the swim team outside, and they were— *quelle surprise*—gossiping about you. One of them lives here with us, and he swears you tried to start something."

"Jerks," Nick grumbled. "So, you live in Powell Hall too?"

Theo raised an eyebrow. "Wow, you didn't even try to deny it. That pretty much confirms the rumor, you know."

Oops.

Nick tried to look nonchalant. "I didn't do anything. It was a misunderstanding."

"I'm sure it was, but by tomorrow morning, people will be saying you punched the captain of the swim team in the throat, or something equally ridiculous. You gotta be more careful."

Paranoia crept up behind Nick. "Did you come here to lecture me? What do you care if I get in trouble?"

Theo held up his hands in surrender. "I have no ulterior motives, I swear. That was a friendly word of caution. No one wants to see you get thrown out of this school over some petty bullshit, including you, am I right?"

Nick eyed him for a moment, but upon seeing no outward signs of obvious evil, he sighed. "Fuck. I'm never going to get used to this."

"To what?"

"Not being invisible."

Theo inclined his head to the side. "Were you not popular at your old school?"

"There's no such thing as 'popular' at a big university. I went to UIC before this, and it has nearly thirty thousand students. Sure, there are cliques and shit, but no one pays any mind to anyone else. They couldn't if they tried. Standing out was next to impossible. Plus, I had a job as a bus boy, and let me tell you, no one looks twice at the guy who's hauling around dirty dishes."

Theo's mouth formed a pensive moue. "I get it. You were a normal-sized fish in a humongous pond, and now you're in a pond so small, you feel like you're the size of the Loch Ness Monster."

"That was . . . descriptive. But yeah, I suppose that covers it."

Theo offered him a kind smile. "I know it's frustrating, but the silliness makes it not worth getting upset about, right? If you absolutely have to punch something, make sure it's inanimate, and there are no witnesses."

It was Nick's turn to laugh. "It sounds like you're not a huge fan of this place either. Why'd you decide to go here?"

Theo shrugged. "It's all I know. I went to the feeder high school, same as half the people here. Hell, I have classmates today that I went to kindergarten with. Besides, despite everything, it's a great school, the campus is beautiful, and it made my folks happy. They're footing the bill, so it was in my best interest to go to their top choice."

"I definitely understand going where money dictates." Now that his initial surprise was wearing off, it occurred to Nick that this meeting was strange in more ways than one. "You never answered my question. Are you staying in this dorm too? How'd you know which room is mine?"

"Yup, this is my dorm sweet dorm." Theo flashed a catlike grin. "And everyone knows you got the attic. It's the best room in the building. A lot of the other students are pissed they couldn't buy their way into it."

Nick looked around the room. It didn't seem any different than the rest of the house. "Why is it the best?"

"You only have to share a shower with one other guy. You should duck into one of the bathrooms on the other floors some morning. Or better yet, don't. The locker room smell lingers something fierce."

Nick scrunched his nose. "I'll take your word for it." He studied the man across from him. Theo was what Nick would term *unconventionally attractive.* His big eyes and bee-stung lips seemed odd on a man's face, but there was no doubt he was beautiful. Nick liked him too. He was frank, and there wasn't a moment when Nick doubted his sincerity. Unlike with a certain someone.

Theo chuckled, and Nick snapped back to reality. "What?"

"I should be asking you that. You're staring at me."

Nick's face grew hot. *I've really got to stop checking out guys. The whole school's gonna know I'm queer before the end of the week.* "Sorry. It's been a long day, and I was lost in thought."

Theo's facial expression was far too neutral. There was no way he'd bought Nick's lie. "You can look at me if you want. I don't mind."

Nick's remaining blood rushed into his cheeks so quickly, he saw spots. "I wasn't— I'm not— I didn't mean to—"

"Man, Seb's right. You're way too easy." Theo leaned back in his chair with a grin. "Much as I hate to spoil the fun, I didn't come here just to chat."

"Oh?"

"I want to talk about Sebastian and Dante. You know Dante, right? Our third musketeer?"

"If he's who I'm thinking of, yeah." Nick made a helpless gesture. "I don't want to sound weird, but I don't know how else to ask this: is he *noticeably* handsome? Like, tall, literally dark, and handsome, with cheekbones that could cut raw diamond?"

For some reason, that made Theo blush. "Yup, that's him all right. He told me you have a class together."

Nick couldn't hide his surprise. "We got out of that lab like thirty minutes ago. How'd you find out so fast?"

Theo gave him a funny look. "We have these things called *phones*. He texted me as soon as he recognized you."

"Oh. Right. I knew that." Nick made a mental note to shove his foot into his mouth later. "I've never spoken to him, though. I'm surprise he knew my name."

Theo offered him a small smile.

"Ah, right. I keep forgetting. New kid. Small pond. Never mind."

"If you'd like, I can share some wisdom with you."

Nick frowned. "What kind of wisdom?"

"Think of it as an Academy survival guide, from someone who's lived here all his life. Anyone who's ever gone to a small university can confirm what I'm about to tell you."

"Okay." Nick had an odd urge to brace himself. "Shoot."

"One." Theo held up a finger. "The rumor mill here runs twenty-four seven. You've already figured that much out. It's about sixty percent accurate, so take from that what you will. Two." He ticked up another finger. "I don't know if you're so inclined, but if you have sex with *anyone* at this school, you'll pretty much be sleeping with the entire university, including some alumni and several faculty members. There's no six degrees of Kevin Bacon here. We have one degree of Charlie Sheen. Got it?"

"Yeah." Nick's lip curled up. "And again, that was descriptive. Overly so."

"That brings me to three." He added a third finger before dropping his hand. "The only way to get any sort of anonymity at this school is to live off campus, away from the mothership. For you and me, that's not an option right now. But when next year rolls around, you might want to consider getting an apartment."

Nick grinned. "You think I'll make it to next year?"

"Dunno. It seems you've caught Seb's attention. There's a reason why people love to hate him. You might never be able to escape notoriety now."

"What's that supposed to mean? I'm not involved with him. He can flutter around me all he likes, but it doesn't mean I have to reciprocate."

"True." Theo rested his elbows on his knees and looked Nick square in the eye. "If you tell me right now that you have no interest in him, I'll believe you. If you want, I'll call him up and make him swear on our friendship to never bother you again. We can pretend this whole conversation never happened."

Nick pressed his lips together. Unbidden, his brain conjured up an image of when Sebastian had talked to him at breakfast. Nick could still hear Sebastian's voice ringing in his ears. *Because I wanted to.* The memory sent sparks up Nick's spine.

Theo gave him a knowing look. "That's what I thought. And that's ultimately why I'm here. Since Seb's my best friend, I figured I should introduce myself. According to him, you're a fascinating person."

Nick's head started to swim. "Can I ask you a question?"

"Sure."

"What's up with Sebastian? Try as I might, I can't figure out his whole hot-and-cold, mysterious-flirtatious routine. It does my head in."

"Yeah, ignore all of that. Sebastian acts cool, but it's a big show he puts on for the other students. He's been doing it so long, I don't think he realizes it's not real anymore. I promise there's more to Seb than his reputation, though. We grew up together, and his life hasn't been all that easy, so he acts out sometimes."

Nick scoffed. "What problems could the poor rich kid possibly have? Does he have to do his own laundry now that he lives on his own?"

Theo's eyes iced over. "You know, financial stability is an incredible privilege, but it doesn't make people immune to misfortune. Sebastian's parents did a real number on him when he was growing up, and having money didn't make him any less depressed. You shouldn't be so quick to make assumptions about Sebastian's life. Or anyone else's, for that matter."

Nick swallowed. "I'm sorry. I'm a little bitter because I'm here on a full scholarship."

"Your parents aren't helping you pay for school?"

"No, they're not." He was surprised how hard his voice sounded. Theo eyed him, as if he sensed there was meaning underlying Nick's words. "I get it. There were times when my family was struggling, and I honestly thought that if we won the lottery, all our problems would be solved. But in the immortal words of the Notorious B.I.G.: mo' money, mo' problems."

"Word. Well, you've listed a couple of reasons for coming here tonight, but somehow I don't think you're really here to get to know me."

"I'm not *not* here to get to know you." Theo winked. "Sebastian's never shown such interest in a guy before, and it made me curious. But you're right, I have other motivations. Honestly, I want to make sure you know what you're getting into."

Nick took a breath to steady his voice. "And what's that?"

"It's entirely up to you."

Nick rolled his eyes. "How can you be so blunt one second and then talk like Yoda the next?"

Theo flashed a big, cheesy grin. "A gift, it is."

Nick wanted to laugh, but it got caught in his throat. "I have a question. Everyone keeps describing Sebastian as a heartbreaker. Has he ever had a boyfriend? Like, a serious, long-term relationship?"

"Very good question. No, he hasn't. His longest relationship was when we were freshmen, and it lasted a month. If you're expecting a tender wooing, you're not going to get one from him."

"I'm not expecting anything, to be honest." Nick shrugged. "As far as I'm concerned, Sebastian's a stranger who keeps popping up when I least expect it, and I don't know what that means yet. I'm not trying to make a splash at this school. I want to catch up and graduate, and that's it. If Sebastian's going to get in the way of me doing that, then I'm going to avoid him. Plus, I'm not trying to broadcast my sexuality, unlike everyone else at this school."

Theo's brow furrowed. "'Catch up'?"

Nick cleared his throat. "I'm a year older than most juniors. I took some time off. For personal reasons."

"Did you take a gap year?" Theo perked up. "Where'd you go? Thailand? I hear a lot of students these days are going to Thailand."

Nick blinked at him. "What's a gap year?"

"Ah. Never mind. It's one of those privileged-rich-kid things. But for the record, about the sexuality thing, you shouldn't worry."

"You're the third person to tell me that, and yet here I sit, still worrying."

Theo shook his head, and his wild red locks shifted like an octopus. "None of the students are gonna care if you're into guys, and they certainly won't blame you for being into Seb. Pretty much everyone is. Man, woman, gay, straight, and all the spectrums therein."

Nick wasn't sure why, but something that almost felt like jealousy sparked up in his chest. "Including you?"

That got a chuckle out of Theo. "No way. Seb and I would never work out. We're way too different."

"But the problem isn't that you're not into guys? You're gay, or whatever?"

"Whatever," Theo confirmed. "I'm pansexual. Sebastian's gay, as I suspect you already know. Dante will tell you his orientation if you catch him riding a caffeine high at three in the morning on the night of a full moon. That's another reason why the three of us are friends. Queer birds of a feather."

Nick nodded. "Makes sense. So, is this you inviting me to join your gang of queer hotties, *Mean Girls*–style?"

With a snort, Theo shook his head again, and the crimson octopus returned. "Not at all, though it bodes well that you make movie references too. Part of me wants to tell you to run as fast as you can. Another part wants Seb and you to fall in love and live happily ever after."

Nick's heart thumped hard in his chest. "Love?"

"And that—" Theo jabbed a finger at Nick's chest "—brings me to the real reason behind my visit, at long last. In the interest of fairness, I'm here to give you a warning. If you don't want anything to happen with Sebastian, you have to tell him to fuck off now."

"What? Why?"

"Because Sebastian is charming and intelligent and gorgeous, and no matter how strong you think you are, or how careful, or how jaded, eventually, you'll fall for him. This isn't a situation where you can get your toes wet. Either jump into the deep end, or get the hell out of the water."

Nick's head was reeling. "If Sebastian's your friend, shouldn't you be talking him up?"

Theo's face was unreadable. "I don't want to see anyone get hurt."

Nick tried to swallow, but his mouth had gone dry. "And you think I would get hurt, if I decided to go for a swim."

"Sebastian has a *lot* of baggage. And not the good relationship baggage, like a broken heart that proves he has one. His baggage involves pain and betrayal and questioning if love even exists, or if most people on this earth are destined to lie, cheat, and die alone. And everyone, *everyone*, thinks they're the special someone who's going to come along and 'fix' him."

"But no one is," Nick finished.

Theo's mysterious smile was back. "That remains to be seen."

Nick swallowed. "Why are you telling me all of this? I gotta admit, this is up there on the strange scale. Ever since I came here, I keep having the oddest conversations with people. What's the point of it all?"

Theo waved him off. "It's just like I said. I'm here to give you a warning. And honestly, I know we don't know each other, but you seem like a cool guy. I'd like for us to be friends." His green-gold eyes met Nick's from across the room, the expression in them unreadable. "For now."

Chapter Six

"Seb."

Sebastian chewed absently on the end on his pencil as he stared off into space. Thoughts darted around in his brain, refusing to settle. They made it difficult for him to focus on anything, including the beautiful-albeit-gray campus around him and the voice calling his name.

"Sebby."

"Don't call me Sebby," he mumbled automatically.

I need to go grocery shopping and change the dead light bulb in my fridge. Maintenance will fix it if I call, but they take forever. I bet I can do it myself.

He made a mental note to look for a hardware store while he was in town. That was his best bet for finding whatever kind of light bulbs he needed. A cool burst of morning air ruffled his hair. He closed his eyes to soak it in. The air smelled like autumn, ready to sweep over campus in all its gold-and-ruby glory.

"Sebastian. Earth to Sebastian."

Sebastian's gaze finally drifted over to the man sitting across from him at their usual table in the quad.

Dante quirked a thick eyebrow at him. "You need another shot of espresso or something? You keep spacing out."

"Sorry. I have a lot on my mind." He looked down at the textbook that was open in front of him. In the past half hour, he'd highlighted three sentences. That didn't bode well. Normally his focus didn't taper off until the middle of the semester. What was up with him this year? "Is it possible to get senioritus in your junior year?"

"Yes," said a dreamy voice to the right.

Theo appeared and heaved a full backpack onto the table. The wood creaked ominously beneath the weight. "Morning, gents. I thought I might find you here."

"Morning," Sebastian and Dante mumbled in unison. The branches above their heads swayed in the breeze as if waving hello.

Dante eyed Theo's bursting bag. "How's that morning lecture treating you?"

"It's great." Theo plopped, boneless, onto the wooden bench like a ragdoll. "And by 'great,' I mean 'it's terrible, and my life is a dumpster fire.'"

Sebastian chuckled. "You're not allowed to call me dramatic ever again."

"You don't understand. There's a reason why literally every list of college advice tells you not to sign up for morning classes. Between that and late-night studying, I'm lucky I live on campus, or I'd never get any sleep."

"I sympathize," Dante said. "Thanks to the late lab I have Thursday nights, I feel like I go to class, sleep, and when I wake up, I'm right back in class. Plus, my mom sent me like twelve frantic texts because I didn't call her before bed like I normally do."

"Man, having parents who love you must be so rough," Theo said, voice dripping with sarcasm. "The last time my dad called, he'd pocket-dialed me from whatever bar he was in. And I know it was a bar, because I heard the distinct sound of karaoke and bad decisions."

Without asking, Dante reached into Theo's bag, pulled an apple out from amongst the books, and traded it for the unopened bag of chips in front of him. Theo grabbed the chips and started wolfing them down.

"I knew your blood sugar was low," Dante muttered.

Sebastian rolled his eyes. "Could you two be more married?"

Dante and Theo both froze for a fraction of a second—long enough to be noticed, but not so long Sebastian wanted to remark upon it—before Dante shot him a far-too-casual look. "You heard from your folks recently, Seb? Are they back in town yet?"

"Nope and nope. They could be dead for all I know."

"Jesus, don't say shit like that. When was the last time the three of you were in the same room?"

Sebastian thought back. "Well, they both attended our high school graduation, though they were seated on opposite sides of the auditorium. Dad spent the whole night with his hand on his assistant's ass, and Mom brought the pool boy as her plus-one. So, I don't think that counts."

Theo flinched. "You never told us that."

"Whatever. Who cares where they are? It's not like I need them for anything."

Dante reached for Sebastian's shoulder, only to drop his hand a second later. "At least this happened after you turned eighteen. It didn't ruin your childhood or anything."

"Oh yeah, my childhood was great." Sebastian's eyes narrowed. "After busting my ass all my life to make them proud, I turned eighteen, and then it was like I wasn't their problem anymore. No more need to put on pretenses for Sebastian. They can have all the affairs they want, right out in the open, and I'm supposed to ignore it."

Theo's eyes were huge. "Sebastian—"

Sebastian realized his voice was rising with every word, but he couldn't seem to stop it. "At least once they're divorced they won't technically be cheating on each other. My only family is falling apart, and everyone acts like I shouldn't care because hey, *I'm not a minor.*"

When he'd finished, mortification crept through him like a choking vine. Dante and Theo both seemed stricken.

"Sebastian, I'm sorry," Dante said." I didn't mean—"

"Let's take a break." Sebastian closed his textbook with a *thump.* "It's the first Friday of the new term. We should do something this weekend. Throw a party. Drink lots and lots of alcohol."

Theo and Dante exchanged a glance, like maybe they were going to insist on talking about what had just happened. Sebastian glared at them, daring them. In the end, they backed down.

"I'm in." Dante shrugged. "Though we're *not* having it at my place. The first party of the year is always the messiest. Remember the one we threw at the start of sophomore year? I had to buy all new living room furniture."

"That's what you get for putting a Slip 'N Slide indoors." Sebastian brushed his thick bangs away from his eyes. "I'm happy to host. It'll have to be tomorrow, however. I'm having company over tonight."

"Oh?" Theo asked. The sunlight streaming through the tree cast dappled patterns on his pale skin, making him look like a Dalmatian. "Anyone we know?"

"Marshall Wallace, that one twinky blond in my West African History class. He asked me if I wanted to get together and 'study' tonight. It's like the college version of Netflix and chill. I wonder if I'll so much as crack a textbook."

"Godspeed," Dante said. "Does this mean you've given up on Nick?"

Sebastian raised a brow at Dante's hopeful tone. "You wish. The bet is still very much on, and I intend to win. Barbzilla *will* be mine."

"If you want to win, why are you seeing other men?" Theo asked.

"I'm single. I can do what I want." He paused. "And Nick has been strangely resistant to my charms so far."

Dante flashed a big, bright smile. "Not falling for your snake-oil routine, huh? Sounds like Blondie's too smart for you."

Sebastian scowled. "*Au contraire.* I'm enjoying the chase. So far, Nick has proven to be a fun distraction. And it doesn't hurt that he's cute too. I love how tan he is. All that bronze skin. Makes me want to lick it and see if it tastes like metal."

"Well, that was far too much information," Theo chirped. "I see that poetry class you took last year paid off. If I can give you some advice: I wouldn't sit on your laurels with Nick for too long. Someone else is bound to come along and snap him up."

"Like you?" Sebastian fluttered his eyelashes at Theo. "Forgive me if I don't see you as a threat. You may share a dorm with him, but unless you happen to bump into him on laundry day, that's hardly an advantage. How often do you suppose the average college guy washes his clothes? Once a month?"

"Gee, if only I'd had the wherewithal to assault him behind the dining hall like you did." Theo flashed a sweet smile. "But as it just so happens, I spent some time in his room last night."

Sebastian's stomach grew cold, as if he'd swallowed ice. "What happened between you?"

"You know I'm not one to kiss and tell." Theo went back to shoveling chips into his mouth, looking for all the world like they were discussing the weather.

Sebastian didn't buy the casual act for a second. "Don't play coy with me. I trademarked that. If you had sex with Nick, I want to know."

"Why?" Theo waggled his eyebrows at him. "You jealous?"

"Of course not," Sebastian said, knowing perfectly well that he was. "I don't want to put time and effort into trying to win the bet if you've done far more than kiss him. I love a good chase, but not if I'm going to end up with a wild goose."

"Fear not. Nick is still totally up for grabs. When I was in his room last night, we talked. About you, actually."

Sebastian's heart couldn't seem to decide if it wanted to skip or race. "What'd you tell him?"

"Nothing you'd disapprove of. I wanted to learn more about him and gauge his interest in you. You're in luck. Despite seeming like an intelligent person, he likes you. Wouldn't shut up about you."

Sebastian's stomach warmed back up, along with the rest of him. "He said that? Like, he directly stated that he likes me?"

"Not in so many words, but it was clear you've got his attention." Theo tapped a finger against his chin. "Although, that may not matter much. If he gets expelled, none of us will get to kiss him."

At that, Dante rejoined the conversation. "Was that a gentle reminder that we could all be expelled at any time? Thanks to the underage drinking and the partying and the general sinning? Or did Nick get into actual trouble?"

"The latter." Theo glanced at Sebastian. "When I spoke to him last night, he'd just come from a confrontation with half the swim team. Seems he ogled the wrong man's boyfriend and almost started a fight."

"Who was he looking at? Was it Robby?" Sebastian scoffed. "I swear, I don't get why everyone thinks he's so hot."

Theo's brows knit together. "Um, priorities? Nick was nearly involved in a violent incident. You know, like a crime? If the administration got wind of it, they'd expel him. Since you're determined to win the bet, I'd think you'd care about that."

If he got expelled, I'd probably never see him again. To his surprise, the idea made Sebastian's guts lurch like a boat caught in a storm.

It's because you don't want the bet to be over before it even begins. It's been fun, and it's taken your mind off your sucky family and how depressed you've been lately. That's all.

Sebastian cleared his throat. "I'm confident you told Nick to watch his back. I'm surprised he needed to be told, though. You'd think he'd know better than to get into a fight."

"I think he was provoked." Theo shrugged. "That's what I heard anyway. One of the swim guys brought up Nick's parents, and he lost it, which confirms that particular rumor. He took a year off for bereavement."

"He's an orphan? Or the adult version of an orphan?" Sebastian rubbed his chin. "I suppose that would just be an adult. Regardless, that must've been rough for him. Or so I imagine, considering my bank account takes better care of me than my parents."

"If I didn't know any better," Dante said, his eyebrows drifting up toward his hairline, "I'd say you were experiencing that 'sympathy' thing."

"So what if I am? It's research for the bet. I'm sure you're going to put in similar effort."

Dante shrugged. "I haven't done shit yet. Haven't even had a conversation with the guy yet, and Theo had *one*, singular. I think you're more invested in Nick than you're willing to admit. Maybe that's the real reason you're hooking up with that blond tonight. You didn't get your first draft pick, and now you're settling for a cheap imitation to scratch the itch."

Sebastian stood up abruptly. "I'm tired of talking about this." He gathered his things. "Once I win the bet, everything will go back to how it was. I'll forget Nick exists, and I'll be the forever owner of one Barbzilla the Great. In the meantime, I'm going to bang the thinking out of Marshall Wallace tonight, and I'm going to start inviting people to our party this weekend. Come Saturday, you'll see for yourself how *not* invested I am."

"Looking forward to it," Theo said with a small smile.

Not for the first time, Sebastian wished Theo would lose his cool. The knowing expression on his face made Sebastian's temper flare.

I'd think my own best friends would know me better than this. Like I'd develop feelings for a stranger after my parents rushed into a disaster of a marriage. No, I'd never fall without making sure someone was there to catch me.

"I'll prove it," he said out loud, not knowing if he was talking to himself or his friends. "I think it's time I upped the ante."

He threw the rest of his things into his bag, slung it onto his shoulder, and stomped off in the direction of Powell Hall.

Nick woke to the sound of Deen swearing violently. He groaned into his pillow, lifted his head, and blinked until the room came into focus.

Deen appeared to be halfway through the process of tearing his desk apart. Papers were scattered on the floor—though only on his side of the room; how thoughtful—and his desk was a mess of books, notes, pens, and more. He was muttering to himself and didn't seem to have noticed that Nick was awake.

The room was dark, thanks to the rain clouds outside the windows. Nick fumbled with his phone, which he'd placed on his desk within arm's length of his bed, and clicked the home button: 10 a.m. Shit. He'd have to hurry to his morning class. What a way to cap off his first week.

He sat up and stifled a yawn with his hand. "Morning. You okay, buddy?"

Deen made a high-pitched noise like something out of *Jurassic Park* and whirled around. His shiny hair was in disarray, and his eyes were wide. "Oh, Nick. I hope I didn't wake you."

"I kinda wish you had. I'm gonna have to wolf down my breakfast." He stuck a finger in one of his ears and twisted it. "That was a hell of a high note you just hit. You should try out for choir."

"Sorry. You usually sleep so soundly. Want me to put a dollar in the Jerk Roommate jar?" He indicated an empty plastic jar of instant coffee they'd set up on the center window sill.

"Nah." Nick attempted to finger-comb his messy hair and winced when he caught on a tangle. "You get a pass this time, since it seems like you're having some kind of meltdown. Need help?"

"Not unless you happen to own a time machine." Deen ran a hand through his own hair, only his silky locks slid through his fingers like ink and fell perfectly into place.

I have never been so jealous of another man's hair.

"I'm fresh outta those, sorry. But I can help you look for something if you like."

"It's the syllabus for my Mechanical Engineering class. I marked the dates of all the exams in my planner, but then this morning, I spilled coffee on it. So now I need the dates again, but *of course*, I don't know where I put the syllabus."

"Ah, college." Nick let his gaze drift wistfully up to the ceiling. "Where pieces of paper have the power to ruin our lives. Pretty soon we'll start having nightmares about sleeping through exams."

"Dude, no joke. I have those during the *summer*. I can't wait for grad school, where I'll dream about getting up in front of the faculty to defend my dissertation, only to discover I'm not wearing pants."

A thought occurred to Nick. "Doesn't your class have an online portal? If so, there'd be an e-version of the syllabus you can download."

Deen stared at him, face reddening, before he sat down heavily on his bed. "Wow. I've been freaking out for ten minutes over *nothing*."

"Better than freaking out for a genuine reason." Nick threw his blanket aside and slid out of bed, his feet hitting the cool, wood floor with a soft sound. "Tell you what. Lemme put on some clothes, and we'll get breakfast together. That'll cheer you up."

"I would love to, but I have three assigned readings to do." His tone suggested he was dying for Nick to give him an excuse not to do them.

"Read while you eat. It's called multitasking, and it's all the rage. We'll bring our books and get coffee and everything. We're roommates. It's important that we bond."

"What about your class?"

Nick waved him off. "We live on campus. Everything's five minutes away. It'll be fine."

"Yeah, okay." Deen looked around at his destroyed side of the room. "Gimme a minute to clear the disaster area of debris?"

"Sure thing. I gotta shower and brush my teeth and all that."

Nick took care of his morning ablutions, and afterward he felt ready to deal with his final day of classes before the weekend.

I should do something besides hang out in the room, he thought as he examined himself in the mirror above the tiny sink. *I could . . .*

I dunno, explore the town. Strike up a conversation with someone in the dining hall. Or maybe I'll hang around the science building and meet some fellow nerds.

If he was ever going to feel like he belonged here, he'd have to put himself out there. Next year, he might get a place off campus—like Theo had advised—and then he'd be invisible. That would be great, except it'd be much harder to meet people. Hell, he might not have anyone to get an apartment with. He had no clue what Deen's plans were, or if he'd even want to live with Nick again.

He sighed as he finished styling his hair. It was curlier here than it was in the city, perhaps because the college was right by Lake Michigan.

His blue eyes looked tired, and his tan was fading, as it always did when autumn rolled around. He needed to get out more, and not just for his appearance. He was already out of clean clothes, and honestly, his wardrobe could use some updating.

"Hey, Deen," he said as he exited the bathroom. "Do you need anything from town, perchance?"

Deen looked up from where he was bent over his laptop, probably logging into his class's online portal. "Not particularly. Why?"

"I was thinking of doing some exploring tomorrow. I need new clothes, and now that my financial aid came in, I can actually buy them. I know clothes shopping with another dude isn't most people's idea of a swell Saturday, but you're always dressed impeccably. I thought maybe you could give me some fashion advice."

Deen glanced down at his pressed black slacks and pullover sweater and then grinned up at Nick. "I would *love* to. I mean, I wasn't going to say anything about your wardrobe, of course, but holes and patches are only acceptable if you're doing a grunge thing. Plus, I can give you a tour of the city. That'll take all of fifteen minutes, but you should see it, and we can grab some lunch too."

Laughing, Nick scooped up his bag and the books he needed for the other class he had that day. "Sounds like a plan. Ready for breakfast?"

"Race you!" Deen grabbed his own bag and took off before Nick could do more than shout after him.

Nick shouldered his belongings and raced after him, barely remembering to lock the door behind him. They bounded down the stairs, dodging other students and egging each other on as they went. Don the RA shouted at them to slow down, but they were gone in a flash. By the time they reached the first floor, Nick had outstripped Deen by a good six feet. He burst out the front door, and his momentum carried him across the porch, down the steps—

—and almost face-first into Sebastian Prinsen.

Nick skidded to a halt like a cartoon character mere inches from knocking into him. "Sebastian?"

Sebastian looked as surprised as he was, gray eyes huge in his handsome face. It was overcast, and in the muted light, they were the same color as the sky. "Nick."

Deen came flying up to them a second later, only he didn't stop in time. He plowed into Nick's back, which created a chain reaction, shoving Nick into Sebastian's warm, firm chest.

Sebastian caught him by the arms and squeezed. There was no reason for the touch to send a thrill through Nick, but it did.

Nick stared at Sebastian, wide-eyed and stunned, for three loaded seconds before he scrambled back. "Hi."

"Hi," Sebastian replied.

"Ouch," Deen said, rubbing his shoulder where he'd impacted with Nick. "Why'd you stop?" He peeled himself away from the weird, horizontal dogpile they'd created. Only then did he notice Sebastian. "Holy shit. Sebastian Prinsen."

Sebastian wrenched his eyes from Nick and offered Deen a smile. "I don't believe I know your name. I thought I knew everyone at this school."

"Oh, I'm nobody. I mean, I'm not *nobody*. Obviously I'm a person, and not Odysseus or anything."

Nick elbowed Deen helpfully in the side.

Deen cleared his throat and slapped on a too-tight grin. "The name's Deenabandhu. Everyone calls me Deen."

Sebastian extended a hand to shake. "Pleasure to meet you."

Deen wiped his palms on his pants before shaking Sebastian's hand. After, he seemed pleased with himself, as if he hadn't expected that exchange to go well. Which was a reasonable expectation, considering.

The smile on Sebastian's face softened as he switched his gaze back over to Nick. "Deen, would you mind giving me a minute alone with Nick?"

"Not at all!" Deen said at the same time that Nick said, "Actually, we're busy."

They glanced at each other. Nick tried to communicate with Deen using only his eyes, but it seemed they hadn't been friends long enough for that.

"One second." Deen flashed a toothy smile at Sebastian before grabbing Nick by the shirt and hauling him a good ten feet away. "*What* are you *doing*? When Sebastian Prinsen asks to talk, you say yes!"

Nick cocked his head to the side. "Was that a mangled *Ghostbusters* reference?"

"What do you take me for?" Deen sniffed. "Of course it was."

"But what about breakfast?" Nick snuck a peek over Deen's shoulder at Sebastian. He was watching them, and when he caught Nick's eye, he winked. Nick looked quickly away. "And we both have class."

In truth, I don't want to hang out with him. It's too confusing. One second he's putting on an act, and the next he's showing up outside my dorm and being nice to my friends. Er, friend.

"Dude, you gotta go with him," Deen said. "If Sebastian says you're cool, you're *in*. You'll get invited to all the parties, and everyone will want to know who you are. You said you wanted to make friends, right? This is your chance to be a proverbial big man on campus."

"What if I don't want to be a big man?" Nick frowned. "There's a sentence I never thought I'd say."

"Then do it for me. You saw what happened just now. Senpai noticed me! If I got invited to one of his parties, I'd *die*. Happy. With a big smile on my face. And my obituary would read 'Deen, a guy who got invited to parties' instead of 'That dude you might've had a class with once, but who can remember?' Please do this for me. Please?"

Nick laughed despite himself. "All right, if it means that much to you."

"You're the best roommate *ever*. Come find me in the dining hall after and tell me everything. Actually, do you think Sebastian would come if we invited him to breakfast? I'd love to—"

"Everything all right over there?" Sebastian was peering at them with an expression of mild concern.

"Yeah, we're good." Deen gave Nick a significant look before stepping away. "It was nice meeting you, Sebastian." He scurried off before Nick could change his mind.

As soon as Deen was gone, the mood shifted. Familiar tension sprang up between Nick and Sebastian, like a magnetic pull. Sebastian regarded him without speaking, and Nick's whole body grew hot beneath the scrutiny.

Nick shoved his hands into his pockets to keep himself from fidgeting. "What did you want to talk about?"

"You, actually." Sebastian's eyes were darting over Nick's face like he was memorizing him. "You said you drink coffee, right?"

"Far, far too much."

"Want to get a cup? It's on me."

Nick hesitated. This was so casual, so different from his previous interactions with Sebastian, he almost didn't know how to react. "Would it be like a . . . date?"

"If that's what you want to call it." Sebastian grinned. "I was more thinking it's morning, and you might be in need of a cup. I know I am."

That's considerate of him. I don't trust it.

"There's coffee in the dining hall," Nick said. "I'm meeting Deen there. I don't want to keep him waiting, so if you'll tell me what it is you want—"

"Don't drink the crap in the dining hall. The coffee cart is way better." Sebastian turned and started walking away. "Come on. We don't want to keep your friend waiting."

Nick stared after him, unsure of what to do.

After a few steps, Sebastian stopped and looked back. "Hurry up."

On instinct, Nick said, "Make me."

Sebastian's smile was sinful. "Tempting."

Damn. That shouldn't be hot, but it is.

A combination of politeness and the tight black jeans Sebastian was wearing convinced Nick to trot after him. He caught up within a few strides and forced himself not to glance at Sebastian every five seconds.

"I heard about what happened with Donahue," Sebastian said after a few steps.

"Who?"

"The guy from the swim team whose boyfriend you ogled."

"I didn't ogle anyone," Nick grumbled. "It was a misunderstanding."

I was only staring at him because he reminded me of you, not that I'll ever admit that out loud.

"Well, whatever you did, it's a good thing it didn't escalate. And I'm relieved to hear you weren't eyeing another guy."

Nick gave in and looked at him. "Why?"

Sebastian met his gaze and smiled softly. He offered no further reply.

The sidewalk curved to the left, and from around a thick oak tree, the coffee cart came into view. There was a guy standing next to it, handing out cups of coffee and swiping IDs as fast as he could. Rush hour happened later on campus than it did everywhere else in the world. The midmorning crowd reminded Nick of a zombie movie: dead-eyed and shambling.

"Stay right here, please." Sebastian started toward the cart. "I have a surprise for you."

This time, Nick did as he was told without rebellion. Sebastian approached the cart. Nick half expected him to bypass the line—since he was Mr. Popular and all—but Sebastian waited his turn like everyone else.

When he reached the front, the coffee guy handed him a cup like he'd been expecting him. Sebastian had a short conversation with him, and then thirty seconds later, he was handed a second cup. He returned to Nick with a grin on his face.

"This is my standing order." He pressed one of the cups into Nick's hand. "Try it. It's my own invention."

Nick took a cautious sip. It wasn't burning hot, to his surprise. The rich flavor rolled over his tongue, and when he swallowed, he actually perked up.

"This is fantastic," he said. "What is it?"

"I can't tell you, but if you want one, ask for the Prinsen special. Oh, but for your own good, don't drink more than three a day."

"Why not?"

"There's a chance you could experience a cardiac event. Actually, scratch what I said before. Drink *four* a day if it's finals week and you're praying for death regardless."

Nick snorted halfway through taking another sip and almost inhaled coffee. He caught himself in time and clapped a hand over his mouth.

Sebastian nudged him. "I'll walk you to the dining hall. Don't want you to miss out on breakfast. Dunno why they don't serve it all day."

"Probably because no one would ever eat anything else."

They took off at a leisurely pace. Campus was as beautiful as ever, even beneath a metallic sky. Nick wondered what it would be like in the winter, blanketed in snow and trimmed with ice. Probably like a postcard. If only he had someone to send one to.

Maybe you will by then, assuming Sebastian doesn't win you over.

Hesitant as Nick was to admit it, he was enjoying himself. Sebastian wasn't bad company when he wasn't being all mysterious or playing games.

That didn't mean Nick wasn't on his guard, though.

He snuck another peek at the same time Sebastian glanced at him. Their eyes locked, and a tingle zinged up Nick's spine. He might not trust Sebastian, but every time he looked at him, Nick found him more and more attractive.

"So." He took another sip of coffee. "Was introducing me to this drink all you wanted? Hoping I'll overdose on caffeine?"

"No." Sebastian's mouth turned down, and he seemed to struggle with words. "I wanted to talk about the almost-fight you got into. When I heard about it, I was . . . annoyed."

"What? Why?"

"Because I don't want you to get expelled." He exhaled, and from the surprised expression on his face, Nick surmised that Sebastian hadn't meant to say that so bluntly. "You're not allowed to disappear, okay?"

"Theo already lectured me. I know I shouldn't have done that, or almost done that, and not just because I would have gotten in trouble." Nick eyed him. "I'm surprised you care, though."

"I don't." Sebastian's voice wavered. It almost sounded like he was trying to convince himself as much as Nick. "I just think it would be a shame if they kicked you out. Didn't you tell me once this is a great opportunity that shouldn't be squandered?"

Nick laughed uneasily. "Oh come on. Don't act like you'd notice if I left." He'd meant for it to sound teasing, but it came out more curious.

Sebastian stopped short and turned to him, eyes searching Nick's face. "Is that really what you think of me? You think I'm that self-involved?"

Nick faced him as well. He debated with himself for a second before deciding the truth was the best approach. "I wouldn't put it like that, but I do think you can be kinda thoughtless at times, and you seem to do what you want regardless of how others might feel. You told me that yourself, remember? 'Because I wanted to.' Did you ever stop to ask yourself if *I* wanted to?"

At the end of his speech, Nick braced himself. He had no idea how Sebastian was going to react. But if there was one thing he'd learned in his short time on this earth, it was that people didn't always respond positively to the truth.

Sebastian was silent for a long moment. Then he moved closer, shrinking the distance between them. "All right. Tell me. How'd you feel about it?"

Nick fought the urge to take a step back. "Huh?"

"Don't play coy, Nick. How'd you feel that day behind the dining hall? When I brushed your lips? You had to know I was thinking about kissing you." His eyes darted down to Nick's lips. "I still think about it all the time. Did you want me to? Were you disappointed when I didn't?"

Words welled up in Nick's mouth. If he were smart, he'd tell Sebastian what he'd done was inappropriate and unwanted. But only one of those things was true.

Before he could process fully, Sebastian stepped closer again. Now they were no farther apart than they'd been earlier, when Nick had knocked into him. "Nick, if you're not into me, say so. I'll leave you alone." He licked his lips, and *damn it*, Nick couldn't stop himself from glancing at them.

"You promise?" Nick was embarrassed to hear how breathy his voice had gotten.

"Of course. I can handle rejection. I don't think you're going to do that, though. I think you're as attracted to me as I am to you, but for some reason, you're fighting it." He met Nick's gaze, and his eyes smoldered. "I would really, *really* like to see you give in."

Nick found the strength to take a step back. "I don't get it. Why do you like me?"

Sebastian's brow furrowed. "Pardon?"

"You've seemed to like me from the moment you saw me. You've been pursuing me pretty relentlessly. Why? Do you have some sort of Pavlovian response to new kids? You see one, and you chase them like a dog chasing a tennis ball?"

For once, Sebastian seemed speechless. He opened his mouth only to close it again. Nick swore he could practically see him debating what to say in response.

Eventually, Sebastian let out a sigh. "I notice you didn't say you're not into me, but fine. I admit my initial interest in you was shallow. You're hot, and you're a shiny new penny. I don't think there's anything wrong with pursuing someone because they're attractive. Though for the record, now that I've gotten to know you a little . . ."

Sebastian dropped his gaze to his red Chucks before looking back up at Nick, his eyes soft. "I like how honest you are. Not only what you say, but your expressions. When you were sketching the other day, I watched you for a sec before I approached. You stared off into space at one point, and your face was so sad. I don't know what happened to you, but"—he lowered his voice like he didn't want to be overheard—"I know what that means. Being sad in the middle of a beautiful morning for no reason. Right then, I decided I wanted to know more about you."

Fuck, Nick thought. *That was a good answer.*

He dithered for a bit longer before waving a hand in frustration. "I'm not going to lie and say I don't find you attractive, but for the record, that's not enough for me. I'm still not interested in a hookup."

"I never said I was either." Sebastian's expression morphed into a triumphant grin. "And you still haven't told me to fuck off. Do you want to get to know me better? You might like what you learn."

Say no, screamed a mental voice. *Say no, and he'll leave you alone. Things will go back to normal. No more confused feelings.*

Nick's head knew that was the right move, but his stomach churned at the idea of saying it. One, because it was a blatant lie. And two, because despite himself, he was getting sucked into the mystery that was Sebastian. Who was he really? How could he be manipulative and arrogant one moment, but sweet and deep the next? What did it all mean?

When I wasn't paying attention, he got under my skin somehow. But that doesn't mean I'm going to make this easy for him.

"So, you don't want a hookup," Nick began. "Is that right?"

Sebastian blinked. "Yes."

"Lying isn't going to score you any points."

"I don't know what you—"

Nick stepped back, shaking his head. "Dude, don't bullshit me. I saw you put on that whole shy act when we talked before, and the second I made it clear it wasn't working, you dropped it. If that wasn't a plot to get into my pants, I don't know what is. How can you expect me to believe anything you say?"

To Nick's shock, Sebastian seemed pleased. "I knew you saw through that. You're very perceptive."

"Flattery will get you nowhere," Nick said even as his face warmed from the praise.

Sebastian reached out—slow enough that Nick could brush him off if he wanted—and touched Nick's hand gently. "It's not flattery."

Bullshit. It's funny how his unctuous charm can draw me in and turn me off at the same time. I've had enough of this.

"You know what your problem is, Sebastian?" Nick pulled his hand away and took another sip of his coffee, making it clear his question wasn't rhetorical. He expected an answer.

Sebastian's smile faltered for a second before he slapped it back on. "Okay, I'll bite. No, I don't know what my problem is. But I bet you're going to tell me."

"You've had it way too easy. You've been a bright, shining star in this tiny community for too long, and you're used to people sucking up to you. My first day on this campus, I had to listen to people talk about you, and I thought it was bizarre, but now I get it. This place is like a small, stagnant pond, and the people here have no idea what it's like out there."

"Out where?"

Nick gestured toward one of the nearby paths leading off campus with his coffee, which sloshed onto the white lid. "In the real world. Where people work shitty jobs and pay bills and are bone-tired every day of their lives because they don't have a choice. I don't know what your plans are for after graduation, but if you end up out there, you're going to be in for a nasty surprise. You're going to learn what it's like to be invisible."

Sebastian's face was blank. Nick almost wished he'd freak out so at least Nick could gauge how he was reacting.

Too late to stop now.

Nick stepped back, putting some distance between them. "You want me to say I'm not attracted to you? I can't. I think you're gorgeous. But I also think you're a liar and selfish and probably a lot more insecure than you let on. So, until you show me another side of you, I'm not interested. Thanks for the coffee."

With that, Nick turned away. For three whole steps, his heart raced with the excitement of a well-earned victory.

Then, a voice called after him.

"You think I don't know what the 'real world' is like?"

Nick paused and glanced back. "What?"

Sebastian looked downright pissed. "You think my life has been nothing but smooth sailing? What, because my *parents* have money, not me? Guess what, sweetheart, I've seen how nasty life can be. You should really do your homework before you judge people."

Nick frowned. "I wasn't *judging*—"

"I accept your challenge." Sebastian's charming smile was back. It seemed to coat him like oil, distorting the genuine emotion Nick had seen on him earlier. "You're wrong about me, Nick. I'm going to prove it, and when I do, you're going to eat your words."

"Yeah, sure." Nick took another step away, walking backward. "You keep wishing on that star."

"And you know what else? You're going to fall so totally in love with me."

Nick stopped dead in his tracks, heart hammering. The utter certainty with which Sebastian had said that made it hard for Nick to breathe.

"N-no way," Nick stammered.

Sebastian simply grinned as he turned away. Watching him go, Nick couldn't help but feel like Sebastian had thrown down some sort of gauntlet.

By the time he got to the dining hall, Deen was halfway through an omelet the size of his head. When he spotted Nick, he stopped cramming eggs into his mouth long enough to ask, "What happened with Sebastian? Did you invite him?"

"Sorry, buddy. It totally slipped my mind." Nick glanced at the coffee cup in his hand. "But don't worry. I doubt we've seen the last of him."

Chapter Seven

Saturday. Glorious Saturday.

Nick was awake long before his alarm—and before Deen, for once—but he stayed in bed, luxuriating in the knowledge that there were no classes he needed to rush off to, nowhere he had to be.

Much as he'd have loved to spend the whole day in bed, simply because he could, that wasn't an option. He had approximately one million chapters he needed to read for class, it was clothes-shopping day, and eventually, he'd have to do all the boring day-to-day shit that was expected of adults. Like showering, and eating actual food, and putting on pants. It was almost enough to put him right back to sleep.

But no, eating was good, and he owed it to both himself and Deen to shower regularly.

Rolling out of bed, he grabbed a change of clothes and tiptoed over to the bathroom. He took his time washing up, brushing his teeth, and towel-drying his unruly hair. The longer he went without cutting it, the more the ends curled up around his ears like golden vines. Pretty soon, he'd look like a Labrador with a husky's eyes.

Once he was dressed and ready, he snuck back out, threw his pajamas onto the laundry pile he'd created under his bed, and debated what to do next.

Deen was cocooned in blankets and snoring cutely. It'd be a crime to wake him when he'd managed to sleep in for once.

I should check my school email. I haven't since Tuesday night, busy as I've been.

It took a solid five minutes for his laptop to whine to life. The wait renewed his determination to find room in his budget for a newer model, even if it meant living leanly for the rest of the school year.

Logging into his email, Nick was surprised to find he had a dozen messages in his inbox. Most were from his professors, sending out e-versions of the slides for next week, along with instructions to print them out and bring them to class. Nick made a mental note to drop by the computer lab tomorrow, since neither Deen nor he had a printer.

One email in particular caught his eye. It was from Dr. O'Connor, the student advisor he'd met with what felt likes years ago. The subject line read *Checking In?*

The question mark threw him off. Was he supposed to contact her, and he forgot?

He clicked on the message and jiggled his leg while he waited for it to load. It consisted of a short paragraph that was signed with a photograph of Dr. O'Connor surrounded by an enviable number of dogs. Nick imagined a similar pack waited at the gates of Heaven to welcome newcomers. It took him a second to pick her frizzy head out of the fluffy animals around her.

A quick scan of the message told him that Dr. O'Connor wanted to meet with him as soon as he was free to see how his first week had gone. It'd been sent Thursday morning, so he was definitely late to respond.

"Ugh," he whispered to himself, mindful of Deen. She meant well, and it was kind of nice to be checked up on for once, but he really didn't want to deal with an interrogation after his emotional roller coaster of a week.

Nice as she was, Dr. O'Connor didn't seem like the sort to take no for an answer, though. With any luck, she didn't check her email over the weekend and wouldn't see his reply until Monday. Which meant he could easily delay a meeting until Tuesday.

He composed a message, stating that he was free early mornings before ten, but Tuesday evening would be convenient, hint hint. Once that was sent, he logged on to Facebook. He was hardly ever on social media—mostly because he had nothing to say—but now seemed like an appropriate time for a status update.

Finished my first week at my new university, he typed. *One down, around fifty-nine more to go.*

He posted it and got a notification all of five seconds later. It was a like from Jacqueline Smith, a girl he'd had class with back at UIC.

She was sweet, smarter than him by a *lot*, and very pretty with doe-like brown eyes the same color as her skin. They'd gone out a couple of times, before . . .

He sighed. *You're going to have to start saying it. Before Dad died. Before you lost your last family member. Before your life got torn apart.*

A comment popped up on his status. It was from Jacqueline and read, *Miss you, Nick! Let me know if you're ever back in Chi-Town.*

Her words made his heart clench, but he appreciated the sentiment. He smiled and closed out of the tab, bringing him back to his email. A new message caught his eye. Dr. O'Connor had responded.

"Shit."

Deen snuffled behind him but thankfully didn't wake up. With no small amount of trepidation, Nick clicked on the message. Dr. O'Connor thanked him for getting back to her so quickly and asked him to meet her first thing in the morning on Monday.

Damn technology. This never would have happened if we were still using carrier pigeons.

Nick considered pretending he hadn't seen her response, but one look at the photo of her buried in happy dogs, and he couldn't do it. He wrote back and accepted the meeting. Might as well get it over with. At least he had a couple of days to brace himself for another round of well-meant prodding.

His stomach growled. First order of business: he wanted eggs and an unreasonable amount of bacon. He considered waking Deen up so they could go together, but Deen was still conked out—face slack, inky hair fanned over his pillow. Nick decided against it.

Eyes on Deen's prone form, Nick grabbed his things, padded to the door, and opened it as quietly as he could. Deen stirred again but didn't wake. Nick breathed a sigh of relief and turned to walk out, only to come face to face with surprised green eyes.

Nick stifled a yelp and jumped back a foot. "Theo?" He remembered to whisper at the last second. "What are you doing here?"

Theo had his hand raised as if he'd been seconds away from knocking. He let it drop and whispered back. "Sorry. Didn't mean to scare you. I texted you last night and again this morning, but you never responded. I thought I'd swing by and make sure everything's all right."

"Oh, shit." Nick dug his phone out of his pocket and squinted at it. Between the cracked screen and the dead pixels, his notifications looked like they were written in cuneiform. "My bad. I didn't get your texts. Can we talk outside? My roommate's asleep."

Theo nodded and stepped back, making room for Nick. Once Nick had shut and locked the door behind him, he turned to Theo. "It's nice of you to check on me." *Today seems to be the day for that.*

"Yeah, well. I hadn't heard from you since we talked the other day. Wanted to make sure I didn't scare you off." He grinned and then reached for Nick's hand.

Nick startled, but a second later, he realized Theo was going for his phone, which he was still holding. Theo took it, and as he examined the obliterated screen, his eyebrows rose up slowly like balloons.

"Wow. This is, um . . ."

"Yeah, I know. Looks like it went twelve rounds with Ali in his prime."

Theo smiled his small, dreamy smile. "I upgraded to a new phone right before classes started. I still have my old one. You want it?"

Nick shuffled his feet. "That's nice of you, but no. You should sell it or something."

"Wouldn't be worth the hassle. It's three generations old, which in technology terms is ancient. Besides, I didn't pay for it or my new one. My parents send me shit without asking if I need it, and now my old phone's collecting dust in a drawer. Someone ought to put it to good use. Is your phone carrier unlocked?"

"Yeah." Nick was caught between gratefulness and guilt. "Don't you want to keep the old phone as a backup, though? In case something happens to your new one?"

"Nah. I could throw it against a wall, and my parents would send me another one. We struggled financially for a while, so when my mom got this awesome job, I guess she decided she had to make it up to me. Now she shows affection with gifts." He smiled, but it was knifelike in its sharpness. "Lucky me, right?"

"I guess." Nick wet his lips. "I don't want to pry, but sometimes you say things that make me think you resent your parents a little bit."

"Maybe a smidge. If I were my mom, I'd be spending money on a divorce attorney, or rehab for my dad, but instead I get sent shit

I don't need while everyone pretends nothing's wrong. That would make anyone resentful, I think."

Nick shrugged. "I dunno. I'd be grateful." *For the phone and for my parents.*

"You say that, but believe me, there are things money can't buy. Anyway, if it's any consolation, my therapist says I'm just acting out." He turned toward the hall. "Follow me to my room, and I'll get the phone for you."

A bit unsettled, Nick followed after him. Theo traversed two flights of stairs to the second floor and strode down a hallway lined with nine identical doors. He stopped in front of one that had a brass number twelve on it, opened it, and waved Nick in.

Nick hadn't had enough time to form any expectations of what Theo's room would be like, but even so, it wasn't what he expected. In many ways, it looked like Nick's room—from the tall windows to the wood floors—but there were several key differences.

One, it had three beds in it, with one pushed against the far wall. Two, the heavy curtains blotted out all light—Nick's room was always suffused with sunlight to the point of irritation. And three, if the bed on the left was Theo's, then he was a complete and utter slob.

"Holy shit," Nick muttered under his breath as he examined what appeared to be a miniature indoor landfill. The desk was *covered* in crap: loose papers, books, clothes, empty soda cans, and chip bags.

Without fail, Theo veered to the left. He noticed Nick staring and rubbed the back of his head. "Yeah, I know. I'm not the neatest person."

"Theo, buddy, you're not in the *vicinity* of the neatest person. The neatest person would take you out back and hose you off before agreeing to come near you."

"I want to be offended, but that was such an artful blend of creativity and rudeness." Theo took a step, and there was an audible *crunch.* Probably a potato chip. "Okay, I admit I have a problem."

"No shit. How did you make this much mess in one week?"

"Okay, I have a *big* problem. This is one of the reasons I wanted to live on campus this year. I figured my roommates could help keep my messiness in check, and so far it's been working."

Nick's mouth almost popped open. "This is what your room looks like when someone's keeping you in *check*?"

"I'm working on it, okay? One day at a time. Stay there on the mainland, and I'll find my old phone for you."

Nick had planned to ask Theo for a third time if he was sure he wanted to give up his phone, but now Nick would do anything to help declutter. "So, your roommates aren't home, I take it? Or are they buried in there somewhere?"

"They're almost never around." Theo shoved a pile of garbage off his desk to reveal another pile. "I can't imagine why."

An item jumped out at Nick from amidst the wreckage. "Why do you have a disembodied Barbie head glued to a—" he leaned forward and squinted "—gold baseball player?"

Theo chuckled. "We call that Barbzilla."

"'We'? As in, you and your roommates?"

"No, Dante, Seb, and me. When we were kids, we were in little league together. We won some local championship and got trophies. After the game, Seb and I were wrestling—I don't remember why—and we broke his trophy. Crushed its head, actually. Sebastian was *pissed*, but thanks to a hot glue gun and Dante's little sister, we were able to fix it. In a manner of speaking."

Nick eyed the hideous thing. "That explains its existence, I guess, but why is it here? In your dorm? Instead of resting at the bottom of a nuclear reactor, where it can obtain sentience and terrorize the town, as befitting its name?"

"It's become an inside joke between us. When we were little, whoever owned it was like the ruler of our little group. Over the years, whenever we've competed over something, we've put Barbzilla up as the prize. Now, it represents our friendship."

"Who would have thought something so creepy could be so cute."

"Seb is actually gunning for it as we speak. He wants it bad. No clue why." Theo wrestled a drawer open and dug through it. "Here we are." He extracted a sleek smartphone and made his way back.

Nick whistled as Theo handed it over. "This is amazing. Not a scratch on it."

"You sound surprised." Theo smiled. "I may be a slob, but I'm careful with my belongings. Unlike you, Cracked Screen McGee.

They say people who are careless with their valuables are careless with other's hearts too."

"Did you read that in a fortune cookie?" Nick turned the phone over in his hands. Three generations old, and it was nicer than anything he'd ever owned. "Can I really have this?"

Instead of answering, Theo took the phone along with Nick's old one, popped the backs off, and swapped out Nick's SIM card. The whole procedure took less than thirty seconds.

When he'd finished, Theo handed the new phone to him. "Do you have an SD card or anything else you want to salvage?"

"No, I'm all set."

"Excellent." Theo tossed the broken phone into the overflowing trash can with impressive accuracy. "You should be good to go, then."

Nick hit the power button, and the phone vibrated to life. "Last chance to at least accept some cash for this. I'm happy to buy it from you."

"You can pay me back by responding to my texts in the future. If you ever leave me on read without a good reason, the deal's off."

When the home screen loaded, Nick imported his contacts and then selected Theo. He typed a short message.

If this is your way of making sure I stay in touch, you could have just asked.

He hit Send. A second later, Theo pulled his own phone out of his pocket, read the text, and laughed. "I know, but this is doubling as my good deed for the year."

"The whole year? I had no idea you were such a philanthropist." Nick slid the phone into his jeans. "My roommate and I have plans to head into town later. You wanna come with?"

"I would, but I have a date with three hundred pages of overdue reading. Before you go, though, there was something I wanted to ask you." Theo glanced up at the ceiling like he was composing his thoughts. Eventually, his eyes wandered back to Nick's face. "I hate to bring this up. It's a sensitive subject, and I know all the gossip bothers you. But . . . I was wondering if what everyone's saying about your parents is true?"

Nick's heart skipped a beat. Not in a good way. "Was there a segue in there somewhere?"

"Sorry. It's because you said earlier that you'd be grateful, but you didn't specify for what. It got me thinking. I don't listen to gossip, I swear, but if what people are saying is true, I want you to know I'm here if you need to talk. I meant it when I said I want us to be friends."

There was a part of Nick that was tempted to brush it off—like he always did—but he had to talk about it sometime. All the bad feelings in him were going to fester if he didn't let them out. And on a less grim note, he liked Theo. He wanted them to be friends too. If opening up would facilitate that, he was willing to give it a shot.

Nick took a breath. "My dad died a little over a year ago. That's why I transferred here. He was helping me pay for college back at UIC, and after he died, I couldn't afford it anymore. I had to go wherever would give me the most financial aid, and that was here. I took a year off to 'deal,' but I mostly worked, paid off debts, and tried not to think about it." He laughed, but it sounded as mirthful as warbling trombone notes. "So there you have it, my whole tragic story."

"Nick, I'm so sorry." Theo's tone was sympathetic without sounding pitying, which was good, because Nick was too raw to handle pity right now. "I shouldn't have brought it up."

"It's okay. Thanks for not asking how Dad died. I hate when people do that. Like it makes any difference. Anyway, it's ancient history, and I'm a legal adult. I'm expected to take care of myself now, right?"

Theo's lips twitched up. "Funny. I heard someone else say something similar recently."

"Who?"

"Sebastian."

"Oh." Curiosity burned inside Nick, but he didn't want to pry, or give Theo the rightful impression that he was interested.

Theo seemed to read his mind regardless. "His folks are alive, for the record. Although, for all the parenting they provide, they might as well not be."

"Ah." Nick shifted his weight. "Does that bother Sebastian?"

Theo gave him an odd look. "Of course it does. They're his only family, and he's not a robot. Granted, he certainly tries to act like it doesn't affect him. It explains a lot of his behavior, in my opinion, but I've been told I take my psych degree home with me."

Nick's thoughts whirred. "I suppose that would explain a lot." *His hot-and-cold attitude, and his alleged penchant for breaking hearts.*

"I'm not saying his situation is the same as yours, but I think Seb and you have more in common than you think."

It was Nick's turn to give the odd look. "Why are you telling me this? One second, you're warning me away from Sebastian, and the next it sounds like you want me to empathize with him. Which is it?"

"Both? I guess I'm trying to look out for Seb and you at the same time, and it's crossing my wires. Seb's my best friend. I don't want him to get hurt. You're my newest friend. I also don't want you to get hurt."

Nick shook his head. "I'm not going to hurt anyone. Sebastian's the one who—"

Theo held up a hand. "Yeah, I know. I don't agree with everything he does—especially when it comes to boys and dating and his whole reputation—but he's a good person who's been through a lot. I want him to be happy." Theo's brow puckered. "Even if it means losing out on something I want."

At that, Nick took a step back. "Theo . . . you're not talking about *me*, are you?"

Laughter burst from Theo, and he clapped a hand over his mouth. "That's a little self-involved, don't you think? One boy pays attention to you, and now you think everyone's in love with you?" His teasing tone took the sting from his words. "No, it's not like that. There's this guy I like, and neither of us has made a move."

"Why not?"

"Well, at the risk of giving his identity away, we've been friends forever."

Nick's heart stopped cold in his chest. "Is it Sebastian?"

"No! Stop guessing. You're bad at it." Theo's mirth drained away, and he heaved a sigh. "The point is, I don't want to risk ruining the friendship I have with this guy—who is *not* Sebastian—and I think he feels the same way. We need to talk about it, but the timing never seems right. Plus, we have a whole group dynamic to think about. It's complicated. Or at least, we're making it complicated." He rolled his eyes. "Boys. Am I right?"

Nick laughed. "Yeah. Since I'm not allowed to ask who he is, can I ask you something else I've been dying to know? Something really important?"

Theo looked wary. "Yeah?"

Nick leaned in and lowered his voice to a whisper. "What's your natural hair color?"

Theo laughed so hard, he fell back a step. "Blond. Like, white blond. My mom *cried* when I dyed it. I thought she was going to hold a memorial service. Personally, I think the red suits me."

"I do too." Nick checked the time. "I should get going. Thanks again for the phone."

"Use it, please. I'm the mom friend, and I worry when you don't call." He winked. "See ya."

"Bye."

Closing the door behind him, Nick was about to head to the dining hall when he got his first new text. Deen wanted to know where he was. Instead of responding, Nick flew back to their room. Inside, Deen was awake and sitting up in bed, though he was wrapped in blankets all the way to his chin. He looked like soft-serve ice cream, topped with a black cherry.

Deen freed an arm long enough to wave. "Morning."

"Morning." Nick flopped next to Deen on his bed. "Ready for breakfast? And after, are you still down to show me around town?"

"I think so." Deen yawned. "It's hard to tell through all the sleep deprivation. When I woke up, I had to convince myself I'm an adult and not a burrito."

"You're a burrito with adult filling." Nick patted where he guessed Deen's shoulder was under the blankets. "We're only a week into the semester, and you're already pushing yourself too hard. What are you going to do when midterms roll around? And then finals week?"

"I'm going to retreat into my cocoon." Deen scrunched his head down into the sheets until only the top half of his face was visible. "A week later, I'll either be a beautiful butterfly, or I'll have failed all my classes."

"Neither of those options sound all that appealing."

"What do you have against butterflies?"

"Nothing, but some of them only live for a couple of weeks."

"Hm." Deen freed a hand so he could rub his chin. "Finals week or death? Now there's a tough decision."

Laughing, Nick got to his feet. "Tell you what, you stay in bed, and I'll go to the dining hall and get us a to-go box full of waffles. We can eat in here and then head into town when you're feeling more human."

"That sounds good. I bet putting on real clothes will help me." Deen's eyes darted to his laptop. Nick would have bet money he was wondering if he had time to tool around on the internet *and* get dressed before Nick got back.

So long as he's wearing pants when I return.

Nick took his leave and made his way to the dining hall. Without classes to draw people to campus, the grounds were quiet. Once inside his destination, he loaded up a box with waffles, as promised, and started to add sausage and bacon until he remembered Deen was Muslim. Nick had no idea if he ate pork or not.

He stood there for a second, wondering what to do, before he remembered Theo's gift. He pulled his new phone out of his bag and—balancing his box of waffles in the crook of one elbow—sent Deen a text.

Within a minute, Deen replied. *I started eating pork around the time I got a tattoo. I figured if I was going to sin, I should do it thoroughly. I also drink alcohol and take Jesus's name in vain, though my deity doesn't care about that last one.*

Chuckling, Nick loaded up on breakfast meats and poured syrup into some plastic containers. Then he carefully, *carefully* transported the small feast back to Powell Hall.

To his immense pleasure, Deen was dressed and sans blankets when he returned. Nick piled onto his bed, and they ate while Deen played viral YouTube videos on his laptop. Nick almost choked on a sausage when a Vine compilation made him laugh mid-bite. It was one of the most normal college interactions Nick had experienced since his last university, and for a beautiful moment, it made him feel like he could really make a life for himself here.

"How do you want to get into town, by the way?" Nick asked when he'd finished eating. "I can look up bus schedules."

"No need." Deen licked syrup off his fingers. "There's one that stops at the front of the university that goes into town every hour on weekends. Or we can take my car."

"You have a *car*? Nice." Nick paused. "We can legit take the bus, though. I don't want to make you drive."

"I actually need to. When I get into hard-core study mode, it sits in the student parking garage for weeks at a time. If I don't take it out every now and then, the battery drains."

"Let's do that, then."

After cleaning up, they walked across campus to the small covered parking garage and found Deen's car: a newish silver sedan. The drive into town took less than ten minutes. Nick was in charge of the radio, though all he could seem to find was either bubblegum pop or country music. He went with the pop and spent the rest of the drive staring out the window at his new home.

Evanston had its charms, he had to admit. There were clean streets, wholesome family-owned stores, and plenty of green grass everywhere he looked. There were even some tall buildings, though they didn't scrape the sky so much as stand on tiptoe and swipe at it.

Deen turned onto a street that was lined with shops and found parking. Once he'd cut the engine, he pivoted in his seat to face Nick. "Any idea where you want to start?"

"Hell if I know." Nick shrugged. "Somewhere that has clothing, preferably. I was sort of relying on your expertise."

"That's cool with me. What's your budget?"

Nick gave him a pointed look.

"Right. We'll start with the thrift shops. But keep in mind, investing in some quality staple pieces can save you money in the long run."

"You sound like one of those makeover shows."

"Good. Maybe we can do a montage later and put it on YouTube."

They got out of the car and strolled down the street until they came upon a consignment shop with a decent selection. Nick chose a couple of T-shirts, some long-sleeve flannels for when it got colder, and a pair of gray Vans yanked from a bin of mismatched shoes. It cost him a whopping eighteen dollars, but he was happy with his choices. Especially the shoes, given that his ratty sneakers were falling apart.

"Well, there's no accounting for taste," Deen said as they left, "but I'll give you points for personal style."

Nick took a long look at Deen's shined shoes, fashionable jeans, and dress shirt. "We can't all rock the night-club-owner aesthetic like you can."

Deen punched him playfully on the arm. "Let's try that place next." He pointed out a small, modern building a block down. It didn't seem like a thrift store, but Nick trusted Deen's judgment. He dutifully followed him inside.

As soon as they entered, they were engulfed in the smell of cologne. The interior resembled a miniature department store, complete with shiny tile floors, colorful displays, and clusters of faceless mannequins sporting three-piece suits.

A sharply dressed woman with perfect makeup greeted them. "What are you gentlemen shopping for today?"

Deen hooked a thumb at Nick. "He needs a new wardrobe. Nothing too flashy or expensive. Some nice jeans, a coat for winter, and maybe one semiformal outfit. You know, in case he decides to take me out for a night on the town." He winked and slung an arm around Nick's shoulders.

Nick turned bright red and was considering stammering some sort of denial when the salesperson giggled.

"I'm certain we can find you something." She turned to Nick. "Do you know your size?"

"Um." Nick thought about it. "I used to, but it might have changed." *There were a couple of months after Dad died where I had trouble remembering to eat.*

"Very well. I'll bring some options." She disappeared into the rows of clothing.

Nick glared at Deen. "Why'd you make it sound like we're a couple?"

"We're two guys shopping for clothes together. She was gonna assume we're a couple regardless. Besides, I'm taking an improv class for gen. ed. credit, and I need the practice."

Pouty as Nick acted, the joke was kind of a relief. He hadn't disclosed his orientation to Deen yet—mostly because it hadn't come up—and he was nervous about it. Much as he liked Deen, there was no telling how any given college-aged male was going to react to learning his roommate was into guys. This exchange gave Nick hope that Deen would be cool when the time came.

The salesperson—whose name tag read *Makeba*—reappeared with jeans, slacks, and a variety of shirt styles draped over one arm. Nick thought he spotted a vest in the mix too.

"Here you are," Makeba said, cheerful as a bird. "I brought a few different sizes. Head into the dressing room over there, and once you find something that fits, I'll bring more."

Nick took the mountain of clothing and headed for the doorway she'd indicated. The stalls were all empty; Nick ducked into the nearest one.

"I'm gonna stay out here," announced Deen's muffled voice. "Call me if you need anything."

"Thanks, *dear*," Nick shouted back. He riffled through the clothing and held a pair of jeans up to his waist. They seemed about right, so he kicked off his shoes and pants and pulled them on first. In actuality, they were a little loose, but he wasn't the sort to walk around in skintight clothing.

He tried on a few more pairs, found two that fit him the way he liked, and set those aside. Then he went for what he assumed was the semiformal outfit: black pants and the vest he'd spotted before. There was no fancy shirt to go with them, so Nick threw on a short-sleeved white tee and left the vest unbuttoned.

Everything fit him perfectly. When he glanced in the mirror, he almost didn't recognize himself. He looked *good*. The well-cut pants lengthened his legs, and the shirt hugged his broad shoulders and flat stomach. But it was the vest that turned the clothes into an outfit. He liked that it was a mixture of formal and informal too. He'd never had a "look" before, but now that he saw what some decent clothing could do, he was tempted to make this his.

Now to see what the peanut gallery thinks.

Nick unlocked the door and—face already hot—walked out. He was grateful there weren't many other customers hanging around, especially when Deen caught sight of him and whistled.

"Damn, Nick. You clean up good."

"Thanks." He rubbed the back of his head and stared down at the ground. "This isn't normally my sort of thing."

"You should make it your thing." Makeba eyes roved up and down his body, but there was no heat behind the look. Nick got the sense she was taking his measurements with her eyes. "It suits you. If you'd like, I can bring some similar options."

"Um. Maybe." Nick hadn't checked any price tags while he was getting dressed. He flipped over the one hanging off the vest, and his eyes nearly popped out of his skull. "Holy shit."

"That bad, huh?" Deen sidled up next to him and peeked at the price too. He huffed. "Ouch. But think of it as an investment. A piece like this will last you for a lot longer than those crappy shirts you got at the thrift store."

"He's right," Makeba said. "And I'm not just saying that because I get commission. Though if you like, we have some less expensive alternatives I can show you."

Nick's blush was getting worse by the second. Unless her options were a third the cost of this, he still wouldn't be able to swing it.

Makeba seemed to sense his unease, because she stepped back. "I'll give you two a chance to discuss it." Her heels clicked on the tile as she retreated to the other side of the store.

Once she was out of earshot, Deen leaned toward him. "Dude, you gotta buy this outfit. It was made for you. I'll weep if you don't."

"I don't know." Nick checked the other price tags.

The shirt was twice what the ones from the thrift store had cost, but not wholly unreasonable for something that hadn't previously been worn. The pants cost less than the vest, which made no sense, considering they had three times as much fabric. Regardless, the whole outfit would take a chunk out of his bank account. If it was between this and replacing his laptop, he had to go with the practical option.

Before he could announce his decision and break Deen's heart, an unfamiliar voice called out to him.

"Nick? Is that you?"

Nick glanced over his shoulder and froze. Dante—the guy from his lab—was standing a few feet away. He had shopping bags in both hands and was dressed in skinny jeans and a scarlet long-sleeved shirt, the fit of which suggested it was actually a glove. He looked like he'd just stepped off the pages of *GQ*.

"Hey." Nick turned to face him. "You're Dante, right? I think we have a lab together."

"Every Thursday." He flashed a perfect smile, and one of his cheeks folded into a dimple.

Hot damn. Nick struggled to think of something to say, but his tongue tied itself into knots with the skill of a Navy Seal.

Something dug into his side. Deen's elbow.

"Gonna introduce me, roomie?" Deen chuckled, seemingly for Dante's benefit, before lowering his voice to a hiss. "How do you know all the most notorious partiers at our school? It's like I'm living with a Kennedy."

"Be cool, okay?" Nick whispered back before clearing his throat. "Dante, this is my roommate, Deen. Deen, this is Dante."

Dante nodded at him. "I'd shake your hand, but . . ." He held up his shopping bags.

"Don't worry about it." Deen laughter was pitched too high. "Rain check."

Dante's attention returned to Nick. "There's someone with me, by the way. Someone I think you'll want to say hi to." His attention shifted over Nick's shoulder.

Heart skipping, Nick swallowed and followed the direction of his gaze. *Could it be?*

Sure enough, Sebastian Prinsen was standing over by a sweater display, having what appeared to be a lively conversation with Makeba. Unlike Dante, he was dressed down in a dark-green V-neck and casual cutoffs that showed off his long legs. Nick's mouth watered a little as his eyes trailed over the chest exposed by his shirt.

I gotta admit, Sebastian's gorgeous.

Dante's voice brought Nick crashing back to reality. "I see I was right."

He shook off his temporary stupor. "Huh?"

Dante merely smiled again. His eyes drifted down to Nick's outfit. "I hope you're planning to buy everything that's on your body right now. It works for you in a big way."

Nick's face got hot for an entirely different reason. "I was thinking about it." Almost against his will, he glanced back at Sebastian.

Sebastian was still talking to Makeba. He didn't so much as glance their way. Nick frowned. He'd expected Sebastian to come over. Say hi. Maybe flirt some more. But no, he seemed to be telling a joke, judging by the way Makeba giggled.

Something pinched low in Nick's belly. He turned his back on them.

"So," Deen said to Dante, "how's the semester treating you so far?"

"Pretty good, though I'm taking sixteen credits."

Deen blew out a breath that made his bangs flutter. "Yikes. Did you have to give up some nonessentials to make your schedule work? Like sleep?"

Dante grinned. "Something like that. Actually, I need people to study with. Nick, I don't suppose you'd want to get together sometime, since we have a class together? I'm only taking it because of a lab requirement, and I hear you're a STEM student."

"Sure." Nick shrugged. "I could use a study buddy. You free sometime next week?"

"Sounds good. Let me get your number." Dante set his bags on the tile floor and pulled a phone from his pocket.

Nick was even more grateful to Theo now than before. He was able to pull his own phone out of his bag without feeling embarrassed about it. "Call me so I'll have yours too."

After they'd exchanged numbers, Dante slid his phone back into the pocket of his jeans—with some difficulty, they were so tight—and smiled. It was amazing how he could turn it on and off like a bulb.

"Great. We'd better be going. See you in class on Thursday. Or maybe sooner." Dante raised his voice. "Yo, Sebby! C'mon." He grabbed his bags and left without checking to see if Sebastian was following him.

Nick's mouth went dry as Sebastian peeled himself away from Makeba and strolled after Dante. As he passed, Nick prepared himself for whatever ostentatious greeting Sebastian was sure to send his way.

But no, Sebastian sailed right by without so much as a sidelong look. He caught up with Dante, and the two of them headed for the door, already laughing as if they'd shared some sort of private joke.

Makeba reappeared at Nick's side. "What a charming young man. He said he knew you both. Are you friends?"

"Yes," Deen said at the same time that Nick said, "No."

She glanced between them for a moment before smiling. "Right. Well, can I help you two find anything else?"

"There are some jeans in the dressing room I'd like to buy." Nick swallowed, bracing himself for potential awkwardness. "Otherwise, I'm all set."

"Perfect." She indicated his body. "Would you like to wear your new outfit out, or shall I box it up for you?"

Sigh. I hate to think I wasted her time.

"Actually, I'm just going to get the jeans. I love this outfit, but it's out of my price range."

"It's already paid for. Your friend took care of it."

Nick's eyes popped open so far, it hurt a little. "What?"

"I thought it was a little odd too, but he insisted." Makeba shrugged. "When he walked up to me, he asked if you were going to buy what you had on. I said you seemed hesitant, and then he insisted on paying for it. He told me to give you this." She produced a piece of paper that looked like it'd been torn from a notebook.

Sebastian had scrawled a message on it in hasty black ink.

My knees actually got weak when I saw you. Wear that to the party I'm having at my place tonight. Be there at nine.

Beneath his message, Sebastian had included his phone number and address.

Nick stared at it, so angry the digits swam before his eyes. *If he thinks this is the way to win me over, he is so, so wrong.*

"Nick?" Deen nudged him. "Are you okay? Your face is all red."

"Yeah," he lied. "Let's go. Suddenly, I'm not in the mood for shopping."

Chapter Eight

S ebastian gazed out over his packed apartment in the manner of
a king surveying his land. The first party of the semester was off
to a raucous start. Music was blaring, drinks were flowing, and tipsy
undergrads were swaying together in the living room, which had been
hastily repurposed into a dance floor.

It was a sea of debauchery and bad decisions. As the number
of people dancing in his living room edged up toward "fire hazard,"
Sebastian couldn't help but feel like something was . . . missing.

"Why so pensive?" a nearby voice called over the din.

Sebastian glanced to the side. Dante had sidled up next to him
with a martini in one hand and a lit cigar in the other. Sebastian
wrinkled his nose. "How many times have I told you not to smoke
inside?"

"Dunno. How many times have I ignored you?" Dante took a
puff. "You seem like you have something on your mind. What's up?"

Sebastian inspected his apartment again. He'd moved in at the
beginning of sophomore year, and though he'd chosen to re-sign his
lease, it'd never felt like "home" to him. Perhaps because he knew he
wouldn't live here past graduation.

The decorating consisted of abstract art, string lights, and
mismatched furniture his father would despise. Which of course
meant Sebastian loved it. Something nagged at him as he looked
around, however. He couldn't quite put his finger on it.

"It's nothing," he said to Dante. "I'm having an off night, I guess.
I normally find parties motivating, you know? They're my reward for
getting through another tepid week of higher education. But this one
isn't doing it for me. I don't know why."

"Maybe you need to drink more." Dante took a sip of his martini. "Or it could be that partying is losing its charm. We do it at least once a month, after all. Perhaps the novelty has worn off."

Sebastian eyed the beer in his hand. He contemplated taking a sip before deciding he didn't have the taste for it. He set it on a nearby table. "I hope that's not the case. It'd be depressing if we got tired of partying before we turned twenty-one."

"Who's 'we'? I'm having a great time." A couple of boys in crop tops and tight jeans walked past them. Dante caught the eye of one of them and flashed a sultry smile. The guy turned red and sashayed away with a pronounced sway in his hips. Dante nudged Sebastian. "I could so have him if I wanted to."

Sebastian debated with himself before asking. "So, have him. What's stopping you?"

As predicted, Dante's eyes dropped to the floor, as if he were afraid Sebastian would read his face. "No reason. I don't want to leave you alone."

Bullshit. He's not the boy you want to take home tonight, and you know it. "Don't let me ruin your good mood."

Dante regarded him. "You're not ruining anything. Something really is up with you. Got a bad case of thinking about the future? After this year, there's just one more left until we graduate and have to enter the big, bad world. I've woken up in a cold sweat at the thought of that before."

"Nah. Furthest thing from my mind." Talking about this was worsening Sebastian's unease. He scanned the crowd, which was pulsating along to the beat of some pop song playing from the speakers. "Where's Theo?"

"Dancing."

A second later, Sebastian spotted a bright-red head in the throng. Eventually Theo looked his way, and Sebastian waved him over.

Theo disentangled himself from multiple dance partners and crossed the living room to the perimeter, where Sebastian had posted up. "Hey, guys. What's up?"

"Nothing much." Sebastian sniffed. "Having fun?"

Theo cocked his head to the side. "Of course. It's a party."

"Not for Sebastian here," Dante cut in. "He's experiencing ennui."

Sebastian glared at him. "Only pretentious college kids use words like *ennui* in everyday conversation."

That earned him a wink before Dante turned back to Theo. "I think he wants us to join him."

"I'm down." Theo smiled. "What are we angsting about?"

"Life. Graduation. Sebastian's inability to enjoy underaged drinking and reckless behavior."

Theo sized Sebastian up. "Since when are you all responsible? Did you try drinking more?"

"I don't want to drink." Sebastian tried to keep his tone from becoming a whine. "I'm in a weird mood is all. I'll snap out of it."

"Could be symptomatic of a larger problem," Theo suggested. "Perhaps something to do with the new semester . . . or your parents. You wanna talk about it?"

"Theo, you know I respect you and your major, but the last thing I need right now is to be analyzed like a rat in a maze. I'm having a rough enough night as it is."

"I think it's about to take a turn for the better." Dante craned his neck to see over the crowd. "Isn't that Nick's roommate who just walked in?"

Sebastian's head snapped toward the entrance. Sure enough, Deen was standing in the doorway, fidgeting nervously like he was waiting for a bouncer to appear and throw him out.

"Finally." Sebastian let out a breath. "If he's here, that means Nick is too." Suddenly, the thing that Sebastian had been missing slotted into place.

"Have I met him?" Theo tapped his chin. "Oh wait. He must be the guy who was asleep in Nick's room this morning."

"You saw Nick earlier today?" Sebastian started to say something else, but then he shook his head. "You know what? I don't care. Let's say hi before they disappear into the crowd."

Dante quirked a brow at him. "A little eager, aren't we?"

"No." Sebastian affixed his poker face into place. "I'm looking forward to making some serious progress on the bet. Hell, I might win it tonight."

"Uh-huh." Dante finished off his cocktail and set the glass down on a table next to Sebastian's abandoned beer. "We'll see about that."

Sebastian wove through the crowd, and he wasn't afraid to shove people as he went. Theo and Dante followed much more slowly and politely, which led to them falling behind. Deen spotted him when he was a few yards away. Between his huge eyes and heavy breathing, he seemed to have dissolved into anxiety.

That's odd. Has he never been to a party before?

"Hey," Sebastian said when he was close enough to be heard over the music. "Your name's Deen, right? Thanks for coming." Despite addressing him, Sebastian's eyes floated right past Deen to the hallway beyond his front door. Nick was nowhere in sight. Had he come in before, or was he late?

"Thanks for having me." Deen's smile stretched tightly over his teeth. "I know you didn't, uh, exactly invite me. I hope it's okay that I'm here."

Out of sheer politeness, Sebastian avoided saying he would have invited a hundred strangers if it meant snagging Nick. "Of course. The more the merrier. I'm still surprised I didn't know you before Nick introduced us. You're not a freshman, are you?"

"I'm a sophomore. And, uh, I tend to keep to myself."

Translation: he's a nerd. This could actually be his first party.

Sebastian smiled, hoping it would get Deen to relax and realize he was actually welcome. "I hope we'll be seeing a lot of you from now on." He made his voice as neutral as possible. "Is Nick with you?"

Deen ran a hand through his hair. "Um, well, the thing is—"

Dante and Theo caught up with him then. Dante had Theo by the arm, as if he'd dragged him through the crowd. "Hey, Deen. Nice seeing you again so soon."

"Likewise."

Theo waved. "I'm Theo. We've actually met before. I got a glimpse of you once while you were sleeping."

"Right." Deen blinked. "Well, I'll be doing a lot less of that from now on."

"Theo, stop scaring people." Sebastian turned back to Deen, praying that he wasn't about to bolt for the door. "So yeah, where's Nick? He did get my invitation, right? And my gift?"

Theo looked sharply at him and mouthed, *You got him a gift?*

Sebastian ignored him in favor of watching Deen. His darting eyes and twitching facial muscles made him seem like a mouse who'd been trapped by three large cats. Sebastian almost expected him to squeak.

"I was getting to that. Um. You see, Nick got your invitation, but he's, um." Deen fiddled with his hair again. "He's not coming."

"What?" Sebastian almost took a step back. "Why?"

"I'm the wrong person to ask, honestly. I told him he should make an appearance. I practically begged him. He's always going on and on about how he wants to make more friends. Coming here would have been a great way to do that, but he wasn't having it. I swear I did my best to convince him." Deen grimaced. "I can still stay, right?"

Sebastian's thoughts were racing too fast for him to answer with words. Instead, he stepped back and ushered Deen in with a hand. Deen scurried off into the crowd.

As soon as Deen was gone, Sebastian closed the front door behind him, hard enough to be heard over the loud music. Several people glanced over, but he ignored them. He stood there for a moment, eyes glued to his shoes, and tried to determine why his stomach felt like it'd sunk down into his toes. He should be annoyed, or even angry that Nick had blown him off. But instead he felt . . . embarrassed? Disappointed? Possibly a combination of things.

"Well"—Dante clapped a large hand onto his shoulder—"that settles that."

Sebastian didn't look up. "Settles what?"

"I'm not trying to kick you when you're down, but I think the message here is pretty clear. Nick's not into you."

At that, Sebastian frowned. "I wouldn't go that far."

"Really? Because from where I'm standing, it seems like every time you do something to win him over, it backfires."

"We don't know that for sure." Sebastian shrugged Dante's hand off. "We don't know why he didn't come. Maybe he had plans."

"Yeah, sure. The new kid, who has one friend that we know of, couldn't make it. No way he had something more important to do than come to the first party of the new semester. If he liked you, he wouldn't miss this opportunity to spend time with you."

"You know, it's not too late to back out of the bet," Theo piped up. "We'd understand if you did. And I swear, we'll only tease you a little. Right, Dante?"

Dante nodded. "Maybe the bet was best left in the past. You gotta admit, it's kinda juvenile. I mean, competing to see who can kiss the new kid first? What a cliché."

Sebastian felt a strange stab of defensiveness, as if he were being criticized instead of the bet. "You two sound awfully eager to call it off. Is there something you're not telling me?"

Dante's head twitched like he was resisting the urge to look at Theo.

Theo smiled far too brightly. "Of course not. It's just that this isn't a high school drama, and we're not angsty teens anymore. We're adults with scary adult responsibilities. We should act like it."

Sebastian wasn't fooled for a second. "If you guys didn't want to participate, you should have said something from the start. I think you're trying to stop the bet because neither of you has made any progress, despite being in much better positions to woo Nick than me."

"That's some grade-A denial there, buddy," Dante said. "Honestly, Theo and I haven't made any real moves yet because we're trying our best to not act like you."

Sebastian squared his shoulders. "What's that supposed to mean?"

"All the ostentatious posturing you've done has blown up in your face. We figure the subtle approach is probably more Nick's style, and sure enough, he likes both of us."

Sebastian bit back a sarcastic comment. There was a grain of truth to that, and it felt distinctly like salt. "Nick likes me, okay? I know he does. I've experienced our chemistry for myself. He's playing hard to get."

"Maybe he really *is* hard to get," Theo said. "Or maybe you're going about this all wrong. What have you been doing so far to get his attention? Getting in his face and being fake and generally acting like this is *Mean Girls*. I don't think Nick is Cady Heron. I think he's Janis Ian, and all the superficial crap you're doing is pissing him off."

Sebastian scoffed. "I am *not* the Regina George of this university."

"You sure as hell aren't Kevin G., babe," Dante said.

"Whatever." Sebastian paused to actually consider what they were saying, much as it irritated him. "Maybe buying Nick that outfit was a bit much, but he looked damn good in it."

Dante glanced at Theo. "Can confirm. Blondie cleans up so good, you wanna get dirty."

"Besides," Sebastian said, "you'd think a scholarship student would appreciate nice gifts."

"He probably doesn't see it as a gift." Theo shrugged. "He might see it as you trying to buy him. I've only talked to him a couple of times, but I don't think he's materialistic. You should have seen his phone. He didn't care at all that it was falling apart."

"Hm." Sebastian mulled that over. "I suppose I *have* been coming at this from the wrong angle. I've been using all the tricks that impress the elitist snobs we go to school with. Nick's not like them. I need to tailor my seduction to his taste."

He thought he saw Dante and Theo roll their eyes.

"Seb, are you sure you want to do this?" Theo asked. "You're being stubborn even for you. Why do you want to win so badly?"

Words weighed heavily on Sebastian's tongue. "Because I want to claim Barbzilla once and for all." He pointed to the fireplace. "I have a spot on my mantel cleared for it and everything."

Dante raised a brow. "You're putting all this time and energy into winning a worthless hunk of plastic? I find that difficult to believe."

"Hey now." Theo pouted. "That's *my* worthless hunk of plastic."

"Not after I take it from you," Sebastian said.

Dante shook his head. "Seriously? You want the trophy that badly? Why?"

Sebastian stared at him for a long moment before looking away, eyes unfocused. *Because my parents are selling the house I grew up in. I feel like I'm losing a part of my childhood along with my family. And once graduation comes around, I might lose you two as well. But if I have Barbzilla . . .*

Out loud, he said, "Because I want to rescue it from that pigsty Theo calls a room. For all I know, he'll accidentally throw it out the next time he cleans. Which should be any month now."

Theo's mouth dropped into an offended O. "I would *never*."

"I call bullshit," Dante said. "This is about Nick, and we all know it."

Sebastian sighed. "I admit that Nick is proving to be a challenge, but now that I've figured him out, he'll crack. I'll win the bet, Barbzilla will be mine, and everything will go back to normal."

Dante did a decent interpretation of the knowing expression Theo adopted when he went into therapist mode. "Don't you think you might be channeling some of your feelings about the divorce into this bet? Your parents hurt you, and now you're lashing out at Nick. This isn't going to solve anything."

Theo appeared impressed. "Hey, not bad. Where'd you learn that?"

"I listen when you talk." Dante winked.

"Enough." Sebastian turned back toward the party. "No more analysis tonight. Since Nick isn't here, there's nothing I can do about the bet, which means I'm free to enjoy all the fun I would have missed out on otherwise." He looked out over the crowd until he spotted Marshall Wallace, the blond from his West African History class. "Tonight's a wash, but come Monday, the bet is back on, and now, I'm done playing."

Nick lay in bed, staring up at his ceiling while anger roiled in the pit of his stomach. His first Saturday at a new school, and he was spending it alone in his room. He was too pissed off to go anywhere or do anything, including some much-needed studying. Instead, he intended to spend a tense evening sequestered away from the general populace, where he could brood in peace.

On the bathroom door hung the outfit that'd started it all: the one Sebastian had foisted on him. He'd specifically put it within view so he could glare at it without having to get up. In some corner of his mind, he knew he was overreacting, but he was too angry to care.

Christ, Sebastian was so . . . Nick had been trying to think of the right word all night. Arrogant. Presumptuous. Manipulative.

Attractive, said a voice in his head.

Nick shoved it away. *More like repellant.*

Thoughtful, it chimed in anyway.

No, fuck that. There was nothing thoughtful about what Sebastian had done.

Nick practically threw himself onto his side and sandwiched his head between two pillows, as if he could muffle his own thoughts. He didn't want to spend the whole night stewing, but since he'd refused to go to Sebastian's party, his alternatives were limited.

If only Deen hadn't gone to the party, he'd at least have some company. But no, Nick couldn't fault him for going. It was like a dream come true for him. Seeing the excitement on Deen's face as he'd picked out his party clothes almost made the infuriating encounter with Sebastian worth it.

If Nick regretted his decisions to stay behind at all, it was only because he'd forced Deen to attend the party alone. Deen had *begged* him to come, pretending it'd help Nick make friends, but Nick saw through his act: his hands had shaken as he'd buttoned up his shirt and combed his hair. He'd been *terrified* of going alone.

And Nick had stuck to his guns and sent Deen off to that piranha tank alone. He was a bad friend.

His phone vibrated on the bed next to him, as if agreeing with him.

He didn't glance at it. It was probably a Facebook notification, and the last thing he needed right now was another friend back in Chicago asking him how he was liking his new school.

But then it vibrated again, and again.

He pushed himself up onto his elbows. Someone was calling him. He glanced at the screen and groaned aloud. Sebastian. Why, of all people, did it have to be Sebastian?

Heart racing, he watched as the call went to voice mail. Thank fuck he'd thought to program Sebastian's number into his phone, or he might have answered. The missed call notification popped up a second later, indicating that Sebastian hadn't left a voice mail. Nick breathed a sigh of relief, only to tense up again a moment later when a text appeared.

He debated checking it for so long, the screen went dark. In the end, he growled and snatched up his phone. The text was one line long, but he analyzed it as if it were one of his textbooks.

You're missing a hell of a party.

That was it. No segue. No small talk. No introduction, like he *knew* Nick had taken his number. Which, of course, Nick had, but that was for avoidance purposes.

Actually, on that note, how had Sebastian gotten *his* number?

Nick's fingers itched to ask, but he held back. He didn't want to give Sebastian the satisfaction. If he were smart, he'd ignore the bastard. Deny him the response he wanted. It'd serve the spoiled jerk right.

Nick held out for five whole minutes before his phone magically found its way into his hand.

How'd you get my phone number? I never gave it to you.

He hit Send, tossed his phone onto the bed, and immediately cursed himself for being so weak. Less than a minute passed before his phone lit up with a response.

Conned it out of Deen.

Nick huffed. He was so going to make Deen pay into the Jerk Roommate jar.

As if reading his thoughts, a second text popped up. *But don't blame him. He resisted for way longer than I expected him to. I had to make him an offer he couldn't refuse.*

Nick was curious to know what Sebastian had given Deen in exchange for his number, but he was still hell-bent on not talking to Sebastian. He threw his phone back onto the bed—probably harder than needed—and flipped open his laptop. He'd started searching for a new one earlier, and there were plenty of options to browse online.

While he attempted to bury himself in retail therapy, his phone buzzed again. He made it ten whole seconds before he sighed and checked the new text.

Why didn't you come to my party?

The text had no inflection of its own, but it felt . . . sad to Nick. Emotion flickered in his chest, something like regret, but he snuffed it out. Let Sebastian be sad. He'd made some shitty choices today.

I didn't want to come.

Another text popped up immediately.

Didn't want to risk being alone with me, huh? There are plenty of other people here, you know.

Nick could practically hear Sebastian's flirty tone. He was having none of that. He wrote back in a huff. *That wasn't my reason.*

Why then?

Because I don't want to see you.

Nick hit Send and waited for a swell of satisfaction, but to his surprise, he felt . . . anxious. As if he were fighting with a friend or a lover or something. Which was ridiculous, so why did he feel this way?

Sebastian replied. *Thanks to my keen powers of observation, I detect a note of anger.*

Oh, I'm pissed all right.

Why? Whatever I did, I'm sorry.

Nick considered ignoring him again, and once more, Sebastian seemed to read his thoughts.

If you don't tell me what it was, I can't make sure I never do it again. To anyone.

Nick frowned. Well, he supposed Sebastian had a point, and it was nice of him to think of others for once. Disarmed, Nick took his phone in both hands and typed quickly.

That "present" you bought me was inappropriate and unwanted.

Oh, is that all? Nick could almost hear Sebastian shrugging. *I was trying to do something nice. Enjoy my altruism. Better yet, let everyone enjoy it. Wear the outfit to my party.*

"Fuck that," Nick said, typing furiously. *No. Bad move. Huge violation of my boundaries. Not impressive or appropriate at all. I'm not so hard up I'll smile while you pull a stunt like that. You made me feel like a charity case. I've worked for everything I have, and I'd never have accepted your "gift" if you'd given me a choice.*

A long minute passed in which Nick received no reply. He'd begun to hope Sebastian had lost interest when another text arrived.

I'm sorry I overstepped. If you think I was trying to buy your affection, I swear I wasn't. I was showing off and being selfish, and I apologize. I wasn't trying to piss you off or make you feel cheap.

Nick shook his head to himself and muttered under his breath as he typed. *Did Theo tell you he also gave me a gift earlier today?*

What'd he give you?

A phone. A nice one. I tried to turn it down a couple of times, but ultimately, I accepted it. You know why?

Sebastian's reply was the last thing Nick expected. *Because you like him, but you don't like me?*

Nick stared at the text, reading it over and over until he thought it might be imprinted on his corneas. More surprising than the text was the realization that washed over Nick. He didn't dislike Sebastian. He liked both Theo and him in totally different ways. He was too angry to admit that right now, so he sidestepped the question.

Theo asked me if I wanted the phone. Keyword: asked. If I'd outright refused to take it, I'm positive he would have dropped the issue. You, on the other hand, didn't bother to consult me. You said you were being selfish, and I agree completely.

Watching as the text sent, Nick realized his heart rate had sped up. This was the kind of frank conversation he usually had when fighting with a lover. Why again wasn't he ignoring Sebastian? How was it that Sebastian kept sucking him back in?

For whatever reason, he needed for Sebastian to understand. The "gift" had solidified in Nick's head every negative opinion he'd formed: Sebastian was an entitled brat who had no idea how his actions looked to people who lived outside his gilded bubble. Nick refused to let him have his way yet again.

For a good few minutes, Sebastian was silent. Nick went back to browsing, but honestly, he didn't read a word. His attention was attuned to the phone on the mattress next to him. Much as he hated to admit it, he was curious to see what Sebastian was going to say. His apology hadn't been half-bad, but if Nick knew him at all, he'd probably turn on the charm next.

The second a notification popped up, Nick's phone was in his hand.

You make my head spin.

Okay, was that a good thing or a bad thing? Before Nick could ask, another message appeared.

I don't know how to describe it. One second, my life is one way, but then the next, you appear, and you make me question everything. I never know what you're going to say. I don't know what you want, and it's frustrating. But I also want to please you.

Nick stared at the words as if he thought he could get them to change if he looked hard enough. This might be the most direct Sebastian had ever been with him, and it roused his paranoia.

Sebastian, have you been drinking?

The response was immediate. *I'm at a party. Of course I've been drinking.*

Nick was about to make a snide comment, but Sebastian texted again before he could. *Not that much, though. I don't want to drink. I don't want to party. I'm standing by myself in a corner texting you while everyone around me is dancing and having fun. Why is that?*

Was that a rhetorical question, or did he expect Nick to answer? Nick told the truth. *I don't know.*

I think I do, and it terrifies me.

That one sentence sucked all the air out of Nick's lungs. He couldn't begin to think of what to say back. He wasn't even sure what Sebastian *meant*, exactly, and yet he did.

Fortunately, Sebastian texted him again. *Come to my party. Please?*

I can't. I'm not going to wear the outfit.

That's not why I'm inviting you. I want to talk. Will you please come? I want to apologize to your face. I'll sweeten the deal: you can yell at me all you like.

That last part made Nick laugh despite himself. When he analyzed his feelings, he was surprised to discover he was considering it. If he could get Sebastian one-on-one, he stood a better chance of getting it through Sebastian's thick skull that he needed to back off.

Is that really why you want to see him? a voice in the back of his head asked. *Are you that determined to lie to yourself?*

Damn it, he couldn't give in now. He needed to show Sebastian that he wasn't going to get what he wanted. Not this time.

Holding down a button on the side of his phone, he watched with satisfaction as it powered off. There. If Sebastian couldn't reach him, he couldn't tempt Nick into coming to his party.

Nick would have preferred to keep his phone on, in case Deen needed him, but Deen wasn't driving, and the party was only a few blocks from campus. He could be trusted to make it home safely. Plus, Nick didn't think he could resist if Sebastian kept saying such confusing things to him. Such thoughtful, genuine-sounding things . . .

He shook his head. This was for the best. He'd go to sleep, and in the morning, he'd think all this over. It would seem clearer in the light of day.

Sans laptop, he climbed into bed, clicked off his lamp, and willed himself to sleep. He spent a few minutes listening for his phone, though he knew it was off, before he rolled over and forced himself to clear his mind.

When he finally dozed off, he was plagued by odd dreams. In one, he was back home. The streets were empty. Chicago's towering buildings bled into a steely winter sky. The city looked different to him now. The streets. The skyline he knew so well. Like a puzzle he didn't have all the pieces for. Was he forgetting it already?

In another dream, he was staring directly into a pair of dark-brown eyes. He thought they might be Deen's, or maybe Dante's, but they blinked and were gone before he could decide.

The last dream he remembered before he woke up was the most upsetting. He was standing next to a picnic bench, looking down at his feet. Next to him, Sebastian sat on the bench, head in his hands. He was clearly crying, his shoulders heaving with sobs. Nick tried to lift his hand and comfort him, but his arm was paralyzed. Sebastian cried so much, he dissolved and was gone.

Nick's churning stomach woke him. He might as well have stayed up all night, because he felt less rested than he had before. Scrubbing the sleep from his eyes, he tried to make sense of his dreams, but they were fading from his memory faster than he could analyze them.

With a yawn, he realized he hadn't heard Deen come in last night. He glanced over at his bed.

Deen was passed out on top of his covers, clothes still on, with a big smile plastered on his face. Nick had to stifle a laugh. Deen was probably going to have a hell of a hangover, but it looked as though it'd been worth it.

Damn, it seems I really did miss out on a great party. At least Deen got to have fun.

What time was it? For once, he didn't know. He grabbed his phone off the desk and pressed the home button. It wasn't until it failed to come to life that he remembered he'd turned it off. Good thing today was Sunday and he had nowhere to be. And that no one ever called him. And that he still hadn't made any new friends.

Besides Theo and Deen, he thought as his phone came back to life. *And maybe Dante, if we end up studying together.*

That raised an interesting question. How was he ever going to avoid Sebastian if they ended up having the same friends?

Nick shook his head as his home screen loaded. The time popped up, declaring that it was after nine in the morning. That was good. He was waking up and going to bed at semiregular times. Maybe he'd avoid becoming nocturnal this semester like he usually did. At least, until finals week.

He was about to set his phone back down on the desk and get dressed when it vibrated in his hand. His heart leaped into his throat. Was Sebastian calling him again? No, it couldn't be. What were the chances he'd call right when Nick woke up?

As Nick watched, a text message popped up. Then another. And another. Too quickly for anyone to be sending them individually.

They must've been sent while my phone was off, and now I'm getting all of them at once. Jesus, how many are there?

His phone went off for a solid thirty seconds. By the time it'd finished, he had seventeen new texts. He almost didn't want to look, but in the end, curiosity won out. He clicked on Sebastian's name in his inbox and scrolled up to the first message he'd sent after Nick powered off his phone.

Are you ignoring me? Do you want me to leave you alone?

Right after that, Sebastian said, *I suppose I should take the hint.*

The time stamps indicated that several minutes had passed before Sebastian sent, *You can tell me to fuck off, and I will. But until then, I'm going to keep trying to make this up to you. I don't want to believe I blew it.*

Nick put down his phone and covered his mouth, needing to steel himself before he read any more. Holy shit, Sebastian was getting more emotional with every text. By the end of this conversation, what would Nick find?

Stalling, he tapped back to his inbox and saw that he also had two messages from Theo and one from Dante. Theo wanted to know where he was, and if Nick was the reason Sebastian was "missing his own party." Gulp.

Dante's text asked if Nick wanted to get together and study sometime soon. Nick replied in the affirmative and asked when was good for Dante. Once that sent, he took an invigorating breath and switched back over to Sebastian.

As Nick read, his eyes got wider and wider until he imagined he must look like an owl. He could sense the night progressing through the messages. Sebastian's spelling and punctuation slipped from time to time, which was a good indicator of his sobriety. Considering the texts spanned the course of hours, he must've had a *lot* to drink.

But then, he'd said he didn't want to drink. Had he hit the bottle when he realized Nick wasn't going to come to his party? He must have, because his texts before had been letter-perfect, right down to the punctuation.

Nick kept reading. As the night went on, Sebastian had stopped pleading with Nick to show up and started describing what he was missing instead. Apparently, Eric Garraffa—whoever that was—had gotten locked out on the balcony and tried to climb down a trellis. *Tried* being the operative word. Two girls named Jackie and Angela had finally hooked up, to everyone's delight.

Nick wondered briefly if that was the same Angela he had class with, before he moved to the next text.

Long stretches of time passed when there were no messages. Around midnight, Sebastian had renewed his feeling that Nick was a puzzle.

I wish i could figre u out. i've never tryd so hard with some1 b4.

The next few messages were more innocuous. Sebastian said the party was winding down and that even Dante and Theo had left. Around one in the morning, Sebastian declared to Nick that he was going to bed. Which must not have happened, since he continued to text Nick. His improved spelling suggested he'd sobered up.

There's a boy in my bed. He's blond and tan, like you. But he's not you.

Nick's heart stopped cold in his chest. He read the next text in double time.

I was going to have sex with him tonight, but I can't. I have no idea why, but I can't do it.

Nick was ashamed to admit he was relieved.

I really am going to bed now. I swear. Soon as my brain quiets down.

The final text was sent at three in the morning, and reading it made Nick dizzy.

I'm staring up at my ceiling, unable to turn off my thoughts. They keep circling back to the same subject: you. Earlier, when the party was in full swing, I looked around and thought to myself that something was missing. From the party. From my apartment. From my life. I couldn't figure out what it was. But now, as I lay here, I think I finally know. It's you.

The air whooshed out of Nick's lungs. He read that last message what felt like a hundred times before he put his phone down and stared off into space.

There was no doubt in his mind that Sebastian had meant what he'd said. It might've been brought on by exhaustion and/or the remnants of booze, but it was real. Real and raw and honest.

Nick had just gotten his first genuine peek at Sebastian, without the reputation and defenses that acted as smoke screens. For the first time, when Nick thought about Sebastian, he saw a passionate, needy young man who was analytical to the point of his own detriment.

And shock of all shocks, Nick kind of liked that person.

This is bad. This is not what I planned.

Nick knew what he had to do.

He picked up his phone again, composed a short, simple text, and sent it off. After, he fell back onto his bed and stared up at his own ceiling, thoughts forming a buzzing swarm in his head.

Chapter Nine

When Sebastian woke the next morning, he had a wicked hangover, a sour mouth, and very few memories.

The second he cracked an eye open, he slammed it shut again. The light streaming through his bedroom windows was agony. And to think, he'd insisted on renting an apartment with floor-to-ceiling windows in most of the rooms. Every time he threw a party, he regretted that decision the next day.

He lay on his side with his eyes closed and gathered his strength. The soft pajama bottoms he'd donned were sandpaper against his skin. He normally slept naked. Why had he put on clothes this time? His brain swam as he tried to think. After a while, he opened his eyes again—gingerly, this time—and glanced at the clock on his nightstand.

Past noon. Damn. He'd really overdone it.

At least he'd remembered to plug his phone in before going to sleep. It was resting next to his clock. He eased himself forward enough to swipe at the white USB cord and ended up knocking his phone onto the floor. A groan poured out of him. Absolutely everything hurt, and if he had to move more than a few inches, he was going to die.

His groan was answered by a small noise beside him. He froze. Suddenly, he had all the strength he needed to whip around and look at the other side of the bed.

A guy who was at least half-naked was lying on his stomach, face buried in a pillow. Sebastian's black sheets were pulled up to his waist. All Sebastian could see was a toned back and messy blond hair.

That explains the pajamas. Is it . . .?

For a fraction of a second, his brain cut to white noise. But then, memories from last night came drifting back. The man next to him was Marshall Wallace, not—

Sebastian scrubbed a hand down his face. God, he needed help. And water. And aspirin. And *water*.

He rolled out of bed as quietly as he could, snatched his phone off the floor, and considered changing into real clothes before deciding water was his top priority. Besides, he was no stranger to walking around shirtless, and he didn't just mean in his own home. He tiptoed out of the room.

His apartment was more or less intact. There were empty beer bottles and red cups lying around—and a rumpled pair of women's underwear on the couch, minus whoever had been wearing them—but it was nothing he couldn't handle. Later. When he'd hydrated himself back to a semblance of personhood.

He made a beeline for the kitchen, pulled a bottle of water out of the fridge, and drank most of it in a couple of swallows. Then he plopped onto one of the stools by his granite island and cradled his head in his hands.

Slowly, he sifted through what he remembered from the night before. His I-don't-feel-like-drinking schtick hadn't lasted. After his talk with Theo and Dante, something in him had snapped. There had been shots. Far too many shots. Of tequila too, which he normally only drank when he was *trying* to get fucked up. He hadn't thought that was his goal at the time, but here he was, piecing the night together.

When had Marshall come into the picture? Sometime between shirtless limbo and a bunch of people getting locked out on the balcony. Sebastian remembered reluctantly making out with him. It'd been sloppy, and Marshall had tasted like stale beer. For some reason, it'd also left Sebastian feeling guilty. He didn't normally feel anything after a hookup. Weird.

After that, things were blurry. Marshall had proposed they sleep together, but Sebastian had a firm anti-drunk-sex policy. He normally didn't let guys pass out in his bed either, but by that point in the night, he'd been too tired to protest, and there'd been no way he was letting Marshall drive home.

Sebastian remembered texting. He remembered texting one person in particular *a lot*.

Cold dread permeated him. It was like his brain had saved the very worst memories for last. Sebastian had spent a large chunk of last night drunk-texting Nick. He'd lain awake, with another guy passed out next to him, and sent Nick a message. He didn't recall now what he'd said, but it'd been emotional. And genuine.

Which meant there was a chance he was fucked.

Lifting his face out of his hands, Sebastian eyed his phone where it rested on the cool granite. Curiosity urged him to scroll through his inbox and see what he'd written, but he wasn't sure he could handle the embarrassment.

He wasn't normally the sort to pour his soul out as soon as he got a couple of drinks in him, but with how volatile he'd been lately, and how strangely he tended to act when it came to Nick, he got the feeling overdrinking wasn't the only regrettable thing he'd done last night.

"C'mon, Prinsen," he murmured to himself. "Rip the bandage off."

With a sigh, he picked up the phone and hit a button. The screen flashed to life. He had a hundred new notifications. Facebook statuses he'd been tagged in. Instagram photos of the party. Too much for him to possibly go through while his head was pounding like a drum.

He bypassed all the alerts and went for his messages. His sight was blurry, he was so hungover, but if he squinted, he could make the letters stop swimming. Sure enough, Nick's name was at the top of the list. He clicked on it and scrolled up to the beginning.

The first messages he remembered. Everything after that, however, was news to him, as was the realization that Nick had blown him off. After their initial few exchanges, Nick had stopped replying.

Which apparently wasn't a deterrent at all for drunk Sebastian. He'd just kept on texting. Photos of the party. Quotes with no context. And oh God, a drunken late-night confession, as he'd suspected.

Sebastian reread the final text he'd sent Nick—the one about feeling like something was missing—with escalating horror. He hadn't meant to be that honest. Hell, he *never* meant to be that honest. And yet, he'd poured his heart out to a guy he hardly knew. What the fuck had gotten into him lately?

But the real kicker was, now that he was rereading it, he remembered writing it. He remembered wanting, with all his heart, to say these things to Nick. He'd sobered up some by the time 3 a.m. had arrived. This, he couldn't blame on alcohol.

Granted, the details were fuzzy, and sober him sure as shit would have done some editing, but he'd known what he was doing. This text was a combination of exhaustion, insecurity, and honest desire.

Desire for what? This isn't you wanting to win the bet. This is something else. What changed, and what exactly do you want from Nick?

He didn't think he was ready to answer that question. Instead, he needed to decide what he wanted to do. Spin this somehow? Call Nick and deny the whole thing? Pretend the texts never happened?

None of those seemed right. Mortified as he was, he didn't regret his words. On the contrary, he was sort of relieved, as if he'd shed a small burden he hadn't noticed until it was gone. Though, he'd have to apologize to Nick for being a drunken mess, and he was dying to know how Nick felt about all this. Grateful as he was that Nick hadn't responded to him, he'd also like to know *why*. Was Nick angry? Confused? Charmed?

I suppose there's no chance he found my display endearing. He's probably filing for a restraining order right now. I should call him and explain. After I drink a lot more water. And kick that other guy out of my bed. And take a long look at my decision-making processes.

Sebastian was about to turn his screen off when he swiped up again and saw a new message.

Nick had, in fact, replied to him. That very morning, while Sebastian had slept.

The text consisted of four simple words: *We need to talk.*

For a second time, Sebastian froze. He'd suspected that Nick would take the texts seriously, as opposed to dismissing them as drunken antics, but now he had proof. Damn. They did need to talk—he knew that—but he'd watched enough sitcoms to know those four words usually spelled trouble.

It's not like he can break up with you. You're not dating.

Why then was Sebastian's heart pounding? He thought back to what Dante had accused him of last night: being in denial. Before he talked to Nick, he needed to figure out what the hell he was doing here.

Why had he gotten so drunk last night? Because he was upset Nick hadn't come to his party? He also wondered if Marshall had something to do with it. Sebastian's no-sex-when-drunk rule was well-known. Maybe Sebastian had overdone it to make sure he couldn't hook up with anyone.

Alarm bells went off in his head. This was getting out of hand. Nick wasn't his boyfriend and never would be. Sebastian had been lying to his face from the start. He had a bet going with his two best friends to see who could kiss Nick first.

There was absolutely no way he could let himself develop feelings for Nick. End of story.

Although, looking back at their short history, it seemed like Sebastian never had much of a choice. Nick was like a natural disaster. Unavoidable. All Sebastian could do was duck and cover. Pray for the best while he got totally swept away.

What made Nick so special? Was Sebastian clinging to him because of what was going on with his parents? His life was falling apart. Maybe he was looking for something solid to hold on to.

That had to be it. Sebastian would pull himself together and focus on the task at hand. This was a game, and it was one he intended to win. *Needed* to win.

He'd talk to Nick. There was no telling how that was going to go. Nick could be furious with him. He might tell Sebastian that he never wanted to see him again. Sebastian might have lost the bet last night.

A thought occurred to him, fuzzy through the dregs of his hangover: he'd lost his chance with Nick the second he'd made this bet. If there was one thing he knew about Nick, it was that he didn't suffer fools, and Sebastian had done something very, *very* foolish. If Nick found out about the bet, he'd never forgive Sebastian.

This bed Sebastian had made for himself was starting to look an awful lot like a rock situated next to a hard place.

Cursing from the bedroom broke him from his reverie. Sebastian sighed. First, he needed to deal with the immediate consequences of last night. Then, he'd think up some way to deal with the bigger ones. And hopefully, some way out of this mess of his own making.

Monday rolled around because life wasn't fair. Nick slept fitfully and was forced to wake up early to make his meeting with Dr. O'Connor.

Deen was still asleep, which was fine by Nick. He'd spent most of Sunday listening to Deen detail everything that'd happened at Sebastian's party. The way he told it, there had been alcohol, an epic round of limbo in which a detachable stripper pole had been used as the stick, and more alcohol.

Nick had listened with patience, for the most part, but a bigger part of him than he'd like to admit was sad he'd missed out. Especially when Deen had told him one interesting piece of information.

"I dunno what you did to the guy," Deen had said, "but Sebastian Prinsen would *not* shut up about you."

"What?" Nick had known he was on Sebastian's mind, obviously, but he'd never expected Sebastian to talk about him. "What'd he say?"

"'Why didn't Nick come to my party?'" Deen had done a pretty decent imitation of Sebastian's cool voice. "'What's he doing? Is he hanging out with other people? Marsha, Marsha, Marsha.' He brought you up every time I ran into him. But naturally, since I'm a good friend, I refused to tell him why you wouldn't come to the party."

"Right, so you just gave him my phone number instead."

At that, Deen had become strangely quiet, muttering something along the lines of, "Well, I had to give the poor guy *something*," before claiming he needed to do some studying.

Now that Monday had arrived, things were no clearer to him than they'd been before. Sebastian had never responded to his text message, leaving Nick to wonder what he was thinking. There was a good chance the texts had been booze-induced and Sebastian was mortified. Possibly too mortified to ever talk to Nick again.

The idea was . . . oddly upsetting.

Nick had considered sending follow-up texts, but he had no idea what to say. Honestly, after having been pursued by Sebastian this whole time, he wasn't about to become the hunter. And he was a little afraid to learn why Sebastian had gone radio silent.

Last week, I would have loved for him to leave me alone, but now here I am. Checking my phone every five minutes to see if he's texted back. What's wrong with me?

Nick got ready for the day and then headed straight for Dr. O'Connor's office. The door was open, so he walked right in and found her sitting at her desk, typing. The dog figurines were present and accounted for.

When she glanced at him as he entered, she had a familiar warm smile on her face. "Right on time, Nick. Take a seat."

Nick did, watching Dr. O'Connor warily as she turned to him. As luck would have it, he had no reason to fret. The whole thing took less than a minute. Dr. O'Connor gave him a once-over with her giant spectacled eyes, asked him how his first week had gone, and then said he could go.

"What?" Nick sat up straighter in his seat. "That's it?"

"Why not?" Dr. O'Connor didn't make eye contact as she quickly typed something up. "This isn't a test. You're wearing clean clothes, you look like you're eating, and you don't reek of booze like some of the other students around here. I'm satisfied you're getting the hang of things." She stopped to flash him a bright smile. "Congratulations, Nick. The hard part's over."

"Good to know." He stood up. "Well, thanks for meeting with me. I'd better get some breakfast before class." For some reason, he hesitated.

Dr. O'Connor turned to face him fully. "Was there something else?"

"No," he said as he made no move toward the door. His head was whirring with so many thoughts, he couldn't find the controls for his feet.

Dr. O'Connor gestured at the seat he'd vacated. "You'd better sit back down."

Nick plopped into it without complaint. "Sorry. I'm sure you're busy. It's just . . ."

"I'm never too busy to talk, Nick. That's my job." She steepled her hands under her chin, elbows resting on the surface of her desk. "Is something bothering you?"

That's putting it lightly. "Kind of, yeah. I don't really know how to describe it. Or even if I should. It's nothing, really."

"Seems like something to me. Does it involve another student?"

Nick nodded.

"Is someone bullying you?"

"No. Actually, everyone's been pretty cool. I know it's only the first week, and this isn't going to bode well, but I've been . . . having trouble concentrating. I need to spend the next few days catching up on my reading."

"Any particular reason you're distracted? Is it your home life? Or your friends? Or a girl?"

Nick chuckled. "It's definitely not a girl. Honestly, I don't know what I'm trying to say. I'm wasting your time. Thanks for talking to me. I'll sort it out." He stood up, and this time his feet were online. He was halfway to the door when he heard Dr. O'Connor's voice behind him.

"If it's not a girl, is it a boy?"

Nick stopped short. Heart pounding, he turned slowly back around. "What?"

Dr. O'Connor looked unmoved. "Will you please shut the door?"

In a daze, Nick did so and once again fell into his seat. "Listen, I'm not—"

She held up a hand. "You don't have to tell me anything if you don't want to. I just want to make it clear to you that while this is a Catholic university, this isn't the sixteenth century. The administration understands that people from all walks of life attend here. No one's going to get expelled for being gay."

"Oh." Nick swallowed. "I see."

"If there was anything you wanted to tell me," she said in a neutral tone, "I would be happy to listen. For the record, this college has had its fair share of queer students. Including one particularly energetic polyamorous woman back in the nineties who I thought was going to give the old dean a heart attack."

Nick opened and closed his mouth, debating with himself. Eventually, he looked away. "I'm not gay, for the record." He paused. "I'm bisexual."

Dr. O'Connor didn't so much as blink. "Was I right when I guessed you were having boy troubles?"

Nick nodded, tense as he waited to see if some sort of trap was going to spring.

"Well—" she sat back in her chair "—if you'd like to tell me about it, I'm listening. Although, you look like you'd prefer to make a Nick-shaped hole in my door, and that's okay as well. We can always meet up another time."

"I'm surprised is all. How'd you know?"

"You laughed when I suggested it was a girl, and then said 'It's definitely not a *girl.*' Psychology can be an imprecise science at times, but I think anyone would have been able to crack that code."

Damn. She's got me there.

Nick nodded. "It's a boy, yeah. His name's Sebastian, and since my first day on campus, we've had this thing."

Dr. O'Connor perked up. "Sebastian *Prinsen*? You're dating Sebastian Prinsen?"

Nick blanched. *Oh shit. He's out, right? Or did I just accidentally out him? There's no excusing that.*

He scrambled for a lie. "Uh, no. It's this other Sebastian."

"This is a small school, Nick. There's only one Sebastian who goes here. Not to mention he's one of relatively few openly gay students. I've had to have talks with him before about appropriate conversation topics at alumni events." She smiled. "Sorry for cracking your code once again. This university can be a bit incestuous at times: everyone knows everyone."

"So I've discovered." The rest of what she'd said caught up to Nick. "Sebastian and I are *not* dating. Not even close. It's more like he's been toying with me, and I'm fending him off. It was easy at first when he was putting on airs, but over the weekend, he said something to me that made me think . . . I don't know. I'm confused."

"Do you have feelings for him?"

Nick blew out a breath. "I didn't used to think so. I mean, I've known from the start I'm attracted to him, but I needed more than that. Unfortunately, he's starting to give it to me."

"Is he the reason you've been having trouble focusing? I don't need to tell you that your grades are much more important than a boy. You're both dealing with a lot right now."

Nick's head snapped up. "What's Sebastian dealing with?"

Dr. O'Connor pursed her lips. "I can't tell you that. It'd be unethical, and your reaction confirmed your priorities aren't in the right place. Try to remember what's important and not fixate on this romance."

Nick couldn't help but laugh at that. "I've been trying all week."

"I know you didn't ask for it, but I'm going to leave you with one last piece of advice." Dr. O'Connor fixed him with a serious look. "Watch out for yourself. I know college is a time to have fun, experience new things, and figure out who you are, but it's also a time for hard work and maturity. I don't need to remind you what's at stake here. It's imperative that you focus on what matters in the long run. No boy is worth losing this opportunity."

"Yeah, you're right." Nick climbed to his feet. "Thanks for this. I feel better."

"My pleasure." Dr. O'Connor stood as well. "You have my email. Don't hesitate to contact me if you need anything."

"Thank you. I will."

Nick exited the office, leaving the door open behind him. As he walked out of the administration building, he was surprised at how much lighter he felt. He'd let this whole Sebastian thing distract him from what he was here to do: get his degree, and get out. That was what mattered. That was why he was here. He shouldn't have lost sight of that for even a moment.

Although, there was a tiny flaw in that plan. Realistically, he could only avoid romance and focus on his studies for so long. He was bound to meet someone eventually. Date. Fall in love. Maybe have his heart broken. He *wanted* to do those things. There was even a part of him that was willing to admit . . . he wanted to do those things with Sebastian. Or at least, the Sebastian who'd shown himself last night.

You should talk to him before you get too much wind in your sail. The texts might still have been a drunken mistake.

Nick reached the dining hall, ducked inside, and remerged minutes later with a box full of eggs and fruit. He found a table in the shade and dug in while he put his thoughts in order.

Priority number one was admitting Dr. O'Connor was right. He needed to make sure, above all else, that college was his primary focus. But he was a young man who wanted to date and have sex and find love. Reconciling those truths was important to his mental health.

Priority number two was Sebastian. Nick was over denying that there was something between them, but if they were going to dance this dance, he wanted to know the steps ahead of time. If Sebastian went back to playing games, Nick would walk away. No questions asked.

But what if he doesn't? What if Sebastian turns out to be as wonderful as you suspect he might be? What are you going to do then?

Nick was far too terrified to answer that question. Ever since his father died, he hadn't let anyone get close to him. Something gave him the feeling that if he let Sebastian in, it would change everything.

His phone buzzed in his hand, and in response, his heart shot up into his throat. He turned on the screen and nearly choked when he saw he had a text message. With shaking fingers, he clicked on it. A second later, he deflated in his seat. It was from Dante. Nick read it quickly.

Hey, still want to get together and study? How's Friday work for you? My place?

A proverbial light bulb went off over Nick's head. Talk about killing two birds with one stone. He needed to focus more on his studies, and he wanted to learn more about Sebastian. What better way to do it than by hanging out with one of his best friends? If Sebastian didn't contact him between now and the end of the week, Nick would find out why from Dante.

Plus, he wouldn't mind getting to know Dante better, and he genuinely needed to study.

Count me in, he texted back. *I'll see you Friday. Around 6?*

Dante's reply was instantaneous.

It's a date.

Chapter Ten

Now that Nick had something to look forward to, time flew. Though it could also have been because Dr. O'Connor was right: he really was getting used to life at the Academy.

He ate in the dining hall, studied in the library, and tried to hit the gym at least twice a week. When he woke up in his attic dorm room to sunlight streaming through the windows, it felt normal. More normal than anything had in a long time. It wasn't home, yet, but he was starting to believe it might feel that way one day.

As the week passed, one thing failed to change: he still snatched up his phone every time he got a notification, expecting it to be Sebastian. It never was, and Nick had no idea why. Intentional or not, Sebastian had once again made himself a mystery.

By the time classes ended on Friday, and Nick was due to make his way to Dante's apartment, he was debating if he should ask about Sebastian after all. Either the guy was busy, or he was blowing Nick off in a big way. Nick had known people who were bad at texting back before, but this was ridiculous.

Whenever Nick went back and reread the texts Sebastian had sent him—which he did more often than he cared to admit—he couldn't believe this was the end. Not this sad, pathetic whimper.

There was never anything tangible between you. You've got to stop acting like you got dumped.

He stopped by his room to drop off his books and get ready to go to Dante's. Deen supervised, excited as a puppy. From his seat on Nick's bed, he shouted fashion advice in a voice that was pitched a whole octave higher than his usual sweet tenor. It was as if he'd been invited as well.

"You can't wear that," Deen said as Nick reached for a rumpled flannel shirt. "Pick something nicer."

"We're studying, not going to prom." Nick dropped the shirt anyway. "No need to dress up."

"Sweet, naïve Nickolas." Deen clucked his tongue. "Did you learn nothing in high school? You don't show up to hang out with the cool kids looking like a nerd. You have to dress for the social standing you want. Plus, Dante always dresses to the nines, and if you're not careful, he'll embarrass you just standing next to you. You should wear the outfit Sebastian gave you."

Nick froze with one hand buried in his laundry pile. "No way."

"Oh, come on. The clothes are yours, and they look great on you. Don't let them go to waste."

"I can't, Deen. It's the principle of the matter."

"Why, though? I get that Sebastian pissed you off, but he's not gonna be there. You can swear Dante to secrecy. Sebastian will never know you wore it."

Damn. That was a good point. But Nick was nothing if not stubborn. "I'd know, and that's enough for me."

Deen sighed. "Sebastian must've really done a number on you. So, what? Did he break your heart or something?"

Nick almost fell over. He jerked his head up and stared at Deen. "W-what?" He still hadn't told Deen he was bisexual. He wasn't sure he was ready to have this conversation yet.

"Your face." Deen smothered his laughter with a hand. "I meant that as a joke, but your reaction was priceless. Guess that confirms my suspicions."

Shit. I've never been a good liar.

"What gave me away?" Nick braced himself. If he'd known he was going to out himself twice in one week, he would have done some stress-reducing yoga.

"I'm not trying to stereotype anyone, but the most notorious gay guy in school bought you an *outfit*. Pretty obvious, no? Plus, when he wouldn't shut up about you at his party, I figured something had gone down between you. Although"—Deen tapped his chin—"you and I have talked about girls, so either you were faking, or you're not gay."

Nick took a deep breath and let it out slowly. "I'm bisexual. Sorry I didn't tell you sooner. I had no idea how you'd react."

Deen waved him off. "No worries. I told myself I was going to wait for you to come to me, but so much for that. Honestly, as the days passed, I was worried I'd done something to make you think you couldn't trust me."

Now that the initial shock had worn off, Nick relaxed infinitesimally. "You didn't. I don't know why I waited. Guess I'm a coward."

"No, you're not. I hear coming out can be harrowing. And hey, I told you I'm religious the first time we met, in name if not always in practice. I can see why you might've had some hesitations. Now that that's out of the way, you wanna tell me what's going on between you and Sebastian?"

With a sigh, Nick took the outfit Sebastian had gotten him off the bathroom door and pulled it on while he recounted *everything*. From the first time their eyes had met, to Sebastian's hot-and-cold attitude, to the drunken texts.

Deen listened without comment, which was good, because the words seemed to rush out of Nick, beyond his control. By the end of it, his mouth was dry. He stopped to fill a glass with water from the sink before he turned to Deen.

"So, what do you think?"

"First of all—" Deen held up a finger "—you look *amazing*."

Nick glanced behind himself at the bathroom mirror. He had to admit, the crisp white shirt and dark pants combo worked for him. The vest was icing. "Thank you. I actually agree."

"Second of all—" Deen held up another finger "—I think you should give Sebastian another chance."

Nick forced himself to swallow the sip of water he'd taken instead of spitting it out. "What? After all that? Rehashing it made me think I should've told him to fuck off from day one."

"I admit the whole thing is a bit bizarre, and *way* overcomplicated for what it is. But what if we uncomplicate it? He likes you. You like him—" Nick tried to interrupt, but Deen glared at him. "You do. It's obvious. I'm not saying it's the greatest love story of all time, but he makes your meatsuit dewy, and you know it."

Nick muttered under his breath. "Fine. That was a terrible reference, though."

"The point is, it sounds like he's realized he made a mistake and is trying to correct it. I think he didn't know when he met you that he was going to like you as much as he does. I know Sebastian's reputation as well as anyone. He's a hit-it-and-quit-it kinda guy. When he met you, he approached you with that intention, but then you called him out, and he's been obsessed with you ever since."

Nick rolled his eyes. "So obsessed he left me on read for five days?"

"Hey, I'm not a mind reader. I don't know everything he's thinking, but it sounds like he's as confused by all this as you are. Didn't he say in one of his texts that he's terrified?"

"Yeah." Nick paused. "I don't know. There's so much about him I don't understand."

"For what it's worth, he really wouldn't shut up about you at the party. There was even this other blond guy hanging all over him, and Sebastian totally blew him off."

At that, Nick felt a pang of something he prayed wasn't jealousy. "I can't imagine why. It's not like we're dating."

"Beats me. But while we're on the subject, I get the feeling something's going on in Sebastian's life. I'm no expert, but he was drinking like he was on a mission, and there were times when he stood on the sidelines alone and seemed downright miserable. At his own party. In my experience, drinking too much and isolating yourself at social gatherings are bad signs."

That reminded Nick of what Sebastian had told him what felt like years ago. That Nick looked sad sometimes, and that Sebastian could relate.

"Maybe." Nick sighed. "But I'll never know for sure if he doesn't tell me."

"Does that mean you'd be willing to give him a second chance if he did?"

Nick pulled his phone out of his pocket. "I suppose. Assuming he ever speaks to me again."

"He will. I'd bet money on it, and gambling is against my religion." Deen winked. "If you don't want to be late, you should get going."

"Right. Thanks for the advice, fashion and personal. I'll see you later." Nick grabbed his bag, slung it over his shoulder, and started for the door. Right as he reached it, he turned back. "Hey, Deen? You're the best roommate *ever*."

Deen grinned. "Right back atcha, buddy."

Nick trekked to the edge of campus and then stopped to check the directions Dante had texted him. Dante lived in an apartment complex five minutes away that wasn't associated with the Academy. According to him, it was much quieter than the party-oriented housing Sebastian lived in and much more anonymous than living on campus.

As Nick walked, he made a mental note to talk to Deen about getting a place there next year. It sounded perfect. Using the navigation on his phone, he found the correct street and strolled down to a modern, two-story apartment complex. Dante's place was on the first floor, number sixteen. Nick found it without ado and knocked. It was only after he did that he felt his first spark of nervousness. The meeting was innocent, but it wasn't every day he went over to a hot guy's place to study. Mere seconds later, the door opened.

"Nick!" Dante greeted him with a brilliant smile. "Glad you could make it. Come on in." He stepped back and opened the door wider.

Nick followed after him, observing first that Dante was dressed impeccably—as Deen had predicted—in white skinny jeans and a black sweater, and second that his apartment didn't look like any college pad Nick had seen. There were no posters taped up, no cheap futon in the living room. It looked *adult*. Real furniture, new appliances, and framed modern art on the walls.

Whistling, Nick checked the apartment out. "Nice place you got here."

"Thanks. My mom and I decorated it together. She's an interior designer, and I think the only reason she let me move away from home was because she got to experiment."

"Well, good taste must run in the family. This place is great." Nick pointed to a white sofa. "May I?"

"Please." Dante walked past him toward an attached kitchen. "You want anything? Water? Beer?"

Nick paused. "Actually, a beer would be great, thanks. I probably should have brought over a bottle of wine or something. Sorry about that."

Dante's muffled voice sounded from the kitchen, along with clinking bottles. "No worries. I know booze is hard to come by for us poor twenty-year-olds."

Nick's conscience prodded him into saying, "Actually, I'm twenty-one. I took a year off."

"Oh, right. I think I heard that somewhere." Dante reemerged from the kitchen, handed a beer to Nick, and clinked his own against it. "Cheers. To the new school year."

"To finding a good study partner." Nick took a sip. He'd never been much of a drinker, but he had to admit, if he could afford beer this good, he might become one of those people who drank one with dinner. For the *taste*.

Dante sat down a comfortable distance from him and waved to an open lab book on the coffee table. "How far into the reading are you?"

Nick pulled his messenger bag into his lap and dug through it for his notes. "I'm mostly caught up. I haven't done the reading for this weekend yet, because I wasn't sure if you had anything specific you wanted to cover."

"I was gonna pull a high school and make some flash cards to be honest."

Nick produced a stack of index cards out of his bag with a flourish. "Dude! I'm so down."

"Nice!" Dante held up a hand, and Nick smacked him five. "Let's never tell anyone we got this excited about flash cards."

They settled in to work for about ten minutes. Nick read aloud from their textbook while Dante made the cards and color-coded them with some highlighters. It seemed like any other study session, until Dante cleared his throat.

"You were missed at Sebastian's party last weekend."

Nick did his best not to tense up. Out of the corner of his eye, he saw Dante glance over at him, but he didn't look back. "I wasn't in a partying mood."

"That's a shame. It was an eventful night. Would have been even better with you there."

"What makes you say that?"

Dante chuckled. "Well, for one thing, Theo wouldn't have been so gloomy. I think he was looking forward to seeing you." For some reason, Dante's voice got tight. "You two have become really close, huh?"

"As close as two people can get in two weeks, yeah." Nick studied Dante's profile. "He's great. Smart. Funny. Empathetic. He's going to be a hell of a therapist someday."

"Gotta agree with you there. It gets a little annoying. Like, sometimes you want to vent, but he wants to discuss how your childhood interactions with your father shape your current relationships, or some shit."

Nick laughed. "Yeah, that sounds like him. Still, he's a good guy. I don't have a whole lot of friends here, so I'm lucky to have him."

At the word *friend*, Dante seemed to relax. It occurred to Nick that Theo had told him a while ago that he had a thing for someone. But neither of them was making a move because they didn't want to mess up their "group dynamic."

Could the guy Theo likes be Dante?

Now that it occurred to him, he wasn't sure how he hadn't realized it before. It made perfect sense. They were best friends, they'd grown up together, and though Nick had never seen them interact, they obviously got along. It also made sense that they'd be scared to take a chance, in case things didn't work out. The prospect of losing a close friend would be daunting for anyone.

"You know," Nick said before he could think through the wisdom of it, "since Theo's such a great guy, he must have a lot of admirers."

Dante jerked his head toward him. "What do you mean?"

"You know. People who want to date him. Since he's such a complete package and all."

Dante narrowed his eyes. "I suppose. Know anyone who's interested in him?"

Nick had to struggle to keep a straight face. He could almost hear the jealousy in Dante's voice. In the interest of not being mean to someone who could be a new friend, he said, "Not that I know of, but Theo told me there's someone he likes."

"Oh?" Dante leaned closer. "He didn't happen to say who it was, did he?"

This close to Dante's handsome face, it was hard for Nick to resist telling him whatever he wanted, but for Theo's sake, he held strong. "No, sorry. But I'm sure it's someone special. The way Theo talked about them made me think he must really care."

Dante let out a breath and leaned back in his seat, flash cards abandoned. "Too bad he'll never make a move. He's more the wait-and-see type, which occasionally drives me batty. Never take him to a restaurant that has a multipage menu. You'll be there all night."

Nick laughed. "Sounds like he needs someone in his life who's not afraid to be decisive. Someone to make the first move. And fast, too. Theo's not going to be single forever. As wonderful as he is, someone's going to fall hard for him."

Dante muttered something under his breath that Nick swore was, "Someone already has," but he let it slide. Dante took a long drink from his beer before setting it down with a pronounced *clunk*. "I have a hypothetical question."

"Go for it."

"What if the person Theo likes is a friend of his? And that person is afraid to make a move because it might ruin everything? What if that person likes Theo so much, they'd rather be friends with him than risk not having him at all?"

Hypothetical. Right.

Nick wanted to drop the act, but he got the feeling Dante needed this pretense. "I'd tell that person that they'll never know if they don't try. That sounds cliché, but it's true. Really strong friendships can survive anything, and it sounds like the risk could have a truly incredible reward. That makes it worth it."

There was a long pause.

Then, Dante let out a breath. "Thank you. That's very good advice. Especially coming from you."

Nick frowned. "What's that supposed to mean?"

"Sorry, I didn't mean it like that." Dante grinned. "But it's a little funny to hear you say 'go for it' when you've been fighting your attraction to a certain *someone* since the start of the semester."

Nick felt himself go red in the face. "I don't know what you mean."

"Oh, come on. You don't have to play coy with me. I'm one of Sebastian's best friends, which means I've heard how he talks about you."

Nick sat up straighter. "What does he say, exactly?"

Dante looked at him sidelong. "Still gonna pretend you're not interested?"

Damn. Busted.

Nick slumped in his seat. "Okay, you got me, but that doesn't really mean anything. Things are . . . weird. I haven't spoken to Sebastian all week, for example. He drifts in and out of my life like a ghost. It's frustrating."

"I can imagine. As I'm sure you've realized by now, his confident schtick is an act, and he actually has no idea what he's doing. Oh, and I wouldn't worry about getting to see him. You two are going to be reunited sooner than you think."

"What makes you—" Nick's sentence was interrupted by a knock on the door.

Dante was on his feet in an instant. "I'll get it."

As Dante walked to the door, Nick watched him with the special kind of dread that came from knowing a trap was about to be sprung but being powerless to stop it.

Dante flung the door open, and for a moment, the setting sun outside shone directly in Nick's eyes. He blinked, and the figure standing in the doorframe came into focus.

Sebastian Prinsen. Of course.

Sebastian was looking at Dante, his handsome features pinched with annoyance. "Dude, I've been calling you for the past hour. Why didn't you pick up?"

"Sorry, buddy. I was a little busy." Dante turned half away from the door to nod in Nick's direction.

Nick swallowed hard.

Sebastian glowered, eyes still focused on Dante. "Well, I can't imagine what was so important. If I'm late to my own party, there's going to be hell to p—" Finally, he glanced Nick's way, and his jaw dropped.

Nick stared at him, paralyzed despite himself. He'd never admit it aloud, but the warmth that washed through him at the sight of Sebastian—especially after a week apart—was like sinking into a relaxing bath.

Eventually, he unglued his tongue from the roof of his mouth. "Hi."

"Hi," Sebastian parroted, eyes wide. They were dark as ink, thanks to the sun behind him.

Dante's eyes darted back and forth between them, his smile growing with each pass. "Well, this ought to be fun."

Chapter Eleven

Sebastian was going to kill Dante. And he was going to get Theo to help him hide the body. There were all sorts of little nooks and crannies around campus where they could bury him. Or better yet, they could sail out to the middle of Lake Michigan, and—

"So," Nick said, looking skittish as a cornered mouse, "long time no talk. How have you been?"

Sebastian's murderous thoughts cut to white noise and then to blinding panic. He should have known Dante was setting him up. That phony text he'd sent Sebastian, claiming there was an "emergency" mere hours before they were set to host another party at Sebastian's place, was classic Dante. It was Sebastian's surprise nineteenth birthday all over again. Present Sebastian wanted to kick Past Sebastian in the shins for not seeing through the ruse.

He'd been silent for way too long. He worked up a lie. "I've been great. Couldn't be better."

Dante stepped back to let him into the apartment. Sebastian followed, glaring daggers at him as he shut the door.

"Glad to hear it." Nick's tone was overly cheerful. "I, uh, haven't seen you around lately."

Sebastian shrugged. "I've been busy. A few of my classes gave out their first assignments at the same time. I was swamped."

That much was true. Sebastian had written his first essay of the semester—a ten-pager worth a sizable chunk of his grade—and he'd had to put a presentation together for another class, on top of his usual reading assignments and studying. It really had been a hell of a week. But it wasn't the real reason he'd never contacted Nick. His radio silence had been caused by sheer cowardice.

On Sunday, as he'd nursed his hangover, Sebastian had debated what he was going to say to Nick. Apologizing for drunk texting him was a no-brainer, but beyond that, he had no idea if he wanted to own up to the texts or play them off. The first route was more honest and appealing, but also more terrifying and confusing. The second was just plain easier. The way his life was right now, easy was too attractive of an option for him to dismiss outright.

The more he'd thought about what he'd done, the more embarrassed he'd gotten, until he'd become convinced that the next time he encountered Nick, he was going to get rejected. So, he'd done what any insecure twenty-year-old would do. He'd avoided Nick like the plague.

It wasn't the most mature solution, but it'd bought him a couple of days of much-needed peace. Except now, thanks to Dante, his avoid-the-problem plan was pressing its nose against the glass after having gone out the window.

"Make yourself comfortable." Dante moved toward the couch. "Nick and I were studying. We have that class together, you know."

Sebastian eyed Dante warily. He couldn't fathom what his purpose was in *Parent Trap*ping them, but there was no doubt Dante would make it known soon enough.

"Are you sure you don't want me to leave?" Sebastian asked. "Since you two are busy and all?"

"No!" Nick said, and then immediately looked down at his lap. "Don't go. It . . . really is great to see you."

Sebastian's heart palpitated. "Oh. Yeah. You too."

"Seriously, stay." Dante flopped onto the couch. The motion seemed casual enough, but Sebastian couldn't help but note how closely he sat down next to Nick. "The more the merrier."

Sebastian was about to retort when Dante slid an arm onto the back of the sofa. Directly behind Nick's shoulders. Like a boyfriend.

To his credit, Nick appeared as surprised as Sebastian felt, and he didn't lean into it, but he didn't scooch away from Dante either. In fact, he stared at him with big, blue eyes that Sebastian couldn't read.

Is this . . . a date?

"Why don't you have a seat?" Dante nodded at a chair perpendicular to the sofa.

Bewildered, Sebastian hesitated for a fraction of a second before walking over to it and plunking down. Silence descended on the room. If Sebastian had ever killed a man, he might confess to it right now just to have something to say.

Thankfully, Nick saved the day. "So, Sebastian, you said you had a busy week. Wanna talk about it?"

There were a lot of things Sebastian wanted to talk about, but schoolwork was not one of them. Although with Dante there, he couldn't very well bring up the texts. Especially not while he was sitting next to Nick, appearing to lean closer to him with every passing second. Was that Sebastian's imagination?

Is Dante finally making his move? Trying to win the bet? If so, why would he invite me over?

As Sebastian speculated, Dante's arm shifted to Nick's shoulders. It wouldn't take much for Dante to put it around Nick and pull him closer. Sebastian's eye twitched.

"I had a big paper to write." Sebastian was shocked by how level his voice sounded. "Ten pages for my art class. You'd think we'd actually paint, but it's mostly a lot of analyzing old dead guys and discussing the *theory* of paint. My professor's more of a Mr. Nolan than a John Keating."

Nick scrunched his nose. "Huh?"

Dante brushed a finger against his shoulder, purportedly to get his attention. "*Dead Poets Society.*"

"Oh." Nick went red in the face, and there was no telling if it was from embarrassment, the touch, or the fact that Dante was *definitely* getting closer to him.

Is he trying to make me jealous? Or is he shoving the fact that he's on a date with Nick in my face? Either way, he must know he's pissing me off.

Then, Dante looked over at him and flashed a bright, knowing smile.

Sebastian's temper boiled over like a pot. He tried to slam a lid onto it, but it was too late. Before he could stop himself, he jumped to his feet. "Nick, can I talk to you? Outside?"

"We're kinda in the middle of something here, Seb," Dante said.

But Sebastian was already heading for the door. He yanked it open, stormed out, and headed for the wrought-iron gate that led out of the apartment complex. He didn't stop until he was standing by the street where he'd parked his car. He braced himself against it with one hand and rubbed his eyes with the other.

Nice move, Prinsen. Way to play it cool.

"Sebastian?"

Sebastian whirled around. Nick was standing a few feet away, blinking at him like Sebastian was a firework that might go off at any moment.

"Hey." Sebastian cleared his throat. "Sorry about that. I was feeling a little claustrophobic all of a sudden."

Nick looked at him askance. "Really? Because I thought Dante drooling all over me might've had something to do with it."

Goddamn it. How does he read me so easily?

Sebastian stared at his sneakers. "I was surprised, is all. I didn't know you two were a thing." He peeked up.

Nick's cheeks were pink. "We're not. I mean, not officially or anything. He really did invite me over to study. But I guess he had other things on his mind."

"Not officially." What the hell does that mean?

Words bubbled up in the back of Sebastian's throat and burst out of his mouth. "DoyoulikeDante?"

Nick startled and took a step toward him. "What?"

Sebastian forced himself to enunciate. "Do you like Dante? It's okay if you do." *That's a big lie.* "I just want to know so I can stop wasting my time."

"Wasting *your* time?" The surprise fell off Nick's face and was replaced with anger. He took another step toward Sebastian, hands on his hips. "You want to talk about wasting time? You wasted a whole week of my life."

"What?" Sebastian pushed away from his car. "How do you figure?"

"You dropped all those emotional texts on me, and then you disappeared. You never called. You never wrote back. Nothing."

"I . . . needed time to think."

"*Five* days' worth of time? What were you thinking about? Why Captain Barbossa died from that gunshot wound before the curse was lifted, but Jack didn't die from being stabbed?"

"No." Sebastian blinked. "Although, now that you mention it, that was a pretty glaring plot hole."

Nick turned away. "I don't have time for this bullshit."

Sebastian watched him go for all of three steps before he called after him. "I was thinking about you."

Nick stopped short, arms limp at his sides. When he turned back around, his eyes were wary. "What?"

"I was thinking about *you*." It occurred to Sebastian that at some point, they'd both moved onto the sidewalk. From feet apart, the tension between them was palpable.

A cool breeze ruffled Sebastian's hair, reminding him that the sun would set soon, and he had a party to get to. And yet nothing in the world could have moved him from this spot.

Finally, Nick sighed. "Sebastian, why didn't you text me back? Tell me the truth."

Lying wasn't an option even without the imperative. "I was afraid of what you'd say when we talked. Afraid I'd ruined this from the start. I was embarrassed, and I told you things I've never said to a guy before. I thought you were going to tell me to leave you alone once and for all. But most of all, I think I was scared that you weren't."

When he'd finished, he dropped his gaze to the grass growing by the sidewalk. His whole body was tense as a piano string.

Something warm touched his chin; he startled and jerked his head up. Nick had reached out, and with gentle fingers, he tilted Sebastian's face back up until their eyes met.

"I wasn't going to tell you to leave me alone." He was standing so close now, Sebastian could see rings of brown around his pupils, like rocks cropping up out of the ocean. "You didn't ruin this. Granted, I don't know what this *is*, but those texts did way more help than harm. They made me think of you in a whole new way."

Sebastian's heart pounded like it was trying to burst out of his chest. The feel of Nick's fingers sent warmth coursing through him. "If you had to guess, what would you call this? Attraction? Something more?"

Nick blushed tellingly and dropped his hand. "I said I'm not sure."

"Bullshit." Sebastian stepped closer, which was starting to become impossible. The air between them was magnetized. "Say it. I need to hear it."

Nick wet his lips, and it took everything Sebastian had not to look down at them. "Why don't you tell me?"

"Nick." Sebastian gave in and stared at Nick's mouth. "Kiss me."

"Whoa, what?" Nick took a half step back.

Sebastian caught him by the arms. "Don't run away from me. Please."

Nick's eyes flashed. "Hey, you're one to talk about running away. You—"

"Nick."

Miraculously, Nick fell silent. He was breathing hard on top of being flushed, and the effect made Sebastian dizzy just looking at him. Somewhere in his head, he knew this was his chance to win the bet, but he also understood, somehow, that it was more than that.

"If you don't want me, fine." Sebastian's voice was steady despite the tremulous emotions within him. "You can tell me."

Nick opened his mouth, and for a second, Sebastian's heart stopped cold. But then Nick's beautiful eyes dropped to Sebastian's lips.

Sebastian smiled. "Can't do it, can you? Kiss me. It has to be you."

"I . . . I . . ." Nick hesitated. Sebastian could see genuine desire on his face, deep and hungry, and it made the air between them crackle. So why was Nick holding back?

Sebastian had no idea, and all of a sudden, he didn't care. He couldn't wait any longer. "Fuck it."

Pulling Nick against him, Sebastian swept him into a kiss that was—all at once—desperate, sweet, and the most brutal thing he'd ever done to himself.

Nick wasn't ashamed to admit he'd imagined what it would be like to kiss Sebastian. Ever since that first day, when Sebastian had touched his face and brushed a thumb over his lips, Nick had wondered about it. In his head, Sebastian was an aggressive kisser who would leave Nick breathless and kiss-bruised afterward.

The reality was nothing like the fantasy, in the best way.

Sebastian's mouth was soft. Velvet soft. Warmer than Nick had thought it'd be, and firm without being forceful. The arms that slid around Nick's waist and back held him close but didn't cage him. Nick could break away if he wanted to. But that was the strange thing.

He didn't.

Nick deepened the kiss without questioning it, tilting his head to fit their mouths perfectly together. Sebastian made a small noise, and it zipped down Nick's spine before pooling in his belly. Teeth nipped at his lower lip, and at the first hot swipe of Sebastian's tongue, Nick thought his knees were going to buckle.

Suddenly, they were moving. Sebastian backed them up until Nick feared they were going to stumble into the street. But then his back hit something big and convex. A car?

There was no time to wonder. Sebastian kissed him up against it with intent. Nick melted into it, grabbing a handful of Sebastian's shirt. For someone so slender, Sebastian was surprisingly strong. Nick could feel the wiry power in his body as he used it to pin Nick in place, back curved along cool metal and glass. And all the while, Sebastian kissed him with the single-minded determination of a man who was precisely where he wanted to be.

No matter how much Nick wanted to deny it, being with Sebastian felt *right*. And not just because Sebastian was a damn good kisser. His body fit up against Nick's like it was meant to, and he used the perfect combination of lips and tongue. And there was something else, something Nick couldn't put a name to, but he felt it. Inside of him, it clicked into place.

It was a good feeling, but it also sent panic rippling through him. He was starting to understand what Sebastian had meant all the times he'd said this was terrifying. One second, Nick was demanding straight answers. The next, he was letting Sebastian kiss him into submission. It was scary how easily his attraction to Sebastian had pushed his valid concerns from his mind.

Stop this. Before it goes any further.

Nick took the hand he'd fisted in Sebastian's shirt, moved it so his palm was flat against Sebastian's chest, and pushed. Sebastian stumbled back, almost tripping, but he caught himself at the last second. He looked up at Nick, panting for breath. His lips were wine-red. "What was that for?"

Nick didn't answer. He was struggling to catch his breath as well. Even as he was glad Sebastian was off him, he mourned the loss of his warmth, the comfort it gave him. Nick debated turning around and walking away, but Sebastian would follow.

As if on cue, Sebastian took a step toward him, his eyes full of purpose.

Nick held up a finger. "Don't kiss me again. I mean it."

"Why not? What's wrong?"

"*This* is wrong. I can't handle all these games."

Sebastian furrowed his brow. "What games? I told you the truth."

"Yeah, this time. What about before? The last time you were honest with me was a week ago, after which you shut me out. Then you asked me if I was attracted to one of your best friends, and now you're kissing me. How is anyone supposed to make sense of this?"

Sebastian opened his mouth, but then to Nick's surprise, he sagged like a sack of flour with a leak. "You're right."

Nick blinked. "Come again?"

"You're right. I fucked up. *I'm* fucked up." Sebastian rubbed his eyes with a hand and then kept it there when he was done, shielding his face. "I'm sorry."

Nick was at a loss. He pushed away from the car and hesitated, unsure if he should put a hand on Sebastian's shoulder, or if he even wanted to. "Do you . . . want to talk about it?"

"No. Yes?" Sebastian wiped his mouth and dropped his hand. His eyes were uncertain as they met Nick's. "Not right now."

"Then I'm sorry, but I'm leaving. I've had my fill of roundabout answers."

Sebastian caught his arm again. "Please don't go. I'm trying, okay? This isn't easy for me."

Nick looked from Sebastian's face to the hand on his arm. "You better say something convincing soon, or I'm out of here, and you *won't* chase after me."

Sebastian released him. "Listen, I haven't been talking to anyone about the shit that's going on in my life. Not even Theo and Dante. I'm not going to tell you—a relative stranger whom I've known for two weeks—things I haven't told them."

Nick narrowed his eyes. "Wow, you're terrible at this." Though the bit about his life was intriguing. Dr. O'Connor had said he had things going on.

"*But*"—Sebastian made the *B* sound pop before ticking the *T*—"I admit I owe you an explanation. So, here it is. My personal life is hell at the moment, and I'm not handling it well. When I sent you all those texts, I meant them. I meant every word. When I thought you were going to reject me, I freaked. I thought if one more thing got added to the pile of flaming crap that is my life, I was going to *lose it*. I avoided you as a result, and I'm sorry."

Nick pursed his lips. "Okay. I suppose I can live with that answer. I wish you'd tell me at least a little of what's going on with you, though. An abridged version will do."

Sebastian's face contorted, but he nodded. "My parents are getting divorced."

Nick waited for more, but Sebastian didn't continue. "Um. I'm sorry to hear that."

"Don't say it." Sebastian held up a hand. "If one more person says it, I'm going to scream."

"Says what?"

"'So? Get over it.'"

Nick shook his head. "I would never have said that."

"Maybe not those exact words, but you were thinking a version of that, right?"

Nick started to lie, but it fell flat on his tongue.

"I know." Sebastian huffed. "I know what you're thinking. People's parents get divorced all the time. It's ubiquitous these days. And it's not like I'm a little kid who's being forced to move and switch schools and leave all his friends behind. My parents weren't happy, either. They should have gotten divorced a long time ago. Why am I upset then?"

It was a rhetorical question; Nick kept quiet, waiting to see if Sebastian would answer it.

Sebastian did. "I'm upset because I thought I was safe. I thought I'd made it to the age where things like this couldn't affect me anymore. But my dad called me at the beginning of the semester and said they're selling our house. I have to pack up all my shit—everything I didn't take to college with me—and put it in storage somewhere. Or I can throw it all away. Family photos, childhood toys, my art trophies. Everything I've ever known and loved. Those were the options they gave me."

Nick piped up. "Your parents don't want any of it?"

"Nope. They're both moving on with their lives. I swear I'm happy for them, but I'm also terrified. They had me young. There's still time for them to have more children, or adopt. Start new families. When the fighting got bad in high school, they'd both spend days away, and it was like they forgot about me. Now that I'm a legal adult, they're not *obligated* to care about me anymore. If they ever did!"

Sebastian's voice had been getting steadily louder as he talked, and by the end of his speech, he was yelling. Nick let him, comfortable in the knowledge that Sebastian wasn't shouting at him. He was shouting at his parents, or the universe, or maybe himself.

When he'd finished, he was panting worse than when they'd stopped kissing. He wiped his mouth again and moved a few steps over until he could slump against the car.

"I didn't mean to say all of that." He sounded dazed. His eyes were glassy as he stared up at the sky, long neck craned back.

Nick was surprised to discover his heart was pounding. The emotion behind Sebastian's words was contagious, and the rawness of it was palpable. He was like an exposed nerve that had been prodded at for too long, until the pain had built to unbearable levels.

Nick's feet moved of their own accord, bringing him closer to Sebastian. "I'm sorry."

Sebastian waved him off without looking at him. "Don't be."

"I mean it. Just because divorce is common doesn't mean it's a picnic. Have people really been telling you to get over it?"

Sebastian nodded. "Oh yeah. My family's a big deal in this town, and Evanston has its own rumor mill. The other day some guy my dad works with walked up to me in the grocery store and told me to 'chin up.' Then he called me 'slugger.' I've never come so close to punching someone. No one gets why I care. My parents are still paying for my college after all, so why should it matter to me if they're not together anymore?"

"That's awful, and so not the point."

"Exactly. 'You're an adult.' I get told that every time I bring it up. They're right, but I wasn't ready for such a big change. I feel like one of the toys I have to deal with. My parents have outgrown me, so they're packing me up and getting rid of me. It's like I've been holding them back all these years, and now that I'm legal, they're free."

"Have they actually said any of this to you? Because if so, fuck them."

"No, I could be worrying over nothing, and I recognize that. But what they have told me doesn't bode well. They're both moving away. They're both seeing other people. They want me to plan to stay in my apartment over the summer instead of subletting it like I usually do. They're not sentimental people. I don't know how they ended up with a son as emotional as me." Sebastian sighed. "I don't want to talk about this anymore. It's depressing."

"Not talking about it is what got you into this mess. Keeping things bottled up isn't healthy. Trust me. I know."

Sebastian studied his face from feet away, eyes bright like pavement slick with rain. "Come to my party."

Nick startled. "What?"

"My party."

"Uh, your party was last weekend. I missed it. That is, unless you've got a time machine, in which case, you should have led with that."

Sebastian shook his head. "I'm having another one tonight to celebrate turning in the Monster Paper of Death. Come to it."

Nick hesitated. "I don't know."

"You have plans already?"

"Well . . . no."

Sebastian looked heavenward. "I'm not going to beg. If you don't want to come, fine. But you wanted me to prove to you that I'm not who you thought I was. So, how come every time an opportunity presents itself, you run the other way?"

A small flame of irritation licked at Nick. "Hey, don't turn this on me."

"It's on you a little bit, though. I get why you didn't come to my last party. I pissed you off. But I apologized for that, *and* I told you what you wanted to know, *and* you said you've seen me in a new light.

I've done everything you've asked me to do. How long are you going to keep me in time-out?"

Damn it, he had a point.

Nick chewed on his bottom lip. "Will Dante and Theo be there?"

"Miss your boyfriends already?"

Nick was about to protest when Sebastian held up a hand. "That was a bad joke, sorry. For the record, I never really thought anything was going on between you and Dante." He paused. "He is a good-looking man, though. I know straight guys who've chosen him as their 'if I had to pick a dude.'"

"Right?" Nick whistled. "Hot damn."

Sebastian's expression soured. "You don't have to be that enthusiastic about it."

Nick fought against a smile. "You're jealous."

To his shock, Sebastian nodded. "Yeah. Sorry about that. I know jealousy's an ugly emotion."

"Uh . . . I forgive you." He paused. "You're really jealous?"

Sebastian looked him right in the eye. "I am. Dante's my best friend. I'd love for him to find someone and be happy. But not you."

Nick struggled to think of something to say but came up blank. His heart and his brain couldn't come to an agreement.

Luckily, Sebastian's gaze drifted off a moment later. "I wish I knew why he invited me over."

"He invited you? That's news to me."

"I use that word loosely. He told me there was an emergency. I dropped everything and drove straight here." Sebastian patted the car he was leaning against, which was a sleek black number that Nick probably could have guessed was his by looking at it. "He must've wanted me to see you two together, but why?"

Nick shrugged. "Maybe he likes me, and he's trying to stake a claim."

"Maybe." Sebastian didn't sound convinced. He pushed off the car and walked around it to the driver's side. "So, are you coming?"

"To the party? Right now?" Nick looked back toward the apartment complex. "I left my stuff at Dante's."

"It's all school shit, right? You can swing by and grab it tomorrow. If you come with me, you won't have to hitch a ride or take the bus."

Sebastian pulled a set of keys out of his pocket and pressed a button. The headlights flashed, and the locks clicked. "Can you tell how badly I want you to come?"

Nice word choice.

Nick still hesitated, which was funny, considering he was no longer concerned that Sebastian was putting on an act. It was actually the knowledge that Sebastian *wasn't* that was giving Nick pause. What Sebastian had said about his parents was real. Visceral and emotional, and it took away a lot of the reasons Nick had used to justify keeping his distance. If Nick went to this party and spent time with Sebastian . . .

There was a very big possibility he was going to start to fall for him. Could he handle that right now? Giving his heart to someone when it was still in pieces from this past train wreck of a year?

While he dithered, Sebastian's face fell in increments. He fixed Nick with a pleading look. "Please say you'll come. Spend some time with me, in my house, away from this campus. After, if I haven't convinced you to give me a chance, then that's the end of that. I'll give up on you."

"I've heard that tune before."

"I mean it. Please?" Sebastian stuck out his bottom lip. "Pretty please?"

Nick laughed and tried not to stare at his mouth. "Okay, I'll come. But only for a little while."

"I'll take it." Sebastian got into the car.

Nick followed after him, heart pounding for an entirely new reason now.

Chapter Twelve

Theo wasted no time getting to Dante's apartment as soon as he'd gotten out of class and eaten something. When he arrived, he didn't bother knocking. Dante had texted him saying the door was open. He let himself in, casting one final look back at the beginnings of a beautiful teal and tangerine sunset before he closed the door behind him.

Dante was seated on the white couch, a pile of flash cards in his hands. He glanced up when Theo entered. "Hey. You got here fast."

"I cut the last five minutes of class and wolfed down what was either a late lunch or an early dinner." Theo tossed his backpack down next to the coffee table and flopped onto the other end of the sofa. "Professor Hopper's voice is better than a lullaby. I'm still trying to wake up."

"Cutting class already? Not a good way to start the semester."

"Imagine how bad it's going to be when we're seniors." Theo fingered his phone in his pocket. "I got your text. What's the big news? I practically jogged here."

Dante swiveled to face him on the couch. "Dude, it *worked*. Like a charm."

Theo clapped his hands together. He'd suspected the news would have something to do with Dante's "study date" with Nick, but he hadn't known for sure. "What happened? Tell me everything."

"Nick came over like we planned, right?"

"Right."

"Well, Sebastian showed up a little after that—also like we planned—and their faces when they saw each other . . . *Priceless*. I've never heard Sebastian trip over his own tongue like that before. I wish I could have taken a video for you."

Theo laughed. "Serves them right for dancing around each other. What happened next?"

"I did what you said and sat a little too close to Nick. Nothing untoward, of course, but when I slid a hand behind his shoulders, Sebastian *freaked*. He didn't say anything, but I thought his eyes were going to pop out of his skull. It took everything I had not to laugh."

"Yes!" Theo pumped a fist in the air. "That confirms it. Sebastian's definitely got it bad for Nick. But how did Nick react?"

"Well, he was happy to see Sebastian, for sure. It was written all over his face. And when Sebastian stormed out of here, Nick went tearing after him. It was like watching a soap opera."

Dante's eyes were bright with mischief as he spoke, and it made Theo a little breathless. He had to exhale slowly and then inhale again before he could speak. "Wow, I didn't expect our plan to work this perfectly. Sebastian's been corked up so tight for so long now, I thought he was going to explode."

"He did storm off. That's an explosion of sorts."

"Nah, that's his automatic response to feelings. We can only hope Nick made some headway when he chased after him."

"Did you see them when you walked up?"

"No, Sebastian's car wasn't parked on the street where he usually leaves it. What do you suppose went down?"

"Judging by the sexual tension that was radiating off them, they're probably headed to Sebby's place."

"Or they might be fighting. There's no telling with those two."

"I doubt it. You would too if you'd seen their faces when they laid eyes on each other. I swear, I thought I heard romantic music swell up in the background."

"Good. This whole past week, I was so sick of watching Sebastian flinch every time I mentioned Nick. He wouldn't come over to watch movies on Thursday like we usually do, because he was afraid he'd run into Nick. Something had to give."

Dante's eyes absolutely sparkled. "Well, it gave all right. Five bucks says Nick comes to the party tonight."

Theo laughed. "Here's to hoping. If those two don't do something soon, one or both of them is gonna burst." He leaned forward and reached for his backpack. "We've got a little bit of time before we need to be at Seb's to help set up. You want to do some actual studying? How much did you manage to get done with Nick before Sebastian showed up?" He glanced at Dante.

Dante's eyes were fixed firmly on Theo's lower back, where he could feel that his shirt had ridden up when he'd leaned forward.

Theo froze, unsure of what to do. A moment later, Dante's eyes drifted back to his face. If he was embarrassed about getting caught looking, it didn't show.

"Actually"—Dante's voice was quiet—"there's something else I wanted to talk about."

Swallowing, Theo asked, "What?"

"Before Sebastian showed up, Nick said you told him you're interested in someone. Which is weird, because you tell me everything, yet you haven't said a word." He wet his lips, and the flash of pink tongue against his brown skin was mesmerizing. "Is there some reason you felt you couldn't tell me in particular?"

All the breath Theo had been trying to hold on to left his lungs at once. He eased back into an upright position, thoughts racing. *Is this really happening? Does he want me to come out and say it?*

Theo licked his suddenly dry lips. "Dante, I—"

Nicki Minaj's "Anaconda" blared at full volume. Dante cursed before snatching his phone off the coffee table and glancing at the screen. "It's Seb. He's probably calling to ask what time we're going to arrive." He made no move to answer it.

Theo laughed, but it came out shaky. "You should get it. He'll blow up your phone if you don't."

"I suppose." With his thumb poised over the Answer button, he fixed Theo with a serious expression. "We'll finish this conversation tonight. Okay?"

Theo's heart skipped a beat, but his resolve had never been steadier. "Okay."

Nick's first impression of Sebastian's third-floor apartment was much like what he'd thought at Dante's place: *Does a college kid actually live here?*

Sebastian's furniture was all leather, dark wood, and glass. Unlike Dante's minimalist approach, everything in Sebastian's apartment was embellished. The white walls were covered in a subtle cream damask pattern, the dining room chairs had high backs like miniature thrones, and in the living room, there were several shelves of leather-bound books the color of red wine. Nick spotted *Teleny* and *Maurice* within seconds and had to stop himself from giggling.

For his part, Sebastian let him in and then stood back, seemingly content to let him explore. Nick examined the books before bypassing the dining room to the left in favor of a balcony dead ahead. Through the glass, there was a charming view of the little city.

There was also an open doorway to the right—through which he could see a large kitchen—and a hallway, which he assumed led to Sebastian's bedroom.

Gulp.

When he'd finished his tour, he spun around and jammed his hands in his pocket. "I like your apartment. It's got you written all over it."

"Thank you." Sebastian watched him from his spot by the front door. The arms folded over his chest suggested he was nervous. "I've lived here since last year."

Nick hated small talk, but he made it anyway. "You're from Evanston originally, right?"

"Born and raised. Though I suppose when I graduate, I can live anywhere I want." Sebastian's eyes drifted out the glass doors leading to the balcony. The beautiful, clear sky was visible through them. "It's freeing but also frightening."

"I know how that feels. When something changes in your life, and suddenly you have all these options." He shuffled his feet. "I'm glad I ended up here."

"Good." Sebastian strolled toward him. "We need to get into party mode. Do you drink?"

"Sometimes. Mostly beer, but on my twenty-first birthday, I bought myself a nice bottle of Scotch."

Sebastian smiled, and the rain clouds that'd been clinging to his handsome features were dispelled. "A man after my own heart. But why'd you have to buy your own birthday Scotch? Your friends didn't want to get it for you?"

"I didn't have many friends." Nick huffed. "Wow, our lives are depressing."

Sebastian reached for his hand. "Dunno about you, but mine has been looking up lately."

Nick's breath caught in his throat. He didn't stop Sebastian from lacing their fingers together, though he didn't help him either.

"If I got you a late birthday present," Sebastian said, his voice soft, "would you accept it?"

"Yes, since it seems you've learned your lesson about forcing gifts on people."

"That I have." Sebastian released his hand and pulled his keys out of his pocket. "I need to go on a liquor run for the party. Since you're twenty-one, how about we pick out a bottle of Scotch? We can enjoy it together tonight."

Nick was admittedly intrigued by the idea, but he still looked at Sebastian askance. "Are you inviting me so I'll get the other liquor for you, oh twenty-year-old?"

"Please." Sebastian gestured at his apartment. "Do I look like the sort of guy who doesn't have a fake ID? I don't use it often, since I'm pretty well-known around these parts, but tonight's a special occasion."

"Fair enough. I'm down."

They got back into Sebastian's car, drove to the nearest liquor store, and to Nick's surprise, had a blast picking out libations for the party. The shop was a little neighborhood establishment run by a jovial old woman whose voice creaked like wood.

They asked her for advice on Scotch, and as luck would have it, she was a connoisseur. She directed them to a bottle of something that had apparently been aged for twenty-five years and tasted like "joy mixed with charcoal and revenge on everyone who's ever wronged you." It was the best sales pitch Nick had ever heard.

When he saw the price tag on the bottle, though, he felt faint. Sebastian must've noticed all the blood draining out of his face, because he said, "It's my treat."

Nick shook his head. "No way. I'm at least paying for half." *Assuming my debit card doesn't get declined, or run away screaming.*

"This is a birthday present. You can't buy your own birthday present. *Again*. Besides, I intend to drink a good amount of this, so it's only fair I pay. Is that okay?"

Nick hesitated for a fraction of a second longer before relenting. If Sebastian had pushed the issue instead of asking, Nick might have refused, but it seemed he'd really learned his lesson.

They loaded up on vodka, tequila, some mixers, plus the Scotch, and then they were on their way.

When they got back, they set up a party station on Sebastian's dining room table, complete with red cups and the liquor they'd bought. Except for the Scotch, of course. They squirreled that away in the kitchen, along with some beer, which was stowed in the incredibly well-stocked fridge.

"Do you cook?" Nick asked. "Or do you have like a maid or something that does that for you?"

Sebastian paused in the middle of pulling two crystal tumblers out of a cabinet to shoot Nick a wry look. "Let me remind you again that it's my parents who have money, not me. While they're paying for college, they're certainly not going to pay for me to have a maid." He paused. "Though I do have a cleaning lady who comes around once a month. But she only does light housework, I swear."

Nick laughed. "I knew it. Are you one of those grown men who doesn't know how to do his own laundry? Because if so, I can tell you right now, this isn't going to work."

Sebastian pouted as he placed the two glasses on the kitchen island and uncorked the Scotch. "I know *how* to do it. Most of the time. I'll admit some of the intricacies elude me. Like when to use warm versus hot water and what it means when there's a little triangle on a shirt's tag."

"That's bleach," Nick answered automatically. "If it's got a triangle, you can bleach it. Unless the triangle is crossed out, of course."

"Oh." Sebastian handed Nick a glass filled with two fingers' worth of Scotch. "Good to know. Where'd you learn that? From your parents?"

Nick scratched absently at the granite counter with a fingernail, trying to push down the sadness that stilled welled up in him. "Sort of. My dad learned from my mom, and then he taught me. Laundry became my job, even after I left for college. Dad *expected* me to come home and do laundry on weekends. For both of us."

Sebastian chuckled. "He sounds fun."

"Yeah. He was."

There was a moment of silence between them, but for once, it didn't feel uncomfortable. It felt like Sebastian was giving him a moment. Nick appreciated it more than he could say.

After a while, Sebastian nudged him with his elbow. "I'm sorry. I'd heard that your dad died, but I didn't want to ask or make assumptions."

"It's okay. It's been over a year."

Sebastian shrugged. "So? Does grief have an expiration date?"

Nick's lips twitched up. "According to everyone I talk to, it seems like it. Kinda like how everyone tells you not to be upset about the divorce."

"I just thought of our toast." Sebastian raised his glass. "To people. Fuck 'em."

Nick snorted and clinked their glasses together. "Fuck 'em."

They took a sip at the same time and then let out identical moans of pleasure.

"Holy shit," Sebastian crooned. "I'm going to Mass on Sunday. This restored my faith in God."

"While you're doing that, I'm going to be in bed, cuddled up to this bottle, reading it love poems." Nick wanted to lick his own tongue so he could get every drop of the honeyed, oaky liquid.

Sebastian chuckled. "That's a much better idea. I might join you."

It was obviously a joke, but the implication made the air between them sizzle. They looked at each other, and tension sprang up like it'd been waiting for them to let down their guard.

"Nick—" Sebastian moved closer, eyes trained on his face "—do you remember why I invited you here?"

Nick swallowed, mouth suddenly dry. "So I can get to know you, or something to that effect."

Sebastian didn't stop until his face was inches from Nick's. It'd be nothing for Nick to lean forward and bring their lips together, and judging by the color in Sebastian's cheeks, he knew it too.

When he spoke, his voice was velvety. "I intended to do that. I wanted to spend this time talking to you, getting to know you as well. So, why is it all I can think about is kissing you again?" His eyes drifted down to Nick's mouth.

Reasons to stop him sprang up in Nick's mind, but to his surprise, they weren't his usual ones. It wasn't that he didn't want to, or that he still didn't trust Sebastian. But rather, if they did this now—while they were alone, and there was a convenient bedroom nearby—Nick didn't know how they'd ever stop.

Sebastian started to close the distance between their mouths, and Nick couldn't work up the desire to protest. Just before Sebastian's soft—so very soft—lips would have brushed Nick's, the doorbell rang.

"Damn." Sebastian glanced past Nick, out of the kitchen and into the living room, before huffing. "That was dumb luck."

"No." Nick smiled. "That was *bad* luck."

Sebastian looked at his mouth again, like he was contemplating kissing him anyway, but then the doorbell rang repeatedly. With a sigh, he poured more Scotch into both of their glasses, put the bottle away, and whisked out of the kitchen. "I'll get it."

As soon as Sebastian was gone, Nick fell against the island and drew a deep, ragged breath. Holy fuck, that'd been close. Now that he'd kissed Sebastian, it was in his system, and all he wanted was more. If he'd realized that before, he might not have agreed to come.

Well no, he still would have. But he would have thought more toward the future. Parties meant laughing and dancing and flirting, and Sebastian had driven him here. What if he wanted Nick to spend the night? What if *Nick* wanted to spend the night?

It was alarming how not alarmed he was by the idea.

Before he could work himself into a tizzy, he heard familiar voices chatting in the living room. He grabbed his tumbler of Scotch and walked out.

Sebastian was standing beside the now-open front door, talking to Theo and Dante, whose arms were loaded with bags.

"Jesus, guys," Sebastian said, "how much are you planning on drinking tonight?"

"A lot," they answered in unison.

Theo caught sight of Nick. His face split into a radiant smile. "Nick! I'd hoped you'd make an appearance."

Nick strode up to his friend and hugged him around the supplies. "Good to see you. Can I help you with those?"

"Nah." Theo hefted the bags. "I got it."

Nick's eyes slid to Dante, and nervousness jolted through him. "Hey, Dante. Long time no see."

Dante smiled pleasantly and edged closer to Theo. There was no trace of his flirtatious attitude from before. "Likewise."

Hm. I wonder if the talk I gave him was fruitful. He made a mental note to ask Theo later.

Sebastian pointed to the dining room. "We've already set up a drink station. We'll help you unload."

Together, they emptied the bags, which contained a frankly disturbing amount of booze.

By the time they'd finished, guests began to arrive in droves. If anyone was surprised to see Nick at Sebastian's party, standing next to him like a cohost, they didn't let on. Nick met a dozen Academy students within the first twenty minutes.

During a lull, Sebastian brought his lips to Nick's ear. "Let me know if this gets overwhelming. We can sneak off and talk."

"No, I'm enjoying it, actually. My big goal when I first came here was to make friends, and now I'm at least meeting new people."

"Look at you two." Theo appeared and gestured at them with the half-full cup in his hands, almost sloshing the liquid out. "Whispering sweet nothings to each other. It's adorable."

Dante took Theo's cup from him. "Wow, you really can't handle your liquor."

"No, I can't." Theo smiled as he addressed Sebastian and Nick. "Hey, you know what you two should do? You should watch the last of the sunset out on the balcony."

Nick almost choked on the sip of Scotch he was taking. "What?"

Sebastian rubbed the back of his head. "I can't leave my own party."

"You're not *leaving*. You'll be right there." Theo whipped a hand around and pointed to the balcony. "Like, fifteen feet away. Grab that bottle of Scotch and scoot before the sun disappears. You've only got

like ten minutes left. Dante and I can greet people, and everyone will
be busy getting a buzz going anyway."

Nick glanced at the balcony. Outside the glass doors, the sun was
hanging low in the sky. Its bright-orange light infused the encroaching
purple evening with a halo of warmth. It was beautiful. Nick couldn't
remember the last time he'd stopped to watch a sunset, let alone done
it with someone . . . significant.

He glanced at Sebastian. "Well?"

Sebastian sighed. "Gimme a sec to grab the Scotch."

As he disappeared into the kitchen, Theo let out a whoop. "All
right! Go team!"

"What team?" Nick asked.

Theo looked over his shoulder as if checking for eavesdroppers
before leaning closer. "Team Sick."

Nick blinked at Theo slowly before it dawned on him. "Is that a
combination of Sebastian and Nick?"

"Yes." Theo frowned. "Though I suppose that's not clear. I didn't
really think it through. What about Team Nebastian? Or Team
Nebby?"

"I . . . can't choose. It's like deciding between poison or a noose."

Sebastian thankfully reappeared with the Scotch, took Nick's
hand, and flashed an award-winning smile. "Please excuse us."

The sound of Theo giggling followed them all the way out onto
the balcony. It had a waist-high stone railing and no screen. The view
of the sunset was unencumbered by tall buildings as it swept over
the town, drenching it in gold. The air was the perfect temperature:
still warm from the day, but night had taken a hold of it with cool,
soothing fingers.

Sebastian set the bottle of Scotch carefully on top of the railing
before turning to Nick. "I'd like to formally apologize for my friends.
What they lack in subtlety, they make up for in obnoxiousness."

Nick waved him off. "Don't worry about it. This was actually a
great suggestion. And I consider them my friends as well."

Sebastian's face lit up. "Yeah, I suppose they are. Listen, Nick, I
was wondering—"

A distinct *click* from behind them interrupted his sentence.

Sebastian's head whipped toward the door. "Oh no."

"What is it?" Nick looked over.

Theo and Dante were standing on the other side of the glass. Their muffled laughter was barely audible.

"Christ," Sebastian groaned.

Nick gasped. "Did they..."

Theo cupped his hands around his mouth. "Have fun, boys! This way, no one can disturb you. We'll come fetch you in a few minutes." He grabbed Dante's hand and tugged him away.

Sebastian sighed. "Those meddlesome bastards. I swear to God."

Nick opened and closed his mouth several times. "They *do* realize anyone inside can unlock the door and come out here, right?"

"Yup."

"Locking it from the *inside* doesn't give us any privacy at all."

"Yup."

"So, what Theo is really doing is—"

"Trapping us out here together. During a romantic sunset."

Nick took a long breath and let it out slowly. When he'd composed himself, he held his glass out to Sebastian. "Well, at least we have Scotch."

Chapter Thirteen

heo's maneuver was juvenile, but Sebastian had to admit, it was
effective. He would have been hard-pressed to get some alone
time with Nick while he was hosting a huge party, but now, at least
they'd have this.

And alone time was something Sebastian really needed. Every
interaction with Nick made two things clear to him: this had stopped
being about the bet a long time ago, and he really didn't know anything
about Nick.

He knew surface things, like what he was majoring in (physics),
his hobbies (drawing), and that he was an adult orphan (devastating).
But if Sebastian was considering dating for the first time in his
life—and potentially giving up Barbzilla forever if he bowed out
of the bet—he needed to know something much more important:
would they even work together as a couple?

And on a different note, Sebastian wondered what Theo's motive
was in all this. First, Dante was clearly up to something, and now Theo
had pulled this stunt. Were they in on it together? Knowing Theo, he
was probably the mastermind behind whatever they were planning.
Dante would never waste time scheming unless Theo put him up to
it. Later, Sebastian would catch Theo after one cocktail too many and
needle it out of him.

For now, he watched the man standing next to him out of the
corner of his eye. Nick was leaning on the stone railing encasing
the balcony, his eyes unfocused as he gazed out over quiet streets
peppered with neat houses. The sunset made his blond hair glow
white-hot, and his tan skin had a distinct pink tinge. It was impossible
to tell if he was flushed or if it came from the pastel sky.

"So"—Sebastian swirled the Scotch in his glass and mourned their lack of ice—"since we're stuck out here, we should probably find something to do."

Nick looked at him askance. "Dude, there's a room full of people inside."

It took Sebastian a second to follow his train of thought. "Wow, so not what I meant." He paused. "Though I'm *thrilled* your mind went straight to the gutter."

The pink in Nick's face deepened, confirming that it hadn't been caused by the sunset. "What were you thinking, then? We could play a drinking game, I suppose."

"We can't play a tawdry party game with a nice bottle of Scotch. This is a sipping liquor. It's not meant for shots."

"You have a better idea?"

"We could plan a daring escape."

Nick gestured at the ground a solid twenty feet below them. "We're three floors up. What are we going to do? Jump?"

"I guess not." He grinned. "But imagine Theo's and Dante's faces if we waltzed into the party a few minutes from now with the door to the balcony still locked. Tipsy as Theo is, I bet we could convince him we're wizards."

Nick laughed. "Dibs on Harry Potter!"

Sebastian made an affronted sound. "Bullshit. If either of us is Daniel Radcliffe, it's me. Only I'm taller and lack his beautiful eyes. You can be Tom Felton."

"Malfoy?" Nick turned to face him. "You think I'm *Malfoy*? On what grounds?"

"You know what?" Sebastian ruffled Nick's hair. "You're not blond enough to be Malfoy. He's platinum, and you're more of a honey." The second his fingers touched Nick's head, they wanted to never stop. Holy *fuck*, Nick's hair was soft. Tangled, but soft.

Nick didn't push Sebastian's hand away immediately, and Sebastian made a note: potential for hair play later. "Seriously, you said you wanted me to get to know you. Now seems like the perfect time for you to tell me about yourself."

"That's a broad topic. What do you want to know about me?"

Nick raised a fine eyebrow. "I can ask anything? You sure you want to hand that kind of power over to me?"

"Fair enough. In that case, you can ask me anything, but I get to ask you anything in return."

For the first time since they'd gotten locked outside, Nick seemed nervous. "And we both have to answer?"

"Well, you don't *have* to, but if you pass too many times, it ruins the spirit of it."

"Hm." Nick shrugged. "All right, I'm in. Though I fail to see how that's much different from a drinking game."

"Just ask a damn question."

Nick looked out over the orange-drenched view and tapped a finger against his chin. After a minute, he perked up and glanced back at Sebastian. "All right, how long was your longest relationship?"

Damn, he comes out swinging.

Sebastian shifted from foot to foot. "I've, uh, never been in a relationship before. I dated this one guy for like a month, but that's not exactly long-term, is it?"

"Oh man." Nick groaned. "I'd hoped that wasn't really the case."

"Hey, what's that supposed to mean?"

"It means you're a flirt who has trust and communication issues. Not exactly the makings of a relationship expert."

Sebastian sniffed. "Touché. You sound like you already knew what my answer was going to be."

"Yeah, Theo told me about your one relationship a while ago. I won't lie: I asked because I was testing to see if you'd tell me the truth."

"I want to be pissed about that, but I guess I don't have the right. It's true: I'm lost when it comes to relationships. Sex is what I'm good at. But to be fair, it's not like I couldn't have dated if I'd wanted to. I've had plenty of offers."

"Why haven't you taken anyone up on them?"

Because for a long time, I doubted if love exists. Though lately, I've been questioning everything I once knew.

"Nice try," he said out loud. "But you don't get two questions in a row. It's my turn."

Nick huffed but nodded, taking a sip of his drink as if he needed it to bolster his nerves. "Go ahead."

Before Sebastian could respond, someone appeared on the other side of the glass door. It was a guy with an unlit cigarette in his mouth. As he reached for the door handle, Sebastian actually wished he wouldn't free them. He didn't want to lose this time with Nick.

Luckily or unluckily, a shirtless and visibly intoxicated Theo appeared and chased the guy away. Literally. The glass muffled most of the sound, but Theo appeared to shout like Tarzan and charge the guy, who ran away in terror. Theo paused long enough to give them a thumbs-up before he disappeared back into the crowd.

Nick whistled. "Our friends are weird."

"Yeah, Theo is one of those people who changes when he drinks. Into what, no one knows. Anyway, back to the game." Sebastian thought for a moment. "Here's a juicy one. How many guys have you slept with?"

Nick's flush intensified, but he met Sebastian's gaze without flinching. "Just guys?"

"Ah. You're bisexual?"

Nick nodded.

"All right. How many *people* have you slept with?"

Nick took another sip before holding up two fingers.

Sebastian looked between them and his face. "You mean two *dozen*, right?"

"What? No! I can't imagine having that many sexual partners." Nick peered at him. "Why? How many have you had?"

Sebastian glanced at his wrist. "Wow, look at the time. I think I'll jump off the balcony after all." He moved like he was going to vault over the railing.

Nick caught his arm, laughing. "Seriously. You can tell me."

"I'd rather not."

"Because of how I reacted? I'm sorry about that. I swear I'm not a judgmental person."

"It's not that. It's just . . . Well, I'm not super proud of my number. Not because I'm ashamed of sex itself or anything. I'm not puritanical."

"Why then?"

Sebastian shifted his weight again and glanced at where his glass was sitting on the balcony. With each passing minute, as more of the sun sank below the horizon, it darkened from amber to a rich, almost chocolatey color. It was like a sundial in a way, alerting him to the fact that his alone time with Nick was running out. If he was going to open up, this was his chance.

"I used to party a lot when I was younger," Sebastian began. "That meant I occasionally got trashed with people I didn't know all that well. There were times when I hooked up with guys whose names I couldn't remember. It's one of the reasons I have a no-drunk-sex policy now. Consent issues aside, I realized it wasn't the healthiest behavior."

Nick's expression was a little too neutral. "Did you feel taken advantage of?"

"No, I always wanted to have sex. I didn't care who with, so long as he was reasonably attractive. I thought I preferred for things to be as anonymous and emotionless as possible."

"Any particular reason?"

That was Nick's fourth question in a row, but Sebastian let it slide. "I was fresh out of the closet and ready to check out the whole 'gay lifestyle' I'd heard so much about. I was also acting out, because while my parents didn't disapprove of my sexuality, per se, they didn't want me expressing it all over town either. So, naturally, I did. And also, I think—" He stopped short. "I was about to say I had a hole to fill, but I realized how wrong that sounds."

Nick, who'd been in the process of drinking his Scotch, snorted into the glass before choking on his laughter. "Oh my God. I'm so glad you caught yourself, or I would have done a spit take."

"I wouldn't have blamed you." Sebastian gave him a small smile. "But in all seriousness, I definitely think I was looking for something in all the wrong places. Not affection, for sure, but maybe validation? Something like that."

Nick nodded. "I get it. Your parents ignored you, so you sought out attention elsewhere. The more I learn about you, the more the puzzle pieces fall into place."

Sebastian eyed him. "In a good way?"

"Definitely in a good way."

Breathing a sigh of relief, Sebastian contemplated his next question. "So, the grand total of two people that you slept with. Who were they?"

"One was a girl named Amanda when I was in high school. She was my long-term girlfriend until we went to separate colleges, failed at the long-distance thing, and parted ways amicably. I still call her sometimes. The other was this boy back home. He was a waiter at the restaurant where I worked to help pay for my tuition. We dated for like six months, but honestly it was never serious."

"Six months, and it wasn't serious?" Sebastian whistled. "You must comprehend a lot in the concept of being serious."

Nick looked him square in the eye. "I do. To me, being serious means I think I might marry that person one day. Is that a problem?"

Sebastian lost their game of eye-chicken and glanced away. "No. Admittedly, I don't think I know what being serious is to me, and here you've got it all figured out."

"I wouldn't say that. It is kind of interesting, though."

"What is?"

Nick smiled. "Us. Together. You have all this sexual experience but no relationship experience, and I'm the opposite. What do you suppose that says about us?"

"That we're weirdly perfect for each other?" Sebastian winked.

"Maybe. Though I'll tell you right now, I don't do casual. You're not going to get any anonymous, emotionless sex out of me."

"Oh, I believe that. I've kissed you. I've felt how passionate you can be." Sebastian eyed him up and down. "You bring that same fire to bed with you, right?"

It might have been his imagination, but Sebastian thought he saw Nick's eyes darken. "Wouldn't you like to find out."

Sebastian wet his lips and stepped closer to Nick. "I would."

At some point, the sun had slipped out of sight, leaving only a faint orange afterglow to suggest it had ever been there. In the houses all around them, lights were flashing on. Illumination from inside Sebastian's apartment filtered out as well. Nick's face was bathed in a delicate mixture of light and shadow. Every aspect of the view was painfully romantic.

Nick's throat moved, indicating that he'd swallowed. "Are you going to kiss me again?"

Sebastian let out a weak breath. "I was thinking about it. Will you toss me over the ledge if I do?"

"No, I'd do something much worse. I'd let you."

Sebastian was finding it difficult to breathe. "Why would that be worse?"

Nick's voice lowered to match his pitch, no louder than the wind wafting past them. "Because there's a party's worth of people right inside, and I don't want them to see. I don't want to share any part of this with anyone else."

Minutes before, Sebastian had been grateful for this chance to get to know Nick. But now, he wished with everything he had that they were inside. Somewhere private. Somewhere he could kiss Nick and hold him and try to communicate all the things he wanted to say but couldn't.

"I won't kiss you," Sebastian said, even as his brain, body, and heart all begged him to reconsider, "on one condition."

Nick frowned as if he were a bit disappointed. "What's the condition?"

"I told you something about myself earlier that I haven't shared with many people. The goal tonight is for you to get to know me, but I also want to get to know you. Tell me something about you. Something important."

Nick looked away, toward the purpling sky. After a long moment, he turned back, wearing the saddest eyes Sebastian had ever seen.

"My dad was my best friend, and when he died, it was awful. I was a mess, so much so I took time off from college. You know what a serious student I am. I'm sure you've realized that for me to do that, I must have been in a bad place." He paused and seemed to steel himself. "My dad's death rocked my whole world, but . . . it was only the second-worst thing that's ever happened to me."

Sebastian had to swallow before his throat opened up enough for him to speak. "What was the first?"

Nick opened his mouth to answer.

And that was, naturally, the exact moment they heard a *click*, and then the sliding glass door opened.

"Guys!" A rumpled Theo stumbled outside. "What are you doing out here in the dark? Come inside and party with us."

Sebastian rolled his eyes. "You're the one who locked us out here, Theo."

"Well, that was then, and this is now, and I want you to come back inside." He started to take a sip from the cup in his hand, but Dante appeared and snatched it away.

"Seriously, guys," Dante said. "Come inside before someone catches a cold."

Nick looked at Sebastian. "Finish this conversation later?"

"Oh yeah." Sebastian reached out and gave his waist a light squeeze. "Count on it."

Nick didn't move away from his touch. In fact, he leaned into it.

If Theo or Dante noticed, they didn't say anything as Dante hauled Theo back inside. Thumping bass poured out from the speakers in the living room, beckoning them to the dance floor.

Sebastian gestured for Nick to go first, and together, they walked into the fray.

Nick had been to his fair share of college parties. In his experience, they came in two forms: raging keggers at frat houses, or pretentious "gatherings" where English majors sat around, drank red wine, and talked about how James Joyce was a latent homosexual.

Sebastian's party, he soon discovered, was a bizarre mixture of the two. On the dance floor, people grinded to The Smiths. People were drinking like it was 2012, but instead of doing keg stands, they were making martinis with actual olives. Someone had broken out a joint—of course—and a discussion concerning the economic effects of government-subsidized marijuana followed it as it was passed around.

It was by far the strangest party Nick had ever been to. He was dying to ask if all Academy parties were like this, or if this was specific to Sebastian's crowd. But as he peeked over at Sebastian standing behind him—so close, Nick could feel his warmth—there was another question on Nick's mind: Were they attending this party as each other's dates?

Did Nick *want* to be Sebastian's date? After spending so much time waiting around to see what Sebastian would do, shit seemed to be moving awfully fast all of a sudden.

It might be time to pump the brakes a bit. It's only been two weeks, and I'm not ready to trust Sebastian after two heart-felt conversations. Plus, this seems like a perfect opportunity for me to make some of those elusive friends I keep talking about.

Nick half turned to look at Sebastian over his shoulder. "As the host, you should be greeting people."

Sebastian nodded. "As a guest, you should be mingling."

"My thoughts exactly. But first, I think I'll check out the drinks station."

"Sounds good. I'll put the Scotch away and catch you later."

They parted ways. Nick dove into the sea of people dancing in the living room. As he waded through, he caught sight of Theo and Dante bobbing along to the blaring music together, but they were too far away for him to say hi. He also spotted Angela—the girl from his physics class—grinding aggressively with another girl while they stared into each other's eyes.

Didn't Sebastian mention something about an Angela getting together with someone? If so, good for her.

Nick made it to the dining room and waited patiently for a couple of boys to grab beers and leave before he surveyed the options. There was enough gin to mistake this place for a 1920s speakeasy, along with bags of ice in a cooler. Nick didn't want to go the martini route like everyone else had. That left tequila—big no to that—or vodka, which was doable.

"Nick?"

He glanced toward the voice. Standing in the open doorway to the living room was none other than Deen. He was wearing his usual fashionable clothes and a huge smile on his face.

Nick's whole mood lightened at the sight of him. "Deen! What are you doing here?"

"I could ask you the same question, but I bet I know the answer. Sebastian convinced you to come." He walked over and slapped Nick on the back. "As for me, it turns out once you get invited to one of these things, you get invited to all of them. Like being on the world's best mailing list. Does that make me a cool kid now?"

Nick laughed. "I dare say it does."

Deen turned pointedly away from him and said nothing.

Nick waited for a moment before tapping him on the shoulder. "Deen?"

He whipped back around, smiling. "I was practicing being too cool for you, now that I'm popular."

"I see." Nick shoved him. "Promise you won't forget us little people?"

"I'll try. You making a drink?"

"Was about to, yeah. You want?"

"*Hell* yeah."

They made screwdrivers and then stood on the edge of the living room/makeshift dance floor, watching the pulsating multitude.

"Man, I love this." Deen took a deep breath. "Smells like teen spirit."

Nick chuckled. "You know, some of the people here aren't teens anymore, myself included."

"You poor things. I don't turn twenty until January, so I'm enjoying the last dregs while I can."

"Think you'll come to a lot of these parties? Now that you're popular?"

Deen shrugged and took a gulp of his drink. "Some of them, I'm sure. But not so many that they stop being exciting. There's a lot more to college than partying, you know. There's movie night once a month in the auditorium and the shows the choir puts on around Christmas. And driving into town in the middle of the night during finals week because if you don't get some Starbucks, you're going to fling yourself off a bridge. Oh, and girls. Have I mentioned girls? I'd like to meet one who makes me want to skip partying on the weekends so we can stay in and watch Netflix."

"That's the dream." Nick held his cup out, and Deen bumped his against it. "Speaking of which, are we doing the whole sock-on-the-doorknob thing?"

"Ew, no." Deen's lip curled up. "We're way too awesome to be that cliché. We'll come up with something when there's an actual need." As Deen spoke, the kitchen door opened and revealed Sebastian. Nick's attention immediately locked onto him. So much so, he almost missed Deen's question. "Although, if you're here with Sebastian, maybe that time has come?"

"Uh, not quite. It's kinda complicated, actually." As if sensing he was being discussed, Sebastian spotted them and made his way through the crowd. Nick took a generous gulp of his drink. "I'll fill you in tomorrow over breakfast?"

"Deal." Deen turned away. "Go get 'em, tiger. I'm gonna get my dance on." He disappeared into the throng.

A minute later, Sebastian appeared in front of Nick. "Long time no see. I would have joined you sooner, but some people were making grilled cheese in my kitchen. It would have been fine, except I have a gas stove, and drunk people plus open flames equals disaster."

"Yikes. Glad you caught them in time." Nick held up his cup. "I got me a vodka and orange juice. The most basic party drink of all time."

"That's actually one of my go-to cocktails. Make me one?"

"Sure. Consider it a small payback for hosting this party." Nick whipped up the drink in record time and handed it over.

Sebastian took the cup, his eyes and fingers lingering on Nick. "Do you want to dance?"

"Um." The heat in Sebastian's gaze made Nick swallow. His initial reaction was to say yes, but he'd said he was going to mingle. Thus far, he'd talked to one person, and Deen didn't count for obvious reasons.

You met more people with Sebastian earlier than you have the entire time you've been at the Academy. Clearly he's better at breaking you out of your shell than you are. Maybe you should stick by his side tonight.

Then again, he was pleasantly buzzed from the going-on-three drinks he'd had. And after all the emotional bonding he'd done with Sebastian, his guard was already down. If they danced right now, Nick was positive they'd end up making out on the floor. In front of everyone.

The Academy's infamous rumor mill would spring to life if that happened. The whole university would know by Monday. Nick wasn't ready for that kind of attention. What if things didn't work out between them? Would he become yet another heart Sebastian had broken? Minho popped into his head, saying, *I told you so.*

Nick believed Sebastian had changed, and there was no denying Nick felt *something* for him, but until he knew what that was, he couldn't risk going public.

Before Nick could decide what to say, a flash of red caught his eye. Theo. He was pulling Dante off the dance floor by the hand, heading for a set of couches that faced each other with a coffee table between them. Currently, they were unoccupied, but Nick suspected Theo was about to change that.

Nick seized the opportunity with both hands. "Why don't we hang out withTheo and Dante? I haven't talked to them the whole party."

Sebastian frowned. "You can talk to them anytime. Dance with me. Please?"

Damn, it's hard to say no.

If only Sebastian weren't so tempting, standing close to Nick, looking at him like he was the only person in the jam-packed room.

Nick scraped together his resolve and held firm. "I want to relax for a bit. Enjoy not being locked on the balcony anymore."

Sebastian's frown had become a full-fledge pout, but he relented. "All right. I guess I can stand to spend some time with my own best friends."

They made their way to Theo and Dante. Slowly. People stopped to talk to Sebastian along the way, and Sebastian introduced Nick to everyone. Nick did his best to memorize names, but he was hyperfocused on how . . . couple-y it felt, having Sebastian by his side, introducing him like a boyfriend.

One thing was for sure, Sebastian made it a hell of a lot easier for Nick to meet people. And to loosen up. And to have fun. Perhaps Nick's nose-to-the-grindstone plan had been holding him back. Come Monday, he'd have to think about finding a good balance between school and his personal life.

They reached Dante and Theo, who had collapsed on one of Sebastian's couches. Theo was talking animatedly about something while Dante fanned them both with a coaster. They were sweaty from dancing and had matching giant grins on their faces. They looked *adorable* together.

If they end up dating, I am so giving myself matchmaker points.

"Hey guys," Nick said when they were within earshot. "Having fun?"

Theo startled a little and moved away from Dante. Nick almost snorted; it was such an obvious guilt reaction. Like a kid who'd snatched his hand away from the cookie jar.

"Hey." Theo's eyes darted between Nick and Sebastian. "Great party, Sebby."

Sebastian answered so fast, it seemed automatic. "Don't call me Sebby."

"Is there a reason you don't like that?" Nick asked.

"Sebby is cutesy. Sebastian is sophisticated and dignified."

Nick laughed. "No, Sebastian is that Jamaican crab from *The Little Mermaid*."

Sebastian shot Nick a sour look. "As a movie aficionado, I reluctantly give you points for that. As a person who didn't get to pick my name, I say fuck you."

"Fine by me." Nick glanced back over at the couches only to find Dante beaming at them. "What?"

"Oh, nothing." Dante batted his eyelashes. "I was watching you two be all cute. Flirting. Bantering. Falling in love. Ah, young romance."

Nick opened his mouth to protest, but before he could, Sebastian slipped an arm over his shoulder and smirked at Dante. "Jealous?" He touched Nick's chin, turned his face toward him, and planted a brief but firm kiss on his lips.

That one interaction, which lasted barely five seconds, was all it took.

Nick heard giggles behind them and wrenched his head around to see. A group of people were watching them, grinning. One guy took out his phone and started typing. Was he telling everyone he knew about the kiss?

Fuck.

And that wasn't the end of it. Sebastian was smiling, but not at Nick. He was looking at Dante, and his expression said it all: smugness with a hint of victory. Nick would have bet all the money in his bank account right then that Sebastian hadn't kissed Nick out of affection or a desire to share his happiness with his friends. He'd done it to stake his claim. To rub it in Dante's face that he'd landed Nick, as if Nick were some sort of trophy.

Selfish, arrogant, egotistical bastard.

Nick was suddenly too furious to speak. He wrenched himself away from Sebastian and concentrated on putting one foot in front of the other while the room tilted. For a second, he thought it was the alcohol, but he'd never felt more sober as anger burned through him.

Plunking his drink down on an end table, Nick pushed his way through the sea of bodies, not certain exactly where he was headed. His only criterion was that he go somewhere Sebastian wasn't. He started to head for the kitchen only to remember there were people in there. Veering off toward the hallway, he made it all the way to the mouth before fingers closed around his arm.

"Nick." It was Sebastian's voice.

Nick shook him off and kept marching.

"Where are you going?"

He ignored the question. The short hallway had three doors: left, right, and straight ahead. The one to the right was closed, but the other two were open, revealing a bathroom and a darkened bedroom. Nick considered locking himself in the former before Sebastian said his name again.

What's going to cause more of a scene? Sebastian pounding on the bathroom door while you shout at him to go away? Or telling him to fuck off quietly in his room?

Nick headed for the center door, feeling around for a light switch and flicking it on. A brief glance gave him the details: navy walls, a white throw rug covering the hardwood floor, and a big bed with black sheets. Above it hung a watercolor painting of a skyline Nick knew well: Chicago. Had he been one iota less furious, he would have asked Sebastian about it.

Footsteps followed behind him, proceeded by the sound of the door shutting, and then a *click*. The lock. Sebastian must've sensed they were going to need privacy. He didn't speak. The only sound was the muted thump of bass and distant voices, which blended together into a meaningless hum.

Nick turned slowly around. Sebastian was eying him from a safe distance, face pinched and wary. For a long moment, he let Sebastian stew while he decided what he wanted to say. The tension between them swelled.

When Nick finally spoke, his voice was harsh as steel wool. "What were you thinking?"

"What did I do?" Sebastian looked him up and down, as if searching for clues. "Why are you angry?"

"You kissed me, Sebastian. In front of everyone. I want to hear the logic behind that decision."

Sebastian's eyes were wide and alarmed. "What do you mean? I was thinking I wanted to kiss you. I didn't realize I needed written permission to do that."

"Well, you do!" Nick made a frustrated sound and sucked in a breath. "I can't help but notice how many times you just used the word 'I.' Did you think about me at all just then? Did you think about how I might feel, being rubbed in Dante's face like a prize? Did it occur to you that I'm not out? Was there a single moment—a fraction of a second—in which you thought about the person on the other end of that kiss?"

Cold realization washed over Sebastian's face. "Oh shit. I didn't . . . Wow, I'm sorry. I didn't think about how you're not out. But is it really a big deal? You don't have to be closeted the whole time you're at the Academy."

"The point is, that wasn't your decision." Nick enunciated each word. "I told you out on the balcony that I didn't want to kiss you in front of everyone, but you ignored my wishes. And don't pretend like that kiss wasn't pure ego on your part. You were *claiming* me. But see, that's a problem. Because I'm not *yours*."

By the time he'd finished speaking, Nick's anger had risen up all over again. He was tempted to push past Sebastian and stomp away again, but he didn't want to face the party outside. He'd stormed off once. If he did it again, tongues would wag in earnest.

Sebastian's expression had morphed from shock to hurt. "Aren't you though, Nick? I thought we were making progress."

"We were. Note the past tense. But we haven't talked about what that means. We're certainly not in a place to make anything official."

Sebastian blew out a breath that scattered his dark bangs. "Do we have to talk about it? Do we have to talk about *everything*? Don't you ever do anything impulsive?" He stepped closer. "Haven't you ever been so swept up in the passion of the moment that you *acted*?"

Nick's body started to heat up with emotion. "No, I don't act impulsively, because I don't have rich, influential parents and safety nets to catch me if I misstep. I wasn't ready to go public about this. You'd know that if you'd stopped being selfish for one fucking second and thought about someone besides yourself."

The hurt fell off Sebastian's face and was replaced with anger, hot enough to match Nick's. "So, that's it, huh? I'm just a spoiled, rich brat who never thinks about anyone else. And you're what? The beleaguered parent who has to teach me how scary the real world is? Because you're so mature and selfless and right all the time? You know, I've had about enough of listening to you preach."

Nick shook his head. "Don't you turn this back on me. You're the one who fucked up."

"You're right, Nick. I did fuck up. I should have asked you before I kissed you out there. But I apologized right away, and I meant it. In my head, I was making plans to do better. Then you started in on me, sprinkling in all these jabs about who I am as a person. Why is that always the first thing you go for?"

Nick pursed his lips. He held out for three seconds before he caved. "You're right. I'm sorry. I'm still mad about what you did, but I shouldn't be so quick to name-call."

"I believe that you're sorry." Sebastian folded his arms over his chest.

Nick blinked at him. "But?"

"But you still think what you said is true. You think I'm selfish."

"I think you have a warped view of the world. You think you're invincible, and I know for a fact that none of us are."

Sebastian rolled his eyes. "Oh, you poor thing. I feel so sorry for you."

Nick took a step forward. "Excuse me?"

"I get it, Nick. Your life has been *so* hard because you had to have a job and pay your own tuition, whereas us rich kids get everything handed to us. That's what you think, right?"

Nick narrowed his eyes. "Not having to worry about how you're going to afford food and clothing and college—one of the biggest luxuries out there, which is treated like a requirement—is a huge fucking advantage. You realize I had to *transfer schools*, right? When my dad died, I had to go wherever the money was. I didn't want to leave Chicago. Chicago was my home. It was everything I knew, and leaving there was like *losing my dad all over again*."

By the end of his speech, he was breathing hard. Electricity coursed through Nick, making his blood buzz.

Sebastian stared at him from a foot away, his eyes hard as graphite. "I'm sorry for everything you've been through, Nick. I truly am. But the contempt you've shown for me and our peers since day one is completely unjustified."

"How can you—"

Sebastian silenced him with a scalding look. "Yeah, a lot of us have had advantages, but you should know that doesn't mean our lives haven't been hard. If you didn't learn that from me, you should have learned it from Theo."

"What do you mean?"

"Has he not told you about his dad, the career alcoholic? His mom who had to become Wonder Woman to give him everything he has? The guilt he feels every day because of it?"

Nick was silent. As a matter of fact, Theo had mentioned that to him. And yet somehow Nick hadn't thought much of it.

Sebastian kept going. "Or what about your new pal Dante? Ever ask him why he's the only one of the three of us who isn't out? Did he mention his homophobic older brother? The years of physical abuse Dante went through, and how he's probably not dating Theo—even though they're *obviously* in love—because a part of him is still terrified of coming out?"

The breath in Nick's lungs burned. He stared wide-eyed at Sebastian, and puzzle pieces fell into place. The heat between them smoldered in a quiet way that somehow worried Nick more than if it were a blaze.

"That's a fraction," Sebastian said, "of the things that are going on in the lives of the people out in my living room right now. I'm not saying they're all saints. Many of them are spoiled and vacuous and petty. But I didn't spend the last year of my life this miserable to have some guy who barely knows me make assumptions about my life based on my parents' bank accounts. Nickolas Steele, you don't have the faintest idea what's going on in the detailed lives of others."

He'd moved closer, and now, they were inches apart. Nick had thought the tension between them was different this time—based in anger and frustration—but now he realized it had flavors of the same magnetism that kept bringing them together.

Nick stared at Sebastian, heart pounding, emotions welling up in the back of his throat that he didn't know how to put words to.

A question formed unbidden in his mind. He stumbled to spit it out. "You know how you asked me if I ever do anything out of pure passion?"

"Yeah." Sebastian's voice was barely a breath.

Nick stared at him, hoping his eyes contained the deep, dark intent that was brewing within him, because he didn't think he could speak.

It seemed they did, because Sebastian wet his lips. "Do you want to make out right now as badly as I do?"

Nick didn't hesitate. "Yes."

They came together in a beautiful blend of fury and calm, like waves drowning the shore.

Chapter Fourteen

In that moment, Sebastian decided that all he wanted to do with the rest of his life was kiss Nick. He didn't want to go to class. He didn't want to graduate and get a job. He wanted Nick, pressed up against him like he couldn't get enough of him. He wanted their mouths, their heat, and the wild, frightening feelings Sebastian hadn't known existed until Nick had come into his life.

Between frantic kisses, Sebastian breathed apologies. "I'm sorry. I'm so sorry about before. I shouldn't have done that in front of everyone."

"No, I'm sorry." Nick pulled away only to feather kisses all over Sebastian's face. "I'm the selfish one. I didn't think—"

Sebastian shushed him with his lips and then wrapped his arms around Nick's waist, needing to feel every bit of him. But no matter how tightly he held Nick, it wasn't close enough. He ended up walking them back, hoping to hit a wall, or—oh God—his bed.

They crashed into his nightstand instead, sending a lamp clattering to the ground, and still they didn't stop kissing, messy and *hot*. Sebastian put a hand on the wall to brace them while the other worked Nick's shirt up in the back so he could get at his skin. For Nick's part, his hands found their way into Sebastian's hair—not pulling it, but squeezing enough to make his scalp sing—while one of his legs slid between Sebastian's thighs.

When Nick rubbed against his cock, Sebastian thought he was going to faint. He was fairly certain he'd been hard since the fight, but at that little contact, he went from turned on to desperate in a flash.

Nick seemed to feel the same way, because he whimpered against Sebastian's mouth. Before Sebastian could return the favor, Nick spun them around. Sebastian barely had time to orient himself before Nick pushed him back, and he fell onto his bed.

For a fraction of a second, he blinked up at Nick, too aroused to process what was going on. But then Nick climbed on top of him, straddling his hips, and the intensity between them reached a zenith.

They were alone, in a locked bedroom, after two weeks of dancing around each other, and something was about to give. Sebastian had never wanted anything more in his life. This. Right now. No more talking. All action.

Now that Nick was on top of him, he seemed to hesitate. Nick's eyes tracked down Sebastian's torso, growing larger and darker as they landed on the bulge between his legs. It sent a little shiver through Sebastian. He grabbed Nick's hips and canted up against him.

The second he did, they both groaned. The answering hardness of Nick's cock—obvious through his jeans—made Sebastian dizzy. Out of all the sex he'd had, this was already the most intense, and they were only getting started.

"Sebastian." Nick's eyes roved over his face. "There's something we need to talk about."

Sebastian groaned for a different reason. "No more talking. Just— *Please*." He rocked his hips up again and was rewarded by Nick making a soft, pleasured sound.

But Nick shook his head. "Earlier, you said you have a strict no-drunk-sex rule. We've both been drinking."

That got Sebastian's attention.

He propped himself up on his elbows. "I appreciate that you thought of that. I had two and a half drinks. I'm a little buzzed, but I definitely don't feel drunk. Haven't for a while, actually. Not since the argument."

"You might've sobered up by now." Nick bit his lip, and the urge to kiss him was almost too powerful for Sebastian to ignore. "I feel sober too. It could be adrenaline, though. I don't want to violate any of your boundaries. That seemed like a big one."

"Yeah, it is." Sebastian took a trembling breath. "But I have that boundary because I did things I regretted with the wrong guys. There's a big difference between then and now."

"Oh?"

Sebastian reached up and touched Nick's face. "I'm not going to regret this, and I trust you."

"Really? But there's still so much we don't know about each other."

"I know." Sebastian grinned. "Isn't it exciting?"

Nick huffed a laugh and tilted his cheek into Sebastian's hand. "There's still the small matter of the room full of people on the other side of the door. I'm . . . not quiet."

Fresh arousal rolled through Sebastian. "You're killing me, smalls. Don't worry about them." He slid his fingers through Nick's soft hair. "Kiss me again, and if you want to stop, we'll stop."

Sebastian was expecting more of a fight, but Nick allowed him to lean up and lock their mouths together. Nick kissed back like he'd been waiting for the invitation.

It was different this time. Before it'd been all frantic passion and need. Now, there was a purpose behind it—a goal they were building toward. One that burned and left Sebastian breathless. When Nick broke their mouths apart only to kiss down Sebastian's throat, mouth open and hot, Sebastian had to shut his eyes against the intensity of it.

"Sebastian."

Reluctantly, Sebastian cracked an eye open. The overhead light was behind Nick, which made his blond hair light up like a halo around him. There was nothing angelic about the expression on his face, though. He looked wrecked, debauched, and Sebastian could only imagine what he'd look like if they actually had sex. Sebastian wanted to find out more than he wanted air.

"I want you so badly I can't think." Nick's voice was deep with arousal. "Show me what you want."

Sebastian almost came from that alone. He shuddered and nodded, unable to form words. Nick was still straddling him, and the insistent press of their clothed erections together sent waves of arousal through him. But it wasn't enough. He slid his hands between their bodies. It took some doing—Nick wouldn't stop rocking against him, and Sebastian wasn't complaining—but he managed to reach his own fly.

The click of the zipper sliding down was audible even over their panted breaths. Nick froze at the sound and sat up enough to meet

Sebastian's gaze. For a split second, Sebastian thought he was going to tell him to stop, or at least slow down, but Nick's pupils were huge, and there was nothing in his expression but deep, raw *want*.

"Be fast." Nick wet his lips. "They'll notice we're gone soon."

Sebastian wasn't sure exactly what Nick wanted him to do, but he didn't care. He wanted all of it. "Okay."

"You sure you want this?"

"Oh God *yes*." Sebastian grabbed his face and kissed him hard. Nick melted into it, warm and heavy on top of Sebastian. Sebastian was almost as turned on by the feel of Nick as he was by what Nick did next. He slid both hands down Sebastian's sides, paused to give his waist a possessive squeeze, and then went for his open fly.

It took everything Sebastian had not to buck up against Nick's hands when they ghosted over the front of his pants. He stopped kissing Nick in favor of panting as the too-light touch both excited him and left him wanting. Despite his best efforts, he ended up arching off the bed in search of satisfaction.

Nick's lips found their way to his ear. "Stop wriggling."

"I can't." Sebastian tossed his head back and whined. "Feels good."

"It'll feel better if you let me—" Nick managed to get his hand into Sebastian's tight pants, beneath the hem of his underwear.

When his fingers wrapped around Sebastian's cock, Sebastian jolted. He'd known he was wound up before, but the second Nick's skin came into contact with his, it was like lightning. Sharp, crackling pleasure burst between his legs and spread through him.

"Fuck, *fuck*." Sebastian grabbed on to Nick's shoulders and squeezed. "That has no right to feel as good as it does."

Nick chuckled. "I've barely touched you. Hold on. I know what we need." He pushed himself up into a sitting position.

Sebastian whined again, wishing Nick's warmth would come back, but when Nick went for his own pants, understanding dawned on him. "Oh, yeah. Good idea." He fumbled to push his clothes out of the way, but he had Nick's increasing nakedness to distract him.

Nick had lifted his shirt up, exposing a stomach that Sebastian wanted to lick things off, and with one hand he unzipped his jeans. He barely had to touch the zipper to get it down. The pressure from his cock must've been something else. Sebastian couldn't wait to feel it for himself.

Meeting Sebastian's eyes, Nick worked his jeans and boxers down much too slowly for Sebastian's taste. Though he had to admit, the tension that built in the air with every new inch of exposed, golden skin was breathtaking.

He managed to get his own pants pushed down. The urge to touch himself was overwhelming. When Nick finally freed his cock, Sebastian's mouth actually watered. It was perfect: not too huge, a shade ruddier than his tan skin, and heavy looking in a way that made Sebastian want it on his tongue.

"Damn," he said without thinking, eyes flicking up and down Nick's body before settling on his face, "you're gorgeous."

Nick let out a tight breath. "You should see the view from where I'm sitting." He trailed a hand down Sebastian's chest. "If I'd had more time with that neck of yours, I would have left some marks to remember me by."

His cock twitched, and as close as it was to Nick's, Sebastian imagined it was trying to bring them together. Nick seemed to have the same idea, because he spread his legs as far as his jeans would let him and situated himself astride Sebastian's hips, groin to groin. Then he aligned their cocks and wrapped one hand around them both.

The first touch was *heaven*. Exquisite to the point of near pain. Nick's skin was warm silk, firm but oh-so-soft. He stroked them once from base to head, and as his hand moved, a shiver visibly worked its way through him. It was one of the most thoroughly erotic things Sebastian had ever seen.

He had lube in his bedside table, but he was too mesmerized by the sight of Nick to move. Nick was staring down at them, thighs tense, one hand clutching his own shirt, which was pushed up to his ribs. The abs that formed every time he clenched his stomach muscles made Sebastian weak. Nick stroked their cocks again, and this time, blond eyelashes fluttered down over his beautiful eyes.

Sebastian decided it was time for him to take things up a notch. He spat on his palm and added his hand to the mix. As soon as Nick felt Sebastian's fingers, he moaned and let his hand fall to the side, tilting his head back. With his eyes closed and his bottom lip caught between his teeth, he looked like he was trying to absorb every sensation.

Long fingers wrapped around them, Sebastian gave their cocks a firm pump, then spat on his hand again and repeated the motion. The slickness was exactly what they needed to take this from good to incredible. Sebastian's fingers slid with ease, wringing little moans from them both.

Sebastian wanted to draw this out, savor it, but the noise from the party on the other side of the door served as a reminder that they needed to be fast. He moved the way he did when he was getting himself off: quick and loose with a little squeeze when he reached the head. Nick seemed to eat it up, judging by the honeyed sounds that poured from him in time with Sebastian's hand.

Honestly, Sebastian felt like he could come from that alone, but then Nick made a strangled noise.

"Fuck, Seb." His breathing was ragged. "So good. Can I— I need—"

Sebastian nodded, too far gone for words.

Nick moved his hips in time with Sebastian's strokes. Nothing but little rocking motions at first, but as they fell into a rhythm, his motions grew more confident.

Sebastian swore under his breath and tried to hold on. Nick had felt amazing nudged up against him before, but now with sweat, pre-come, and his thrusts in the mix, Sebastian was seeing stars. He gripped one of Nick's thighs and concentrated on keeping his rhythm, but with Nick on top of him, practically riding him, it was impossible to think.

The moaning wasn't helping either. Nick hadn't been kidding when he said he wasn't quiet. It wasn't the volume so much as the deep, wanting quality his voice took on. Sebastian swore he could almost hear Nick getting close.

His own orgasm was looming over him. When Nick leaned down for a sloppy kiss—all desire and no coordination—it was almost too much.

The closer Nick got, the less room Sebastian had to maneuver. He released their dicks and gripped Nick's hips, letting him move how he wanted to. And Nick did, sliding their cocks together with single-minded purpose. The clumsy desperation behind every motion made it hard for Sebastian to breathe. This was so like penetrative sex—all thrusting and slick bodies—but the pleasure was vastly different. Shallower, but needy. Immediate.

Nick's groans were getting louder, too loud. Sebastian covered Nick's mouth with his. If he didn't, someone was going to hear them for sure.

Goddamn. If this is how he reacts to a little frottage, I can't wait to get him naked.

"Seb, I'm close." Nick spoke against his mouth, murmuring despite how loud he was being otherwise.

"Me too." Sebastian had been on the edge for what felt like years. The tension mounting in him was unbearable. He was going to burst if something didn't give soon, and Nick was *everywhere*. On top of him. All around him. The smell of his sweat and whatever soap Nick used was in Sebastian's nose, the taste of his skin on Sebastian's tongue. He was drowning, and he never wanted it to stop.

Nick made a noise that was part gasp and part sob and started moving faster. "Seb, I—" A tremor worked through his whole body. "Oh God, I want to— You—"

All Sebastian did was slide a hand down Nick's back and grab a handful of his ass, and Nick came unraveled. He thrust hard against Sebastian a few more times before he came to a shuddering halt. Despite his earlier noise, his orgasm was silent, right up until the end, when he made the smallest, most broken sound and breathed, "Christ, *Seb*."

Sebastian had held on until then, but at his name, he fell apart. He shoved a hand between them and barely touched his cock before he orgasmed with such force, the room went black.

He babbled jumbled syllables that might've been Nick's name, if it'd been fed through a paper shredder and then glued back together at random. The heel of his hand found its way into his mouth, and he bit the hell out of it in his attempt to keep quiet. And all the while, pleasure worked through him, deep and sharp.

When it was over, Sebastian fell back against the bed, boneless and panting, eyes closed. The mattress depressed next to him, presumably from Nick's limp body. Sebastian had no idea how long they lay there, but when his heart rate returned to a semblance of normalcy, he forced an eye open.

Nick was, in fact, lying on his side next to Sebastian, eyes lidded and his mouth slack as he breathed deeply. Sebastian was rendered momentarily speechless from watching him: sweaty and disheveled and . . . gorgeous.

After a second, however, Sebastian shifted, and his attention diverted to his sticky clothes. And body. And pretty much everything. No amount of cleaning up could hide what they'd done.

"Fuck," he said to himself without emotion.

Nick jolted up next to him. "Are you okay?"

Sebastian lolled his head toward him. "I'm great. Why?"

Nick looked him up and down, as if checking for signs of trauma. "You swear? Should we not have done this?" He reached out like he was going to touch Sebastian's face, but he stopped shy of it, hand hovering uncertainly.

Sebastian snorted. "You're adorable. Everything's fine, I swear. Better than fine, actually. That was . . ." He blew out a breath. "Yeah. I feel *great*."

Nick relaxed infinitesimally. "No regrets?"

"I regret not taking our clothes all the way off. I was too caught up in the moment to think it through." He gestured to his jeans, which were sporting an impressive assortment of fluids. "Now we're going to have to change."

Nick glanced down at himself. His clothing hadn't ended up much better. "Oh shit. I didn't consider that."

"Don't worry about it." Sebastian grinned. "You were a little preoccupied, what with humping me and all."

Nick's face turned red in a blink, like a flash sunburn. "Sorry. I got a little carried away."

"No need to apologize. A little frottage never hurt anyone. And I meant it when I said I feel great. I've never . . ." He chewed on his lip.

"What?"

Sebastian debated with himself before looking Nick in the eyes. "It's never been like this before. Sex, I mean. After, I usually can't wait to shower and kick the guy out. But now, I'm considering ditching my own party and staying in here all night with you."

Nick's flush deepened. "Since when are you so sentimental?"

"I guess you bring it out in me. What was with you calling me *Seb*, by the way? You never call me that."

Nick laughed. "I hate to break this to you, babe, but your name so doesn't pass the can-you-moan-it-in-bed test."

Sebastian squawked. "It does so!"

"Uh, no. Way too many syllables, and I really didn't want to start picturing the singing crab in the middle of sex."

In lieu of a response, Sebastian grabbed one of his pillows and hit Nick square in the face with it. Nick toppled over like a Jenga tower and giggled. Sebastian scrambled on top of him and pretended to press the pillow over his face. Nick's muffled laughter continued, and then he flipped Sebastian over, grabbed the pillow, and tossed it away.

Sebastian snorted as well. Although, when he realized they were both still partially undressed and were now in the same position they'd been in a minute ago, his mirth died in his throat.

Nick's expression sobered too, as if he'd realized the same thing. Slowly, he put a hand on either side of Sebastian's head. He leaned down, and it seemed as if he was going to kiss Sebastian.

At first, Sebastian thought nothing of it, but then icy understanding swept over him.

If he kisses me, I win the bet. I'd almost forgotten about it.

Sebastian thought back on their sex. Had there really been no point whatsoever in which Nick had kissed him first? Sebastian raced through his own memories and came up blank. Nick had kissed his face and his neck, but at no point had he initiated an on-the-lips kiss. Fucking technicalities.

How much do I still care about the bet honestly? Should I come clean right now, or let this happen and beg for forgiveness later? Is it already too late? But we just had sex. That would be the worst timing ever. I could lose Nick and the trophy. The hunk of plastic that has no value to anyone but me. The thing that started it all.

The idea was paralyzing. Before Sebastian could decide what to do, Nick stopped his slow descent, eyes studying Sebastian's face from inches away. "We need to get out of this room, or we really will be in here all night. Fun as that sounds, you can't disappear from your own party."

Sebastian nodded. "You gotta get off me, then."

Nick did, rolling off the bed and standing up. He pulled his jeans up but didn't button them. "Can I borrow some clothes? Maybe some sweats, since you're skinnier than I am?"

"Everyone's going to notice the wardrobe change." But Sebastian pointed to a drawer in his bureau anyway.

"We've been in here for like half an hour. There's no saving face now." As Nick dug through Sebastian's drawer, he sighed. "I'll deal with it somehow."

"Is it really so bad? Having people know we're a thing?"

Nick shrugged without looking at him. "Seems a little fast to me, is all. But it's going to depend on how things turn out."

Misery threaded itself through every inch of Sebastian. Not because Nick still doubted him, but because he had every right to. Sebastian had never regretted keeping a secret from someone so much in his life. When he told Nick the truth, what then? Would this be over right as things were looking up?

Words tingled on the tip of Sebastian's tongue, but he held back. He moved over to the closet to get some distance, both physical and mental. *Nick's been through enough. I don't want to ruin his night any more than I already have. We'll go back to the party, we'll enjoy this time together, and then tomorrow, I'll deal with this mess I've made.*

He pulled on clean jeans—*not* skinny jeans—along with a black shirt. As he stripped, he made no move to cover himself. Nick was silent behind him, but Sebastian could feel his eyes on him as he got down to his underwear, threw the messy clothes in his hamper, and then yanked on the new ones.

Under other circumstances, it probably would have been hot, having Nick watch him. Sebastian might have even done a little striptease for him. But right now, it made him feel vulnerable. Exposed. He dressed as quickly as he could without tripping himself and then turned around. "Ready?"

Nick nodded. "After you."

Sebastian unlocked the door, and they emerged from his room. Sebastian almost told Nick to wait a few minutes before following after him, but Nick was right. That ship had sailed.

The party was precisely as they'd left it. People were dancing, and liquor was flowing. The door to the balcony was open. A deluge of people had spilled out onto it.

No one paid them any mind as they emerged. Sebastian found his drink where he'd left it on a table. It was way watered down now, but he took a big gulp anyway.

Nick appeared next to him a moment later. He glanced at his own cup only to frown. "Is it cool if I make a new drink?"

"Help yourself." Sebastian smacked his lips. "Actually, I'm coming with you."

They made it halfway to the dining room before Dante and Theo appeared in front of them. Judging by the sweat on both their brows, they'd been on the dance floor.

"There you guys are." Theo fell into step beside Nick. "I was worried about you when you stormed off. I thought maybe you'd killed Sebby and then climbed out a window. If you'd run away to Mexico without me, I'd be really hurt."

Sebastian sighed. "Don't call me Sebby."

Dante gave them a once-over and whistled. "Lookin' a little worse for the wear, Seb. Were you guys fighting or fu—"

Theo elbowed him in the side, and he fell silent.

Red in the face once more, Nick cleared his throat. "We're about to freshen up or drinks. You want anything?"

"Nah." Theo shrugged. "I did tequila shots a minute ago with this girl I've never seen before. I don't think she goes to our school. Anyway, that's going to kick in any second now, so I'm gonna get back on the dance floor." He spun around and held a hand out to Dante with a dramatic flourish. "Dance with me."

Dante rolled his eyes, but he was grinning as he leaned closer to Sebastian. "I swear, just as I thought he was sobering up. If he does another Tarzan yell, someone's gonna fall off the balcony and die."

They disappeared into the crowd, which was thinning as the night wore on. Nick led the way to the dining room, where they made new drinks. After, they stood on the threshold of the living room, an unspoken question hanging between them.

Now what?

Sebastian was mentally scratching his head when Nick solved his problem.

"You don't have to spend the whole night with me, you know." Nick glanced at him. "I didn't mean to commandeer you for so long. I'm sure there are people you'd like to talk to."

"Actually, everyone I want to talk to is right here."

Nick indicated a sofa on the far wall. "Sit with me?"

The couches were free of people for once. It was the closest they could get to privacy without locking themselves in a room again.

Sebastian nodded and held out a hand, indicating that Nick should go first. To his surprise, Nick took his hand and tugged Sebastian along behind him.

Sebastian's heart leaped up into his throat. "You sure you want to hold hands with me in front of everyone?"

Nick looked over his shoulder at him. "The damage is done, remember? No sense in pretending anymore."

They took seats next to each other on the sofa. Nick sat with his leg on the cushion, turned to face Sebastian. He took a sip of his drink before setting it on the coffee table. "So."

"So." Sebastian took a gulp of his own to wet his dry mouth and calm his nerves. "There's something I want to ask you. Actually, there are a couple of things."

"Should I be nervous?"

"No, but I sure as hell am." Another drink, and then Sebastian set his cup down as well. He squared his shoulders toward Nick. "You remember why I wanted you to come here tonight, right?"

Nick nodded. "You wanted to show me the real you."

"Have I done that?" Sebastian held his breath.

There was the briefest of pauses. "You have. And for the record, I like the person you've shown me tonight."

Air left Sebastian's lungs in a *whoosh* that he hoped only he could hear. "That's a relief." It really was. Maybe this situation wasn't as hopeless as he feared. All he needed to do was magically get his shit together and figure out what he wanted. Easy enough, right?

The latter bit was what was tripping him up. What did he really, truly want? He liked Nick—that much had been undeniable from day one—but did Sebastian like him enough to change who he was? To give up single life and alter his whole philosophy on love? To forfeit Barbzilla, the representation of his only happy childhood memories? Terrifyingly enough, after two short weeks, Sebastian suspected the answer was yes. If only he had more *time* to figure all this out, to come up with a plan. Nick had been suspicious of him from the start, and if he didn't find some way to spin this . . .

Oblivious to his inner turmoil, Nick fiddled with the drawstrings on the sweats Sebastian had given him. "I owe you an apology."

The statement surprised Sebastian from his thoughts. "For what?"

"Making assumptions about you, and everyone at the Academy, really. I let my bitterness at my own circumstances color my first impressions. I'm no better than the people who spread gossip without caring if it's true."

"No way. And to be fair, it's not like your assumptions were all wrong. There are people at the Academy who fit the 'rich kid' stereotype. They grew up knowing they would go to college one day, and that it would be paid for. When they graduate, they're going straight to work at their parents' companies. They'll never know what it's like to job hunt or be unemployed. They're the same tools who say shit like 'dress for the job you want' and 'pound the pavement.'"

Nick laughed. "I see. So, you forgive me?"

"I do." *Tomorrow, will you be able to forgive me?*

"Thanks for that." Nick chewed on his lip. "You said there was something else you wanted to ask me?"

"Yeah." Sebastian surveyed his apartment. Midnight had come and gone, and now there were only a dozen or so people left, including Dante and Theo. Pretty soon, they'd be alone, unless Nick decided to leave. If Sebastian wanted to prevent that—and he very much did—he needed to act fast.

It's now or never, Prinsen.

He took a breath. "Before I say anything, I want you to know that no matter what you decide, you won't hurt my feelings."

"All right. Now I'm nervous. Ask me already."

Sebastian steeled himself. "Nick, will you spend the night with me?"

Nick's eyes widened. He didn't answer right away, which prompted Sebastian to babble.

"Nothing has to happen. In fact, I plan to do some more drinking after this, so nothing *can* happen, but I want you to stay over. We can talk in the morning, and honestly, I don't want to be apart from you. Which is really weird for me, by the way. But again, whatever you decide is fine. If you want to go home, I'll call you a cab. It's totally up to you."

Sebastian must've sounded as nervous as he felt, because Nick chuckled. He reached out and took one of Sebastian's hands. "I'd love to spend the night. I was actually dying to ask if I could, but I didn't want to be presumptuous."

Sebastian's heart skipped a beat. "Really? You were?"

"Yeah. When you hit me with that pillow before, my first thought was 'Ooh, is this goose down?' I definitely want to take those babies for a spin."

Sebastian shoved him playfully, Nick shoved him back, and the next thing he knew, they were pseudo-wrestling on the sofa. Things were seconds away from becoming heated when someone coughed next to them.

Simultaneously, they looked to the right and found Dante observing them from a few feet away, a hand clapped to his mouth as he tried and failed to smother laughter.

"Wow, you kids are so gosh-darned cute." He giggled. "Sorry to interrupt, but I gotta jet. It's nearly one, and as much as I'd love to stay, I have to be up for Mass in the morning."

Sebastian disentangled himself from Nick with reluctance. "I can't believe you still keep up the pretense of going to the chapel on campus."

"Hey, some of us take the Lord's word very seriously." Dante downed the drink in his hand and plunked the empty glass on the coffee table. "Don't worry. That was water. I stopped drinking a couple of hours ago."

"How are you getting back to campus? Need me to call you a cab?"

"Nah, I'm okay to drive. I'm going to take Theo's drunk ass home." He jabbed a thumb over his shoulder at where Theo was talking to the remaining people in the living room, whom Sebastian recognized as the guys who lived down the hall. "I'll try to get some water in him before he passes out. Wish me luck."

The neighbors broke away from Theo a moment later and waved goodbye as they headed for the door. Sebastian waved back and shouted something performative about doing this again soon, but his focus was on Theo, Dante, and Nick. The final countdown.

Finished with his conversation, Theo wandered over. He stopped next to Dante and smiled knowingly at Nick. "You need a ride home too? We're headed your way."

Sebastian groaned inside his head. *Theo is so going to pay for that later.*

Nick coughed. "Uh, no, thanks. I'm going to stay for, um, a bit longer."

"Uh-huh." Dante winked. "Get Sebastian to make you French toast in the morning. It's his specialty."

"What's that one charming phrase?" Sebastian tapped his chin. "Oh yeah. It's 'Get out of my house.'"

Theo laughed. "It seems we've overstayed our welcome. C'mon, Dante." He headed for the front door.

Dante followed after, still grinning. "See you guys later."

They disappeared, leaving Nick and Sebastian finally alone.

Nick turned to Sebastian on the couch. "You tired?"

"No. You?"

"No."

There was a pause. Sebastian wet his lips. "You know one thing we could do to wear ourselves out?"

Nick's eyes widened. "Build a fort out of couch cushions?"

Sebastian, who was reaching for his drink, laughed so hard he couldn't hold it. Nick joined him, and together they giggled like kids until Sebastian was out of breath.

"Come on." He climbed to his feet. "Grab your drink. I have an idea."

He led the way back to his bedroom. He listened for the sound of feet following behind him and didn't relax until he heard Nick shuffle in. Then Sebastian made a beeline for the wardrobe across from his bed.

"Um, Sebastian?" Nick was standing in the doorway, looking curious. "When you said we weren't going to have sex tonight . . ."

"I meant it." Sebastian held up his drink and took a big gulp. "See? I may not have been drunk before, but I definitely am now. No more sex."

"Okay, I was just checking." It might've been Sebastian's imagination, but he thought Nick looked both relieved and disappointed as he kicked off his shoes and plopped onto Sebastian's bed, cross-legged. "So, what's the plan?"

Sebastian opened the wardrobe, revealing a flat-screen TV. "I thought we'd watch a movie until we fall asleep." He yanked on one of the bottom drawers, which was loaded with DVDs. "Sound good?"

"Hm, watching a movie and cuddling on a Friday night. That sounds . . . domestic." Nick grinned. "I like it."

They picked some action flick. Sebastian put it on, and after changing into sleep clothes similar to what he'd given Nick, he settled into bed. They pretended to sip their drinks and maintain some space between them for a solid ten minutes before Nick finally cracked and snuggled up to his side.

Sebastian piled pillows around them and covered them with blankets. Soon, even the movie's explosions couldn't keep his eyes from closing. Nick's head was on his shoulder, and with every breath, he could smell Nick's hair. Just as Sebastian was drifting off, Nick spoke.

"I've realized something."

Sebastian leaned back so he could glance at Nick. "What?"

Instead of looking at him, Nick tilted his head back. His eyes landed on the painting of Chicago above Sebastian's bed. "Did you paint that?"

"I did. After spending a week there one summer with my mom. One of my few fond memories from high school. Why?"

Nick was silent for a long moment. "The day we met, your eyes were the first thing I noticed about you."

Sebastian wasn't exactly tracking this conversation, but he suspected Nick had a point. "I get that a lot."

"I really mean it, though." Nick yawned and laid his head back down on Sebastian's chest. "This is silly, but your eyes reminded me of something. I couldn't think of what until I saw that painting. I loved growing up in Chicago. The city comes alive in the summer, but in my head, it's always winter there. Icy and stark, with steely skies that make the skyscrapers blend into the clouds.

"On the coldest days, when the streets were slick with sleet, and the wind was so harsh it burned, my dad would tell me knock-knock jokes to distract me. The worse the joke, the better." Nick's voice got quiet. "When I first looked at you, I saw Chicago. I saw home."

Sebastian was breathless. He'd never been so disappointed that he couldn't see someone's face. His first instinct was to tease Nick to diffuse the tension—call him cheesy or something—but he couldn't do it. That was possibly the most romantic thing anyone had ever said to him. Despite lying perfectly still, his heart was pounding.

He struggled to think of something to say back, but no words came. He waited so long, Nick must've drifted off, because he heard the deep sound of his breathing over the TV.

Sebastian ended up snuggling closer to him, kissing the top of his head, and closing his eyes, though it was a long time before his racing pulse allowed him to sleep.

Chapter Fifteen

Nick woke the next morning to sunshine heating his face. He opened his eyes gently, anticipating a hangover, and blinked the room into focus. It was much the same as last night, though thanks to the strong light pouring through the windows, Nick noticed details he hadn't seen before: discarded shoes next to the closet, textbooks piled on the bureau, and single framed photo that was too far away for him to make out the subject.

Sebastian was cuddled up to his side, eyes closed, his chest rising and falling evenly. In repose, his face was soft. He looked peaceful in a way he seldom did when he was awake. Or at least, when he was around Nick. Their interactions were always so . . . charged.

Watching him sleep, Nick experienced an odd clash of emotions. Affection. Anticipation. Little hints of regret. Much as he wanted to lie back down in this warm bed and pretend everything was fine, he couldn't.

When he agreed to go to Sebastian's party, he'd had no idea how much would change. He'd meant what he'd said last night: he liked the person Sebastian was when he dropped the act. But in the span of one afternoon, they'd argued, made up, argued again, and were now in some weird purgatory where they weren't *dating*, but they were definitely *something*.

Nick almost wanted to grab his clothes and sneak out so he could have some time to think before he talked to Sebastian again. There was so much to process. So much had happened in such a short time. There was no denying one thing, though. Somewhere along the way, Nick had begun to have feelings for Sebastian.

That should have been a good thing, or just another part of life. Dating. Falling in love. Under normal circumstances, those things weren't complicated. In Nick's case, they were too frightening for words.

After the emotional turmoil of the last year—the grief and upheaval and the loss of everything he knew—he didn't think he could handle the thing that sometimes came after falling in love: heartbreak. He was still in such a fragile place, and his relationship with Sebastian was undeniably tumultuous.

He'd let himself get swept up in the party and the excitement and Sebastian's charm. He hadn't asked himself an important question: Did he trust Sebastian not to hurt him?

I wish I had more time to think.

Extricating himself from the bed, Nick tiptoed to Sebastian's bathroom and slipped inside, closing the door as quietly behind him as he could. He went through his usual morning routine, skipping showering in favor of washing his face. He borrowed Sebastian's deodorant and rubbed some toothpaste on his tongue. It was about as fresh as he was going to get in someone else's bathroom.

When he'd finished, he glanced at his reflection. He looked like a different person, partially thanks to the fact that he was wearing Sebastian's clothes. His eyes were tired as they looked back at him. They reminded him of that first car ride to the Academy, what felt like years ago.

Why couldn't this have been simple? Why couldn't I have met someone and fallen in love and had this one thing in my life that wasn't a struggle? Dad, I wish I could talk to you. You'd know what to do.

With a sigh, Nick crept back into the bedroom. Sebastian was still sleeping. Nick scrounged around for his clothes, brought them into the bathroom with him, and cleaned them as best he could with a damp washcloth. Then he put them on, leaving Sebastian's sweats folded on the counter. After that, there was nothing left to do but pluck up his courage, wake Sebastian, and see how things went.

Despite his trepidation, as Nick approached the bed, he smiled at the sight of Sebastian. Curled up in the sheets—his pale skin stark against them, and his hair splayed softly across his pillow—he looked like a black-and-white photograph.

Miraculously, the shifting mattress didn't wake Sebastian as Nick knelt next to him. Sebastian made a small, content noise, but his eyes stayed shut. Emotions swirled in Nick, from fondness to wariness, contributing to his increasing heart rate.

It didn't seem right to shake Sebastian awake after an intimate night of cuddling, so Nick went for a subtler approach. Bending down, Nick brushed his lips along the curve of Sebastian's face until he reached his mouth. Then, he planted a gentle but firm kiss directly on his lips.

Despite how soundly Sebastian had been sleeping before, at the touch, he shifted. He kissed Nick back without opening his eyes. "Mmm."

Nick pulled away. "Morning."

"Morning." Sebastian rubbed his eyes with one hand, a smile creeping over his lips. "Can I hire you to be my alarm clock?"

Nick laughed. "I'd be worried about some sort Pavlovian response. What if you jolted awake every time I kissed you?"

As if cued by his words, Sebastian jerked his head up. "What?"

"Nothing, not my best joke. Do you want to get some breakfast?"

"You kissed me." Sebastian touched his lips. His eyes were wide and wild as they stared at him. "*You* kissed *me*." His tone suggested Nick had committed some kind of crime.

Nick gave him a once-over. "We've kissed plenty of times."

"No, I've kissed *you* plenty of times. You've never initiated before."

Nick furrowed his brow. "Sebastian, I don't think—"

Sebastian crawled backward on the bed until he was as far from Nick as he could get. "Nick, I am so, *so* sorry."

"For what?"

"Everything."

Sebastian's thoughts buzzed like an upended hive. He didn't think he'd ever woken up so quickly or thoroughly before.

I won the bet. I won Barbzilla. This whole thing can end right here and now, and then—and then—

And then what? What was his next move?

"Sebastian?"

Nick was staring at him like he'd announced he intended to give up worldly possessions and become a monk, and Sebastian couldn't blame him. This all must be so confusing. Hell, Sebastian was confused, and this whole convoluted plot was his doing.

After all the times he could have kissed me and didn't, why'd he have to do it now? Before I could come up with a plan?

The easiest thing to do would be to tell him the truth—in its entirety, starting from the day they met—right now, and let the chips fall where they may. But that would also be the hardest thing to do.

From the beginning, Nick had rejected every show of insincerity Sebastian had made. If Sebastian told Nick this had started as a bet, he'd lose him forever. Nick would never speak to him again, and everything they'd been through, the foundation they'd begun to build, would crumble away. Nick would never trust him again. He might even hate Sebastian, and Sebastian would have no one to blame but himself.

What else could he do, then? Never tell Nick about the bet? Take that secret to the *grave*? Mentally, Sebastian shook his head. There was no way. Not only was that reprehensible, but Theo would never allow it. He considered Nick a friend. He'd tell him the truth, and then Nick would *really* hate him. For the lie, and for not having the decency to tell Nick himself.

God, I am so fucked. Every chance I had to do the right thing, I ignored it, and now I'm out of chances. I set myself up to fail from the start. If only I'd somehow known the random new kid was going to turn out to be . . . to be . . .

Sebastian's eyes stung. A little choked sound escaped from his throat before he could stop it.

"Sebastian?" Nick moved closer, lifting a hand to touch him. "Are you okay? You're starting to freak me out."

Sebastian turned his back on him. He couldn't look at Nick right now. "Hold on for a second. I have to . . . I have to think about something."

It was decision time. Options scrolled through his head at light speed. If he was fucked anyway, he could do it thoroughly and choose Barbzilla. He could call Theo right now and claim his prize.

Nick would hear him and figure out what was going on, and he'd hate Sebastian forever. Sebastian labeled that plan C.

He could tell Nick the truth and then beg for forgiveness. There was a chance Nick would forgive him, but it was so slim it was translucent. That was plan B, then.

What if he called off the bet? Theo and Dante had offered to let him out of it before. They might agree to that again if he explained. Sebastian could turn back around, blame his weirdness on a lingering nightmare, and make Nick French toast before coaxing him back into bed. They could start over. Date. Be happy.

But no, that would be the same as never telling Nick about it. He couldn't pretend for the rest of his life.

The rest of your life. Is that how long you want to be with Nick?

Holy shit, he was the world's biggest fuckup. He'd lived up to his heartbreaker reputation yet again. This was who he was. The party guy who'd never been in love before, the one who used men and then tossed them away. The emotionally stunted asshole who knew nothing about love, and it was obvious to everyone who met him.

How had he ever thought he could do this? Be in a normal, healthy relationship with a guy he genuinely cared for? Of course he'd fucked it up. That was all he ever did.

Maybe this is for the best. If it wasn't the bet, it would have been something else. You would have found another way to ruin things. You don't know how to be in a relationship. It's better this is ending now, before things got serious.

At least he'd get Barbzilla out of this. With perfect clarity, he understood that the trophy had no real-world value whatsoever. But to Sebastian, it meant something. It meant he came from somewhere.

When the house he grew up in became someone else's house, and he graduated from college and moved away, and Theo and Dante had their own lives going on—the only people who'd loved him no matter how badly he fucked up—at least he'd have that. Proof that there had been a time when he'd had a family. When he'd looked forward with hope instead of back with regret.

Nick was mercifully quiet as Sebastian muddled his way through this paradigm shift. Coldness washed over him as a plan A began to take shape in his head, stealing bits and pieces from the others

and cobbling them together. It was a mangled horror worthy of
Dr. Frankenstein, but it was what Sebastian had to do.

He'd tell Nick what he needed to hear.

Swinging his legs over the edge of the bed, he plucked his phone
off the nightstand and found Theo's name in his contacts. It only rang
twice before Theo answered.

"Hey, Sebby. What's up?"

For the first time in Sebastian's life, he didn't correct him.

"I won." His voice cracked. "I won the bet. I got Nick to kiss me."

"What?" Theo sounded both confused and horrified. He said
something else, but Sebastian's ears were ringing.

He cleared his throat. "I'll drop by your dorm to pick up Barbzilla
on Monday before class. We can talk then." He hung up the phone.

Silence followed in the wake of the call. Sebastian became
hyperaware of the lack of motion behind him. Perhaps Nick was
frozen with shock. Perhaps he was processing, trying to fit the pieces
of the conversation into a picture that made sense.

This was it. The moment of truth.

"Theo, Dante, and I made a bet at the beginning of the year."
Sebastian didn't look behind him as he talked. "It was an old favorite
of ours from high school. Since we've known pretty much all our
classmates since grade school, whenever there was an interesting new
kid, we'd bet to see who could kiss him first. It sounds childish, I know,
but we were bored, and you know what they say: kids are mean."

He paused, praying Nick would interrupt so he could stop. Nick
didn't. There was no sound from behind him whatsoever.

Sebastian continued. "As I'm sure you've figured out by now, you
were the subject of our bet. It wasn't enough for me to kiss you, though.
You had to initiate. I had to make you want to kiss me. That's why I
approached you that first day. That's why I pursued you so relentlessly.
I would have done anything to win, and now I have."

There were ways Sebastian could explain this that would make
him sound less terrible. He knew there were, and yet he wasn't using
them. If anything, he was going out of his way to play up the awfulness
of it. Why?

*Because you deserve this. After everything you've done, you deserve to
have Nick hate you forever.*

He took a breath. "You saw through me from the beginning, and instead of letting it go, I did everything I could to get you to like me. I told you things about me that I've never told anyone. But it wasn't real. It was all because I wanted to win the bet. I lied to you so many times and in so many ways. I can't ask you to forgive me or to trust me ever again."

His throat tightened on that last sentence. He was horrified to realize he was close to tears. Thank God his back was turned to Nick. If he looked at him right now and saw whatever combination of anger, betrayal, and pain that was surely on his face, he'd lose it.

His confession was followed by several long seconds of silence that ticked by in Sebastian's head like a doomsday clock. With each one that passed, he grew more tense, like he could snap at any second. Hurt and bitter anger, all directed at himself, bubbled in his stomach.

Eventually, he cracked. "Please say something."

There was another interminable pause. And then Nick's steady voice replied, "I have nothing to say to you."

Somehow, that felt more final than all the condemnations in the world. Sebastian resolved to do one final selfish thing: deprive Nick of the chance to scream at him.

"Please go." Sebastian waved over his shoulder in the direction of his door. "Get your things and go."

He expected Nick to put up a fight, but to his surprise, he heard shuffling. Nick's weight rose up off the mattress, footsteps walked to the door, and then the hinges creaked as they opened and closed again, followed by a *click* that might as well have been a gunshot.

For a long time afterward—Sebastian didn't know how long— he stayed sitting on the edge of his bed, feet on the cool wood floor along with his eyes. His mind was blank except for one thought that repeated over and over.

He didn't even care enough to say anything. He had you figured out from the start.

Theo took a bite of eggs and moaned. "Oh my God, this place is amazing."

"Glad you approve." A smile tugged at Dante's lips as he watched him devour an impressive bacon omelet. He had a plate of eggs in front of him as well, but his were scrambled with a side of fresh fruit. He hadn't overdone it as badly as Theo had last night, so he didn't need the extra grease.

A cool morning breeze swept through the outdoor patio of Dante's favorite breakfast place. It was a block from campus, and several Academy students were seated around them, eating what were clearly their own hangover cures.

Leaves swirled in the wind. In autumn, they'd form tiny dervishes that flashed red and gold. Watching them was almost as much fun as hunting down the crunchy ones while he walked to class.

"Something on your mind?"

He glanced up.

Theo was studying him from across their table for two. His green eyes were gold in the light and currently hanging shamelessly around Dante's mouth.

He grinned. "I might ask you the same thing. See something you like?"

Theo swallowed, and his eyes found their way back up to Dante's. "Sorry. I was just, uh, thinking about last night."

"Before or after you ended up coming home with me? Feel free to be specific."

Smiling, Theo looked down at his plate. "I was actually talking about the *party*."

He's cute when he's shy. I shouldn't tease him ... but I'm going to.

"Oh, right. I keep forgetting about the party, considering the after-party was so much more fun." Dante flashed the thousand-watt smile that he knew made Theo weak. "You were so cute when you insisted you wanted to hang out more only to immediately pass out on my couch. But my *favorite* part was when you woke me up climbing into bed with me this morning."

Theo's cheeks filled with color, but when he glanced up, he was grinning. "That's the best way to wake up, yeah?"

"Yup, and long overdue." Dante steeled himself. "We should talk about what this means. I've been joking about it so you don't spook and bolt or anything, but this morning . . . It meant everything to me, Theo."

Theo set his hand on top of Dante's where it was resting on the table. "I'm not going to spook. If anything, I'm worried about you. You're the one who's had to hide who you are all this time. I was starting to think this was never going to happen for us. I was so happy being your friend, I'd almost convinced myself I didn't need anything more."

Dante shook his head. "I should have come out a long time ago. I shouldn't have let what my family thinks stop me for a second. And most of all, I should have told you how I felt sooner. But we were friends, and we had Seb to think about—"

"And it was all so complicated. I get it. For the record, I could have been more upfront about my feelings too. Now that we're here, though, I want you to know I'm in this."

"I'm in this too." Dante squeezed his hand. "So long as you'll have me."

"Okay." Theo smiled. "But seriously, about last night. Do you think our plan worked?"

"It's so hard to care about Seb's drama right now, but all right." Dante dutifully turned off the charm and pondered his question, lips pressed together. "Yes and no. The make-Seb-jealous bit definitely got him to acknowledge his feelings, and it was a great sign that Nick was at the party, but I don't know if it's enough. Last we talked to Sebastian, he was still determined to win the bet, and Nick only recently defrosted toward him. One wrong move, and the whole thing could topple."

"You worry too much. I'm sure once they both realize their feelings aren't going away, they'll be adults about it, have an honest conversation, and everything will work out fine."

Theo's phone buzzed on the table. He ignored it, until it buzzed again, indicating that someone was calling him. "Sorry about this." He glanced at the screen. "It's Sebastian. Speak of the devil."

"He might be calling to tell you that Nick spent the night, as if we don't already know." Dante grabbed a spoon and went for his fruit. "Go ahead and pick it up. If he starts to gush, I can tease him about it until one of us dies. And if he's the one to go, I'll get a Ouija board."

Chuckling, Theo accepted the call. "Hey, Sebby. What's up?"

He must've put it on speaker, because Dante heard Sebastian loud and clear.

"I won. I won the bet. I got Nick to kiss me."

Theo, who was halfway to taking another bite of eggs, dropped his fork with a clatter. "What?"

There was a pause. Sebastian sounded like he was taking a deep breath.

"Sebastian, no." Theo's voice was panicked. "What did you do?"

"I'll drop by your dorm to pick up Barbzilla on Monday before class. We can talk then."

The line went dead. Theo held the phone up and stared at it, as if expecting it to continue the conversation.

Dante looked between him and it in rapid succession. "What the hell was that?"

"That was Sebastian claiming his victory. As in, he still cares about the ridiculous bet. As in, our plan failed, and he and Nick aren't madly in love like we'd hoped."

Dante blew out a breath. "I knew he was in denial, but this is going way too far. And after they practically announced they were a couple in front of everyone. Do you suppose he told Nick the truth?"

"He'd better have, or I'm going to be pissed. Nick's my friend too."

It was surprising to hear an angry edge in Theo's airy voice. In a good way. Dante wasn't thrilled by this turn of events either. How could Sebastian insist on clinging to the bet when he had a real shot with Nick?

Reminds me how all my feet-dragging almost cost me Theo. I can't let Seb make the same mistake.

Out loud, Dante asked, "What should we do?"

Theo shrugged. "I was thinking go to Sebastian's apartment and slap some sense into him."

"Calm down, Tyson. You can't do that. Not because it's illegal—Sebastian would never be able to make the assault charges stick after my testimony—but because there's someone else who needs you more right now."

Theo exhaled hard. "Nick. I should talk to him. I wonder where he is."

Just then, Theo's phone buzzed again. At the same time, Dante's began to ring.

"It's a text from Nick," Theo said.

"It's a call from Sebastian," Dante replied.

They exchanged a look that Dante swore was as good as words. *Breakfast is officially canceled.*

"I'll talk to Sebastian." Dante stood up. "You go find Nick and see if he's okay."

Theo got up as well. "I will."

"Oh, and Theo?" Dante grinned. "I want to hear *everything*."

Theo smiled. He glanced down at the table. "Can I buy you breakfast?"

"No, I got it. Nick needs you. Go make sure he's okay."

"Has anyone ever told you how sweet you are?" Right then and there, Theo cradled Dante's face and kissed him. There was a moment when Dante panicked—they were in public; people could see them— but then the warmth of Theo's lips swept all his worries away. It was like the sunlight tickling his face, only it came from within. From one particular place in his chest, he suspected.

Dante kissed him back for good measure, letting the call go to voice mail. "*Go.* But maybe come over later?"

"You know it." He shook his head. "I can't imagine what Seb is thinking. Good thing I had that talk with Nick, or this would be a disaster. As it is, there's a chance we can salvage this if we can get Seb to come to his senses."

Dante crossed his fingers and dialed his phone. It only rang once before the line clicked. "Sebastian, you had better have a damn good explanation for this."

Sebastian said something in response, but Dante's eyes were on Theo as he walked away. Right before he would have disappeared around the corner, Theo turned back and looked at him. When their eyes met, he blew Dante a kiss before ducking out of sight.

Dante's face hurt, he was smiling so hard. Much as he wanted to be disappointed in Sebastian, he was having a hard time feeling anything other than pure, unadulterated happiness.

Chapter Sixteen

Two Weeks Earlier

"I'd like for us to be friends. For now."

Theo was sitting at a desk in Nick's dorm room, watching him process all the new information Theo had laid upon him. Though they'd only just met, Theo had gleaned a couple of things from their short conversation: Nick was smart, down-to-earth, and had been hurt in the past. It was all in his wary eyes and the way he skirted around talking about his life before now.

With every passing second, Theo was more and more convinced Nick and Sebastian were made for each other. Good thing too, because he'd come here with a very specific plan in mind.

"What's that supposed to mean?" Nick's expression was tense.

Theo waved him off. "Sorry. I've been told I have a talent for sounding unintentionally ominous. I mean I hope that one day we'll be *close* friends. Like best friends, you know?"

"Oh, okay." But Nick was still eying him with the wariness of a cornered mouse. "Why are you telling me all of this? I gotta admit, this is up there on the strange scale. Ever since I came here, I keep having the oddest conversations."

"It's like I said. I'm here to give you a warning and maybe make a friend. Nothing else, and certainly nothing sinister."

Nick looked adorably confused. "I'd like to be friends too, though your whole riddle-me-this schtick is making my head hurt."

"Which is why I'd like to tell you the truth." Theo sat back in his chair. "We made a bet about you."

Nick's brow furrowed. "What? Who?"

"My friends and me. Sebastian and Dante. We made a bet. It's this silly thing we started doing in high school after watching *Cruel Intentions* one too many times. We'd pick someone—usually a hot new boy—and bet to see who could kiss him first. Oh, but the guy has to initiate. That's what makes it a challenge: getting him to like you enough to do that."

Theo studied Nick's face. Was he going to get angry? Kick Theo out of his room? Theo hoped not, or his plan might be ruined before it began.

But Nick didn't do either of those things. He studied Theo right back. "Why are you telling me this?"

"Because the bet is shitty. It is and always has been cruel and mean-spirited. I don't want anyone to get hurt. Now that I've told you what's going on, you can't be caught unawares."

"I'm confused. If you think the bet is terrible, why participate?"

"That's where our new friendship comes in." Theo leaned forward in his chair. "I know I have no right to ask this of you, but I need a favor. Sebastian is going through some shit right now. Serious shit that none of the adults in his life are being very adult about. This bet is his way of . . . I dunno how to explain it. Lashing out? Getting some company for his misery? The point is, I'd like you to play along."

"Seriously? You want me to kiss Sebastian?"

"No, I want the opposite. Resist him. Resist him for as long as you can. Drag it out until you can't anymore."

Nick frowned. "But I could do that forever."

You think that, but you haven't met the real Sebastian yet. The guy I know and love. Once you two get to know each other, I don't think that'll be a problem anymore.

"If that's what you want, sure. Feel free to reject Sebastian over and over again. Just don't let him know you're onto him. Okay?"

Nick looked off to the side. "I dunno. That's a tall order. What's this subterfuge supposed to accomplish?"

"It's going to make Sebastian realize the bet is a mistake. He doesn't really want to hurt anyone, you see. He's looking for a distraction, and I think getting him to realize that on his own will be better in the long run. That, and his life is kind of a dumpster fire right now. He doesn't need his own best friends telling him he's a jackass."

"Dumpster fire, huh?" Nick cocked his head to the side. "I have to admit, I'm intrigued."

Theo smiled. "I know I'm asking for a lot, but it's for a good cause, and honestly, once Sebastian realizes his mistake, I think you two will get along swimmingly. And I know Dante thinks you're cool. In other words, I'm pulling a *Mean Girls* and inviting you to sit with us at lunch. Play along, and you'll get three new friends out of it."

Not the absolute truth, but also not a lie. Let's see what he says.

Nick chewed on his bottom lip, seemingly lost in thought.

Theo was taut with anticipation, but he was careful to keep it off his face. His plan depended on Nick being willing to go along with it.

After an interminable pause, Nick nodded. "All right. I'll do it. But I have some caveats."

Theo's relief was profound. "Name them."

"I reserve the right to back out of this at any time. Sebastian seems like a nice enough person, but he's also . . . weirdly intense. If shit gets too real, I'm out."

"That's fair. Anything else?"

"Yeah, one more thing. You said the bet's to see who can get me to kiss them first, right?"

"Right. And Sebastian's going to do whatever he can to—"

Nick got up from his desk, walked over, and before Theo could so much as sit up in protest, he planted a brief but firm kiss on Theo's lips.

"There." Nick pulled back with a grin. "Congrats, you won the bet. And it only took a day too."

Theo blinked at him. "*Ooh.* Nice thinking. You're going to fit in great around here."

Nick moved over to his bed and flopped onto it. "So, you wanna watch some Netflix or something?"

"I'm calling it early: this is the start of a beautiful friendship."

Present Day

Nick walked back to his dorm in a daze, using his phone to navigate from Sebastian's place to campus, since he'd only ever been driven there. It was only a few miles away, but it felt like he was moving through molasses. He'd been semi-dumped by his not-boyfriend, and though he'd seen it coming, it still didn't seem real.

This was your decision, Nick. You kissed him. You let him think he won knowing he might do this. You have no right to be surprised.

But as he trudged up to Powell Hall and climbed the steps to his room, he discovered he *was* surprised. As prepared as he'd been for the possibility that Sebastian was only pretending, an equal part of him had been hoping for the opposite.

And that part of me is a complete chump.

When he walked in, the first thing he did was glance at Deen's bed. For once, his roommate wasn't home. He was probably off in the dining hall, stuffing his face to chase off the vestiges of the party.

Unbidden, images from the night before flashed through Nick's head. Getting to know Sebastian. Fighting with him. Having desperate, fantastic sex with him. Sleeping next to him and waking up to his peaceful, handsome face.

At that last one, Nick slammed a mental door shut on his memories. He couldn't. He was still too raw.

He started to reach for his bag on instinct—the first thing he did whenever he entered his room was toss it onto his bed—only to remember he'd left it at Dante's apartment. Great. He'd have to go back there and pick it up. Sebastian might show up there again, and then Nick would probably die.

Someone knocked on his door, dispelling the macabre thought. Nick didn't bother to look through the peephole. He flung the door open and said wearily, "Hi, Theo." Then he slumped over to his bed and tossed himself onto it.

Theo walked in and shut the door behind him. "I got your text." He dug his phone out of the pocket of his jeans—the same ones he'd been wearing last night, Nick noted absently—and read aloud. "'I'm so sorry, Theo. I couldn't keep up the charade any longer. Shit with

Sebastian was getting way too real, and I had to end it.' Care to tell me exactly what the hell happened?"

Nick sighed. "I decided to kiss him, and right after, he called you. Then he confessed the whole sordid scheme to me and told me to leave."

"He didn't beg for forgiveness or anything?"

"Nope. Wouldn't even look at me. I knew from the start he was playing me, and yet I let myself get caught up anyway. How naïve am I?"

To Nick's surprise, Theo walked over and threw his arms around him as best he could while Nick was lying down. Awkward as it was, Nick buried his face in Theo's shoulder. The warmth from his body was a small comfort.

"You're not naïve, and you didn't do anything wrong." Theo pulled away and perched on the edge of the mattress. "Sebastian, on the other hand . . . There are a few choice words I'd like to use to describe his recent behavior."

"Actually, right up until he asked me to leave, he was great. Charming. Sweet. I'd even say romantic." Nick heaved a sigh. "I really started to think he liked me. He should change his major to drama. He'd make a hell of an actor."

Theo's brows knit together. "What makes you think he was acting?"

"Um, the part where he kicked me out as soon as he got what he wanted."

"Believe me when I say he's going to hear from me about that, but for the record, I know Sebastian. He's *never* been as besotted with a guy as he is with you. It's written all over his face. I can't explain why he did what he did, but I'm telling you right now, it's not because he doesn't care. If he didn't, he wouldn't have taken the time to explain everything to you. I don't believe for a second he was faking it."

The words were meant to be comforting, Nick was sure, but all they did was smart. "It doesn't matter if part of it was real. He still chose the bet over me. He could have come clean at any point, but he didn't until I forced his hand." Nick sighed. "Anyway, I wanted to tell you I'm sorry I didn't hold out longer. I know you wanted me to keep up the ruse forever, but I couldn't do it anymore."

Theo mumbled something like "—wasn't the point—" but Nick couldn't quite hear him.

"What was that?"

"Nothing." Theo put a hand on his shoulder. "Get some rest. Eat something. Do whatever it is you need to do to feel better about this. Oh, and Nick?"

"Yeah."

"I'm sorry."

Nick quirked an eyebrow at him. "Why?"

"This is all my fault. I never should have dragged you into this. I thought . . . Well, I thought Sebastian was more of a grown-up than he is. I thought he would make better choices. Regardless, I gambled with your happiness in the hopes that things would work out one way, but I knew they might not. For that, I apologize."

"It's okay. I just dunno what I'm going to do come Monday. Everyone saw Sebastian and me together at the party. When they find out he's dumped me, or whatever you want to call it, I'm going to join the list of guys he's tossed aside." Nick exhaled a tight breath. "I really didn't want that to happen."

"I wouldn't worry about that." Theo stood up. "I know it's hard to see anything good about Sebastian right now, but I know for a fact he's not going to broadcast what went down between you two. He's going to bottle it up."

"What makes you think that?"

"It's his way, but also because if he *does* say anything, I'll snap his neck." Theo winked. "All teasing aside, Sebastian may surprise you yet. I'm not saying any of this to excuse what he did—you should be furious with him—but I don't want you to worry."

"Thanks, but forgive me if I don't hold my breath."

"You gonna be okay? I told you about the bet ahead of time so it wouldn't blindside you, but it seems like you're still taking this pretty hard."

Nick wanted to deny it, but he respected Theo too much to lie to his face. He paused, took stock of himself, and then shook his head. "I don't think it's fully hit me yet. I'm sure the next couple of days are going to be a roller coaster."

"Want some company? We could go do something. Take your mind off things. Want to see a movie? Or go to brunch and get you good and drunk on mimosas?"

Nick groaned. "No alcohol. Ever again. I think I'd like to take a nap. I'm exhausted all of a sudden. And then I have a lot of reading to catch up on. Actually, are you going to Dante's house between now and Monday?"

For some reason, Theo's cheeks filled with color. "Yeah, why?"

"I left my bag there with all my notes and shit. I can pick it up, but I'd rather not go anywhere I might accidentally run into Sebastian."

Theo nodded. "Don't worry about it. I'll bring your bag by later tonight." He started for the door. "If you need anything else, text me, okay?"

"Okay." Nick grinned. "So, going to Dante's today, huh? You two have plans?"

"Oh, nothing serious." Theo's voice was neutral as he opened the door and paused in the threshold. "We have some things we need to talk about, since we had sex this morning and all."

Nick sat straight up in bed. "You *what*?"

But Theo giggled and disappeared out the door, shutting it behind him.

Bastard. I'm so happy for them, though. At least one good thing came out of the party last night.

At that thought, Nick's excitement drained away, leaving him limp. Before he could stop it, his memory of that morning replayed in high-definition. Nick got to experience again all the twisted emotions he'd felt when Sebastian had confessed to him and asked him to leave.

He repeated his reasoning for ending the charade in his head, as if hearing it for the hundredth time would be more impactful than the previous ninety-nine. So much had happened at the party. Nick had no longer been able to deny that things were getting serious between them. Walls were breaking down. Sebastian had said he'd told Nick things he hadn't told anyone else, and in truth, Nick had done the same.

Nick couldn't have allowed this to go any further without being a hundred percent sure it was real. The bet had to end, and he'd had to see—for good or for ill—how Sebastian really felt.

So much for that.

He shook himself as melancholy crept over him. This was silly. He'd known what he was getting into, so why couldn't he shake off this shock?

Because what Theo said was right. Sebastian may have let you down in the end, but there's no way all of that was fake. For a while there, you two really had something. And he let it go. The bet was more important to him than you, and that hurts. It hurts more than you ever thought it would.

Fuck this. Nick wasn't about to spend his day wallowing. Sebastian had never been his; therefore, he hadn't really lost anything.

Shoving those thoughts aside, Nick looked around for something to distract himself with. His sketchbook caught his eye first. He'd set it on his desk two weeks ago and hadn't picked it up since. Too busy. He moved to get it, but at the last second, he remembered the subject of his most recent drawing: Sebastian's eyes.

He snatched his hand back.

His laptop sat on the bed next to him. It seemed like the most obvious way to distract himself—he could stream Netflix, or, God forbid, study—but then he thought about what would load as soon as he opened it. He'd left his browser open to Facebook. He had a dozen new friend requests from classmates, and Sebastian himself.

There had been a tiny part of Nick that had wondered if Sebastian had added him so he could send him a relationship request.

Again, so much for that.

Is there nothing I can do to take my mind off him? Am I doomed to dwell on this forever? He wasn't my boyfriend.

And yet, no matter how many times he told himself that, the ache in his chest worsened with every beat of his heart.

He ended up burying his face in his pillow and fighting back tears. He refused to cry over this. The last time he'd cried had been at his dad's funeral, and this was *nowhere* near as painful as that. Sebastian didn't deserve his tears.

Without warning, the door opened. Nick pushed himself up enough to see a rumpled-looking Deen trudge into the room. Bags had appeared under his eyes, and for once, he was wearing normal clothes: a T-shirt and baggy shorts. It was like seeing a teacher outside of school for the first time.

Deen spotted him right away. "Hey, you're alive. I was starting to worry."

"Am I alive?" Nick let his head fall back onto his pillow. "I don't feel like I am."

"Did you overdo it too? I swear, I've never been so hungover in my life."

"Yeah," Nick lied. "Have you already eaten?"

Deen moved over to his bed and climbed gingerly onto it, wincing whenever the movement rocked his head. "Yeah, after waiting for you until I couldn't anymore. We had a date, remember? You said you'd fill me in over breakfast."

Nick groaned. "Oh God, I totally forgot. I'm sorry."

"Don't worry about it." Deen lowered himself onto his mattress with the care of a bomb defuser. He lay on his side so he could look at Nick. "When I left Sebastian's party last night, you'd run off with him somewhere, so I figured you two were . . . busy." He grinned. "Wanna talk about it?"

Nick swallowed. "I'd rather not, if it's all the same to you."

"Not one to kiss and tell, huh? I promise I won't go all straight guy on you about it."

"No, really." Nick's stomach lurched. "There's nothing to tell."

"What? But you didn't come home last night. I took that to mean you'd slept over at Sebastian's. I was gonna text you if you didn't show your face soon, but I wanted to give you a chance to bask in your new romance." Deen put a wrist to his forehead as if he were swooning. "Ah, young love."

Nick wasn't sure what it was, but something snapped within him. The next thing he knew, the tears he'd been holding back welled up in his eyes. He couldn't bite back the little sob that escaped from him.

He tried to wipe his cheeks, but he was too late. Deen saw and gasped. "Dude, are you okay?"

Embarrassed, Nick turned his face away, burying it in the crook of his elbow. He ordered himself to stop, but a second later, something brushed his back. Warm arms slid around him, followed by a face pressed to his shoulder, and the tickle of soft hair against his cheek.

Deen didn't ask him what'd happened again. He didn't say anything else. He just hugged Nick and didn't let go until Nick had finished crying. Then he hugged him some more.

By the time Monday arrived, Sebastian was exhausted. He hadn't slept through the night since he'd told Nick the truth, and nothing could distract him from his catastrophe of a life.

For one, his sheets smelled like Nick no matter how many times he washed them. It was impossible, and yet every time he lay down at night, he smelled Nick's shampoo on the pillow next to him.

For another, every few seconds, he swore his phone vibrated. He'd snatch it out of his pocket and check it, praying for a text or a call from Nick, only to find nothing. He was beginning to wonder if heartache had hallucinatory effects.

To top it all off, Dante and Theo were being insufferable. Dante kept trying to get him to talk about it, which was usually Theo's job. Dante was relentless, no matter how many times Sebastian told him to leave it alone.

Theo, on the other hand, was suspiciously mute on the subject of Nick. Sebastian had asked him a few times if Nick was doing okay, but Theo refused to answer. Funnily enough, every time Sebastian asked what time he should come by on Monday to get Barbzilla, Theo would laugh and say, "I'll get back to you." It was like he knew something Sebastian didn't, but Sebastian couldn't fathom what that was.

The weather was gorgeous as he trekked onto campus: sunny and bright, with fluffy clouds sailing by overhead. It was the kind of cusp-of-autumn day he'd cherish if his mind weren't filled to the brim with anxiety.

As he slogged past the dining hall and caught sight of Theo's dorm, his heart started to pound. Powell Hall looked more intimidating than it ever had before. What if he ran into Nick? That was how they'd met in the first place, after all. They'd spotted each other from across campus, like something out of the many movies they'd compared their lives to.

Damn tiny university. If he didn't run into Nick today, he was bound to run into him eventually. What would happen then? Would Nick scream at him? Or worse, would he ignore him?

Sebastian was grateful Nick hadn't said much before, but now he was burning to know what Nick was feeling. How was he taking this? Did he care at all?

He has to care. There's no way he doesn't care. Not after everything we shared.

A wave of melancholy washed over him. Sebastian gave his head a brief shake to dispel the gloom. If only Theo had given him some sort of news. He could ... He could ...

You could what? What exactly do you want to do when it comes to Nick? Apologize? Beg for forgiveness? You fell on your own sword because you were convinced he'd never forgive you, but now you want to see how he feels?

There was a part of him that screamed yes, but another part was terrified. If Nick rejected him, his heart would break all over again. If Nick forgave him, then Sebastian would have to do something he'd never done before. Something too frightening for words.

He'd have to be in a relationship. One where he cared deeply if it worked out or not.

The thought made him queasy, not because he didn't want Nick, but because he'd never let himself be vulnerable that way before. What if they dated, and he kept ruining things? What if he hurt Nick again? What if they fell in love, and then everything fell apart?

But what if it doesn't? What if it works out?

The thought made him stop short in the middle of the stone path. It figured he'd start being optimistic after he'd obliterated his chances. Jesus, what was he going to do?

He was on the threshold of Powell Hall now. His attention had been so focused on the front door—which he'd expected to swing open and reveal Nick at any moment—he hadn't looked at his surroundings.

Somehow, he'd completely missed the two figures sitting at a picnic table under a tree. The same one he'd strolled up to while Nick sketched. Sure enough, sitting in the same spot as that day, was Nickolas Steele. And he wasn't alone.

QUINN ANDERSON

Sebastian's brain supplied a name the moment his eyes slid over to the man sitting suspiciously close to Nick. Minho Ghim. A notorious gossip hound and a former paramour of Sebastian's.

Well, *paramour* might be a bit strong. They'd hooked up once back in freshman year, and then they'd never spoken again. It wasn't by design; neither of them had pursued the other.

Though now that Minho was talking to Nick, Sebastian's interest flared up like a roman candle. Horror scenarios ran through his head. Minho could be telling Nick all about their brief fling. Nick could be doing the same. They could be commiserating. Congratulating each other on dodging the bullet that was Sebastian "Fuck Up" Prinsen.

Before he could work himself up into a proper tizzy, Nick glanced his way. For a second, his eyes slid past him, but then they snapped back like they were attached to rubber bands.

The emotions that rolled over Nick's face were as easy to read as bold print. Surprise, followed by awkwardness, and then a healthy dose of anger. He turned to Minho and said something. Minho looked over at Sebastian too, and Sebastian swore his heart actually skipped a beat.

His first instinct was to about-face and hightail it in the opposite direction, but then Nick spoke again, inaudibly. Minho nodded, and with one final glance at Sebastian, he scuttled away. His phone was already in his hand. He was probably going to text the whole exchange to everyone he knew. Awesome.

Keep in mind, you brought this on yourself.

With a sigh, Sebastian approached the picnic table. Nick watched him. It wasn't until he was about three feet away that Nick seemed to make a decision. He jumped to his feet and moved like he was going to flee into Powell Hall. Sebastian almost let him, miserable as he was, but his hand acted of its own accord.

He grabbed Nick by the shoulder. "Wait."

Nick stiffened beneath his touch and didn't look at him. "What do you want?"

"To talk." It was true. Sebastian wanted—needed—to explain himself to Nick. If there was even the slightest chance this was salvageable, he had to take it.

"I told you before: I don't have anything to say to you."

240

Sebastian's throat tightened. "I deserve that, but I don't think it's true. I bet there's a lot you'd like to say to me. Loudly. While a jeering crowd throws tomatoes at me."

Nick laughed and then narrowed his eyes, like he was mad at himself. "I hope you didn't come here to see me, because I have a date with the dining hall, and then class after."

"No." Sebastian swallowed, which made his tight throat ache. "Honestly, I came to see Theo and claim Barbzilla. Running into you is both a bonus and a nightmare."

Nick laughed again, but this time, it was without any trace of remorse. "Barbzilla? Good luck with that."

Does he know whatever it is that Theo's not telling me?

He was itching to ask, but he held back. "Give me five minutes of your time. Please. I want to apologize again and explain some things."

"Look, Sebastian, if you're going to lie to me again—"

Sebastian put his hands up. "No, I swear. I'll be totally honest. I was honest with you the last time we talked, but there were some things I left out. Things about me. I need for you to know them. As an added bonus, if you want to yell at me after, I'll sit there and take it for as long as you need."

Nick shook his head. "No. I can't believe you'd ask me for a favor after everything that happened."

"Please?" He wet his lips. "Please talk to me? I'll beg."

The pause that followed was endless. Sebastian heard nothing but his own heart jackhammering in his chest. Then, Nick shifted his weight.

"Okay. Five minutes."

Chapter Seventeen

Nick followed Sebastian across campus with no small amount of trepidation. Sebastian was silent as he escorted them "somewhere private" to talk. As they walked, Nick debated if he could still make a run for it. He'd sworn a hundred times this weekend to never think about Sebastian again, and after the hundred and first time, he'd decided he could at least promise never to speak to him again. And yet here he was, strolling by Sebastian's side like everything was fine.

After his miserable weekend, however, part of Nick had been hoping for some closure. He'd thought he'd get it through self-reflection and maybe some binge drinking, but he wasn't opposed to going straight to the source.

Actually, this might work out for the best. They'd never had a chance to tie up loose ends. Now they could talk, get everything out in the open, and then go back to being indifferent acquaintances.

He told himself that, and yet when he snuck a glance at Sebastian, his heart throbbed. Simply walking next to him made Nick feel an electric current between their bodies. It brushed his skin like a physical touch, that unnamable *something* that had been between them from day one. Only now, there were real emotions behind it.

Nick wasn't trying to be mean, but it definitely wasn't caused by Sebastian's looks this time around. He was visibly exhausted. His gray eyes—the feature Nick had originally been entranced by—were overshadowed by dark circles and bags. His brow was pinched, and his mouth, which Nick normally had a healthy appreciation for, was pressed into a thin, tense line.

And yet somehow, Nick still responded to him. Body and heart.

Maybe going somewhere private to talk isn't such a good idea.

Nick gave himself a mental slap across the face. There was no way he was going to let hormones distract him from telling Sebastian off. He'd lied to Nick, he'd hurt him, and though he'd come clean in the end, it was too little too late. Good thing Sebastian had shown his true colors before things got serious.

Serious like you both talking about your issues with your parents and meeting each other's friends and having sex and sharing a bed together? Oh yeah. Bullet dodged.

Before Nick could argue with himself in earnest, they approached an old, gorgeous building Nick had never been to before. It almost looked like a cathedral, with its stained-glass windows and brick pinnacles laced with white stone.

"This is the auditorium," Sebastian said before Nick could ask. "Remember when I asked you to skip class and hang out with me?"

"Oh yeah." Nick stared up at the beautiful building, drinking in the details. "You said there was a room in the auditorium no one ever used. I remember thinking it sounded like trouble."

"You're not wrong. The theater majors used to use it to smoke weed and make out, but then the administrators found out. It got raided a few times and then abandoned. Now it's used sparingly. Actually, when Dante and Theo announced they were taking an acting class together for gen. ed. credit, I kinda hoped they'd use it to, um"—he grinned—"*bond.*"

Nick nodded. "Looks like they didn't need to. They ended up together anyway."

"What?" Sebastian rounded on him. "What did you say?"

Nick blinked. "Dante and Theo. Did you not know they hooked up?" He would think Sebastian would be the first person they'd tell.

"They *what?*" Sebastian dug his phone out of his pocket like he intended to call them right then and there, but then he stopped. "God, how could I have not seen it? They went home together after my party, and they were together all weekend. Was I honestly so caught up in my own shit that they didn't think they could tell me?"

Nick didn't know how to answer that. Actually, judging by Sebastian's dazed face, he might not know he'd said that aloud. Nick shifted his weight from foot to foot. His instincts were telling him to comfort Sebastian, but his brain was crowing over the pain on his face.

Serves you right, you jerk.

Eventually, Sebastian sighed. "I'll call them later and apologize. I don't want to hold you up. Follow me."

They entered the auditorium, and for a moment, Nick was stunned. It was beautiful inside, with a vaulted ceiling, rows of red velvet chairs, and frescos on the walls beneath the stained-glass windows. It could have been the inside of a European church.

Once again, Sebastian seemed to read his mind. "The choir performs here around the holidays. You should go to the Christmas concert. When the stage is lit up with candles, and you can see snow falling outside, it's magical."

Nick could picture it. Campus was probably gorgeous in the winter. He hadn't thought that far ahead, focused as he'd been on getting here and getting settled. Surprisingly, he was excited to see it. This must be what school spirit felt like.

Sebastian walked along the back of the theater to an open hallway that ran down the length of it. It was lined with doors and bisected with another hallway, which he headed down.

Nick followed after him. Sebastian stopped in front of a door near the back and opened it, revealing a disused dressing room. There were old costumes hanging on a rack, boxes piled against the back wall, and an assortment of old chairs. Plus, a red couch in the middle that was the only thing not covered in dust.

"This is it." Sebastian walked in and waved at a makeup station with a cracked mirror lined with blackened light bulbs. "Glamorous, huh?"

"I think it's cool." Nick checked the place out, hands shoved in his pockets. "So, you had something to say to me?" The sooner they got to the point, the sooner he could flee to safety.

"You want to get comfortable first? This could take a minute."

The sofa was the easiest to get to, but Nick wasn't about to sit on what was obviously a make-out spot with Sebastian. He freed a rickety stool from a pile of junk and perched on it. It was uncomfortable and groaned like a dying animal, but he stayed stubbornly on it. Then he crossed his arms and looked expectantly at Sebastian.

Sebastian shrugged and took a seat on the couch, as close to Nick as he could get. There were maybe five feet between them, and every inch was magnetized. "I'm sure you have some idea of what I want to talk about."

"If you were to say politics and religion right now, I'd be relieved."

Sebastian's lips quirked up, but he sobered quickly. "I want to apologize for lying to you."

"Which time?" Nick was being tart, but he didn't care. He'd agreed to hear Sebastian out, but that didn't mean he had to make it easy for him.

Sebastian flinched. "Every time. I'll start at the beginning. I never should have brought the bet back in the first place. I was angry at all the things in my life that were going wrong, and I decided to make someone else feel as miserable as me. It was callow and mean-spirited. I'm surprised Dante and Theo didn't try to talk some sense into me."

"They did, in their own subtle way. According to Theo, they were hoping you'd realize your mistake on your own." Nick narrowed his eyes. "Guess that never happened."

"No, it did." Sebastian ran a frustrated hand through his hair. Nick watched it fall across his brow like a bird's wing. "As soon as I got to know you, I realized I'd made a mistake, but I kept lying to myself. I acted like the scared child I guess I am inside. By the time I came to my senses, I was so deep in it, I thought for sure you were going to hate me forever no matter what I did."

Nick shifted in his seat, and the wood creaked worryingly. "The jury's still out on that."

"I know, and I deserve that. I get it now, I promise."

"Do you? What brought on this grand epiphany?"

"Talking to you. Being with you. Realizing about halfway into it that this was so not about the bet." With a sigh, he glanced at Nick. "I should have come clean long ago, and I'm sorrier than I've ever been. You don't have to forgive me if you don't want to."

Nick shifted in his seat again. This was starting to sound like Sebastian wanted him back, and it was making Nick uncomfortable. He'd come here under the assumption that Sebastian had been playing him all along, but now it seemed like Sebastian had played himself. "If you don't want forgiveness, then what do you want?"

"I want you to understand. I've never been in a relationship before, like I told you on the balcony. Clearly, I have no idea what I'm doing. I fucked up, and I'm not saying my inexperience is an excuse, but I'm hoping you can at least get how . . . *lost* I am." Sebastian blew out a breath. "I make the wrong choices every chance I get, and I don't know why."

Despite himself, Nick's chest panged with sympathy. Sebastian was gazing off into space, his face pinched with pain and mortification. It was obvious he was pouring his soul out. "I remember you telling me that. How you're lost when it comes to relationships, and sex is what you're good at."

Nick almost bit his tongue. He should have thought that through. The words hung in the air between them, carrying an entirely different kind of tension. One that sizzled.

For a moment, Sebastian's eyes darkened in a way that sent tingles up Nick's spine, but then he looked away. "Anyway, I'm also sorry I asked you to leave. It was more avoidance behavior on my part, and it was selfish. If there's anything you want to say to me, you can say it now. For closure. And I know it's horrible of me to ask, but . . . is there any chance you'll forgive me someday? With time and a lot of groveling?"

Yeah, this was getting into dangerous territory. Nick had expected Sebastian to apologize, and some of Nick's anger had ebbed away, but he couldn't just forgive him. Forgiveness could be a slippery slope that might lead to them giving this disaster another shot. He'd been ready to put this behind him and move forward. He was *not* ready for the return of Team Sick.

Oh God, I don't know what to do. Quick, say something.

He cleared his throat. "Don't worry about it. It's not that big of a deal."

"Yes, it is. You don't have to pretend for me. I know you're angry, and you have every right to be."

"That's the thing, though. I'm not *angry*. Hurt, sure, but not angry. When I first realized you were picking the bet over me, I was a little blindsided, but if anything, I was angry at myself. I let myself get swept up in this whole whirlwind. I'm normally so good at keeping my feet on the ground."

Sebastian winced. "Sorry again. It must've been quite a shock when I told you it was a bet all along."

"Not at all." Nick looked at him askance. "Theo did tell you, didn't he? I knew about the bet from the start."

Nick hadn't expected his statement to get much of a reaction, but it was like he'd pulled out a firecracker and lit it right in the middle of the room.

In an instant, Sebastian was on his feet. "You *what*?"

For the second time in fifteen minutes, Nick was left blinking at him. "I ... knew all along?"

"How could you possibly have known?"

"Theo. My first day here, he came to my room and introduced himself. Then he told me everything. About you, your friendship, and the bet. He said he wanted to warn me so I wouldn't get hurt." Nick shrugged. "Guess that happened anyway. Oh, and by the way, you didn't win the bet. Theo did. I kissed him then and there. Platonically, of course, but it still counts."

Sebastian stared at him, his expression incredulous. For several seconds, he was silent. Then, he exhaled a sharp breath. "I can't fucking believe you."

"Wait, what? What did I do?"

Right then, Nick's wobbly seat gave out beneath him. One leg broke in half, sending him to the floor like a ragdoll. He landed awkwardly, and while it didn't hurt, the surprise of suddenly being on the ground left him blinking.

For several seconds, Sebastian glared at him, as if he thought Nick had broken the chair on purpose. Then with a sigh, he offered Nick a hand.

Nick took it, and when Sebastian pulled him up, it brought their faces close. His mouth went dry. He might've read into it, but Sebastian was still glaring at him.

"You lied to me." Sebastian's eyes narrowed.

It was Nick's turn to be incredulous. "Excuse you?"

Sebastian dropped Nick's hand and jabbed a finger at him. "This whole time, you were playing me. I *knew* there was something up with you. You were so resistant to me, and I kept wondering and wondering why you were holding back. Well, now I know."

Nick bristled. "*I* was playing *you*? Spare me."

"It's true. You let me make the worst mistake of my life and never said a word. You lied to me every bit as much as I did to you, and then you had the nerve to be angry at *me*?"

"You should be grateful I knew about the bet. If I were you, I'd call Theo and thank him. We wouldn't be talking right now if he hadn't warned me. Do you have any idea how horrible I would have felt if I hadn't known?"

"Yeah, you'd feel how I feel right now! Maybe I'm a hypocrite, but so are you. Acting all betrayed when you've been pretending all along. How many times did you tell me to drop the act and be honest? Did it ever occur to you to do the same?"

They fell silent, but the words resonated between them. Nick's heart was pounding, and Sebastian was staring at him with such intensity, it scalded. Nick begged himself to look away, but he couldn't.

Distantly, he realized Sebastian was breathing hard. Nick's own pulse had sped up, as it so often did around Sebastian. He'd told himself he wanted closure. He'd told himself that this would be the last time he'd talk to Sebastian. But standing here, in yet another heart-pounding confrontation with him, Nick had to wonder if the magnetism between them was more like a gravitational field, and they were destined to pull each other in again and again.

"Okay." Nick swallowed hard. "Fine. I owe you an apology as well."

Sebastian scoffed.

"I'm serious. I shouldn't have gone along with the bet in the first place. And then every move I made after that compounded my initial mistake. Worst of all, I lost sight of the fact that this wasn't real."

"Not real," Sebastian parroted. "That's what you think?"

"Don't you?"

"Nick, you already know the answer to that."

Nick opened his mouth to protest, but the words lodged in his throat. After this conversation, he couldn't pretend Sebastian was the heartless bastard he'd spent all weekend building up in his head. "There were times when I thought . . . But it was too hard. It's not supposed to be this hard."

A long beat of silence passed between them.

"There's one thing I can't figure out," Sebastian finally said. "Why'd you do it? Theo was a stranger to you when he asked you to lie. Why agree?"

"Because I was desperate to make friends." Nick shrugged. "It was my first day at a new school, and I was scared and lonely. And I really wouldn't call it *lying*. Omission isn't the same as what you did. Honestly, that's why I kissed you when I did. This was getting way too involved."

That, Nick learned, was the wrong thing to say.

"You're unbelievable." Sebastian stepped closer to him. "Acting like some poor put-upon victim who was dragged into this, when in reality, you practically volunteered. You had no qualms about lying to me. I may have done it first, but you did it worst."

Nick rolled his eyes. "Well, if it rhymes, then it must be true."

"No, fuck that. By agreeing to go along with this, you were complicit. For the record, I'm pissed off at Theo as well—and Dante, because there's no way he wasn't in on this—but at least they had good intentions. I've admitted that what I did was wrong. I've apologized and explained myself. But you're still trying to act like you didn't actively manipulate me, right down to deciding where and when the bet ended. Twice."

Nick wanted to argue with that, but there was a lot of truth to what Sebastian was saying. "Okay, fine. I'm sorry I lied. I guess we're both guilty."

"You say that as if you think our wrongs cancel each other out somehow. They don't. I can't believe I've been beating myself up this whole time, and here you are, without a shred of remorse."

Nick's temper flared. "You think I don't regret what's happened here? You think I didn't spend this whole past weekend praying for a mulligan? I would give *anything* to start over. I thought this place *was* my fresh start, and then day one, I run into you. You're handsome and charming and mysterious, and the next thing I know, I'm swept up in this whole intrigue, and all I want to do is not get hurt again, but in the end, I still do. No matter what."

Sebastian paused, and when he spoke again, his voice was quiet. "If you could start over—if you could go back to that first day, and do it all over again—would you make it so we never met?"

Hurting as he was, Nick almost said yes, but the lie caught in his throat. "No. I don't regret getting to know you. When you told me you trusted me, it meant a lot. I realize now that I betrayed that trust. I don't think it makes what you did any better, but you're right. I'm not blameless here. Try to understand, though. Knowing about the bet only made what happened marginally easier. I still had to sit there and question every conversation we had. I had to watch you choose every day not to tell me the truth."

Hanging his head, Sebastian nodded. "I get it. I'm not making excuses, but for the record, right now, I'm thinking back on the past two weeks and seeing everything you did in a completely new light."

All of a sudden, I'm exhausted. It's time to wrap this up.

Nick shrugged. "We should put this disaster behind us. Pretend it never happened."

"Is that really what you want? Because I'm never going to be able to forget this."

Me neither.

Out loud, Nick said, "There's one more thing I need to know. Theo told me he and Dante offered to let you out of the bet, but you didn't take them up on it. Why? Theo made it sound like the bet barely had any stakes."

That seemed to give Sebastian pause. He stared down at the floor, face pinched. They were standing so closely together, Nick could hear his breathing.

Several seconds passed before Sebastian looked at him again. "I can see why you'd think that. To an outsider, the bet would look like it was for nothing. But to me, it was for something that mattered more than anything. It was a chance to claim something I thought I was losing. I wanted it so much, I was willing to ignore what I felt for you to get it."

Nick sucked in a breath. "What you felt for me?"

"Yeah, note the past tense." Sebastian glanced away again. "I'm not going to force my feelings on you. I invited you to talk because I had this tiny little flicker of a hope that we could patch things up, but I guess I was deluding myself. Tell me this one thing. When you were pretending to not know about the bet, were you also pretending to be interested in me? That thing you told me about how I reminded you of home . . . Was any of it real?"

Nick was so stunned, he took a half step back. "You think I was faking?"

"I don't know what to think. Try to see this from my perspective: I found out my own best friends set up an elaborate charade with a complete stranger. Then that stranger insinuated himself into my life, became friends with my friends, and basically tricked me into falling for him. Now he wants to put it behind us! How would you feel if—"

Sebastian seemed to realize what he'd said, or maybe Nick's face was as rigid as it felt, because he cut himself off.

"You . . ." Nick swallowed hard. "You fell for who now?"

"I . . ." Sebastian's eyes searched his, wary and frightened. "I'm emotional. I don't know what I'm saying."

"No, don't back down from this. Are you saying you fell in love with me? In two weeks?"

Sebastian made a frustrated sound. "I don't know! I don't know, okay? I have nothing to compare these feelings to. I haven't had the best role models for love. I . . . I know I feel *something* for you. It's dizzying and frightening, and it makes me . . . It makes me . . ."

Nick was suddenly awash with emotions he couldn't name. "It makes you what?"

"I don't know," Sebastian repeated. "This is all so confusing." He took another step toward Nick. "I know you're attracted to me. We've proven that time and time again. But is that it? Can you really walk away from this?"

Fear hit Nick like a sledgehammer. "You can't ask me that. Not after everything that's happened."

"I am asking you, though. For both our sakes. Answer the question."

Nick opened his mouth only to close it. His lungs felt like the small room was running out of oxygen. "All of this happened so fast. Too fast. Way too fast for it to be love."

"But could it be love someday?" Sebastian's expression was pleading. "What do you feel for me, Nick?"

Nick backed away a step, feeling strangely giddy. "I'm not sure."

"I don't believe you." Sebastian stepped forward again, invading his space. "I think we've both known what this was from day one, and we've been getting in our own way. I think we're both scared of this for surprisingly similar reasons. Neither of us wants to get hurt, so we lied to ourselves and distanced ourselves and sabotaged ourselves." His smile was sharp like cut glass. "It's remarkable how similar we are, really."

Nick laughed, and the sound was all air. "I can't think. Not with you so—"

"So what?"

Nick shook his head.

"I know you feel something for me. You as much as said it. Why won't you tell me what it is? Why are you so afraid to admit you feel it too?"

"Feel what?"

"*This.*" Sebastian fisted a hand in the front of Nick's shirt. "Us. This thing that keeps drawing us back to each other no matter how much we try to deny it. Tell me you don't feel it, and this time, I really will leave you alone. Forever. No more talking it out. No more second chances. It'll be like none of this happened. We'll graduate and go on with our separate lives, and one day, we'll struggle to remember each other's names. Tell me that's what you want, and it's yours."

It was so far from what Nick wanted, his thoughts wouldn't so much as form the lie.

His silence must've been all the encouragement Sebastian needed, because he moved closer again. So close, the world around him blurred, and all Nick could see were eyes. Gray, gray eyes. "Nick?"

When asked later, Nick would swear he'd had no idea what he was going to do until the moment he decided to do it.

He grabbed Sebastian's face in both hands, closed the last of the distance between them, and kissed him with all the ferocity he had in him. The second he did, it was like the emotions smoldering between them bubbled over. Nick felt so much, his brain cut to static: relief, uncertainty, fear, and incontrovertible want.

Sebastian seemed to feel the same, because he made a deep sound in the back of his throat and kissed Nick back with alacrity. They came together like puzzle pieces. Face to face. Chest to chest. Both pushing against each other as if they could close some imaginary gap.

Their kisses in the past had been intense, but they didn't compare to how Sebastian kissed him now. He kissed Nick like he was air. Like he was necessary. Like this was the last kiss Sebastian was ever going to have, and he was trying to make the most of it. Hands everywhere, all desperation and need.

Before Nick knew it, he was being crowded backward. He didn't try to resist, intent as he was on kissing Sebastian with everything he had. The backs of his calves hit something. The sofa.

Sebastian stopped moving forward but didn't stop what his hands and lips were doing. He was giving Nick a choice, and for once, Nick didn't hesitate.

He fell back onto the couch, tugging Sebastian after him. Sebastian followed, and they hit the cushions in a tangle of limbs. The couch smelled musty, and tall as they both were, there was hardly enough room for them to stretch out, but Nick couldn't have cared less. Sebastian was warm and heavy on top of him, and as they moved together, Nick lost the ability to think about anything other than how *right* this felt.

Until Sebastian reached down and palmed Nick through his jeans.

He was hard, and the knowledge rocketed through him. Suddenly, reality came slamming back into focus through the cloud of his arousal. They were in an unlocked room in the university auditorium, and as amazing as it felt to be with Sebastian again, Nick couldn't. For one very important reason.

Nick wrenched his mouth away and sucked in a breath that trembled. "Wait."

Sebastian buried his face in Nick's neck and groaned. "Don't say that. Anything but that."

"I'm sorry. *Believe me*, I'm sorry. But we can't do this. Not right now."

Sebastian supported himself on his palms. "Are you still mad about that silly bet thing? Let's just call it even and go back to making out."

Okay, that made Nick snort.

"Yes, I'm still mad, but no, that's not the reason." Nick propped himself on his elbows, which brought their faces dangerously close together. "This is the third time we've done this. We fight, passions run high, and then we make out like that fixes everything. But it's only a bandage. We have issues, and we can't fuck them out."

Sebastian pouted. "How will we know if we don't try?"

Nick laughed again and had to fight to smother it. "I want to propose a compromise. There's something I need to tell you."

That got Sebastian's attention. "Does it have to do with what you told me at the party? About how your dad's death wasn't the worst thing that ever happened to you?"

Nick nodded. "I need to tell you that first for two reasons. One, it'll help you understand me and where I've been coming from this whole time. And two, it'll give us some distance. Once we've had that, we can decide where we stand without hormones dictating our actions."

"All right. Go ahead, then. I'm all ears."

Nick pushed Sebastian gently off of him and sat up. "First of all, I can't talk while you're on top of me. It's . . . distracting. Second of all, I can't do it here. We could get interrupted."

"Then what do you want to do? Meet up later?"

Nick debated with himself for a moment. "No, I can't wait. I need to tell you this now."

Sebastian raised an eyebrow. "We both have class to get to. In fact, if I leave right now, I'll still be late to my first lecture."

Nick chuckled, and this time, he didn't try to stop it. "Then I suppose there's only one thing we can do. Skip class with me. Let's go somewhere private and talk."

"There's a certain poetry to that. Two weeks ago, I was the one trying to convince you to skip, and now you're convincing me."

"Look how far we've come. So, what do you say?"

Sebastian only hesitated for a moment. "Where do you want to go?"

"I don't know. I'd say my dorm room, but Deen could be there." Nick steeled himself. "Your place?"

"You think that's a wise idea?" Sebastian flashed a wicked smile. "That's where my bedroom is."

Nick took a breath. "We're adults. The kiss from before aside, I think we can handle being alone together. Besides, after I say what I need to say, I doubt you're going to be in the mood."

"I'm always in the mood around you. Even when I'm furious with you." Slowly, Sebastian leaned forward, giving Nick plenty of time to push him away if he wanted.

Nick didn't. He allowed Sebastian to place a chaste but potent kiss on his lips. It only lasted for a second, but it shot through Nick like lightning.

Sebastian pulled away with a shiver. "Let's get going, yeah?"

"Yeah. Did you drive here?"

Sebastian nodded. "We'll take my car."

The drive to Sebastian's place was simultaneously tense and uneventful. They didn't look at each other the whole time, but Nick was aware of Sebastian's presence with every fiber of his being. The journey seemed to take far too long and be over far too quickly simultaneously.

Nick didn't relax until they were inside his apartment, and even then he couldn't seem to decide what to do with his hands. They stood awkwardly together in the living room—neither of them speaking— until Sebastian finally exhaled.

He inclined his head toward the balcony. "Join me?"

Nick waved toward it, indicating that Sebastian should lead the way. Outside, the air was starting to lose its morning chill and take on the warmth of afternoon. There was a decent breeze that kept it from being uncomfortable, however. As Nick settled against the parapet, his discomfort came purely from within.

"So." Sebastian smiled. "Let's hear it."

Nick took a breath and let it out, gathering his words. "This is something I haven't told anyone. And I mean anyone. Not Deen. Not Theo. Not Dr. O'Connor, the counselor. No one."

The smile fell off Sebastian's face. "Okay. I'm a little scared."

"Don't be." Focusing on keeping his breathing steady, Nick began. "I've told you a bit about my dad's death. How it changed everything. How it led me here. How I grieved, and how I'm still grieving. But I haven't told you about my mother."

Sebastian's eyes widened. "That's right. She died when you were young. I assumed you were too little to remember her, so maybe it wasn't that bad. From your tone, I'm guessing that's not the case?"

Nick swallowed hard. "I never said she died."

Sebastian gasped. "She's still alive?"

"Last I heard, yeah. She left when I was five. Dad got full custody, and we never heard from her again. No birthday cards. No visitation. Nothing. When I got older, I asked Dad why she left, and he said she realized too late that she wasn't cut out for marriage and children. I always thought there had to be more to the story. I mean, how can someone have a kid and then decide they *never* want to see them again?"

Sebastian nodded. "I'm guessing when your dad died, you found out what happened?"

"In a manner of speaking." Nick breathed through his tightening throat. "I found out there *wasn't* more to the story. That really was it. When Dad died, he left some things to her in his will. Nothing valuable. Oddments they'd collected during their brief marriage that he wanted to return to her.

"The attorney I hired to deal with all the legal bullshit tracked her down to let her know. I thought . . . I thought that was going to be my chance, you know? Like in a movie. You lose one parent, and you get reunited with another. I thought she'd come to the funeral, we'd end up talking, and we'd reconnect. I thought she'd sweep me into her arms and tell me some story about how she was kidnapped, or she was in witness protection. She'd say she hated leaving me, but that she'd had no choice. I thought we'd be a family."

Sebastian sidled up to him. His warmth was a comfort against Nick's side. "That didn't happen?"

Nick shook his head. "She didn't come to the funeral. She had the items Dad had left her shipped to somewhere in Utah. I guess that's where she lives now. I wouldn't know, though, because she made no effort to contact me whatsoever. When I tried to reach out to her, I got radio silence."

"But you're her son. Isn't she obligated to do *something*?"

Nick smiled bitterly. "I'm over the age of eighteen. She's no longer responsible for me in any way unless she wants to be, and she made her feelings on that score perfectly clear. Honestly, it was like she really had died. Like I really was an orphan."

"Christ, that's terrible. I'm so sorry."

Nick shrugged. "Your parents suck too. I'm sure you can relate."

Sebastian fell silent for a moment. "I can, but it's not the same. You actually just made me appreciate what I have. At least my folks acknowledge my existence. I know I said it felt like they were moving on with their lives without me, but they still call me every weekend." He peeked over at Nick. "I think you gave me some of that 'perspective' shit I keep hearing about."

"I'm glad. Though, for the record, I'm not trying to compare our pain. It's not a competition where the winner is the one who gets to be sad. You've been hurt too, and you've shown me how it's affected you."

Sebastian sized him up. "Well, look who was listening all those times I lectured him on not making assumptions about others."

Heat seeped into Nick's cheeks. "I'm a big enough person to admit you taught me a valuable lesson. One I needed to learn too."

"Same here. Man, you keep making me build my character. Can't have that, now can we?"

They both laughed. Companionable silence filled the space between them as they looked out over the city. Nick thought he could smell cut grass and hot pavement on the breeze. It was familiar and comforting. Maybe someday, he'd think that was what home smelled like.

Eventually, Sebastian shifted next to him. "I'm glad you shared with me, though I'm curious as to why you felt like you had to tell me right away."

"I know why." Nick exhaled. "Because things were getting real again."

"What do you mean?"

"It's the same reason I kissed you when I did and 'ended' the bet. And the reason I resisted you as hard as I did from the start. My dad's death devastated me, but my mom shattered my heart. Absolutely crushed it. I managed to glue it back together again before I came here, but then I met you. The more time I spent with you, the more invested I became, and the more worried I was that I'd get obliterated again. After all, my first introduction to you was people telling me you were a heartbreaker."

Sebastian muttered something that sounded like, "Fucking Minho."

Nick snorted. "As I got to know you, I had this constant war going on in my head. I kept telling myself not to get involved, that you were lying to me, and that I couldn't risk getting hurt again. But I knew deep down what we had was real. I couldn't stay away from you. When my feelings got to the point where I couldn't deny them anymore, I did the cowardly thing and walked away."

"That's why you kissed me," Sebastian said. "That's why you acted like this didn't mean anything, and why you pushed me away when it seemed like we were going to reconcile."

Nick nodded. "I didn't realize it until we met, but I've been pushing people away ever since Dad died, always with the excuse that I was protecting myself. I've been saying I want to make friends, but I've kept everyone at a distance. You. Dante. Theo. Even Deen. I can't go through the rest of my life like this. At some point, I have to realize that the possibility of getting hurt can't keep me from living my life."

He turned to face Sebastian. They were standing inches apart on the little balcony. The intimacy of it grated against his skin, warning him to back off, but he stood firm. "That's why I decided to tell you this. I'm done pretending like I can stay away from you. Telling you about my mom was the proof. I don't have any more secrets or excuses to hide behind. I haven't entirely forgiven you, and you don't have to forgive me either, but you once said you trust me. Is that still true? Because I think I'm ready to trust you."

After his speech, Nick felt like all the air had been let out of his body. But then, when he breathed in again, he realized what he'd let out wasn't air. It was all the pain he'd been carrying with him, and without it, he was free to fill the space inside him with whatever he wanted. Air. Light. Maybe love.

There was a pause while Sebastian studied his face. There wasn't a single iota of Nick that regretted saying what he'd said—it was the truth, simple and pure—but as the seconds ticked on, worry rose in him like a cold tide. His chest tightened in preparation for his heart, which he'd guarded so carefully this past year, to shatter once again.

But then Sebastian brushed the backs of his fingers against Nick's cheek. His hand drifted down to Nick's, and he twined their fingers.

"I think we've said everything we need to say." His voice was soft as his touch. "We've both apologized, and all the lies—even the ones we told ourselves—are out now. There's nothing more I need to hear from you. I want to be with you. If you'll let me, I want to show you that I trust you."

Nick swallowed. He knew the answer to the question he was about to ask, but he resolved to ask it anyway. "How?"

"When we first met, there were so many times I told myself to hang back and let you kiss me, but I couldn't do it. Kissing you was like hearing the truth in a completely different way. When we had sex before, it was so easy to let go. To give in to what I wanted and be raw and honest with you in a way I couldn't be with words. I want that again. I want that now, and for as long as you'll have me."

He moved closer, and Nick's breath caught in his throat. His eyes wanted to flutter closed as Sebastian leaned forward until their lips were almost touching. "This time, it won't be a bandage. It'll be more like stitches. The first step we need to take to heal. I've spent my life having sex for all the wrong reasons, but this time, it feels right. With you, it'll be different. I know it will. Will you let me show you? Nick, will you be with me?"

Sebastian's breath tickled his skin. It reminded Nick of when he was a kid, and on the fourth of July, he'd hold his hand close to a lit sparkler and let it brush his skin. Gone too quickly to hurt, but with lingering heat.

Nick swallowed all his doubts and worries—all the trepidations that had held him back from the moment they'd locked eyes—and said the one word he'd been longing to say to Sebastian.

"Yes."

Chapter Eighteen

As Sebastian led him inside by the hand, Nick's heart pounded like it was trying to escape. Every step toward Sebastian's bedroom made it beat harder. Not with nervousness, but with anticipation.

It was funny. After everything they'd been through, Nick hadn't expected this to feel so perfect. He'd had so many doubts and uncertainties previously, but as they entered the bedroom, and Sebastian closed the door behind them, Nick didn't think he'd ever been more eager to have sex. It was as if all the obstacles they'd put in their way had been broken down. Now that they'd finally let go, it was flowing like water. Natural and sure.

Sebastian used their entwined fingers to tug Nick toward him. Nick came willingly, molding their bodies together. Sebastian tilted his head up for a kiss, but Nick held back, soaking in the moment: chest to chest, forehead to forehead. Happy to bask in Sebastian's warmth and the spicy-sharp smell of his cologne.

Eventually, Nick gave in and kissed him, and when he did, it was slow, but in no way lacking heat. It built between them, like embers being stoked into a blaze, until Nick's hands were fisted in Sebastian's shirt, and Sebastian had wrapped both arms around Nick.

"You know," Sebastian breathed between searing kisses, "now that I have you here, I wish I had a fireplace in my room." He swiped his tongue along Nick's bottom lip.

The light touch made Nick gasp. "This is an odd time to discuss your future renovation plans."

Chuckling, Sebastian mouthed down his neck. "You don't remember? I once joked that you don't hook up, you make love in front of a roaring fire. Joke's on me, because all I want to do right now is lay you out and touch you in all the ways I've imagined for weeks now."

The arousal that swept through Nick left him light-headed and much, much too hot. He'd been turned on before, but at that image, sex went from something he wanted to something he *needed*. He used his hands on Sebastian's chest to guide him back until they reached the bed, and then he pushed Sebastian none-too-gently onto it.

Sebastian landed with a *thump* and blinked up at Nick, eyes dark. "Holy fuck, I'm so turned on right now."

With more confidence than he'd ever displayed in his life, Nick stepped forward, between Sebastian's spread legs, and grinned. "Just you wait."

He kneeled on the bed next to Sebastian's thigh. Sebastian took the cue and scooted back, kicking off his shoes as he went. Nick crawled after him, hovering close enough to feel the heat from his body. He wanted to kiss him, but he held back, drawing it out. He thought he could almost see Sebastian twitching with anticipation.

When they were in position—Sebastian splayed out beautifully under him, and Nick with a thigh between Sebastian's legs and a hand on the mattress by his head—Nick leaned down and brushed their lips together. It wasn't a proper kiss, but it sparked and crackled in a way that made him dizzy.

"So"—Sebastian spoke against his skin, breath tickling—"how do you want to do this?"

Nick had imagined having sex with Sebastian enough times that a dozen possibilities sprang to mind. The aforementioned sweet lovemaking. Frantic, desperate sex that left them both sweaty and weak. He'd even thought about some adventurous balcony sex, though that wasn't quite suitable for a first time.

Right now, there was only one thing Nick wanted.

He brushed his mouth against Sebastian's again, flicking his tongue out to taste skin. "I know you were joking about making love, but I would really like to do that with you." He kissed Sebastian's temple. "Spread you out." Then his cheek. "Finger you open." The corner of his mouth. "And fuck you."

Sebastian actually whimpered. "*Hell* yes. I want that. Want you so much." He slotted their mouths together, and this time when they kissed, it was deep and needy.

If Nick had any doubt how much Sebastian wanted him, it was obliterated when Sebastian rolled his hips up and rubbed their groins together. Nick jolted when Sebastian's erection met his. It wasn't just that Nick was hard, it was that he hadn't realized how fucking hard Sebastian was. Solid and warm. The heat of him could be felt right through his jeans.

"Oh fuck." Nick shivered. "Clothes off. Now."

"I *love* this commanding side of you." Sebastian scrambled to comply, yanking his shirt off and then diving for his jeans.

Nick sat up, astride Sebastian's hips, and peeled his own shirt off. He didn't intend to make a show of it, but when the fabric cleared his head and he looked down, Sebastian was staring at him. More specifically, his torso. Sebastian's mouth was slack, and his pupils had dilated.

"Damn," Sebastian said under his breath. "Why have I never gotten you shirtless before?"

"Same to you." Nick leaned over Sebastian again and brushed a hand along both of Sebastian's distinct collarbones. "I've never been a biter, but I'm itching to mark up this skin of yours."

"Don't do it anywhere visible, and I'm game." Sebastian got his jeans open and wriggled them down his hips along with the black boxers. Now naked, he lay between Nick's legs in no particular pose, and yet the sight was going to fuel Nick's fantasies for years to come.

Nick reached behind him to pull off his shoes before starting on his own pants. To his surprise, Sebastian knocked his hand away. "Allow me."

As he looked down, the gorgeous man under him, whose dark eyes were latched on the bulge in his jeans, worked Nick's fly open in three seconds flat. It was one of the most erotic things Nick had ever witnessed. When Nick's cock sprang free of his underwear, Sebastian actually licked his lips, and Nick thought he might swoon.

He had to take a breath before he could move. Sliding off the bed, he shucked all remaining clothing before crawling back on. It felt weird not to have Sebastian beneath him for even that brief moment. He had a feeling that after this, he was going to be seriously spoiled.

Back in position, he took a moment to appreciate the splendor that was naked Sebastian. His skin flushed pink in all the most tender places: lips, neck, armpits, groin. It was a roadmap Nick intended to follow with his tongue.

Unabashed in his nakedness, Sebastian threw an arm behind his head like a pillow and grinned. "You come here often?"

Nick didn't miss a beat. "No, but you will, if I have anything to say about it."

Sebastian laughed and hooked a leg around Nick's waist, bringing their hips together. With their pesky clothing out of the way, the touch of flesh on flesh was raw and intimate. It made Nick's arm tremble as it held up his torso.

He took a shuddering breath. "Do you have condoms and lube and all that?"

Sebastian pointed to the nightstand and then rocked his hips, making their cocks slide together. "Hurry."

Nick scrambled to obey, though he couldn't help but tease him. "I thought you wanted me to make sweet, slow love to you?"

From over his shoulder, Nick heard a growl. "I do, but I also need you to fuck me *yesterday*, so if you can find some magical way to make both happen, that'd be great."

Rummaging through Sebastian's nightstand, Nick gathered the necessary supplies and dumped them onto the bed a foot away from Sebastian's head. Then he straddled him again, picked up the bottle of lube, and drizzled some onto his fingers.

Sebastian watched with his plump lower lip caught between his teeth. As Nick slicked his fingers, he shivered. "I thought you were the long-relationships guy. Not the sex-god guy."

Gently, Nick skimmed the back of his lubed hand down Sebastian's stomach, then between his legs. "Why can't I be both? Considering all my relationships lasted over a year, I bet I've had more sex than you have." His fingers found Sebastian's hole, lubed it, and then slid in.

Sebastian tensed only to take a breath and let it out slowly, his body going slack. "Don't say 'bet.' Too soon."

Huffing a breath, Nick kissed Sebastian's collarbones as he fingered him. "We're in bed, and I'm inside you. Stop making me laugh."

He added a second finger and angled them the way he liked best when he fingered himself. With utmost satisfaction, he listened to the honeyed moan that poured from Sebastian.

"That's enough." Sebastian pawed at his shoulders. "Fuck me."

"Is not. I just started."

Sebastian whined. "I can't wait any longer."

Nick bit down on the collarbone he was kissing. Sebastian's startled groan of pleasure was almost as good as sex. "I could do this for hours. I could finger you until you're a sweaty, mewling puddle under me."

"Oh God." Sebastian wriggled beneath him, panting. "This is your revenge, isn't it? You're going to tease me to death."

Nick was tempted to answer in the affirmative, but then Sebastian bucked beneath him, and Nick's vision blurred.

"Fuck it." He removed his fingers and reached for the condom. "Spread your legs."

"Oh fuck yes." Sebastian did as he was told, as far as he was able to with Nick's thighs caging him in. "I've wanted this since the day I met you."

Nick tore open the condom and rolled it on. As he got into position, he looked Sebastian in the eye. "I've wanted you for longer. I've been searching for you for a long time."

Sebastian made a sound that had nothing to do with sex. He leaned up and kissed Nick with feeling. Nick kissed back as he guided himself into Sebastian's body and slid home.

They gasped together, mouths still touching. Sebastian was apparently flexible as hell, because he hooked a knee over Nick's shoulder like it was nothing. Nick had to adjust the angle of his hips a few times before he found what worked, but just being here—*finally* with Sebastian—felt so good, he almost couldn't handle it. He moved slowly, trying to get a hold of himself while also milking the sheer pleasure that was being skin to skin with Sebastian, inside and out.

Sebastian was no help at all. The smallest motions wrung throaty moans from him. When Nick thrust into him, his leg flexed around Nick's waist, like he was trying to draw him deeper in. Nick glanced at him and almost came then and there. Sebastian looked exquisite and *wrecked*: eyes clenched shut, brow kissed with sweat, and head thrown back, exposing his long neck.

As if sensing Nick's gaze, he opened his eyes—the winter-sky eyes that had first drawn Nick to him. Their gazes met, and something raw and intimate passed between them. The concrete knowledge that they were here, right now, together. Sebastian craned his head up and pressed the softest but most deliberate of kisses onto Nick's lips, and it zinged down Nick's spine like lightning.

Suddenly, drawing this out was no longer a priority to Nick.

He started fucking Sebastian in earnest, and the pleasured sounds that earned spurred him on. He gave one particularly hard thrust, and when Sebastian gasped and clenched around him, his own moans joined the mix.

"Nick, I—" Sebastian quivered from head to toe, and Nick felt it all over. "Fuck, that feels good."

"You feel good." Nick skimmed his lips up Sebastian's throat. "So gorgeous." He got his hands under Sebastian's hips and propped him up, allowing himself to sink deeper into him.

Sebastian threw his arms around Nick's neck and buried his long fingers in blond hair. Nick had a serious weak spot for having his hair pulled, and before long, his rhythm faltered.

"Shit. I'm close. Want me to slow down?"

Sebastian shook his head, his expression balanced on the delicate knife-edge between pleasure and exquisite agony. "I've been close since we were making out. In fact, I think . . ." He reached between their bodies and gripped his dick. "*Oh.*"

Nick didn't stop fucking him, but he did look down to watch. Sebastian's reddened cock slipping between his beautiful fingers was going to linger in Nick's memory for a long time.

It seemed as though Sebastian barely stroked himself before he tensed up. "Oh fuck, oh fuck, *oh fuck.*"

He unraveled like a tapestry. Seeing his composed, aristocratic face caught in throes of pleasure would have been enough to do Nick in, but then Sebastian grabbed Nick's shoulder and dug in his blunt fingers.

The burst of pain was so sharp and at odds with the ecstasy of being buried in Sebastian, it heightened the entire experience. Half a dozen quick rocks of his hips later, and Nick came so hard he saw stars.

His eyes slammed shut automatically, and he shoved himself as far into Sebastian as possible. His hips gave a stilted little thrust, milking the pleasure racing through him, and even that small movement was almost too much sensation. He stilled, heart pounding, breath coming in labored pants, and luxuriated in it.

He thought at some point Sebastian might have said something, but he couldn't hear anything but his own thundering pulse.

When the last shockwave had worked through him, Nick collapsed on top of Sebastian as gently as he could. Sweat and skin made a smacking sound as they came together. Sebastian slid soothing fingers through his hair until their breathing returned to normal, and then he pushed at his chest. "You're heavy."

"You're such a romantic." But Nick obeyed, sliding out of Sebastian and slumping to the side. He managed to dispose of the condom in a little bedside trash can, but that was the end of his cognizance. He snuggled up to Sebastian's side, throwing one arm over him and collapsing.

Sebastian kissed his temple. "Hey."

"Hey." Nick didn't open his eyes.

"How are you?"

Nick chuckled. "Good. Much more awake than I was this morning."

"Exercise will do that to you." Sebastian kissed his temple again and then foisted himself up. Nick watched him through slits.

Like a true millennial, now that they were finished having sex, Sebastian grabbed his jeans off the floor and pulled his phone out of one of the pockets. He checked it and groaned, and not in a sexy way. "I have three missed calls from Dante and a pointed text from Theo."

Nick willed himself to lift his head, only to decide eye contact was overrated. "Why?"

"Theo stopped by your dorm room around lunchtime. You two had plans?"

"Fuck, I forgot. Lemme guess, with you not responding and me missing, he put two and two together?"

"Yeah, and it equaled sixty-nine, judging by this text."

"What does he want?"

"Allegedly, they want to hang out, but that means they want to harangue me and interrogate you. Rest assured, if we ever break up, they'll be completely on your side."

At that, Nick summoned the strength to prop himself up on his elbows. "If we break up? As in, we're together?"

Sebastian shot him a wry look, though he was noticeably blushing. "We crammed three years' worth of relationship issues into less than three weeks and had two rounds of spectacular sex. I think it's safe to say we're dating."

Nick's heart was so light, it felt like it was floating in his chest. He grinned. "I did it. I tamed Sebastian Prinsen, the infamous heartbreaker. Wait till the student body gets a load of this. I'm going to be *popular*."

Sebastian snorted. "Probably."

"More popular than *you*."

The indignant squawk that came from Sebastian was worth getting hit in the face with a pillow right after.

"Anyway"—Sebastian rolled onto his side to face Nick—"we should probably tell Dante and Theo before we do anything else. Or before they break down my door. You up for a hang-out sesh?"

"Yeah, sure. Tell them to come in an hour, though. I want to shower and eat something before we have this conversation. Oh, and I have to call Deen. He sort of hates you."

"Why would he—" Sebastian sighed and started texting back. "Never mind. Silly question. I'll tell Dante and Theo to head over in an hour. I want to have a conversation with them anyway about how they conveniently forgot to tell me they hooked up. If I play my cards right, I can milk that until winter break."

Nick laughed. "I'm so glad I came to this school."

That afternoon ended up including a number of firsts for Sebastian.

Obviously, it was his first time going all the way with Nick, but it was also his first time being intimate with him. Or anyone for that matter. And later, as he made sandwiches for them in his kitchen while Nick sat at the island and kept him company, it was his first time being domestic with someone.

And most importantly, it was the first time, in a long time, that Sebastian could remember being truly, deeply happy.

They'd just finished eating, and a damp-haired, extremely kissable Nick was helpfully doing the dishes, when there was a knock at the door. Sebastian opened it without looking through the peephole. Sure enough, Dante and Theo were standing on the other side, still with their school bags on their shoulders. They must've come right from campus.

Sebastian had been prepared to spend all afternoon dropping subtle hints about them until they confessed, but when he opened the door, he saw that they were holding hands.

He glanced between them, keeping his expression neutral. "Honestly, it's about time."

They broke into grins, crossed the threshold, and each threw an arm over him.

"Happy for us?" Dante asked.

"Ecstatic. Though the real question is, how am I going to be *both* of your best mans at your wedding?"

"Oh, I wouldn't worry about that," Theo teased. "I'll ask Nick to be my best man. That won't be awkward, right? Considering you two are *so* over."

Nick chose that moment to appear in the doorway to the kitchen. "Yeah, about that."

"*Quelle surprise.*" Theo tossed Sebastian a sharp look. "Care to tell us what happened?"

The two couples brewed some coffee and sat opposite each other on Sebastian's twin couches. Between sips and giggles, Nick and Sebastian related (most of) the story of their reconciliation. Leaving out the more salacious details, of course.

Dante and Theo listened attentively, though they abandoned their coffee mugs in favor of holding hands, Theo's head on Dante's shoulder. There was a miniscule part of Sebastian that twanged with awkwardness every time he glanced over and saw his two best friends cuddling, but when Dante ran his fingers through Theo's bright hair, and Theo gazed at him with eyes that were liquid bliss, that awkwardness evaporated, never to be seen again.

"So, this is it, huh?" Dante gestured at the room as if to encompass them all. "Happy endings all around? It almost doesn't seem real."

Theo shushed him. "Don't jinx it, darling."

"*Darling*?" Sebastian's lip curled up. "Please don't tell me you're going to be a cutesy-pet-name sort of couple."

"Oh, absolutely." Theo grinned. "And the sort to engage in PDA. In fact, I feel a bout of bunny kisses coming on." He leaned over, and Dante rubbed their noses together while they both made cooing sounds.

Sebastian pretended to retch.

"I think it's sweet." Nick slid his arm behind Sebastian's shoulders on the sofa. "I was rooting for you two from the start."

"Same for you guys." Dante glanced at Nick. "When Theo first proposed we *Parent Trap* you, I thought it was a longshot, but look at you now. Someone finally defrosted Sebby's icicle of a heart."

Sebastian opened his mouth to deliver his usual rebuke, but Nick beat him to it.

"Don't call my boyfriend Sebby." Nick smiled over at Sebastian. "He doesn't like it."

Sebastian's whole body warmed with happiness.

"Adorable," Dante said. "And disgusting."

"You're officially not allowed to make fun of us ever again," Theo said. "And I mean *ever*. Not even if Dante and I wear a couple's Halloween costume and start calling each other pookie."

That devolved into a round of good-natured ribbing that had Sebastian laughing harder than he had in a long time. And all the while, he couldn't get over how right this seemed.

For so long, it'd been just him, Theo, and Dante. The three musketeers. Licking each other's wounds and shutting everyone else out. But Nick fit right in with them. It made Sebastian wonder if maybe the future—and all the changes that were sure to come with it—wasn't so scary after all.

"So, what's next for you two?" Dante asked after they'd settled down. "You worked through all your issues, and now it's smooth sailing?"

"Mostly." Nick shrugged. "Obviously not *everything*. We both have serious baggage when it comes to our parents, and there's a lot we don't know about each other still."

"And I've never been in a serious relationship before, so I have a lot to learn." Sebastian squeezed Nick's hand. "We're going to take it one step at a time."

"Plus, I know I need to work on my communication."

Sebastian chuckled. "We *both* need to work on that. No more secrets from here on out. And the bet is officially retired forever."

"Oh hey, that reminds me of something." Theo leaned down and reached for where he'd thrown his bag at his feet. After some rummaging, he produced a worn and admittedly hideous trophy. "This is for you."

"Barbzilla!" Nick and Sebastian said at the same time.

Sebastian peered at Nick. "How'd you know that's Barbzilla?"

"I saw her in Theo's room once. Besides, I sincerely hope you don't have a *second* mutant Barbie hanging around."

"Nope, it's one of a kind." Theo plunked it down on the coffee table between them. "Technically, since I won the bet, I should have permanent ownership of it. But Dante and I talked about it, and we realized for Sebastian to go so totally overboard trying to win this thing, it must mean a lot to him. So—" he flashed a smile at Sebastian "—it's all yours, buddy."

Sebastian's eyes widened. "I can have this?"

"Yeah." Theo's grin was evil. "And to think, if you'd asked me for it in the first place, this whole thing could have been avoided."

"But then we might not have ended up here." Sebastian started to reach for the trophy, but then he stopped. "On second thought, I don't want it anymore."

"Really?" Nick nudged him. "Are you sure? You said it means so much to you."

"It used to. I've realized a lot in these past two weeks, including the fact that I don't need to cling to the past. And I definitely don't need some old trophy to remind me where I came from. Or who my friends are." He glanced at his friends. "Thanks, you guys."

Dante pretended to wipe away a tear. "It's like a Hallmark card. But I'm not taking it, and now that I'm with Theo, it can't stay in his room either. The thing gives me the creeps."

"I know who it should go to." Theo turned his gaze to Nick. "To the newest member of our little group."

Nick pointed at himself. "Me?"

"Sure. Call it a consolation prize for all the trouble we put you through."

"I dunno." He nodded at Sebastian. "What if Sebastian and I break up tomorrow? I'll have your beloved childhood heirloom as my hostage."

"Somehow, I think Seb and you are gonna make it in the long run."

"Me too." Sebastian snuggled closer to Nick. "Think about it: if I ever piss you off, you can send me photos of you about to throw Barbzilla onto a grill."

Nick laughed and took the trophy, setting it in his lap. "Actually, I can see us having a lot of fun with this thing. We could have a dinner party, set a place for it at the table, and when people ask about it, we can pretend we don't know what they mean."

Sebastian snorted. "We can refer to it casually in conversation like it's a person."

"When we take Christmas card photos, we can cradle it like a baby."

"Oh my God, I bet that would freak my parents out enough that they'd insist on spending the holidays with us."

"Good." Nick rested his head on Sebastian's shoulder. "I want to meet them."

"You two are weirdly perfect for each other," Dante said.

"Yeah." Sebastian's face hurt from smiling so much. "We are."

Dante and Theo hung out for a bit longer before they excused themselves. They had their own date planned. Sebastian didn't mind at all that they were hanging out without him. He had everything he needed in his apartment right now.

When they were gone, he took Nick by the hand, nervousness fluttering in his stomach. "I have to admit, what Dante said about this seeming surreal gave me pause."

Nick quirked a brow at him. "No worries there. I vividly recall the half a dozen fights, lies, and missteps it took us to get here."

"Touché. Do you think we'll be able to start over?"

"No."

Sebastian startled. "What?"

Nick touched his cheek. "We can't start over, and I don't want to. I don't want to pretend the last couple of weeks didn't happen, because that was what got us here. I grew a lot, and I think you did too. I wouldn't have it any other way. Would you?"

Sebastian put a hand on top of Nick's. "No, though I might have ditched the bet and just asked you on a date."

"You know something?" Nick leaned in for a kiss. "I would have said yes."

Wrapping Nick in his arms, Sebastian shared a kiss with him that reached deep into him and soothed all his worries about the future. No matter what happened—no matter what tribulations they faced—Sebastian knew with utmost certainty that they could handle it. Together.

Epilogue

Graduation Day

When asked later, Nick would say all he remembered about graduating from college was worrying his tassel was on the wrong side, being blinded by a dozen camera flashes, and praying *Don't trip, don't trip, don't trip* as he walked across the stage.

The truth was much more detailed and bittersweet.

The ceremony took place in the auditorium, which—ringed by May flowers—seemed to get more beautiful every time Nick saw it. Inside, white candles in tall, gold sconces adorned the wooden stage. A gorgeous May pre-sunset filtered through the stained-glass windows. Two hundred spectators filled the red velvet seats: family, administration, and some of the students who had become Nick's friends over the years.

He had to admit, he'd wondered at times if this day would ever come, and now here it was. After five years, he was graduating from college with a degree in physics.

This ceremony represented both accomplishments and regrets for Nick. He remembered when Dad had first packed him up for college. They'd driven to his new dorm together and set up. Dad had joked about only seeing Nick when he needed food money, and they'd both thought that in a few years, Dad would watch him get his diploma.

As Nick looked out across the auditorium, he thought, *I did it, Dad. I made it.*

But Nick wasn't alone on this day. There were three very important people graduating with him, and a guest he'd invited personally, sitting somewhere in the stands. It was with extreme pleasure and pride that Nick watched Dante, Theo, and Sebastian cross the stage, while Deen cheered them on, louder than any of the proud parents sitting around him.

After, everyone poured out into the courtyard, where a formal reception was being held. Tables had been set up with hors d'oeuvres, and as the sun slowly lowered, lights flickered on in the windows facing them.

Campus was as beautiful as the day Nick had first set foot on it. The redbrick buildings were unchanged, though the creeping vines were determined to claim the face of the gymnasium as their own. The trees were full of new leaves, and the smell of fresh-cut grass was sharp in his nose.

Dr. O'Connor was standing off to the side, looking particularly willowy in a gauzy green gown. She spotted him and waved, a huge smile on her face that spoke to him as clearly as words: *Congratulations. Be proud.* It made him feel like the sun had briefly stopped setting so it could shine on him in particular.

He couldn't see Powell Hall from here, but he could imagine the beautiful old building that'd been his home for a hell of an eventful year. Sometimes, when he woke in the morning, he still expected to open his eyes and see sunlight pouring through attic windows.

As if summoned by his reminiscing, a familiar voice called Nick's name. He turned toward the sound just as Deen broke through the crowd. Deen was wearing a nice suit jacket, which was only somewhat diminished by the tuxedo shirt he'd put on under it.

"'Gratz, Nick!" His brown cheeks were red with excitement. "You did it! You didn't trip, and now I know what to expect when I graduate next year."

"I'm so glad you could make it." Nick tossed an arm over Deen's shoulder and held up the fake diploma they'd handed him. Each student had gotten a symbolic piece of paper tied with red ribbon. "What they say about college is true: you go through all that work, and at the end, they hand you a lousy piece of paper."

"You'll change your tune when the real one comes in the mail. My parents already bought this giant embarrassing frame for it. It has a tassel and a slot for a photo of me in my cap and gown and everything. It's way over the top." Despite his words, he was grinning.

"You're loving this, aren't you?" Nick squeezed his shoulders. "Getting a glimpse into the future. I bet you're going to be the only college kid ever to experience reverse senioritus."

"Probably. But enough about me. This is your day. You must be so jazzed to finally be free. I'm going to miss having you around, though."

"We'll always have Powell Hall. Besides, we had this whole past year to get used to living with other people. Speaking of which—" he scanned the crowd "—where's Andi?"

Deen pointed to a woman standing a few feet away, talking to two elderly Indian people: Deen's parents. Deen had said they were flying in for a "visit," aka a thinly veiled reason to meet his girlfriend.

Andi, who played on the Academy's basketball team, would have towered over Deen's parents on a normal occasion, but she'd donned a sundress and heels for the ceremony, making Nick wonder how he hadn't seen her sooner.

She noticed them staring and waved, a big smile on her face.

Nick waved back. "I'm gonna miss her. What am I going to do when I go grocery shopping and need something off a top shelf?"

"I know, right?" Deen giggled, sounding utterly gleeful. "I still can't believe we've been dating for nine months. How lucky am I?"

"Congratulations. Invite me to the wedding?"

Deen crossed his heart. "Of course. Listen, I know graduation is a prime time for everyone to make mushy, emotional speeches and blah blah blah, but promise you won't forget about me when you move back to the big city?"

"I'll *never* forget you, Deen." Nick pulled him into a fierce hug. "You were the first friend I made here, after all. You can visit me in Chicago, and I'll visit you here. The bus route from Chicago to Evanston is one I know well. Although, promise you won't let me crash any college parties and talk about what things were like in my day."

"Deal." Deen patted him on the back. When they both stepped back from the hug, Deen's eyes latched on to something over Nick's shoulder. "Well, that's my cue."

Before Nick could ask what he meant, Deen said, "My folks are taking Andi and me out for dinner, but maybe we can meet up later for a celebratory drink? I'll call you." Deen about-faced and left as quickly as he'd appeared.

Nick understood why a moment later, when someone brushed up against his side. "Hey, handsome."

"Sebastian." Nick turned around and threw his arms around his boyfriend. "Congratulations, fellow graduate. We made it."

"Yup. We're *alumni* now." Sebastian slid his arms around Nick's waist. "How's it feel?"

"It hasn't hit me yet. Probably won't until I'm holding my diploma. I loved getting to watch you walk across stage, though. I thought you said you were going to high-five the president?"

"Yeah, but I made the mistake of telling my mom about that little plan, and she threatened to disinherit me." He shrugged. "It wasn't *quite* worth it."

"Fair enough. How is she, by the way? I haven't talked to her since that dinner party."

"Good. She and Dan are somewhere in the Galápagos right now. They want us to come on their next Christmas cruise with them."

"Will your dad be cool with that?"

"Yeah, so long as we spend Thanksgiving with him this year." Sebastian shook his head. "I never would have guessed he'd be the one to start nesting after the divorce, while Mom runs around doing all this traveling. He sent me a photo of him the other day holding a pie he'd baked from scratch, and he was wearing an *apron*. It had *ruffles*, Nick. When I was growing up, he didn't know where we kept the baking sheets."

Nick laughed. "Things certainly have changed these past few years. So, where are—"

He was interrupted by a loud popping sound followed by raucous cheering. The crowd parted, revealing Dante and Theo over by the refreshments, holding a freshly opened bottle of champagne.

"Drinks all around!" Theo shouted while Dante handed champagne flutes to everyone in the vicinity.

Nick whispered to Sebastian out of the corner of his mouth. "He does know it's nonalcoholic, right?"

"Yeah, but he's been so excited all day, I'm surprised he didn't get a megaphone. Besides, he hasn't touched alcohol since that party we threw last semester."

"The one where he kept trying to go streaking, and Dante had to handcuff him to the kitchen sink?"

"That's the one." Sebastian crinkled his nose. "I never did ask Dante where he got those handcuffs from. And so fast. We're probably better off not knowing."

They laughed, and a second later, Dante and Theo strolled over to them. Dante had a glass of champagne in each hand and one tucked into the crook of his arm. Theo had one and a bottle of champagne, which he probably wasn't supposed to remove from the refreshments table.

Nick wisely chose not to say anything and took the glass Dante handed him. "Cheers, guys. Anyone want to make a toast?"

"I do." Dante raised his flute. "To making it count."

Sebastian tsked. "You can't steal the toast from *Titanic*. Come up with your own."

"Fine." Dante glared at him. "To final chapters and new beginnings."

"Nice one, darling." Theo clinked their drinks together before doing the same to Nick and Sebastian. They all repeated the toast and took a sip.

The bubbles tickled the roof of Nick's mouth, providing proof that this was, in fact, really happening. "What an incredible two years it's been. I almost can't believe it's over. We're college graduates."

"Cheers to that," Dante said.

"I have a toast as well," Sebastian said.

Theo groaned. "Oh God, are you going to toast to Nick and say something cheesy? Like, 'To the love of my life' or 'To finding my better half'?"

Sebastian frowned. "Well, *now* I'm not."

"Uh-huh. If you don't mind, I have an actual toast."

"All right. To whom are you toasting?"

"Dante!" Theo raised his glass. "The love of my life, and my better half."

"Aw, thanks, honey. How original." Dante leaned over and planted a kiss on Theo's cheek.

Theo winked at Sebastian, ignoring his scowl. "But seriously, we have great news. Dante heard back from Duke. You're looking at a future doctoral student."

"You got into grad school!" Nick clapped Dante on the shoulder. "That's great! I'm so happy for you."

"Thank you. I'm excited too. And terrified. Like, a sixty-forty ratio of excitement to abject terror."

Theo leaned toward Nick and spoke in a stage whisper. "More like thirty-seventy."

Nick laughed. "I don't mean to be nosy, but Theo, what are you going to do when he leaves for Duke? I thought you two were planning to move in together?"

"We are." Dante grinned. "He's coming with me."

"Wow! Really?"

"Of course." Theo waggled his eyebrows. "Considering I'm going to school there too."

"Holy shit, two future doctors in the house!" Nick gave Dante a high-five.

"Not quite," Theo said. "I'm only getting a measly master's degree. But it'll be fun to get out of this town after living here our whole lives, and North Carolina is beautiful. Those trips we took to see the campus convinced us more than anything else."

Sebastian held up his glass. "That definitely deserves a toast. Congratulations, you two. If you're ever missing Illinois, you can stay with Nick and me."

"You can count on hosting us on a regular basis." Dante clinked their glasses together before turning to Theo. "Want to see if we can't find a bottle that has some kick to it?"

Theo drained his glass in one gulp. "Way ahead of you."

They raced off. Nick watched them go, a smile creeping over his face.

"Hey." Sebastian touched his chin. "What are you thinking about?"

"Lots of things. The future. The past. How much has changed, and how glad I am I ended up here."

"Me too." Sebastian took his hand. "To think, two years ago, you were just a cute boy I wanted to kiss, and now we're moving in together. Starting our adult lives in a new city. Dante's right: it's both exciting and terrifying."

It was all Nick could do not to sigh with pleasure as he imagined life as a "real" adult. With a job he could hopefully tolerate, an apartment, and maybe a dog. Hell, he'd pay taxes with a smile, so long as he got to do it on his own terms. And of course, with a certain someone by his side.

Nick laced their fingers together. "What's your ratio? Fifty-fifty?"

"Nope, I'm ninety percent excitement. I suppose you're a hundred, since you got that job offer right away."

"What can I say? Physicists are in high demand. And let's not overlook your art internship, Mr. Sebastian 'the new Botticelli' Prinsen."

"I got very lucky in many ways. It was your sketch of that old hotel we stayed in that inspired my most popular painting, and you were the subject of all my best portraits." He lowered his voice. "And some nudes the world will never see."

Nick chuckled. "Who would have thought we'd be an artsy couple?"

"Or that Sebastian Prinsen, notorious playboy, would paint tributes to the love of his life." Sebastian kissed his hand. "You'll always be my favorite subject."

Nick gave him a squeeze before scanning the courtyard, eyes roving over the familiar trees, benches, and buildings. "I'm excited to get back to Chicago, but I gotta admit, this place was a damn good home."

"It was. But now we get to make a new home that's all ours."

Dante and Theo reappeared then with another bottle. Theo opened it with an exaggerated wrist-flick and refilled their glasses. "What are you guys talking about?"

"We're reminiscing," Sebastian answered.

"Oh, on that note—" Dante glanced at Nick "—now that you two are moving, I was wondering what's to become of a certain trophy we gave you a hundred years ago."

Nick looked to Sebastian and quirked a brow.

Sebastian took the cue. "Barbzilla is going into storage, along with the rest of the things we're not taking with us. When my dad got all domestic, he offered to hold on to some childhood knickknacks, including that. So, if you'd like to discuss visitation rights, take it up with him. As far as we're concerned, it's time to start fresh."

"You're not nervous about leaving it behind?" Theo took a pointed sip of champagne. "You don't want to take it with you to remind you where you came from?"

"I have you guys for that." Sebastian smiled. "The group may be splitting up, but you're not getting away from us that easily. You're invited to our housewarming party, and you can bet we're going to road trip to see your new school. Assuming you're not living in the dorms."

"Well," Theo said, "about that. I do still have trouble waking up for class on t—"

Dante covered his mouth with a hand. "No, we're going to get an apartment. Definitely. And you're welcome to stay with us anytime."

Nick gestured to campus with his champagne. "I feel like we should do something to commemorate the moment. This is the last time we're all going to stand here together as Academy students. We should savor it."

"We should." Theo looped his arm around Dante and looked out over the courtyard. "So long, Academy. It's been real."

Dante in turn slid an arm over Sebastian's shoulders. "Thank you for everything you've given us."

"Yeah." Sebastian took Nick's waist. "And you've given us so much."

As the sun set on their final day at the Academy, Nick pictured the twisted path he'd walked to get here. A path dotted with change, grief, healing, and growth.

He had no idea what the future held, but out of all the lessons he'd learned here, there was one that mattered most. No matter what happened, or where he ended up, friendship and love would always find him.

Dear Reader,

Thank you for reading Quinn Anderson's *The Academy*!

We know your time is precious and you have many, many entertainment options, so it means a lot that you've chosen to spend your time reading. We really hope you enjoyed it.

We'd be honored if you'd consider posting a review—good or bad—on sites like **Amazon, Barnes & Noble, Kobo, Goodreads, Twitter, Facebook, Tumblr,** and your blog or website. We'd also be honored if you told your friends and family about this book. Word of mouth is a book's lifeblood!

For more information on upcoming releases, author interviews, blog tours, contests, giveaways, and more, please sign up for our weekly, spam-free newsletter and visit us around the web:

Newsletter: riptidepublishing.com/newsletter
Twitter: twitter.com/RiptideBooks
Facebook: facebook.com/RiptidePublishing
Goodreads: tinyurl.com/RiptideOnGoodreads
Tumblr: riptidepublishing.tumblr.com

Thank you so much for Reading the Rainbow!

RiptidePublishing.com

ALSO BY
Quinn Anderson

The Long Way Around
Fourteen Summers
New Heights
On Solid Ground
All of the Above
The Other Five Percent

The Murmur Inc. series
Hotline
Action
Cam Boy

ABOUT The Author

Quinn Anderson is an alumna of the University of Dublin in Ireland and has a master's degree in psychology. She wrote her dissertation on sexuality in popular literature and continues to explore evolving themes in erotica in her professional life.

A nerd extraordinaire, she was raised on an unhealthy diet of video games, anime, pop culture, and comics from infancy. Her girlfriend swears her sense of humor is just one big Buffy reference. She stays true to her nerd roots in writing and in life, and frequently draws inspiration from her many fandoms, which include Yuri on Ice, Harry Potter, Star Wars, Buffy, and more. Growing up, while most of her friends were fighting evil by moonlight, Anderson was kamehameha-ing her way through all the shounen anime she could get her hands on. You will often find her interacting with fellow fans online and offline via conventions and Tumblr, and she is happy to talk about anything from nerd life to writing tips. She has attended conventions on three separate continents and now considers herself a career geek. She advises anyone who attends pop culture events in the UK to watch out for Weeping Angels, as they are everywhere. If you're at an event, and you see a 6'2" redhead wandering around with a vague look on her face, that's probably her.

Her favorite authors include J.K. Rowling, Gail Carson Levine, Libba Bray, and Tamora Pierce. When she's not writing, she enjoys traveling, cooking, spending too much time on the internet, playing fetch with her cat, screwing the rules, watching Markiplier play games she's too scared to play herself, and catching 'em all.

Connect with Quinn:
Facebook: facebook.com/AuthorQuinnAnderson
Twitter: @QuinnAndersonXO
Tumblr: QuinnAndersonWrites.tumblr.com
Email: quinnandersonwrites@gmail.com

Enjoy more stories like
The Academy
at RiptidePublishing.com!

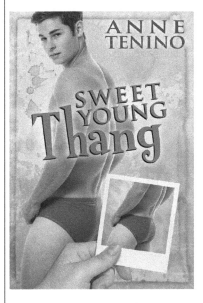

Sweet Young Thang

When Plan A fails, turn to Man A.

ISBN: 978-1-62649-033-8

Apple Polisher

This straight-A student has a dirty little secret.

ISBN: 978-1-62649-035-2

CPSIA information can be obtained
at www.ICGtesting.com
Printed in the USA
LVHW01s1755130918
590068LV00003B/582/P